750

THE BIG BEAR

ALSO BY RONALD L. RUIZ

Giuseppe Rocco
Happy Birthday Jesús

THE BIG BEAR

BY

RONALD L. RUIZ

Ron Ruiz
5/31/03

Arte Público Press
Houston, Texas

This volume is made possible through grants from the City of Houston through The Cultural Arts Council of Houston, Harris County.

Recovering the past, creating the future

Arte Público Press
University of Houston
452 Cullen Performance Hall
Houston, Texas 77204-2004

Cover design by Giovanni Mora

3 4 5 6 7 8 9 0 1 2   10 9 8 7 6 5 4 3 2 1

The man smiled at him a sly smile. . . . Something of age and youth and their claims and the justice of those claims. . . . Above all a knowing deep in the bone that beauty and loss are one.

Cities of the Plain
Cormac McCarthy

PART I

CHAPTER 1

He sank into the chair on the other side of my mahogany desk, and even before his eyes met mine, he said, "I didn't kill her."

I hadn't expected it so soon. Most first meetings are laden with different shades of denials. Everything from outright lies to minimizations, omissions, and simple denials. But not so quickly. He had shaken my hand and said, "My name's Alan Newsome. I'm sure you've heard about my case. It's been in all the papers and on television for days. Doctor kills his wife. . . ." Then he sat down and said, "I didn't kill her."

I too had just sat down and was about to look at him when he said it. I heard it, but didn't see it, didn't see his eyes, didn't measure their steadiness and directness, didn't see his mouth—was it firm, set? In thirty-four years of representing people accused of crimes, I had come to value my clients' denials. They usually said as much about them as they did about the case.

"Steve Rafferty referred me to you. He once represented me in a malpractice suit. And so did Frank Bassett. He's a close friend of one of my colleagues." The recommendations of two fellow lawyers were worth all the ads on a dozen yellow pages.

"Tell me about yourself," I said, reaching into the top drawer of my desk for a yellow legal pad, thinking as I did that I was interested in the case: why else go through the trouble of taking notes? But the last thing I needed was another high-profile case. I had all the cases I could handle, and I was long past needing to see my name in the paper or my tired old face on television.

I had heard of the case, had heard lawyers talking about it in court as we waited for the calling of the calendar. I heard their speculation as to who would get it. I had stopped at the newspaper

3

racks outside the courthouse to examine the amount of front-page coverage the San Francisco papers were giving to a Santa Clara County case. Substantial. I was interested in the case even then.

I studied him as he gave me his name, address, age, occupation, and the fact that he was married, correcting himself, had been married, with a nine-year-old daughter. His mouth was weak, soft; it had little conviction. Still, it would be months, maybe even years before a jury got a glimpse of him. By then he would be accustomed to speaking about the homicide. There would be little of the awkwardness or embarrassment that he was exhibiting now. By then he would have adopted a version, true or not, that was most favorable to him and would have come to believe it, or at least accept it, before he told it to a jury.

His skin was a pasty, timid white. But he was white. Sandy, thinning hair and blue eyes. Better than being brown or black. He would be tried by a jury of his peers.

Most importantly, he was a physician. Years ago a judge had told me as a young lawyer, "In order for a jury to convict a defendant, Gabby, they must decide two things. First, they must decide that he did it, and, second, they must decide that they want to convict him. Usually, they'll decide that he did it, or did something. It's the second prong that can be troublesome. Because the more you can make those jurors identify with your client, the more difficult it will be for them to vote guilty." As I looked across my desk at that fragile, troubled, not particularly attractive man, I thought: Any lawyer worth his salt ought to be able to find much in a physician for a jury to identify with.

"What happened?" I asked. The quickness and directness usually took them by surprise, and he was no exception.

"What happened?" he repeated.

"Yes, what happened on the night your wife was shot?"

"I don't know. I wasn't there."

Our eyes met for the first time. Now there was no hesitancy in his blue eyes. They were firm and had purpose. Maybe he hadn't killed her.

"Let's try it this way. What did you do that day, beginning

with the morning?"

"What day?"

I rolled my eyes. "Look, anything you say to me, Doctor, even at this stage of the proceedings, falls within the attorney-client privilege, which means that ethically I can't repeat anything you tell me, and, even if I did, it couldn't be used against you in a court of law. So what did you do that day, beginning with the morning?"

"I got up around 6:30, showered and shaved, and made breakfast for Amy and myself. We ate, and then I changed Amy and her bed, washed the dishes, straightened the house, and then got dressed for work and glanced at the morning paper as I waited for Amy's nurse. She got there a little after eight, and I left for my office."

"How long were you at your office, Doctor?"

"Most of the day."

He had to be too precise a man for that answer. "What time did you leave your office, Doctor?"

"Around four."

Too precise. "Well, was it 4:15 . . . 3:45 . . . 3:30?"

"It could have been as early as 3:30."

I would come back to it. "What time do you normally leave?"

"Five, five-thirty."

I paused, but he didn't explain. I would come back to it. "Did you go out for lunch?"

"No, that's not my custom."

"Did you eat lunch?"

"Yes."

"Where?"

"In my office."

"What time did you get home?"

"Five-thirty, quarter to six."

Again I paused, and again he didn't explain. "How do you fix the time?"

"Rachael has to leave by five forty-five."

"And Rachael is?"

"My wife's nurse."

"Where were you between three-thirty and five-thirty?"

He shifted in his chair and rearranged his mouth. He reexamined whatever he was examining on the far wall. He sighed and said, "I went out and had a couple of drinks before I went home," adding weakly, "I think I have a drinking problem."

None of it rang true. "Where did you go drinking?"

He looked at me, looked away, and then looked at me again, as if he was trying to decide if he could trust me. Finally, he released it, "I went to The Rendezvous."

"The Rendezvous?" I asked. The Rendezvous was a dance hall, bar, and restaurant that hosted rock-and-roll bands almost nightly, everything from local garage bands to big name groups making their way to and from San Francisco. It was patronized by the eighteen-to-twenty-eight-set, and Alan Newsome wasn't far from fifty. Maybe he did shoot her. "What were you doing in The Rendezvous?"

"Drinking."

"At 3:30 in the afternoon?"

"Yes."

"Have you told the police that?"

"No."

That story alone would have made him a suspect. "Did anyone see you there?"

"The bartender. Although he probably wouldn't remember because I didn't sit at the bar."

He was lying. Most of them did at one time or another. I suppose I expected more from a doctor. "Where did you sit?"

"Around the back near the dance floor."

"Was there music then?"

"No."

"Then why sit around the back near the dance floor?"

"I wanted to be alone with my thoughts."

"Have you told the police this?"

"No."

I looked away. Poor bastard. "What time did you leave The Rendezvous?"

"Sometime after five, five-fifteen maybe."

"And the entire time you were there, you sat alone with your thoughts back around the dance floor?" I couldn't leave it alone.

He nodded.

"You went home and relieved your wife's nurse?"

More nodding.

"What was your wife's illness?"

"It was a flu-like condition. Chills, cold-sweats, aching of the joints, constant fatigue, no appetite, exhaustion, loss of weight. I had her examined by the best specialists available. She had a complete workup at Stanford and at the Centers for Disease Control in Atlanta. She's had every test conceivable. I've had her . . ."

The list went on, each proof positive that he couldn't have killed her. He was rushing through them. Wild horses couldn't have stopped him. I watched him, paying little attention to the names and procedures, more confused than convinced. When he finally stopped, I asked, "Once you were home, what did you do?" bringing him back.

"I prepared dinner, like I do every night. We ate together in our bedroom, watching the evening news. Then I cleaned up."

"And then?"

"I went to my office."

"Your office?"

"Yes. Since Amy's illness, I began spending at least two nights a week and Saturday afternoons working at the office to make up for the hours I spent caring for her during the week, as well as paying for the costs of her care and the costs of having our nine-year-old daughter live with her aunt in Ohio."

"Was anybody home with your wife when you left?"

"No."

"You left her alone?"

He turned in his chair, rubbed his lips together, and nodded.

"Did you usually leave her alone when you worked nights?"

"Yes," nodding.

"I don't understand why you would have a nurse for her all day and then leave her alone at night."

"I was only gone for a few hours, and she usually slept then anyway. And, believe it or not, the cost of a private nurse is enormous."

"The night she was shot, how long were you at your office?"

"Two hours at the most."

"And then you went home?"

He paused, gathered his breath, looked in every direction but at me, and then said, "No."

"Where did you go?" softly.

He sighed and said, "To The Rendezvous."

I waited for an explanation but there was none, and with each passing moment, as tension rose, I became more and more certain that there would be none, not that day anyway. I offered him an answer, "Drinking?"

He nodded, but even the nods were weak. I let it go. I wasn't his lawyer yet. There would be ample opportunity to return to it once he retained me, if he retained me.

"How long were you there?"

"An hour at most."

"How do you know that?"

"I watched part of the late evening news at home and that comes on from 11:00 to 11:30."

"Did you hear any shots fired once you were home?"

"No. The police place the time of the shooting between 8:00 and 11:00 that night. I wasn't there when the shots were fired."

"Whose gun was it?"

"Mine. But Amy had access to it."

"Did you tell the police about your second visit to The Rendezvous?"

"No."

"They don't know?"

"No."

"Why didn't you tell them about The Rendezvous?"

"I was too ashamed to tell them that I was out drinking while my invalid wife was home alone."

"Why The Rendezvous?"

"I like that kind of music. I guess in that respect I've never grown up."

"The police don't know that you frequented The Rendezvous?"

"Not that I know of."

"How did you account for your time?"

"Not very well. They caught me lying. I told them I worked until 5:30, but my nurse told them that she had cancelled my late appointments. I told them that I had gone to see patients at St. Luke's hospital after I left the office later that night, but St. Luke's told them that I had no patients in their hospital that night."

"Why did you tell them that?"

"Again, I was too embarrassed to tell them that I was out drinking when I should have been home with my wife. I never dreamed that I would become a suspect, that they would check out everything I said. To me, this was a suicide."

"Have they questioned anyone else that you know of?"

"They've tried to question Lupe Rodríguez."

"Who is Lupe Rodríguez?"

"She's one of Amy's former clients. Amy was a psychiatric social worker, and Lupe Rodríguez is a paranoid schizophrenic who was devoted to my wife, she visited Amy almost daily over the past two years."

"What's she told them?"

"I don't think she's talked to them. I know that they've tried to talk to her but she's very paranoid, very ill. Amy's death has probably made her much worse than she normally is."

"How do you know that, Doctor?"

"Her sister is a patient of mine."

"Is there anybody else they questioned or talked to?"

"They're looking for Kathleen Powers."

"Kathleen who?"

"Powers."

"Who is she?"

"She worked in my office, but only briefly, as a receptionist shortly before this happened."

"Why do they want to talk to her?"

"I don't know."

"Have they?"

"I don't think they've been able to locate her."

"Anyone else?"

"No, not that I'm aware of."

I was out of questions, except for one or two and the answers to those I wanted to see as well as hear. So I stopped and rocked back and forth in my chair, looking at the ceiling as I did. When I was sure I had his undivided attention, I asked, "Why did they arrest you?"

"I think because I lied to them."

"Are you lying to me now?"

"No." His look was soft, blank, doe-like. "I think it was suicide. She didn't have much of a life."

"Do you have any idea at all who would have wanted to kill your wife?"

"No."

We sat in silence—he looking at whatever he was seeing on the far wall and I rubbing the smooth, soiled horsehide of a baseball that had been given to me years before and which now rested on my knee below the desktop. I kept that baseball in the middle drawer of my desk and seldom did a day pass that I didn't take it out and rub it, careful not to touch and eventually blot out the autograph on it. I rubbed it then.

There was still the matter of fees.

I have long thought that the hardest part of practicing criminal law is the extraction of fees. It has nothing at all to do with the practice of criminal law, and yet it has everything to do with it. Without it one couldn't practice criminal law unless, of course, one were a state-paid public defender. Too often it reduces itself to greed. The extraction of fees. Sometimes I saw myself like a Nazi soldier, bent over a corpse on a railroad track outside a concentration camp wrenching gold from the mouth of a skeleton-like body.

There was a time as a young lawyer when I took virtually

every case that walked in the door. The clients were mostly poor. But I was in the business of helping people then, of making a difference. Once I tried a homicide case for $700 and paid for the psychiatric expert and investigation out of my own pocket. Court-appointed cases sustained me during those early years. Gradually I realized that I had to charge for my services. Rebecca turned my law practice into a business. Everyone was charged; no one was gouged. As my practice grew, time constraints dictated that I be more selective in the cases I took. When I decided to specialize in criminal defense cases, that cut into the number of cases I could handle as well. The court-appointed cases now were both complex and heinous, taking up at least half my time. With Rebecca gone, the privately retained cases brought me back to the business of extracting fees. Those cases usually involved hardworking, blue-collar families whose sons or grandsons were charged with serious felony violations. It was never easy or pleasant setting a fee in those cases.

These days, accepting a new, privately retained case came down to whether I wanted to take the case or not. If I didn't like the case or the client, I would either quote an exorbitant fee or say that I was too busy to take the case. I wanted Alan Newsome's case, which meant that we would have to discuss fees.

"When do you go back to court?"

"A week from Friday."

"That's only nine days. . . . I take it that you've already been arraigned and that your next appearance is for plea and identification of counsel?"

"Yes. That's what the judge said."

"That doesn't give you much time to retain a lawyer." I assumed that if he hadn't already been to Tom Jacobsen's or Stuart Orwitz's offices, he soon would be.

He nodded, examining my desktop.

I could hear Jacobsen insinuating, as only he could, with his slicked-back hair and glinty eyes and cocksure voice, that he had never lost a big case. I could see Orwitz leading Dr. Newsome down the halls of his ornate office, jovial, flashing his biggest, toothiest smile, slapping him on the back a time or two as he paused before framed newspaper articles that broadcast his courtroom victories before showing him impressive reference books that listed him among the best of the best.

"I don't know if you're planning to consult with other attorneys, but if you are, I'd advise you to do so as soon as possible."

"I've already spoken to some other lawyers."

I was glad to hear that. In all likelihood, the parameters of my fee had already been set.

"Who did you consult with?"

"Actually, I've spoken to three lawyers. A Mr. Orwitz, a Mr. Jacobsen, and a younger woman, Valerie Johnson."

Valerie Johnson came as a surprise. She had recently left the Public Defender's office and I hadn't expected her to be traveling with that kind of company so soon. But then, she was an excellent trial lawyer, probably better than the other two.

"Do you mind my asking what kinds of fees they quoted you?" It was important that I ask him before he asked me.

"Ms. Johnson was quite reasonable, considerably less than the other two. But then, she's just starting out. In private practice, that is."

The ability to garner a fee and to try a case were not necessarily related. But he wasn't answering my question.

"What kinds of fees were Mr. Jacobsen and Mr. Orwitz asking?"

"Substantial. I may have to sell my house or, at the very least, refinance it. But they were surprisingly close."

"What did they quote you?"

"They both asked for $250 an hour plus investigation and expert costs. Mr. Jacobsen was willing to put a cap of $250,000 on his fee. Mr Orwitz said only that his fee could exceed $250,000."

Two hundred and fifty thousand dollars. That was a lot of money. Two hundred and fifty dollars an hour. That too was a lot of money. Four dollars and twelve cents a minute. I thought of my father and the backbreaking work he had done in blistering heat and freezing cold for eight dollars a day. I would be making more walking from my car to the courtroom on any given morning than he would have made in an entire week. Even by today's standards, was any one man worth $250 or $300 or $350 or whatever ridiculous hourly fee the big law firms were charging? My father had been a good, decent, hardworking man. Uneducated, yes, but intelligent. Was I 249 times more valuable than my father?

"What kind of a fee did Valerie Johnson quote you?"

"She said somewhere between $150 and $175 an hour with a cap of $100,000. But from the looks of her office, it was clear that she was just starting out. My life, liberty, and livelihood are at stake here, and I'm not about to start cutting corners for my legal representation."

I turned in my chair and looked out my fifteenth-floor window. For years I had practiced out of a storefront office and had driven an unadorned Chevrolet, determined that I would never let appearances define my competence. When the store was sold out from under me, I graduated to a plain, antiseptic downtown office building, mainly because of the low overhead. After several years, a disagreement with an associate brought me, almost by accident, to the plush offices of Jones, Kennedy, and Marcus, one of San Jose's most prestigious law firms. My overhead was still very reasonable.

"Is there a connection between a lawyer's ability to represent you and his office furnishings?" I couldn't restrain myself.

"Of course there's a connection. It may not be absolute, but I would think that any lawyer would have to be successful to afford these kinds of furnishings."

I looked about the room. None of the furnishings, including my beloved desk, which had been with me through so many similar conversations it was almost like a companion, was mine. They belonged to Jones, Kennedy, and Marcus. On the other hand, I had never made as much money as I had since coming here.

"What would your fee be?"

I looked at him. I thought I could like him, and I knew I wanted the case. I would certainly do as good a job as Orwitz or Jacobsen. The thought of him selling his house flickered across my mind. But Valerie Johnson had underpriced herself. Did I need four dollars and twelve cents a minute? Was I worth it? I fell back on a trump card.

"What do you think my services are worth?"

He studied me. Few things are worth more to men than their money.

"You come highly recommended. As high as Mr. Jacobsen or Mr. Orwitz. And I have to tell you something. Five or six years ago I was subpoenaed by the District Attorney as a witness in a child abuse case. As it turned out, I didn't testify. But I watched you cross-examine the pediatrician in that case. You destroyed him and I told myself that if I were ever in trouble and needed a lawyer, you would be the one. Do you remember that case? The mother was a young, teenaged girl and it was dismissed."

I did and I nodded. But he still hadn't answered my question.

We looked at each other across the desk. There was trust in his eyes.

"What do you think is fair?" he said, putting the ball in my court again.

I knew then that the case was mine.

"I'll charge you $200 an hour. If my fees exceed $200,000, I'll absorb 50 percent of all costs, investigation, psychiatric, ballistic, fingerprint, whatever."

He smiled for the first time, took out his checkbook, and said, "I'm prepared to write you a check for $50,000 now and the balance of whatever your retainer fee is within two weeks. That's what Mr. Orwitz wanted. Is that agreeable?"

"Yes."

He put his pen to his checkbook, stopped, and looked up again. "Who should I make this out to? Jones, Kennedy, and . . ."

"No, make it out to me, Gabriel García."

As I watched him effortlessly write out his check, I thought: You've come a long way, Gabriel Garcia.

Once he was gone, I looked out of my huge window at the foothills that were just turning green and chided myself for my reaction. And I thought of a man that I had never met, a man I had thought of often over the years as I had made my way through my professional life. He was the father of George Jackson, a revolutionary black inmate of the early seventies who had been shot and killed by prison guards as he allegedly tried to scale a prison wall. One glance at that enormous wall established the absurdity of that claim forever.

George Jackson had recounted a prison visit he had with his father in a book he had written more than twenty-five years before. His father was a Los Angeles postal worker who had come to admonish him about his revolutionary prison activities. Each man had left the visit disenchanted, and George Jackson had subsequently written that his father would go to his grave accepting the condition and role that the white man had carved out for him long ago.

If George Jackson had named his father or given a physical description of him, I didn't remember either. Yet I knew and understood the man, and he had always been there for me as a reminder. After a while I gave him a name. I called him the house nigger.

CHAPTER II

I was born and raised on Joe Pavlovitch's table grape ranch in the southeastern corner of the great San Joaquin Valley. My father had happened on the ranch when he was scarcely more than a boy from Mexico. He had worked hard and efficiently through several harvests before Joe Pavlovitch kept him on year-round, housing him for two years in an old chicken coop and then in one of the six, small, new houses he built for his foremen. It was then that my father sent for my mother. Ever since I could remember, my father was Joe Pavlovitch's foreman.

Joe Junior, or J.J. as I called him, was Joe Pavlovitch's only son. Three months older than I, he had four sisters, and in the vast isolation of that huge ranch, we were destined to become brothers, he the light one and I the dark one.

My first memories of us are in the vines nearest the main house navigating our tiny metal cars along the countless roads we had engineered in the loose sandy soil and mud of the irrigation ditches, protected from the merciless sun by the great green leaves of vines that were three times our height. We were very busy then, seldom speaking, maneuvering those tiny cars over obstacle after obstacle.

I can still see us in the lower branches of the mulberry trees that surrounded the main house, the only trees for miles, or until you reached the next main house. I see us walking, our faces red with cold, the main house disappearing twenty feet behind us as we pierced the thick white tulle fog, waiting for and then witnessing the miracle we had come for, the reappearance of the vines, leafless and twisted, harnessed together by the wire that will support next summer's fruit. And always I can see Joe

Pavlovitch, short but powerful, broad but not fat, never fat, wheeling about the workers with his tireless energy, his brow furled, forever furled, back up into his bald head. Then he would see us, or rather, see J.J., and he would come, smile, tousle J.J.'s hair, and say, "How's it going, Champ! You behaving yourself, taking care of business?" And J.J. would nod, and the gruff man would bend and kiss J.J. lightly on the forehead, and turn and leave, cloaking himself in that fierce energy again, without even a glance for me.

I remember Mrs. Pavlovitch, too, a tall, warm woman, taller than her husband, my protector, always reassuring me, without a word, that it was okay for me to be in their house. Because none of the other Mexican kids ever came into the main house. At times I'd hear her say in a quiet, diplomatic voice to her irritated husband, "I did tell Joe Junior that it was all right if he stayed for dinner." I was always on guard for Joe Pavlovitch's squints of annoyance whenever he came into the house and first saw me.

Papá used to ask Mrs. Pavlovitch in his broken English, "You choor he no bother?" And she would smile and shake her head and say, "Oh, no, José, he's no bother at all. We all love him." I knew one that didn't. But I never said anything to Papá.

And Papá used to say to me when we were alone, "You better behave good when you're over there. You know, none of the other kids on the ranch gets to go over there." I knew.

My father was a good man. Tall for a Mexican, he stood five-foot-ten. His face had the lines of a white man: a sharp fine nose, thin pursed lips, a straight jaw, narrow cheeks, and a high brow. He once told me that his father had been the son of a wealthy Spanish family who had taken a liking to one of the maids. Once my grandmother was found to be pregnant, she was forced to leave the household. My father spoke softly and said little, but when he did speak, those around him listened. When he approached his men, as he called them, it was with respect and purpose. They loved him.

He was the antithesis of Joe Pavlovitch, yet he was Joe Pavlovitch's most trusted foreman. The most difficult and important jobs were assigned to him. He had the best crew and was the first man in the field each day and the last to leave. There was little of the ranch's operation that Joe Pavlovitch did not discuss with him. They were a familiar sight. The two men standing in the broiling sun shaded only by the brims of their hats, the taller thinner man bent to one side, listening and nodding to the shorter, thicker man, who spoke not only with his lips but with his head and hands and arms, pointing and moving and gesticulating in every direction. Every now and then, the smaller man would stop and look up at the taller man, who in turn would stop nodding and say a few measured words before the smaller man began moving and talking again.

It was my father who raised me. Because my mother was never feeling well. "*Tu mamá no se siente bien.*" I had heard that explanation ever since I could remember. It was all he ever said, but it was all that needed to be said. Because one had only to look in the direction of Catalina Garcia to know that she wasn't feeling well. But you couldn't always see her. Because she kept our house closed and dark, and as the sun moved across the sky, she too moved, to the darker parts of our little house. I could count the number of times she left our house on her own. My father said she was afraid to go out, that she had convinced herself that there was evil outside, and when I saw her shaken condition the few times she did go out, I was almost convinced, too.

She was a thin, frail woman who wore the same dark clothes day after day. Six months out of the year she wore a heavy black shawl over the black cotton dress that hung from her bony shoulders down to her ankles. Much of the time she rarely spoke, and whenever she moved within the house, it was silently. As much as I would have liked her to speak, like J.J.'s mom, I shuddered when one of her speaking bouts began.

How she withstood the summer heat in that closed clapboard furnace I never knew. "*¡Abre las ventanas, mujer!*" my father would say every evening when he came from the field, as he went from window to window, raising first the shade and then the window, letting loose the trapped heat while I waited in the doorway until some of the suffocating heat had been released. And she would move, retreat, as rapidly as she ever moved, without a word, as if surprised, startled, frightened by my father's evening ritual, to the back of the house where there were no windows.

If it hadn't been for Joe Junior, my life would have been very different.

At school we were inseparable. We sat next to each other both in class and on the school bus. After school we played together until dusk or until Joe Pavlovitch or my father left the fields. Summers brought us closer. Whoever woke and ate first would go to the other's house and wait until he was ready. Then we would roam across that huge ranch, cooling off in and drinking from irrigation ditches, armed sometimes with slingshots and J.J.'s B.B. gun, hunting birds and jackrabbits, dazzled by the fall of an unfortunate bird, touching the still thumping breast of that tiny twitching thing, climbing on the ranch's giant machinery, driving it to far-off places for great adventures, hiding in the different sheds and coolers. Sometimes we would make our way to the county road and cross over to the vines that were beginning to shade the road's shoulder. There we would lay looking down at the shimmering heat a hundred yards away, making it whatever we chose to make it, a pool, a lake, a river, the unimaginable: water in the midst of that desert's relentless fire. At first we chased it, ran toward it, laughing, knowing even then that we would never catch it, that it would always move as fast as we ran. At other times we were content to just lie on the shoulder for hours and guess at the make and license plate of the first blur of a car far down that isolated road.

Lunch we ate at J.J.'s house every day of the summer except Sundays. He and I alone at the small kitchen table because Mrs. Pavlovitch didn't want us tracking through the rest of the house. He, relaxed and hungry, talking with his mouth full, loudly, about anything and everything. I, wary, eating quickly and quietly with an eye on the door, happy and honored to be in that big, clean, airy, light-filled kitchen and yet wanting J.J. to stop talking and eat faster so that we could get out of there before Joe Pavlovitch walked in and found me in his house again. It was in that kitchen that I learned to eat and like "their food," as I called it, meats and breads and vegetables and desserts that I had never tasted before.

About mid-afternoon J.J. would start watching the backside of the big storage unit. As soon as its shadow had crept two feet out, he'd say, "Let's go!" and run to retrieve his bat and balls and glove. Then he would stand in that slit of the shade as the first batter, and I would stand in the sun with his glove as the first pitcher, lifting one foot and then the other to escape the ground's fire in between pitches, most of which landed in the vines far behind me. After each third hit I would turn and half-run, half-walk after the three balls until sweat was streaming down my face and the sun felt as if it were sitting on my head and I'd say, "It's my turn to hit," and he'd say, "Okay" and I'd stagger to the shade.

At school J.J. was the best baseball player, the best football and basketball player, the fastest runner, and the strongest wrestler. He was always the first captain, and he always chose me first. It was a thrill to stand with the others as he looked us over and said what we all knew he would say, "I'll take Gabby," not because I was the best, but because I was his friend.

We must have been eleven when we started waiting for the Bakersfield newspaper on those late summer afternoons along the county road at the Pavlovitch mailbox. We had discovered the sports page and line scores. Major league baseball had not yet come to the West, and down at the bottom of *The Kern Republican*'s front page was a small box reserved for the games that had been completed or were in progress somewhere across the country. There was a tiny string of numbers, most of them zeros, that ended under an R, H, and E: runs, hits, and errors. Beneath them, in equally tiny letters, appeared the names of pitchers and catchers: Feller and Hegan, Newhouser and Cochrane. And sometimes HR: Williams, DiMaggio, which meant that my Splendid Splinter or J.J.'s Yankee Clipper had hit a home run in a distant city that I never dreamed I would visit. We spent almost as much time deciphering the line scores of today's games as we did reading the wire service accounts of yesterday's games. The line scores left so much to our imaginations. We could make whatever we wanted of those games.

Joe DiMaggio and the New York Yankees were J.J.'s favorites. Ted Williams and the Boston Red Sox were mine. DiMaggio was everybody's hero and the Yankees were America's team: they always won. DiMaggio was a gentleman, a nice guy, everything a hero was supposed to be. Boston always lost and Williams was hated by many. Still, I loved the way he refused to tip his cap to the cheering crowds, after hitting a home run, as was baseball's sacred tradition, and the way he refused to speak to reporters, and jumped into the stands to chase abusive fans, all of which heroes never did. For a long time, during our afternoon games J.J. was Joe DiMaggio and I was Ted Williams.

Jackie Robinson was in his second year then. I can still hear J.J. asking his father, "Why shouldn't a Negro be allowed to play with white men?" And I can still hear the exasperated answer, "A nigger is a nigger. Someday you'll understand. These are professionals. They make a lot of money. They shouldn't be forced to play with niggers. It's just not right." As for me, I was in awe of a nigger not only playing with white men, but playing *better* than white men. Secretly, I rooted for Jackie Robinson.

J.J. saw it first. We were sitting under clusters of young grapes, and J.J. had just finished straightening out the front page of *The Kern Republican* when he said, "The Indians beat the Yankees 3 to 1. Garcia and Hegan. Hey, is that your uncle or big brother? Garcia WP, winning pitcher." I laughed.

I thought he was joking, poking fun at me. "No, look, Gabby, it says Garcia and Hegan." I looked and looked again. It said Garcia, G-A-R-C-I-A. I took the paper from J.J. and brought it up close to my eyes, blinked several times, and then looked again. G-A-R-C-I-A.

I asked Papá.

"No, I never heard of a pitcher named Garcia. But I'm sure there must be one. Garcia is a pretty common name, and, you know, they play baseball in Mexico, too. They have the Mexican League, and they're pretty good . . ."

"No, no, Papá, I'm talking about the major leagues, here in

the United States. I saw it with my own eyes. Garcia. Just like ours. And he's good. He beat the Yankees 3 to 1."

"Well, I've never heard of him. So what can I tell you? I don't think he's related to us. Because all of my brothers and sisters, all of our people, all of your mother's people are still in Batopilas."

I waited the rest of that day and the next for *The Kern Republican*. The next afternoon I made sure that J.J. and I were down at the county road when it came. I took it from the driver's hand before he could slip it into the mailbox.

The wire service blurb was no more than two inches, but I didn't get past the first sentence. "Visalia's own Mike Garcia, The Big Bear, showed more of his 1949 rookie year form in limiting the powerful New York Yankees to three hits and one unearned run in a masterful 3-1 win in Yankee Stadium."

"J.J., where's Visalia? Isn't it around here someplace?"

"Yeah, it's on the way to Fresno."

"How far?"

"I don't know, but it's closer than Bakersfield. That's where my Dad catches the plane whenever he flies someplace."

Closer than Bakersfield. My mind was racing. "Have you ever been there?"

He looked up from the line scores. "Why do you want to know?"

"I just do."

"Yeah, I've been there. It's kind of like Delano."

The Big Bear. I tried to imagine what he looked like, why they called him that. He had to be big, but that was as far as I could get.

"J.J., they call him The Big Bear."

"Who?"

"Mike Garcia."

"So?"

"Why do they call him that?"

"How should I know?"

He wasn't interested. But I was. From that day forward, whenever we played baseball, I was The Big Bear, whether I was running, hitting, or fielding, but especially pitching. It made little difference what I called myself, J.J. still pounded everything I threw far and wide. Sometimes when J.J. rounded the bases I thought of giving up the name: I was disgracing The Big Bear.

And then, about four weeks later, I saw his picture. There he was in *Sports Magazine,* in a colored full-page photo, side by side with Bob Feller, resplendent in his white Cleveland Indians uniform with Chief Wahoo grinning wildly down from his cap. He was huge and he was dark, darker than me. I held the picture up to my arm, just to be sure. Darker than me. I was relieved. His face was round and brown, shielded from the sun by his cap. I compared it to Feller's shaded face. Much, much darker. Then I made out the dark, black, semicircles under his eyes, and I understood why they called him The Big Bear. And there was no escaping his size. He was bigger than Feller and much bigger than Papá, and I could hear Papá telling me over and over again that we weren't big people, and I hoped against hope that he was one of us. He had to be.

The magazine had just come, and I knew that J.J. hadn't seen it. So I hid it under a stack of old magazines until I could return the next day armed with one of Papá's razor blades. I waited until J.J. went to the bathroom, and then I sliced the photo from the magazine, carefully folded it, and put it in my back pocket where I carried it for almost a year until Papá accidentally washed it with my pants. But not before I took it out of my back pocket time and time again to admire him and dream. Someday the photo would be of me and The Big Bear. They would call me The Little Bear.

Still, I wasn't sure. So one day I went to the field where the workers were with the photo in my back pocket. In those days I stayed away from the workers as much as I could. I didn't like them then. They were poor, dirty, and dumb, a constant reminder of what I could be. I went just before noon and waited for them to emerge from their rows to the dirtroad where their lunches were stored in their beat-up, dirty old cars. Slowly they came, one at a time, down that long line of rows, straightening themselves and stretching after six hours of crooked labor, with another six before them. Out they came with effort, as if from a hole rather than a lush, green row.

They were not a pretty sight. Their heads and necks and faces were covered with hats and rags and bandannas to protect them from the merciless sun. Their bodies were wrapped in layers of clothing, the first sweat-soaked layers already acting as coolants against the burning heat that had yet to reach its peak. Their feet and legs were caked with white dust, and splattered all about them were the sticky streaks and splotches of the fruit's juices. They congregated in small clusters under whatever shade they could find at the head of the rows and began unraveling and baring their heads before they ate. Over the course of several harvests many had tried to speak to me, but I had stood mutely, and probably contemptuously, staring back at them, as if I didn't understand them, as if I didn't speak Spanish, emphasizing, perhaps mostly for myself, by my silent stare that I wasn't one of them.

Now I needed them and was uncomfortable in that need. Still, I had to examine them, make myself sure. I took the worn and creased photo out of my back pocket and studied the face and skin that had long since been engraved in my mind. When I was sure I remembered his face and his skin, I folded the photo, perhaps for the thousandth time, and put it back in my pocket. I walked toward them. Now it was impossible not to acknowledge them, say hello at least, answer yes or no at least, as I stopped and stared, impossible not to admit, at least, that I spoke Spanish. *"¿Buscas a tu papá?"* "No." They knew I was the boss's son— maybe not the big boss, but their boss. *"Tu papá ya se fue."* I let them ask and say whatever they wanted, while I in turn stared. Their faces were one and the same: dark and dirty. But their skin was dark. I looked closer for circles under the eyes but could see none. Worse, they were half his size.

September came bringing school and the end of the 1951 baseball season. The Big Bear was a twenty-game winner for the first time, but the Indians didn't win the pennant. For a week J.J. and I huddled outside the principal's door each day during our lunch hour to listen to a few innings of the World Series being sent across the continent to our tiny country school by radio. We didn't care who won nearly as much as we wanted to be recognized as baseball fans. After the World Series, *The Kern Republican*'s sports page shrunk, as did our interest. We had all but stopped reading it when I saw the article: VISALIANS TO HONOR MIKE GARCIA. I read and reread it. J.J. was sitting across from me but I said nothing. Later, as I folded that part of the paper, he asked, "Anything good?"

"Naw," I said, hoping he wouldn't look. He didn't.

Papá was already home when I got there. I motioned him outside as I always did when I didn't want Mamá asking her crazy questions. When he came, I said, "They're having a parade for Mike Garcia in Visalia next Sunday. Can we go, Papá, just me and you? Please, Papá, please." "What?" he said, wrinkling up his nose. I raised my voice, "You know, Mike Garcia, the baseball pitcher I've been telling you about . . ." I looked back at the screen door and windows that he had just opened. If she heard, we would never go.

I asked him twice more before he understood. Then he looked out over the quiet, resting grape fields and the vast reddening horizon behind them and tipped his hat a bit and scratched his forehead a bit and sighed. "Please, Papá," all too aware that there hadn't been an immediate, irrevocable no. "Please, Papá." Somewhere in that dying sky he was dealing with her, seeking his counsel. How to leave her alone for the only part of the week that we were supposed to be together. Then we heard her at the screen door, "¡José!' and he straightened his hat and said, "We'll see," which meant yes if I was on my best behavior between then and Sunday. I jumped for joy even though I knew she was watching. "I didn't say yes," he mumbled under his breath, "but you'd better not say anything to her." "I won't, Papá."

He waited until the next night to tell her. The October dusk was short and swift, and it was dark outside when Papá finished cooking dinner and asked me to move my homework from the kitchen table. There was a bite to the night air at the open window. Outside, crickets were bleating like goats. They came early now and left early. "*Catalina, está listo.*" She waited until the places had been set before slipping out of the darkness of their bedroom. Thin and silent and dressed in her eternal black, she took her place, opposite Papá's, at one end of the wobbly, wooden unfinished table, stained and smoothed by countless meals. I sat between them, facing the black rectangular openings of the two bedrooms.

Papá served us, his big brown hand taking up most of the handles. He seemed to be giving her smaller portions. I wanted to tell him that it wouldn't work, that no matter how little he served her, she would always leave half, unless, of course, he was thinking that half of nothing was nothing. She sat erect as she did all day, staring straight ahead at whatever it was that she was seeing. Her hair was silver and straight, framing and enriching the brown of her creased face. She sat motionless until Papá picked up his fork, and then, as if on cue, she picked up her fork.

With his first mouthful, Papá began. "Catalina, this Sunday Gabriel and I have to go to Visalia. *El jefe* wants me to see about a tractor. And you know I'm not too good at making *gringos* understand me or me understanding them. So I'll have to take Gabriel as my interpreter." I made no pretense of eating. I sat, fork in hand, turned and watched and waited for Papá's words to wind their way past that implacable front, through the twisted byways of her mind until they registered. Sometimes it took longer than others. I waited. She gave no sign of hearing although I knew she heard everything. Finally, she looked at her fork and poked at a bean. I was elated. I was going to see The Big Bear.

I didn't tell J.J., I didn't want him to go with us. I didn't want to share The Big Bear with him. The fact that he was my best friend and shared everything with me didn't matter. He had everything to share. The Big Bear was the first thing that I ever had that he didn't have. And maybe I didn't even have The Big Bear. I wouldn't know until Sunday.

The next morning on the bus I said I was sick, not feeling good, and I stayed in at recess and lunch and was still not feeling good on the way home. Because I didn't want to talk to J.J.; I didn't want him to ask about Sunday. I went straight home from the bus stop, straight to the darkness and suffocation of our tiny house, prepared to stay in that cramped darkness the rest of the week, if need be, so that J.J. wouldn't find out. But one afternoon of that darkness, of being enclosed in that tiny space with another human being who wouldn't move or breathe or speak, but who was aware of every breath I took, of every move I made, who had to know how I longed to pull down the towels and rags that she had draped over the drawn shades and pull up those shades and open those windows to breathe air that she hadn't breathed or rebreathed, one afternoon of that made me well.

Well enough to answer on the bus the next morning when J.J. said, "My Mom's taking us to Delano on Sunday to see a Roy Rogers movie and you're invited."

"I can't go."

"How come?"

"I have to go to Fresno with my Dad on Sunday to see a man about a horse."

"Fresno?"

"Near Fresno."

"A horse. My Dad won't even let *me* keep a horse on the ranch. How's he gonna let your Dad keep one?"

"It's not for us, it's for my cousins." I had to think fast.

"Why do you have to go?"

"Because my Dad wants me to."

"I'll ask my Mom if I can go with you. I love horses."

I looked away. "We can't take you."

"How come? We take you everywhere we go."

"Because my cousins will be there and they wouldn't like it."

"I thought you said you were seeing a man."

"We are. But my cousins will be there, too, and they're Mexicans and Mexicans are funny people."

I waited for Papá at the head of the white sandy road. Behind me were six small white houses, three on each side of the road, stilted on the untreated white clay that had once been that part of the valley. Those houses sheltered us and the families of five other

year-round workers. We didn't have a car and would be taking one
of the ranch's trucks, and Papá would have to give Joe Pavlovitch
a reason.

"Tell him we have to go see a man about a horse for my
cousins near Fresno."

"Why?"

"Because that's what I told J.J."

"Why did you tell him that?"

"Because if I told him the truth, he would want to go, and I
didn't think you'd want to take him."

"He can come if he wants to. They take you every place, and
we never take him any place."

"But we never go any place, Papá. And besides, you don't
understand, Papá. I just want to go with you, do something with
you, just me and you, Papá."

I slept in bits and pieces on Saturday night, and even in that
sleep I saw him, huge and in his white uniform and blue cap with
that crazy-looking Indian on top. Always he was smiling at me,
shaking my hand or tossing me a ball or standing next to me in
my new Indian uniform about to be photographed.

I was sitting in the truck half an hour before we left. Once we
started, I asked every minute or two, "How much longer, Papá?"
"How many more miles, Papá?" Twenty minutes into the trip
Papá said calmly but firmly, "You ask me one more time, and I'm
turning this truck around and we're going back home." Then I had
to rely on the road signs: Visalia 30, which would never come.
Visalia 25.

We stopped at the first gas station to ask. A tall, pimply-faced
white boy stared down at us next to the pumps. Papá turned to me.
"Where's the parade?" I asked. "What parade?" "For Mike Garcia," I gasped. "What?" "Let's go, Papá," I said. Fear and shame
were crushing me. When we reached the street, Papá stopped, not
knowing which way to turn.

A stiff, old white man dressed in his Sunday best was shuf-
fling down the sidewalk toward us. "Ask him," Papá said. As soon
as the man reached us, I stuck my head out the window and said,

"Do you know where the parade for Mike Garcia is?" "What's that?" he said, coming closer. "Where the parade for Mike Garcia is?" "Say again," stooping, cupping his ear. I repeated myself. He came closer, looked me in the eye, leaned forward until he was inches from me and said, "What was that?"

"Let's go, Papá," was all I could say. I was about to cry.

Half a block down the street we saw a short, sturdy Mexican man walking down the empty sidewalk as if he owned it. "Ask him, Papá." Papá pulled up alongside the jaunty man in a tasseled white hat and asked him in his best foreman's Spanish, "Excuse me, but do you know where the parade for the great baseball pitcher Mike Garcia is?" The man stopped, thought, rubbed his chin, thought some more, and said, *"No, señor, no sabría decirle."* Papá asked him again and again, each time adding more details. But each time the answer was, *"No, señor, no sabría decirle."* "Let's go, Papá," I said.

Papá saw me crying and said, "In Mexico, whenever they have a parade, it always ends up in *el centro.*"

"This isn't Mexico, Papá. This is America." I wanted no part of Mexico.

Papá found Visalia's two-block downtown anyway. But all we saw there was the flashing red light of a police car. A fat, broad-brimmed policeman greeted us with, "Where you boys headed?" as he looked into the truck's cab. Papá was terrified. "Let's see your driver's license and registration, Mister," the policeman said. Papá sat dumbfounded. I started crying again. All I wanted was to be back at the ranch. The policeman said, "What's the matter, boy?" And I blurted out through my tears, "We came all the way from way past Delano to see the parade for Mike Garcia, and now there's no parade." Then from deep within me came the uncontrollable moan of a broken heart.

The policeman let me cry. When I quieted down, he said, "So you're a baseball fan, are you?"

I nodded.

"Came all the way from way past Delano to see The Big Bear, did you?"

I nodded, soaked and choked with tears.

"Well, no wonder your Dad went through that stop sign. I probably would have, too, if I was from way past Delano looking for Mike Garcia. Well, we ain't exactly having a parade for The Big Bear. It's more like a reception. We're real proud of The Big Bear here. Have your Dad follow me and I'll take you to the hall."

He led us to a wide, flat new building on the edge of town behind which the grape fields extended to the distant foothills where orange trees were beginning to take hold. Over the doors of the building was a yellow banner with black lettering that said, "WELCOME HOME, BIG BEAR." We were at the right place.

We drove into the parking lot. People were everywhere, milling around the parking lot, waiting by the doors. It was only after we parked that I saw that they were all white, more white people than I had ever seen in one place. Papá had to have noticed, too, because his face was tense and tight. Neither of us even hinted at getting out of the truck. We sat for a long while watching, the only sound the buzzing of a big black-and-green fly darting around the cab.

"You want to get down?" Papá said.

"No."

"You want to go home?"

"No. . . . Do you think he's here?" I asked.

"I don't know. But nobody's going inside. Maybe he hasn't come yet."

"Let's wait, Papá."

We sat there, safe in the truck, out of sight yet close enough to see, for at least half an hour. Several times Papá tried to make small talk, but either his voice deserted him or it was punctuated by a small awkward laugh that made no sense at all.

Then there was a big cheer, and I heard, "He's here! He's here!" and I looked to where they were pointing and saw him, big and unmistakably brown, sitting atop the backseat of an open convertible, smiling and waving as the convertible approached. Kids ran alongside the car, shouting and laughing. Then he was close enough to confirm forever: the skin dark, far darker than mine, the thick black hair, the round Indian face. Even the big circles under his coal black eyes said it.

"He's a Mexican, Papá! He's a Mexican!"

Papá just stared straight ahead, his face tense and tight. At the front steps everyone surrounded him, shouting and holding up balls and papers for him to autograph. He laughed and began signing. I had brought an old grey ball that J.J. would never miss. I fingered that ball. "I have a ball, Papá. Let's go over there." But Papá didn't budge, except for the slight shake of his head no. His hands were gripping the steering wheel, and I saw that his veins had become exaggerated green welts on the back of his hands. I was sure we were going home then. But Papá didn't move; he just kept looking straight ahead.

Then a loudspeaker blared, "Hey, you kids and people, let Mike come inside. We've got some presentations to make, and we're already running an hour late. We got to get started. I'm sure Mike will be happy to sign your balls and things after the ceremony. Come on now, let him get in the hall."

The surge around The Big Bear receded, and he made his way, smiling and waving and shaking hands as he went into the hall.

"Can we stay, Papá, please?"

Papá said nothing. He just kept staring straight ahead. But he hadn't said no and we hadn't left.

We sat in the fading October heat with the windows rolled down and the truck's roof shielding us from a sun that would have cooked us just a few weeks before. Once they were in the hall, Papá released the steering wheel and then sat back, resting his head on the back of the cab, his eyes on the visor, saying nothing, which at least wasn't no. I too said nothing, not wanting to give him another chance to say no. The minutes dragged by as I held my breath, reminding myself that he still hadn't said no. Inside the hall we could hear applause and cheering.

Then a big surge of people poured through the doors. Squarely in the middle of them was The Big Bear. Once on the landing, more and more people swarmed around him, patting his back and his shoulders and anything they could touch, laughing and shouting, shaking his hand and pulling at his shirt, begging for his auto-graph. And they were all white.

The loudspeaker blared out again, "Hey, you people, form a line! Somebody's gonna get hurt. Form a line over here. Mike said he'd sign everyone's ball. So form a line."

A long line formed, curling around the side of the hall. Slow-ly, it shortened as kids and adults walked away from The Big Bear smiling, holding up their balls and papers for everyone to see. When there were no more than ten in the line, I promised myself that I would ask him again when there were five. I had little to lose then. Just then he said, "*Vamos.*" I didn't know if we were going home or going to the line. But he opened the door, and my heart jumped for joy.

The parking lot was almost empty as we walked over its newly painted lines. My heart was pounding. As we neared him, I saw the look of complete adoration on the faces of the last white kids. And even though I knew, was as convinced of it as I was of my own name, I wanted to, needed to hear him say it. So I said, "*Pregúntale, Papá, pregúntale.*"

"*Pregúntale ¿qué?*"

"*Pregúntale.*"

"*¿Qué?*"

"*Si es mexicano.*"

Papá tsk-'tsked and shook his head. "*¿Estás loco?*"

We got in line and my eyes went to him. God Himself could not have been more awesome, more radiant. He was huge and his smile was just as big, and I understood why everybody loved him. But when it was our turn, when I was finally next to him, I couldn't look at him. I looked at my feet instead, even after he said "Hi!" in that big friendly voice. Still, I was able to mumble, "*Pregúntale, Papá, pregúntale,*" and when Papá didn't answer, I said loudly, "*Pregúntale.*"

"Ask me what?" he said in that big clear voice. "What do you want your Dad to ask me, big fellow?"

I couldn't speak.

So Papá said, "*Si eres mexicano.*"

"Of course, I'm a Mexican and damn proud of it!"

My heart exploded, and I looked up at him in adoration, too. And he said, nodding, "And don't you ever forget it!"

I still have the ball he autographed. I kept it in my office desk; many a day I rub it. When I gave him J.J.'s old battered ball, he shook his head and took out a shiny brand new ball and signed it "Mike Garcia." I was thrilled, but not satisfied, and I must have shown it because he said, "What's the matter?"

"You didn't sign your whole name."

He laughed and ruffled my hair and took the ball from me and slowly added "The Big Bear."

CHAPTER III

It was late October of 1952. J.J. and I were in the sixth grade at Jefferson Elementary School. The harvest was over, but Joe Pavlovitch was "mad as hell," as J.J. repeated, that he had to come to school for a parent-teacher conference. Mrs. Pavlovitch was in Los Angeles, and Miss Adams, our teacher, felt that the situation had become intolerable.

"Wait for me, Gabby, don't go home on the bus. My Dad's mad as hell. I don't know what she's gonna tell him, but it ain't good, and he's gonna be more mad as hell when she's finished. It'd be better if you were in the car when he drives me home."

We were outside swinging on the bars when Joe Pavlovitch drove up. As soon as J.J. saw the white truck, he jumped off the bars and ran to room four where Miss Adams was waiting. Joe Pavlovitch bounded out of the truck in one motion, flipping the door behind him as he reached the ground. I had seen him mad as hell hundreds of times out on the ranch, and he was mad as hell then. He walked past me without seeing me, his mouth set, his jaw jutting, each step firm, quick, and loud. He walked through room four's open door without knocking, pausing, or speaking.

I hung motionless on the bars straining to hear, but I couldn't hear anything. I dropped to the ground and moved to the edge of the sand pit. Nothing. I didn't want to get caught eavesdropping, certainly not by Joe Pavlovitch, so I went back to the bars. But I stopped before jumping up, lowered my head, and leaned toward room four. I would have given anything to hear what was being said. Nothing. Which made me all the more curious because Joe Pavlovitch was not a soft-spoken man, especially when he was mad as hell. I went back to the edge of the sand pit, bent over for

34

several silent moments and then crossed over onto the asphalt walkway. I approached a few steps at a time, starting, stopping, listening, then starting again. I was at room three when I heard Joe Pavlovitch, "I don't believe it! I don't believe it!"

Then Miss Adams, "Well, you may not believe it, but it's true, Mr. Pavlovitch, and the only person it's hurting is J.J. Frankly, I'm tired of watching it."

"I don't believe it!"

"Well, ask J.J. He'll tell you."

"Tell me it's not true, Joe Junior," softly, pleading. But there was no answer.

Miss Adams again, "This is a serious matter, J.J. I think you owe your father the truth and an explanation, if there is one." Still no answer. "Well, if there's any doubt about this, I'm sure Gabriel Garcia can confirm it and he's outside."

"What's he doing here?"

"He's waiting for a ride home," which was the first time I heard J.J.

Before I could move, Joe Pavlovitch was at the door, fifteen feet away. We were both surprised. "Get in here!" he scowled as if he owned me, which, in his mind, he did. There was little difference between me and the thousands of Mexicans he had brushed past in twenty years of harvesting grapes, even though I was his foreman's son and J.J.'s best friend. I followed him into room four without hesitation.

J.J. was standing at the front of the room with his head down. Miss Adams was standing alongside her desk with her arms folded. Joe Pavlovitch looked at me sideways as if I didn't deserve a full look. Everyone was silent and solemn. I didn't know what J.J. had done, but I now understood that I was involved and I didn't like it. Miss Adams wasted no time. "Gabriel, how many times have I caught J.J. looking over your shoulder during tests?"

I looked at J.J., who had his chin on his chest, at Miss Adams, who sensed victory, at Joe Pavlovitch, who was squinting at me with cold accusatory eyes, as if I were solely and completely responsible for everything. I looked from side to side, as if the answer were elsewhere.

But Miss Adams wouldn't be denied. "Gabriel, how many times has J.J. copied your homework or, worse, had you do it for him?" Fear resonated through me. There was no way I would ever tell on J.J., especially with Joe Pavlovitch standing there. Now I too was looking down, and when the silence refused to pass, knowing that they were all looking at me and waiting, I started to cry, weak, whimpery sniffles.

J.J. must have heard me because he said, "Stop it! Leave him alone! He didn't do anything. I did it. It's my fault. I made him give me his homework when he didn't want to. I made him let me see his tests when he was scared that Miss Adams would see. Gabby's my friend. He did it 'cause he's my best friend."

It was a long ride home. And a silent one. Surprisingly, Joe Pavlovitch said nothing. He was in a state of shock. There was nothing more for J.J. to say, and I sensed that the less I made my presence felt, the better. Because I knew even then that I could not or should not outdo J.J. in anything, especially in a setting where Joe Pavlovitch was present. He had watched as J.J. had run through twelve hapless boys for touchdown after touchdown, had made basket after basket, and registered strikeout after strikeout. He was proud, and the look on his face always said, "This is how it should be." Time and again I had seen Joe Pavlovitch wave his hand over the expanse of his ranch and say to J.J., "I did this all for you, son. Someday it will all be yours. I did it without an education. Imagine what you'll do with an education!" What had happened in room four that day was not in the scheme of things.

Joe Pavlovitch's silence was not the only surprise on the drive home. The other was that he seldom looked at us. When he did, it was not at J.J., who was sitting next to him, but rather at me, and each time he did, it was not with a look of anger, but rather of confusion.

When we reached the ranch, Joe Pavlovitch drove directly to my house. I left the truck without a word and made my way to the front door until the truck had turned. Then I, too, turned and ran to the new refrigerated storage buildings. It was at least two hours before Papá came home, and I didn't want to sit in that dark suffocating air with Mamá until he did. Huge refrigerated trucks were being loaded with grapes that would be shipped across the country. In three to five days, depending upon who was telling it, people on the East Coast would be eating our grapes. The whole process fascinated me, and I watched pallet after pallet loaded onto the trucks. And I wondered: would any of those grapes make their way to The Big Bear's table in Cleveland?

I walked home with Papá in the warm orange dusk. I helped him with dinner. We had no sooner sat down to eat when Mamá stood up and ran to their bedroom. Someone was coming. She always knew or sensed it long before we did. She was seldom wrong and wouldn't come out until the person had left. Papá and I continued eating as we waited.

It was Joe Pavlovitch. I was in for it now. Papá went to the door. They would talk outside. No one was ever invited in, not even Joe Pavlovitch. Whether it was because of Mamá or because of the cramped, cluttered way in which we lived, I never knew. Joe Pavlovitch wasted no time. Even before Papá reached the door, he said, "I want the boy out here, too." I rose. Joe Pavlovitch's wish was our command.

I moved past Papá, avoiding his eyes, not wanting to let on that I already knew that I was a transgressor, through the open door to the frail, brave little tree in our patch of front yard where Joe Pavlovitch, my judge and my jury, stood. I didn't look at him, either.

"What's the matter, *patrón,* what's he done?"

I waited for the hammer to fall, watching big red ants making their last run of the day.

"He hasn't done anything." My eyes widened and I looked around. "He's a very smart boy. You should be proud, José. He's gonna be thirteen pretty soon, isn't he?"

Papá nodded and I wondered.

"Well, I think it might be about time that he started learning what this business is all about. As big as we're getting, we could always use somebody with brains around here."

Papá looked at me, as bewildered as he was proud. "I don't understand, *patrón.*"

"I want the boy to be with you, after school and on Saturdays. Don't worry, I'll pay him."

"With me to do what?"

"With you to watch and learn. He doesn't have to do any work. I just want him to follow you around and watch and learn. And you know how you use Manuel to interpret for you with the truckers and all the other Americans. Well, no more Manuel. Any time the boy's with you, I want him to interpret."

That was how it began.

It was about that time that I saw a photograph in *Sports* magazine that I never forgot. It was of The Big Bear and his new bride. They were in an open convertible in a downtown Cleveland street surrounded by hundreds of cheering people, all of them white. She was white, too, redheaded and beautiful, a beer company beauty queen, the caption said.

I clipped that photo out as well when J.J. wasn't around, and I hid it under my pants in the bottom drawer of my dresser. For months I took it out every night, when I was sure Papá and Mamá were in bed, to admire it. Gradually, I forgot about it. Then one night, as I climbed into bed, I remembered and went to my dresser drawer. The photo was gone, disappeared. I looked and looked but couldn't find it. Mamá.

It was soon after that Mamá made her infamous walk. Mamá never left the house, but on a brisk November Saturday morning while I was at the new ranch with Papá, she did the unexpected— she left the house. She didn't go very far, only to J.J.'s house, which was about a city block away. She took a large brown paper bag with her.

By then I was spending Sundays with J.J. The day began with a drive into Delano for church, which I had been doing with J.J. and his mother and sisters for years. It was just recently that Joe Pavlovitch had joined us, or rather, would drive his truck into town behind us, park behind the Pancake Palace, get into Mrs. Pavlovitch's car, and drive the rest of the way with us to church. "It's good for business," he'd say. "We're getting so big my accountant says that people should see me in church." After Mass he stayed long enough so that everybody could see him talking to and laughing with Father Flanagan outside. Then he would drive us back to the Pancake Palace, where the rest of us had breakfast while he drove back to all the things he had to do at the ranches.

That year, after Sunday lunch, Mrs. Pavlovitch had begun driving us into town and dropping us off at the movies for the rest of the afternoon. Most of the time I was the only Mexican in the theater. That hardly mattered because everyone knew that I was J.J.'s best friend. What started to matter was that I didn't look cool. Suddenly, clothes had become important. J.J., and most everybody else, dressed in Levi's, Pendleton shirts, and Converse tennis shoes, none of which we could afford. As it got colder, J.J. sported a leather jacket. For years Papá had bought me two pairs of cords, two white short-sleeved shirts, a sweater, and a pair of boots at the beginning of the school year. Now I stood out. J.J. felt almost as awkward as I did about my wardrobe. His eyes said so.

He must have talked to Mrs. Pavlovitch about it because one night while we were eating, she came to our house. Mamá had left the table before we saw the sweep of the car's headlights. Papá went to the door. I could see Mrs. Pavlovitch's silhouette, tall and slender in the doorway.

"José, I'm sorry to interrupt your dinner. I should have guessed that you'd still be eating." Her voice, gentle and kind, was an accurate reflection of the person. "I don't know quite how to put this. . . . Well, you know how Gabriel goes everywhere with J.J. And I love to see that, believe me. But boys their age are becoming very clothes-conscious. How they look has become important to them. They want to wear clothes that make them look good. We may think they look just fine in the clothes we buy them, and they do, but they have other opinions. Anyway, I noticed that all the boys are wearing Levi's and Pendleton shirts. So yesterday, when I was in Bakersfield buying school clothes for J.J., I thought that Gabriel might like to have some Levi's and Pendletons, too. So I bought him some. I hope I'm not insulting you. Don't be embarrassed. It's not a big thing. It wasn't that expensive. So here. I hope they fit." With that, she raised a large brown paper bag and held it out for Papá.

I don't know how much of that Papá understood. But there before him was Joe Pavlovitch's wife with a big bag of something for me. Sounds caught in Papá's throat, precursors to an awkward laugh. He opened the screen door and reached for the bag, nodding nods that were just short of bows, mumbling words and sounds that had to be thank-yous.

She left without another word and Papá turned to me, perplexed, and asked, "*¿Qué es esto?*"

"I don't know, Papá." And I didn't, until I felt and looked into the bag and saw two pairs of Levi's, a Levi jacket, and two Pendleton shirts. "Levi's! Levi's!" I had long since promised myself that someday I would have a pair of Levi's. "Levi's!"

Mamá came out of the bedroom. She had heard everything, knew everything, heard more from her corner of the bedroom than Papá or I ever did. Still she asked, "*¿Qué es esto?*"

"Mrs. Pavlovitch brought me some Levi's," I said, looking at Papá, sensing that I was in need of his support.

She went to the bag, looked in, felt the clothes, and said, "You already have clothes. Your father just bought you some." The words were for me, but her eyes were directed toward the bag, not in it or even at it, but far away, back to her mind where the images of what she spoke were clear and immutable. "I've told you too many times that you should not be with that boy. They are rich and we are poor," she said, her voice flat and low without any hint of emotion. "They are white and we are Mexicans. They will hurt you. They will laugh at you. They will throw you away when they are through with you. She brings you clothes because yours are not good enough. She is telling you that you need these clothes to be good enough. Will you ever be good enough?"

I looked at Papá and he at me: she had to be endured. She went on. "You should be with your own kind, where you can just be you. I don't know how many times I have told you about that boy and that family and those people and . . ." On and on and on. But it didn't matter. Because Papá wasn't listening either. I could keep my Levi's.

When she finally went to their room, I took Papá into my room, took out the Levi's, and held them up to me.

"*Están muy grandes*," he said.

"I know, Papá, you have to wash them."

"But they're not dirty."

"They shrink when you wash them. They will get smaller and fit me. But you'll have to wash them two or three times before they fit me."

"Two or three times. Why couldn't she just buy some that fit?"

"Papá, that's how everybody does it."

That night I went to bed with my Levi's. I laid them flat and smooth on my bedspread, I did the same with my Levi's jacket and Pendleton shirts, creating a patch-like quilt. Then I carefully crawled into bed, took a deep breath, smiled, and slept as soundly as I had ever slept. The next morning I quickly made my bed and carefully laid out my Levi's again and went happily off to the new ranch with Papá, reminding him that he had to wash my new Levi's three times before Monday.

Betty, J.J.'s younger sister, saw Mamá first. She watched her for a while, got scared, and then ran to the kitchen to tell everyone. J.J. said that he and his mom and other sisters went to the front-room window and watched her. She was dressed all in black and was carrying a brown paper bag. She kept walking back and forth in front of the house, looking at no one and nothing, going to one end of the house, turning, returning to the other end of the house, and then turning again. They watched for a long time, thinking she'd tire and leave. But she didn't. Finally, Mrs. Pavlovitch went out to talk to her, maybe even to take her home or to the hospital if need be. Mrs. Pavlovitch first tried to talk to Mamá from the porch steps, but Mamá didn't or wouldn't hear. She tried again from the walkway, and when Mamá wouldn't acknowledge her, she stood directly in Mamá's path and waited. When Mamá returned, she gave no indication of having seen Mrs. Pavlovitch until she was a foot or two from her. Then she stopped, opened the bag, turned it over, and let all the pieces of my neatly cut-up Levi's and Pendletons fall to the ground.

The day after Mamá cut up my Levi's, she had her worst talking bout.

I was ten when Mamá had her first talking bout. One evening as Papá was preparing dinner and I was doing my homework at the kitchen table, Mamá came out of the darkness of their room before Papá called her. She came out talking. At first I thought she was talking to me, but then I saw that she wasn't looking at me, nor at Papá.

She came to the table and seated herself as she spoke, past me to the wall beyond, with her back to Papá at the stove. She spoke in a normal tone of voice, spoke more words probably in the next five minutes than I had heard her speak in the past five months. It wasn't that she was speaking nonstop, because she would pause, as if she were listening to someone and then answering, but in normal flowing sentences rather than in the spare, curt words that usually came from her. She was talking about washing sheets in the river and the need to be finished before Don Pedro got home, about people and events that I didn't recognize. Later Papá told me that he thought that she had been talking to her mother and her sisters at the river that ran alongside Batopilas, their village in Mexico. She talked through our meal with Papá occasionally interrupting her and reminding her that she had to eat her dinner.

She would stop, look at Papá for a moment, eat a few bites, and then start talking again. She continued talking in their room when she left the kitchen. As we washed the dishes, I smiled uncomfortably at Papá several times. It wasn't until she had fallen asleep that he said quietly, "It's nothing to worry about. She had an aunt in Mexico who'd go around like that for days and then stop. She never hurt or bothered anyone." Mamá resumed her talking the following morning, but when we came home that evening, she had stopped.

The talking bouts recurred three or four times a year. There was never any indication of what precipitated them. Mamá always seemed to be talking to people in Mexico about subjects that most of the time were unfamiliar even to Papá. The bouts could last for several days, but when they began extending through the night so that Papá couldn't sleep, he said, "I know how to fix this."

That was how we began driving a ranch pickup truck to the Virgin of Guadalupe Church in Bakersfield on Sunday afternoons three or four times a year. Papá always said that if any one of our neighbors ever learned that Mamá was *mala de la cabeza*, and told Joe Pavlovitch, he would lose his job because nobody wanted a person that was sick in the head living on their property. That may well have been, but both Papá and I were deeply ashamed of Mamá's condition. *Catalina no se siente bien.* I must have heard Papá say that hundreds of times to anyone that asked, and often to those who hadn't asked. I, too, became skilled at saying, "My mother doesn't feel well."

Papá didn't have to explain to me why we had to drive fifty miles to Bakersfield rather than ten miles to Delano to go to church. Nor why we waited until Sunday afternoon to go to church when it was empty rather than go on Sunday mornings when it was full. Nor why he drove the pickup onto our tiny patch of fragile lawn and parked it two feet from our front door and spoke loudly into Mamá's stream of words for all the neighbors to hear as we quickly loaded her into the truck. But he did tell me that people in Batopilas used to take Mamá's aunt to church and bless her with holy water to make her better.

Papá was not a religious man, but he believed in God. He believed in heaven and hell. If you lived a good life, when you died, you went to heaven; if you lived a bad life, you went to hell. He believed there was a devil, a fallen angel, who roamed the world causing evil and making people evil. For Papá, church-going was unimportant; the measure of one's goodness lay in how one treated one's fellow man.

When we got to Bakersfield, Papá asked me to sit in the truck with Mamá to make sure that she didn't get out while he went into the church to see if it was empty. When he returned, he had me carry a brown paper shopping bag stuffed with rags and empty jars into the church as we walked alongside Mamá who was still talking. As soon as we entered the church, we stopped at the vestibule next to the holy water font, and Papá dipped and filled the jars with holy water and then capped all of them but one. He sprinkled us with holy water. Then, placing one of his large brown hands on Mamá's bony shoulder, and saying, "This will make you feel better," he poured nearly half of the opened jar's holy water over Mamá's head. Mamá shuddered and shivered as the holy water ran down her face and over her body onto the floor. But she stopped talking. "*Es el diablo,*" Papá nodded and began mopping up the holy water on the floor with the rags. When it looked like Mamá was going to start talking again, Papá took her by the arm and led us down the center aisle to the second pew from the altar railing where we knelt and prayed, as Papá held Mamá with one hand and the open jar of holy water in the other. Every time Mamá said something, Papá poured holy water over her and she stopped. When she stopped altogether, Papá nodded, mumbling that even the devil couldn't exist under those conditions.

Our long ride home was celebrated by silence. Once we were home Papá sprinkled the whole house and everything in it with holy water as Mamá watched in silence. If I hadn't believed in God before our first trip to Bakersfield, I would have after it.

The day after Mamá left the many strips and squares of my Levi's strewn in front of the Pavlovitch home, the talking bouts returned. This one was markedly different because Mamá was scared. She kept looking around as if someone were going to sneak up on her. Now she mumbled an almost steady stream of indiscernible phrases that ended in screams of "*¡Es mi hijo! ¡Es mi hijo!*" "He's my son! He's my son!" At first I knew she was being punished for cutting up my Levi's. But as the night wore on, the terror in her face began to haunt me and I forgave her. I even knelt down next to Papá and pleaded with God that she had been punished enough, that all was forgiven. But the screams continued, and Papá took to gagging her, to stuffing rags in her mouth so the neighbors wouldn't hear, and then tying her hands behind her so that she couldn't take the rags out.

That was Friday night. We couldn't go to Bakersfield until Sunday. Saturday was a busy workday. There was no way Papá could leave the ranch on a Saturday with Mamá and me in a company pickup. So we waited until Sunday, with me left in charge of a tied-up, gagged Mamá so that the neighbors wouldn't hear. Through the rags she still made groaning, grunting sounds. But only I could hear those, just as only I could see her tear-filled eyes above the rags, see them so clearly that by mid-morning I wouldn't look anymore as I pleaded with her to stop, that we were going to take her to church the next day, as soon as we could, that she would be better then, that God would make her better, that it was the devil, but God would chase him and she would be better.

Late Sunday morning Papá saw Doña María across the road working on her patch of front yard. "Nosy bitch! She never works out there. Why now? She must have heard something. She must know that we're going to leave with your mother. Nosy bitch! She'd be the first one to tell the *patrón*. She can't wait for her lazy husband to have my job." Every few minutes for the next two hours, while Mamá groaned and grunted through her rags, Papá would peek out the front window and then back away from it with, "Nosy bitch!"

Finally, Papá said that we could wait no longer, and he went for the pickup and parked it inches from the front steps. Then he came in and took the sheets off their bed, threw them over the bound and gagged Mamá, rolled her over into a ball, and tied the corners of the sheets over her in a big knot. When he stepped out of the house with his big bundle, he smiled across the road to the nosy bitch and said loudly, "We're going to the laundry," tossing his bundle onto the truck's seat. Then we left.

Only after Papá had made sure that the church was empty did he unwrap and untie and ungag Mamá. At the vestibule he poured a whole jar of holy water over Mamá, and she immediately stopped mumbling. In our pew we knelt and prayed, while Papá held an open jar of water and I the rags that we only had to use twice before it seemed that even this talking bout had passed, too. Then Papá said, *"Era el diablo,"* and I nodded. Just then the church doors banged shut behind us.

An old priest and a small brown woman covered by a large black shawl stood at the back of the church. "I'm sorry," the priest said, "but I'm locking the doors for a few minutes while we celebrate a birthday. You're welcome to stay. It'll just take a few minutes and we'll probably need your help anyway." They came down the aisle to the pew before us, which the woman awkwardly entered as the priest excused himself to put on his vestments. As the woman bumped herself getting into the pew, I saw that she too was carrying a big bundle, but on her back, covered by the black shawl.

Then the woman leaned carefully back in the pew until the bundle was resting on the bench seat. She loosened the shawl, freeing herself from the bundle, and covered her head with yet another black shawl that had been draped around her shoulders, and began to pray. I could see the side of her face, her head slightly bent, her eyes trained on the altar's gold tabernacle, her hands clasped together before her, and her lips moving rapidly, fervently. She was talking to God with an intensity that made me stop and watch.

Until I heard the voice of a child. I looked around the church but saw only the four of us. I heard the voice again and realized that it was coming from the bundle next to the woman. Then there were movements, jerkings in the bundle that caused the shawl to unravel and expose a sight that shocked me and made Mamá groan and Papá stir. There, spread out on his back next to her, was a startling distortion in diapers. It was an infant whose head was larger than its body.

It was clad only in a diaper and a white undershirt. It lay on a blanket on the seat of the pew with its enormous head next to its mother facing me. Its tiny unused legs appeared to be those of a six-month-old, and he bent them and held them up like any infant and kicked them when he saw us. His body fit his legs perfectly. Then came the gigantic head, there was no neck, only the pear-shaped head that began with a delicate chin and then expanded and exploded in every direction, culminating in a massive forehead that went on and on, upward and outward, so that the head appeared at least three times the size and four times the weight of that baby's body. Only the fingers and hands, and perhaps the arms, too, gave any hint of the distortion's true age. Because there was a dexterity to those fingers far beyond that of any infant, a dexterity in the way he manipulated the skin under his great round eyes to see anything that wasn't directly above his immobile, ponderous curse, which he did to see me, pulling and stretching the skin under each eye to see the noise or movement he must have heard or felt. And when he saw me, he smiled, an innocent, pure smile totally removed from his predicament, and said, "*Mamá . . . hombre*," in the light, clear voice of a two- or three-year-old. "*Mamá . . . hombre*."

I expected the woman to turn, and I struggled to hide my horror before she turned. But she didn't turn. She was talking to God in a way that I never would or could. The infant continued to watch me, stretching those large, bulging fish-like eyes, pressing and shifting the skin on either side of his nose to watch as I knelt in the pew behind him. We looked at each other, my face shocked and scared; his face was open and innocent, breaking into unsolicited smiles from time to time, flashing his tiny fish-like teeth, assuring me that nothing was wrong.

Then the altar lights came on, and the old priest, now wearing his vestments, came out from behind the altar and stood at the edge of the altar steps just beyond the opening in the altar railing. Remnants of unruly white hair ran in every direction above his loose, creased face. He stood for a moment and then motioned for the woman to come forward. She, in turn, looked at me and the priest said, "Would you help her please, my son?" I looked at the priest and then at the woman and then at the priest again, and then at Papá: How was I to help her? "Help her bring the child up here. The head is heavy. It's too much for her unless she straps him on her back again." I looked at Papá again, but he only shrugged. I was the closest to the aisle and the infant. "Help her, my son," the priest said to me again. I looked down at the baby who was already looking at me, as if waiting, with trusting eyes. I looked at the woman, and her eyes said, "Help me."

The idea of touching that little thing repulsed me, but I had no choice. I moved into their pew. "You take the child's head. It'll be easier that way," the priest said. I nodded. The baby's great eyes followed me as I bent toward him, his tiny fingers pulling at the skin above his eyes. Just as I lifted his huge melon of a head, he smiled. It seemed as if I were carrying a long, dense, heavy watermelon except that the flesh was soft and warm and there were wisps of delicate hair on that massive head, hair not unlike that of a baby rabbit. And regardless of how much revulsion I might have been showing, he kept smiling at me, as if I were a dear friend, or, worse, his brother. We knelt at the priest's feet, she with the body and me with the head, holding him up as if in some offering. For a long while the priest looked at the infant, as if examining him for God. Finally, he clasped his hands together and, tilting his head back, looked up at the highest point in the church's ceiling and said a long, loud prayer in Spanish, raising his voice to just under a shout, as if making certain that it reached to and through the roof. When he finished, he took a gold instrument from his vestment and sprinkled the infant with holy water, muttering Latin words as he did so. The woman's face radiated happiness, and even before the priest finished, while the infant was still blinking, she bent over and kissed the priest's feet. Then the priest said, "There is no greater faith than yours, my child, and God will have a special place in heaven for you. You have come here on this day every year for the past fourteen years to give thanks to Almighty God on your son's birthday. The doctors told you that your son would live at most until he was eight. He's sixteen today. How little men of medicine and science know of the ways of God. I believe you when you say that these blessings on his birthdays are the happiest moments of your life."

The woman bowed in thanks and began spreading the big black shawl on the altar floor. Then she motioned and nodded for me to put the giant head down. We laid the baby on the shawl, and then she sat and leaned back over him, with her back just inches above him and began bringing the ends of the shawl to her, loosely at first, then gradually tightening them until the baby was a large lump on her back. Slowly but steadily she rose and then turned and smiled at me, blessed herself, and walked down the aisle. "*Vaya con Dios*," the priest said.

As the woman walked slowly down the aisle with her big burden, the priest said to us, "She asks nothing from anyone and certainly doesn't want to be pitied. I've offered her rides home, but she's always refused. I don't know where she lives or even her full name. I call her Señora Filomena. She carries him on her back like that for God only knows how far. She covers him up like that so that no one will see him, so that they won't gawk or ridicule him, and maybe so that he won't become aware of how different his life is from theirs. . . . But on his birthdays I have seldom seen anyone happier. She has accepted God."

Just as the woman reached the vestibule, the infant began to cry. The woman tried to hush him with "*M'ijo, m'ijo.*" Mamá erupted, screaming, "*¡Es mi hijo! ¡Es mi hijo! ¡Es mío! ¡Es mío!*" knocking me over as she forced her way into the aisle, where she fell face-down with a loud heavy thud and began convulsing, writhing, and gasping, "*¡Es mi hijo!*"

An ambulance took Mamá to the hospital. Papá and I followed in the pickup. We waited for several hours before a nurse came and told us that they were going to keep Mamá overnight. Papá said to me in Spanish that he wanted to see Mamá. When I asked the nurse, she shook her head and said that Mamá was in no condition to see anyone. The next evening we waited well past dark to take a pickup down an irrigation road onto a side road off the ranch and start for Bakersfield. At the hospital another nurse told us that Mamá was going to be in the hospital for at least another two weeks. When I asked her why, she said that they were going to give Mamá shock treatments. I told Papá what the nurse had said, and he asked me what shock treatments were. I told him I didn't know, and we left it at that, too uncomfortable to ask anything more.

Almost three weeks later we learned, if nothing else, what the effects of shock treatments were. When they brought Mamá out from one of the hospital wards, she was alive but lifeless. If she recognized us, she didn't show it. Her eyes were fixed straight ahead: they didn't blink, shift, or twitch. Her body was there, but she was somewhere else. She stood absolutely motionless, not wanting to or needing to move, moving only when one of the technicians led her. Papá stared in disbelief. Finally, he went up to her, put his hands on her arms, shook her gently, and said, *"Catalina, soy yo."* There was no reaction from Mamá. Her eyes remained as fixed as they were when they had first brought her out. It didn't matter that Papá had put himself in her line of vision, that his face was filling up her entire field of vision, she still didn't see him. They told us that the doctor wanted to see Mamá in two weeks. We left with that.

It took some time to become accustomed to living with a lifeless, speechless human being who simply sat or stood or lay in bed, staring constantly at some far-off thought or incident or object. Mamá could not or would not do anything for herself, and yet she had needs. Papá fed her spoonful by slow spoonful, as he would have a baby. He tried to make her use the toilet, but with little success. Her incontinency made me want to vomit every time I came in from the outside, not to mention the pile of smelly laundry that mounted by the days. Papá tried to make Mamá sleep. But I never saw her with her eyes closed, and Papá said that they were always open when he turned out the light at night and open when he woke in the morning. When Papá tried to undress Mamá to bathe her, she stiffened. Apparently, the suggestion of nakedness, and perhaps intimacy with Papá caused a reaction in Mamá.

Papá was convinced that no one knew about Mamá's condition. No one had seen us take her to Bakersfield that Sunday afternoon, and no one had seen us bring her back from the hospital late at night three weeks later. No one ever visited Mamá, and Mamá never went out. Best of all, there had been no rumors or gossip on the ranch about Mamá's condition. As for the return visit to the hospital, Papá told everyone that Mamá had to have some teeth pulled. All was well. Papá wouldn't lose his job, we wouldn't have to move, and no one needed to know.

Then Mamá stopped eating. She drank water but took nothing else. Try as Papá did, by cajoling her, threatening her, forcing her, she wouldn't eat. Each day, several times a day, Papá told me not to worry, that eventually she would eat. My worry paled in comparison to Papá's. If anything, he made me worry all the more. By the end of the week, Mamá was weak and losing weight that she didn't have to lose. Papá was beside himself. "We have to take her to the doctor, Papá." He didn't want to hear that. "She's going to die if we don't." But Papá had other considerations: "If we take her to the doctor again so soon, everybody will know." "It doesn't matter what anybody knows, Papá, if we don't, she'll die."

That night, after everyone on the ranch was asleep, we took Mamá to the Bakersfield hospital. They kept her for four days. When we returned to the hospital on the fourth night, Papá was certain that someone on the ranch had seen us leave and that Joe Pavlovitch would be waiting for us when we arrived with Mamá. Before she was released, a doctor came out to give Papá instructions on feeding her. When the doctor saw how distraught Papá was, he said to me, "Why don't you feed her?" "Me?" "How old are you?" "Fourteen." "There's no reason why you can't feed your mother, at least until this situation settles down a little. I think you should feed her." When I told Papá what the doctor had said, he was quick to agree.

Joe Pavlovitch wasn't waiting for us when we got home that night. But Papá was waiting for me in the kitchen the next morning with a bowl of hot cereal and Mamá sitting at the kitchen table seeing whatever it was, if anything, she stared at the opposite kitchen wall. I took the bowl and a spoon and positioned myself squarely in front of Mamá so that she could see only me, and I said, "Mamá, it's me, Gabriel, *tu hijo*. The doctor said I should feed you. Please eat, Mamá, we don't want to take you and leave you in the hospital again. Please, Mamá, please, you have to eat," I pleaded. When I finally looked down below her eyes, I saw that her mouth was open. I fed her spoonful after spoonful, encouraging each spoonful with anything and everything I could think of. "That's it, Mamá." "You're doing so good, Mamá." "We'll never have to take you back to that hospital if you keep eating like this." "Mamá, we love you." When Mamá finished, Papá was stunned.

At dinner, I had only to say, "Mamá, it's me, Gabriel, *tu hijo,* you need to eat your dinner," for Mamá to open her mouth. When she had eaten most of the refried beans, Papá said, "Gabriel, let me try." We traded places. But even before Papá could raise the spoon, Mamá closed her mouth. She kept it closed, no matter what Papá said or did. When Papá gave me back the spoon, Mamá opened her mouth again. I fed Mamá all of her meals for the next fifteen months.

Then there was the matter of Mamá's incontinency. During the four days that Mamá had been in the hospital, Papá had aired out our house, washed Mamá's clothes and bedding, and scrubbed the floors and even some walls until Mamá's foul smells were gone. What a pleasure it was to walk into a house free of those odors. But it was just a matter of days after Mamá's return that our house reeked with those smells again. Five days of that wretched stench and Papá said, "Take your mother to the bathroom."

"What!"

"I'll say it again, Gabriel, take your mother to the bathroom."

"But Papá, she's my mother."

"What's that got to do with it?"

Everything. But I couldn't mention a word of it, not to him. At fourteen sex was everywhere. There was no other topic that dominated my friends' conversations more than sex. Jennie's tits. Debra's ass. Becky's pussy. The way Wilma walked said that she had to have it. Their sexual exploits were amazing: in the rows of

vines, in the tall grass along the irrigation ditches, in alfalfa
stacks, in the front and backseats of cars with every known and
unknown girl begging for it. Everyone had had their share except,
it seemed, for me. The closest I had come to nudity were the one-
piece bathing suits that the girls had worn for the eighth-grade
graduation picnic, and that had been as much as I could handle.
And now I was to see my own mother naked? Everything, Papá,
it has everything to do with it. But I couldn't say that.

"If she eats for you, maybe she'll go to the toilet for you.
You've seen how many times I've put her on that toilet. And she
won't go, at least not until she gets off of it."

"But Papá . . ."

"Oh, you don't have to touch her."

"I didn't say I was going to touch her."

"And you don't even have to look at her."

"I didn't say I was going to look at her."

"All you have to do is take her to the toilet, lift up her dress a
little bit, sit her down, and wait."

"But doesn't she wear underpants?"

"She does."

"So how do I get those out of the way?"

"That's never been a problem because she's never gone on the
toilet. She's gone everywhere else except on the toilet."

"So how do I get her underpants down?"

"Once she's on the toilet, just take her hand and put it under
her dress and have her pull on them."

"And if she won't pull?"

"Let's cross that bridge when we come to it."

I took Mamá to the toilet. I sat her on the toilet seat without a
problem, lifting her dress just enough so that I could drape it
around the bowl. Then came the hard part. I might not have done
it except that Papá was standing at the door behind me, watching.
I took her right hand in mine and put it under her dress, brought
it up to her waist, inserted her thumb past the waistband of her
underpants, drew back, squatted, so that our faces were inches
apart and said, "Mamá, it's me, Gabriel, *tu hijo,* you need to pull

your underpants down. You need to go to the toilet in the toilet, but you need to pull your underpants down first." Mamá pulled, but only the right side of her underpants came down. So I repeated the process with her left hand. This time the underpants came down. Still squatting, I said, "Now go, Mamá, please go." I waited and then heard first the trickle, then gas passing, then a heavy plop in the water. Papá came in and hugged us.

Overjoyed, he kept saying, "We did it! We did it!"

A week later Papá said, "Your mother's not wiping herself, neither in the back nor the front." I stopped Papá right there. "I'm not wiping her, Papá, I'm not wiping her! I'm not even going to help her wipe! I'm not!" Papá heard my resolve. He didn't mention wiping again.

But I did agree to help Papá bathe Mamá. My help consisted of taking Mamá to the bathroom, of saying, "Mamá, it's me, Gabriel, *tu hijo.* Papá needs to give you a bath. Papá needs to make you clean. Let him, Mamá." Then I would turn my back while Papá undressed and bathed her, turning again only after Papá had dried and dressed her.

For the next fifteen months I was Mamá's caregiver. I fed her twice a day and took her into the kitchen with me when I got home from school. There we spent two or three hours together until Papá came in from the fields. I usually found her where I had left her in the morning: in their bedroom sitting in the old wicker chair next to their bed. "Hi, Mamá," I'd say, "How you doing," as I kissed her on the forehead. I kissed Mamá three times a day. In the morning when I left, at night before I went to bed, and late in the afternoon when I returned from school. The afternoon kiss was special because then she reacted. She quivered when I kissed her then, much like a cat being petted. That quiver confirmed what I was already convinced of: some things reached her, wherever she was. The kiss, for certain. My words: "*Mamá, soy yo, Gabriel, tu hijo.*" My touch: the slightest pressure I exerted on her arm in any given direction, moved her in that direction.

I couldn't imagine what it must have been like to be Mamá. All those hours, day after day, spent in that tiny house in the middle of nowhere with nowhere to go and no one to see and nothing to do. Getting up in the morning: for what? Going to bed at night: for what? So I tried to include her, make her a part of my homework world each day for those two or three hours. I tried reading all of my assignments aloud in Spanish, but translating as I read was cumbersome, too time-consuming, and some were seemingly of little interest to her. What did Mamá care about solving equations: if x equals 6 and y equals x minus 4, then y plus . . . ridiculous. English grammar was equally as bad. But I did read my history assignments aloud in English and summarized paragraphs in Spanish, adding bits of information to give them a fuller meaning for Mamá. I worked on my English compositions out loud in Spanish, and that gave me the idea of thinking aloud, of trying to say everything I thought aloud in Spanish until Papá came home. I don't know if I added anything to Mamá's world over those fifteen months, but I do know that she loved me. The afternoon quivers told me so. And I do know that I loved her.

Mamá died eighteen months and four days after the first time we brought her home from the Bakersfield hospital. She died in her sleep. Rather, she died in her bed sometime during the night. Whether she was asleep or not we never knew, because her eyes, as always, were open and fixed when Papá realized that she was dead. Papá used to say that she was like horses who stood through the night; you never knew if and when they were asleep.

The mortician's assistant came for the stiff, ice-cold, brown-green body. He said that Mamá had died of a heart attack. That was accepted by all. Now I wonder. No sooner had the assistant left when Papá told Joe Pavlovitch that we had to go to the mortuary. At the mortuary Papá had me tell the mortician that he had had a change of heart, he wanted Mamá cremated. The mortician was surprised. He asked if we were Catholic and Papá said yes. He told us that some people believed it was a mortal sin for a Catholic to have his loved one cremated. Papá said that he had heard that, too, but that he still wanted Mamá cremated. I understood.

Papá had Mamá's ashes sent to Batopilas to be spread along the river that she had so often talked about.

CHAPTER IV

Washington Junior High School brought about many changes. The biggest was the beginning of the inevitable separation between J.J. and me. It was the girls. They came at J.J. from every direction, in every size, shape, and color. There were screeches in their voices and flames in their eyes. "J.J.! Oh, J.J.!" They met him in the hallway after each class and jockeyed for positions closest to him on the short walk to the next class. They fought over seats nearest him in the classroom and on the bus. They surrounded him at lunch and brought him special goodies from home. And I watched from further and further distances.

Then the parties began, parties in the homes of twelve- and thirteen-year-old girls who had convinced or reminded their mothers that the time for romance had arrived. Parties to which I was never invited.

It was Katherine Pavlovitch who changed that, seeing to it that J.J. invited me to his sister Mary's birthday party near the end of the seventh grade

"I don't wanna go."

"How come?"

"I don't like parties."

"You haven't been to any, so how can you not like them?"

"It'll be just like school. All the girls will crowd around you, and everybody will forget about me."

"No, we have someone for you. She's already been invited. We told her all about you, and she really wants to meet you."

"Who?"

"I'm not telling. You don't know her anyway. So it don't matter."

She really wants to meet you. Words as bright as the sun, as dark as the deepest cave. She was at once as beautiful and blonde as any girl who had ever crowded around J.J. and then as awkward and ugly as any. I looked at myself more times in the mirror in the next twelve days than I had in the previous twelve years, concluding, more often than not, that the older I became, the more handsome I was becoming. And I imagined her, blonde, blue-eyed, budding, and beautiful.

I was shaking as I waited in J.J.'s room a half hour before the party, thinking that I shouldn't have come. I could hear them downstairs making the final arrangements, hear Mary protesting from time to time that it was her party, not theirs. I must have changed my mind a dozen times, deciding to leave, go home, no stay, reversing myself each time I thought of her, blonde and budding and wanting to meet me.

I heard the first cars arrive, and waited some fifteen minutes until after the last car had arrived, my heart thumping at the thought of her downstairs somewhere below me, maybe ten or fifteen feet away, waiting and wanting to meet me, having been told all about me and still waiting for me, blonde and budding.

As I descended, J.J. came up to me and said, "Where've you been? My mom picked up what's-her-name and she's been waiting and waiting for you." Then he took me by the arm through the crowd of thirteen- and fourteen-year-olds to the far side of the room and brought me face to face with her and said, "Uhm, I forget your name, but this is Gabby Garcia, my best friend. He really wants to meet you."

I looked at her and writhed and squirmed as if I were trying to set myself free from a bad dream.

She, in turn, smiled. "My name is Eufemia Oropeza. Very pleased to meet you." And as much as I tried to deny what was before me, the image wouldn't change or fade: dark skin, darker than mine, coal-black eyes, pitch-black hair. I looked and I looked, but it was true, all of it, all of her.

And then the room came rushing in at me, and I was aware of all of them, individually and collectively, watching us, though I dared not look, couldn't look, felt myself burning with shame. Because they all knew what I had coveted, what I had reached for, even though I had to have known I could never have it.

"You two should dance," J.J. said, pushing me to her, and she, who was so ready, willing, compliant, raised her right arm, and I took her right hand, as cold as mine was hot, and shuffled my feet, though I had never danced before, so that J.J. would leave and take some of the other eyes with him. I shuffled to the darkest corner of the room, trying to hide who she was—neither blonde, nor blue-eyed, nor budding.

We shuffled back and forth in my selected corner, stiff, awkward, and silent, as I desperately searched for something to say, not because I needed or wanted to speak to her, but rather, to show the others that I was having fun, that I did not want or need one of theirs. But I could find nothing to say.

When the music stopped, she asked, "Why did they invite you?"

"Because I'm J.J. Pavlovitch's best friend. That's why."

"I don't know why they invited me. I just know that your Mrs. Pavlovitch and my Mrs. Pavlovitch both wanted me to come so I came."

The music began again, and we shuffled about again, our legs occasionally bumping, stiffening us all the more. We ground on, not to their music, but to ours, to the strains of self-consciousness, doggedly, determined. Because we had to. When the music stopped, she said, "I'm scared, too."

"Scared! Who's scared?"

"Me."

"What're you scared of? There's nothing to be scared of!"

"Shhh," she said, lowering her eyes.

"Well, what're you scared of?"

"We're the only Mexicans here."

"So! What difference does that make? They're no better than us! We're better than them!"

"Shhh. They'll hear us. They're looking at us."

"Who cares if they're looking. Let them look. That doesn't

bother me."

"Don't feel bad, I'm scared, too."

"How many times do I have to tell you, I'm not scared!" in a hushed tone, through gritted teeth.

"Okay, okay, I'm the only one scared here."

Again the music and again she held her arm and hand up and I matched them. But as we shuffled this time, I saw that there was a large, empty semicircle around us, larger than any space on the otherwise crowded floor.

"They're moving away from us."

"They're not moving away. We're the ones who are moving into this little corner. Pretty soon we won't be able to move."

"I didn't ask you."

"I'm telling you."

"Look, can you see anybody that has as much space around them as we do?"

"So let's dance over by them."

"No."

"Why not?"

"Because I don't want to."

"Why don't you want to?"

"Because I don't, that's why."

So it went, song after song, every break, every dance had its own brand of humiliation. I would have left, gone home, but walking through that room and out that door, running for all to see would have been the biggest humiliation. We trudged on, stiff-legged and aware, she with icy hands and me with clammy, sweaty hands.

That was December of 1952, when the descendants of the first wave of Slovenian, Armenian, and Italian immigrants that had settled in the southern part of California's great Central Valley were beginning to taste the enormous success, wealth, and growth that could never have been foreseen by their parents and grandparents. Hard, hot, arid wastelands were being transformed into rich growing fields by harnessed mountain streams and soil treatment programs. Advances in refrigeration were now allowing the shipment of table grapes for time periods and to markets that had never been dreamed of. Acres and acres of previously unwanted land had been bought up for pennies by the astute descendants of those first humble settlers. Joe Pavlovitch and his brother, Pete, were foremost among that band of growers. Pete Pavlovitch's first ranch and his subsequent acquisitions rivaled Joe's. Located some ten miles south of Joe Pavlovitch's ranch, Pete and his family were not only relatives but neighbors.

Katherine Pavlovitch was a frequent visitor to the Pete Pavlovitch ranch. She and her sister-in-law, Jackie, were close friends. It was there that she met Eufemia Oropeza, the daughter of Pete Pavlovitch's foreman, Nacho, and the playmate of her niece, Jennie.

After Mary's party I seldom thought of Eufemia. To think of her was to think of humiliation. But from time to time Katherine Pavlovitch mentioned Eufemia and would always insert, "She's such a pretty girl. She's so beautiful." I didn't think Eufemia was pretty or beautiful. It would be more than forty years before I could see that Eufemia had been not only pretty but beautiful. But Katherine Pavlovitch's comments allowed me to at least see that Eufemia was acceptable, and after a while that was enough.

The following year Katherine Pavlovitch had me invited to another party. Eufemia was there. Neat and clean and trim, as she would always be, smiling when she saw me. No one had to direct me to her, or her to me. We knew with whom we belonged.

"Hi."

"Hi," the smile lingering, "I'm glad you came."

"Yeah," was all I could muster.

But it was not like before. This time we danced and stood among the others. This time some of them spoke to us, came up to us, and laughed with us. This time when Mrs. Pavlovitch came up to us and said, "Eufemia, I promised your mother I'd have you home by 9:30," and asked, "Did you have a good time?" Eufemia answered, "Yes, I had fun." And I said, without being asked, "So did I."

So it went, Eufemia and I, over the next several years, together, always together, expected to be together at almost every social gathering in that tiny corner of the world, pleasing ourselves and our hosts and their guests. Welcomed and accepted without question. Occasionally, we would hear, "I'm so happy to see you here. You know, there's a lot of people who say we're prejudiced against Mexicans. Having you here just proves that we're not. I love to tell people that some of my daughter's best friends are Mexicans, that she even goes to parties with them, and we don't mind."

We talked about it.

"Don't lie to me, Femi. You like being here, don't you?"

"Why shouldn't I, or do you think I should be getting ready for a life on the ranch waiting for my husband to go into town and get drunk and spend all the money and then come home and beat me. Or would I rather be at one of those little fiestas we have on the ranch twice a year in April or October, because it's too hot or too cold the rest of the time and the houses are way too small for a party, so that it has to be outside, and the only music you have is the blare of Mexican music from those little wooden radios, and the men sit on one side of the yard drinking, and the women sit on the other side of the yard talking, but really watching, and we're supposed to sit with them and watch, too. Or would I rather be living in town now with all those low-riders having my second baby and school gone and nothing to look forward to but the welfare checks or the fields, and the only thing to remember is the four or five times I dressed up to go to a Mexican dance in Bakersfield before I got pregnant. No, I'd rather be here."

"Don't get mad."

"I never said I don't like being here."

"Why do you think they invited us?"

"I don't care why they invited us. I'm here and it's a lot better than being where all the other Mexicans are right now. And I know you feel the same way, Gabby. You're ashamed of the other Mexicans. I hear the way you talk about them, all of them, the ones from Mexico who pick the fruit, the ones who live on the ranches with us, the ones in town. You make fun of them. You say hateful things about them. You laugh at jokes about them, as if you're not one of them. I see how you get all embarrassed when one of the maids comes out of the kitchen to pick up the dirty plates and glasses, or when they come out with the food and can't speak English and only grin that silly grin whenever they're asked anything. I see how you get. If you weren't so brown, so dark yourself, you'd turn red."

It was true.

"I'm sorry, Gabby, but we both want to be here."

Kern Union High School broke down into many groups. Eufemia and I were our own group. For four years we were together before and after school, between classes and at noon. We met in the halls or at the quad or at the bus stop, and together we sat or stood or strolled through the campus. Together we faced the challenges of high school just as we had faced the challenges of the first parties and then the barbeques and the picnics. She was my best friend.

As I began high school, Joe Pavlovitch had definite plans for me. I had been Papá's exclusive interpreter. I had run errands for him and helped him with whatever was at hand on Saturdays. For this, Joe Pavlovitch had been paying me. At the beginning of high school, he raised my pay to that of a seasonal worker. Papá was shocked and I was ecstatic. It was pennies to Joe Pavlovitch, but it had the desired effect on me. The ranch was becoming more than my home, it was becoming my future.

"He has big plans for you, *m'ijo*. He just bought another ranch and more land. He knows you're intelligent. He's told me many times. When you finish your high school, you will have a very good job waiting for you here."

On the other hand, once high school began, J.J. fell almost

completely out of my life. We had few classes together, and when I did pass him and his friends on the sprawling Kern Union High School campus, it was with a quiet uneasiness.

By the time we were juniors, Eufemia Oropeza had her life planned out. She wanted to be married by nineteen, start a family at twenty, limit that family to two children, a boy and a girl, work for Pete Pavlovitch in the office, save up and buy first a car, and then put a down payment on a house. She hadn't identified her husband yet, but everybody, including me, assumed that it was me.

"You two make a perfect couple," women would say at parties or barbeques. "My, just look at you, just like a little old married couple." "When are you two getting hitched?" we'd hear from classmates. Even Joe Pavlovitch had commented, "You kids were made for each other."

We were not the perfect couple. I had misgivings even then. What she said she wanted was attainable and even comfortable in our setting. But not for me. I always felt as if I were being cheated, that her plans would put an end to my life even before it had begun. And I never lusted for Eufemia. She never caused the stirrings in me that the white girls did at school. When I masturbated, it was the white girls I wanted. Other boys were always bragging about their exploits with their girlfriends. One night, out of a feeling of necessity if not compulsion, I grabbed at Eufemia's breasts. She slapped me and moved away saying, "I'm not that kind of girl, Gabby. I'm saving myself for my husband." More than anything, I was relieved. I had no idea what I would have or could have done if she had let me touch her.

Joe Pavlovitch continued to court me all through high school. He went out of his way to talk to me whenever and wherever he saw me. He was beside himself when he learned that Eufemia and I were a couple. By our junior year he was telling Eufemia about all the wonderful opportunities that awaited me on his ranches when I graduated from high school.

At the beginning of our senior year Joe and Pete Pavlovitch merged ranches to become, as Joe Pavlovitch boasted, "the biggest table grape growers in the country." Then Joe Pavlovitch began pursuing Eufemia as well. "Pete's told me all about you, honey, believe me, we've talked about you. We've got big plans for you. Our main office is gonna be on my ranch, the main ranch. We're gonna build a nice new office over by the refrigeration units. We're gonna need somebody sharp to run the office. My Aunt Bertha's getting too old. I know once you kids get married, you're gonna want to start a family. If you have your babies in December and January, that shouldn't be a problem. And we'll get you real good sitters, not young girls, older women, women who have had a lot of kids, to help you." Eufemia lit up with the word *married*, and got even brighter with the mention of babies. The following year J.J. was leaving to attend a big university in Los Angeles, and after that, to study to become a lawyer. I at least wanted to go to junior college.

The summer after graduation didn't end at the beginning of September as it always had. It stretched on through September and deep into October with me rising at 5:30 every morning to the smells of Papá cooking and leaving the house at exactly 5:55 to the cooler and darkening mornings to begin another day in the fields. I missed school. I never could have imagined how much. After thirteen years, school was suddenly, irrevocably gone. No more classes, no more books, no more learning about something other than grapes, and, strangest of all, no more homework to fill the lengthening nights.

When the harvest began, Joe Pavlovitch made me a foreman. A foreman at nineteen was unheard of. My first crew consisted of thirteen men and three women. The first morning they looked at me in disbelief when I told them that I was their foreman. An old man asked, "How old are you, son?" "I'm old enough to be your foreman and don't you be calling me son. I'm Mr. Garcia to you." I watched them and I pushed them, insisting that their picking be fast and thorough and clean. They were my crew, and they were not going to be just another bunch of dumb, lazy Mexicans. By the third day I began weeding some of them out, letting them go. There were plenty more where they came from. Then, some stopped coming on their own. By the end of the second week I had a whole new crew.

Papá talked to me. "What's going on with your crew?"

"What do you mean?"

"I mean they're all leaving."

"They're lazy. They're sloppy. They won't work right. They want something for nothing."

"None of the other foremen is having that problem."

"Maybe I'm not like all the other foremen. I want my people to work hard, do a good, quick job. I think that's what Señor Joe wants, too."

"Gabriel, that's hard dirty work that these people do in this *infierno*. If you don't believe me, get out there and do it with them. You've never picked. I have. Believe me, it's not easy. And you have to give people their dignity. These are people, too, just like you and me. You'll get a lot more out of people if they like you."

"I'm not here to make people like me, Papá."

"Then at least make them respect you, not hate you."

The first person I fired was the first person who had questioned me, the old man. He had fallen behind from the first day, making me return to him time and time again to see what the problem was. By the second day he was almost a full row behind the others.

"What the hell's the matter here!" I said. "What the hell's the matter here?"

After several moments he slowly turned his wrinkled neck to me, looked at me with his milky eyes, and then returned to the vine.

"Goddamn it, I said what the hell's the matter here!"

Again he turned, slowly, and said, without looking at me, "I'm doing the best I can."

Twice that day I had to have other workers help him with his row. At the end of the day I said to him in front of the others, "You'd better get a good night's sleep, old man, because I'm not going to put up with your slowness much longer."

The next morning he trudged past me without looking at me. That day I was determined to watch him closely. Within the first fifteen minutes he fell behind. I waited, giving him a chance to catch up. After another fifteen minutes he fell further behind. I went to him again. "Look, I can't put up with this anymore. You're going to have to go." He kept picking. "I said you're going to have to go!" He kept picking. I grabbed his bucket from him, and when he turned those milky eyes on me, I said, "Get out!"

And he said, "Sonny, I've been picking grapes before you were even a thought."

I erupted. "You lazy, dirty, old son of a bitch! Don't you ever talk to me like that! You no good . . ."

Other workers gathered. When I finished, he was still looking at me, still staring at me with those milky eyes. Then he said, "You can talk to me like this in front of everybody because I am old. But someday you too will be old," and left.

On the last Sunday in October we celebrated the end of the harvest. Katherine Pavlovitch prepared a sumptuous feast of dove and polenta. There was beer and wine, and Katherine and Joe and Suzie and Eufemia and I were joined by Pete Pavlovitch and his family. It had been the biggest and best harvest ever, and the brothers were ecstatic. The more Joe Pavlovitch drank, the louder and more he talked. Some of his talk was directed at Eufemia and me.

"You kids were great! We couldn't have done it without you. And you're just beginning. You have a great future here! Don't they, Pete? You'll make a great couple. And to show you how much I mean that, tomorrow the carpenters are coming. They're gonna start working on Mamá and Papá's old house up by the road, gonna fix it up real nice. And guess who it's for! Not me, not Pete, not Katherine. No, it's yours! As soon as you kids get married, it's all yours! You'll like it. I promise. It's gonna be real nice. Let's drink to that!"

Eufemia and I had not talked about marriage. Over the past three-and-a-half months we had talked very little, talking mainly when I drove her home in Joe Pavlovitch's pickup after Sunday dinner at the Pavlovitches's, which had become our custom once

J.J. and his two older sisters left for college. Usually, we would stop at one of the ranches and walk deep into the deserted vines as the sun sank, coloring the sky in its descent, content with the silence and relief of the otherwise busy fields. Mostly, we held hands and meandered. Occasionally, we stopped and kissed, more like friends than lovers.

Nor did we speak of marriage on that late October Sunday evening, even though it was clearly on our minds, she excited and I troubled. But when the carpenters came the next day and the house was raised and a new foundation poured and a steady hammering followed, we talked about it.

"Are we going to get married, Eufemia?"

"Are you asking me?"

"Not really. Not now, anyway. But everybody seems to think that we are, and I just wanted to know what you think."

"Oh, Gabriel, I don't know. It's not something you rush into."

"I'm not rushing."

"Neither am I. . . . We could do a lot worse. And I don't see anybody else around for either of us."

"So you think we are?"

"I don't know."

"When will you know?"

"I guess when you ask me."

I was afraid to ask, afraid to even think about asking. It seemed so final, as if my life would end even before it began. It meant that, like Papá, I would be there for the rest of my life, watch the sun come up over those vines every morning and watch it go down over another set of vines every evening for the rest of my life. I wanted more, even though I didn't know what more was. And, like Papá, I would become another one of Joe Pavlovitch's possessions. Joe Pavlovitch already had too much say in my life.

But the hammering continued every day, it seemed, from sunup to sundown. I could hear it all over the main ranch and sometimes, I thought, down at the Emerian ranch eight miles away. And now it seemed that Joe Pavlovitch had arranged my schedule so that at least three days a week I was at the refrigeration units at noon, close enough to Eufemia so that we could have lunch together, so that she could say, "Let's go look at the house, Gabby." Now that the harvest was over, it was my job to drive her home. "Did you see what they did to the house today, Gabby?" It even carried over to Sunday dinner. "All right, you kids, I think we'd better take a walk over to the house so that you can give me some ideas about the kitchen. They're starting on it this week, you know. Kathy, I think you'd better come, too. You've spent more time in kitchens than me." Across the harvested vines we went to the house that Joe Pavlovitch had grown up in, with Joe Pavlovitch out in front with his short, quick, efficient steps, and Eufemia and Katherine behind him happily chirping about kitchens, and me following like a captured, condemned man with a noose around my neck, silently cursing, "That fucking house. That fucking house."

They finished remodeling and refurbishing the house in early January. For the first time ever, I welcomed the hated tulle fog. Because it hid the house, made it disappear from the world fifty feet beyond it. Only to have it resurrected by Joe Pavlovitch every chance he got, every time he saw us together, taking a set of keys from his pocket and dangling them before us, "The minute you kids say the word, it's yours, all yours."

Eufemia was so excited the first time we saw the refinished house alone that she dropped all pretenses, using the word "we" openly and unashamedly. We could put a sofa there and a loveseat here. We could have end tables there and there, with big ceramic lamps. We'd need a dinette set. Katherine had told her that McMahon's in Bakersfield had one just like theirs on sale. We really had to look at it before they sold it. I looked and listened, saying little except at one point asking how she intended to pay for everything. "We can buy it on credit, Gabby. We're both working. We both have good steady jobs. We'll have good credit. That's how Kathy and Joe did it when they started out. In fact, they'll even co-sign for us if there's a problem."

Just as the fog lifted in the third week of February, Eufemia lost interest in the house. "I really don't want to," she said to

Bertha several times when Bertha asked if we were going over to look at the house. Nor did she ask to see the house when we were alone. She became increasingly quiet when I drove her home. "What's the matter?" "Nothing. I'm just tired." When she began staying home on Sundays because she "had a lot of things to catch up on," even I knew what the problem was. Sundays without her were aimless and lonely. I had no one to see and nowhere to go. We had not only survived but advanced in that world of grape fields. Now I felt as if I were losing my grip. If nothing else, we were friends.

On one of those Sunday afternoons, Papá said, "She's hurt and embarrassed."

"I know." I was lying under that small tree in our patch of yard looking up through the new green leaves at the soft spring sky.

"She just expected what everybody else was expecting, that you'd marry her."

"I know, Papá. But I never promised her, I never said a word. I swear."

"Well, it must be that you two were together for so long. It seemed like you made a perfect couple. Everybody just thought . . . I've talked to her father. Her parents like you. They're proud of you, son. They see what you've done. In one year you've done more than most of us have in twenty-five. We were just waiting. We even joked about who was going to pay for the wedding. Now Nacho doesn't know what to think. And Señor Joe spent all that money on the house . . ."

"Papá, I never asked him to."

"I know, son, but he likes you. He calls you "his kids." He wants the best for you. And Señora Katherine, she's heartbroken. She keeps asking me what happened, all sad-eyed. Even the workers are asking. They thought you'd get married last summer. Gabriel, I know I'm not as intelligent as you, and I know you've had a lot more schooling than me, but I have lived twenty-six years more than you, and I love you and I too want the best for you, so I can tell you with a clear conscience that you're not going to do any better than Eufemia. She's a good, intelligent girl, and she'll make you a good wife and a good mother to your children. You can't ask for more than that."

We were married two months later. It was a small wedding held on the main ranch on a late Saturday afternoon, with only our parents and the two Pavlovitch families in attendance. That was what we wanted.

Because of the impending harvest, our honeymoon was postponed until November. We spent the first night of our marriage in our remodeled new home. It was dusk when we left our parents and the Pavlovitches and walked hand in hand down the white sandy road, through the rising remains of the heat, around rows of leafy vines to our new home. I was giddy with champagne, laughing at almost everything. Eufemia opened the door to the smell of new carpet and then stopped just outside the threshold, blocking my path, and turned and asked, "Aren't you going to carry me over the threshold, Gabby? I'm Mrs. Garcia now." I laughed a long, head-back laugh and then said, "Okay." Eufemia sidled up to me, put an arm around me, and then hopped up on me. I caught her but dropped her. She fell hard, let out a groan, and started to cry. She cried and cried until I offered to take her to a doctor. "No. No. This is our wedding night."

We rose and walked into the house. "I'm sorry, Eufemia, I'm . . ." "Shh, this is our wedding night." Then she kissed me as she had never kissed me, pressing herself against me openly and firmly so that I could feel her breasts and thighs and maybe more. It was a long kiss. I was overwhelmed. When she released me, she said, "It's already dark. Don't you think we should be going to bed?" "Yeah," I said, fighting back champagne laughter. "Good. Wait for me here. I need to change in the bedroom."

I was excited. During the two months of ambivalence since I had asked Eufemia to marry me, the only constant was the thought of nightly sex. Any sex was better than no sex, better than my hand. Now I was about to realize that. I fended off my excitement by moving about the front room, fingering the new furniture she had bought on credit at McMahon's. Then the bedroom door opened, and she stood in the doorway in a sheer white nightgown, her nakedness outlined by the light behind her. She was smiling. "You like my new nightgown, Gabby? I hope so. I bought it just for you." I looked in disbelief, her body so different than mine. "Come over here, Gabby, and kiss your wife." I needed little encouragement. I kissed her again, a long, hot kiss, feeling the nakedness of her back on my fingers. "Aren't you hot, Gabby? Why don't you take off some of those clothes and get ready for bed." I took one step away from her and started to undress. It was then that I realized that I wasn't hard and another form of excitement welled up in me, panic. I got hotter and hotter as if I had contracted an instant fever. She was standing there, watching, waiting. I stripped down to my shorts, hoping she wouldn't notice. "There, don't you feel better, Gabby?" She held her hand out and said, "Take me to bed, Gabby." I took her hand and led her to the bed, shivering, not from lust, but from fear. We stood at the side of the bed and she said, "Take it off." I didn't know which one she meant so I chose her nightgown. "Do you like me?" Yes, I nodded, a hundred quick yeses, too short of panicked breath to answer, too staggered by fear to breathe.

"Put me to bed, love," taking my hand and putting us both to bed. "Kiss me, love. Kiss your wife. I told you I was saving myself for my husband and now I'm all yours." She pressed herself to me, and I kissed her and ran my hands over her body as her breathing got heavy and she let out little "Ohs," and I felt nothing and thought nothing except that I wasn't hard. She got hotter, and I was about to burst, but not from lust, never from lust, touching her over and over again, somehow hoping that I could fend off the inevitable. Not so. She began tugging at my shorts. "Take them off." I resisted. She pulled harder. "What's the matter? Take them off. You're my husband. I want to see you." I stopped struggling. She pulled them down to my knees and looked and looked and looked. "Oh, my God!" she finally said, "Oh, my God!" and then turned and covered herself and shifted herself to the farthest edge of the bed and cried. I looked at myself and saw myself smaller than small, hidden somewhere at the base of a mass of wrinkled uncircumcised skin.

I didn't sleep that night. If I did, I don't remember. Eufemia didn't sleep much either. From time to time I could hear her or feel her sobbing. I got out of bed at the first grey of morning. I left the bedroom and sat on the cheerful new couch and wished I were dead. I sat there for hours, not daring to go outside, somehow believing that they all knew or would know, and dreading the first sounds in the bedroom.

Eufemia came out of the bedroom just before noon, wearing more clothes than I had seen her wear all summer. "Let's go to town," she said. "I don't feel like seeing anybody now, and if we stay here, we will, and I don't want to go to the Pavlovitches's for dinner today." I drove to town. As we neared it, Eufemia broke her silence.

"Have you seen a doctor?"

"A doctor? For what?"

"You know what."

"No, I don't know what."

"About not being able to get big."

"I can get big."

"Was it me, then?"

"No, I can get big."

"What was it then?"

"The champagne."

"Please don't lie to me, Gabby."

"No, I get big all the time."

"How do you know?"

"What do you mean, how do I know? I get big, big as hell and I come all over the place."

"Are you sure?"

"Sure I'm sure. I've been getting hard-ons since before I can remember, and I've been coming since I was thirteen."

"Can you tonight?"

"Sure."

We drove on through Delano and into Bakersfield. We had lunch at a Mexican restaurant and went to a movie to escape the heat and wait for "tonight." We sat through two full-length Technicolor films of which I remembered nothing, staring instead at the huge screen, gulping at "tonight." I fondled myself several times in the darkness of the theater to make myself hard. Nothing. Not even the slightest stirring. In fact, it seemed to be running away from me, getting smaller and smaller, sinking down into my testicles. I told myself it was because I was in a theater with people all around me. But I knew better, and I didn't want the second movie to end.

We had dinner at the same Mexican restaurant, more to pass the time than to eat. We drove home in absolute silence with "tonight" rapidly approaching. When we arrived, she slammed the pickup's door with finality. It was dusk again, twenty-four hours later. I closed the front door and swallowed. We turned and looked at each other. "Well," Eufemia said. I brought her to me, hugged her and kissed her, telling myself that she wanted it, that she had to have it, over and over again. Nothing. But I could try again, because we had been careful not to press our pelvises against each other. I kissed her again, this time moving my hands over her body and calling up the repetitive fantasies of my masturbations, a big buxomy blonde female who not only wanted it and needed it, but was begging me for it. Nothing. I inserted Eufemia as the female. Nothing, less even. But I felt her arousal and released her.

She was out of breath, and I feigned the same. She came back to me, saying, "Oh, Gabby, I love you." I kissed her again, long and hard, my hands moving, and I inserted a big-busted, big-thighed, big-assed blonde, the staple of my fantasies, and felt a stirring, and started taking off Eufemia's clothes, pulling at them before it left, deserted me. And Eufemia, in turn, helped me with mine, as I thought harder and harder of the blonde through the gritted teeth of my mind, and fell on Eufemia and all her little "Ohs." And I tried to do what I knew I had to do, without ever having been taught or told. But nothing. And Eufemia, panting, took that frightful stub in her hand, gently, touching it ever so delicately, massaging it, rubbing it. But nothing. Rubbing it harder and harder. Nothing. And then grabbing it as hard as she could, fingernails and all, determined to pull that tiny thing out of its cat-acomb until I screamed in pain.

Then she cried, there on the entry floor, until it was dark, when she slunk off silently to the bedroom. I, in turn, slept what little I could on that cheerful new couch as I did for the rest of our marriage.

The next day everyone, including Papá, greeted me with smiles, telling me that it was clear that I wouldn't be getting much sleep for a while. Even Bertha remarked, "You better let that girl get some sleep, Gabby. She didn't do much but yawn around here all day."

Sleep we eventually got over the next two months, she sleep-ing in the bedroom with the door closed, and I was on the couch. We hid our condition from everyone, careful in what we said and how we appeared in public and quickly eradicating each morning any possible sign that we were not sleeping together. The harvest was soon in full swing, and with my long hours we seldom saw each other. Eufemia was already locked in her bedroom when I came home from the fields and was still there when I left in the morning. We didn't try again. Neither of us wanted to risk the pain.

When J.J. came home from summer session, he cornered me in the field and asked me what it was like getting it every night. I grinned as best I could but said nothing. The next day I drove my company truck to town, parked it on Main Street behind the Grey-hound depot, got on a bus, and didn't return until twenty-one years, three months, and two days later.

It was for Papá's funeral. I wore a three-piece suit and recog-nized only a few people and spoke to even fewer. At the cemetery J.J. said, "You didn't recognize her, did you?" pointing to a fat grey woman holding a small child in each hand. "That's Eufemia and her two grandkids." I hadn't recognized her. I would never have imagined that her tiny bones could have carried that much weight. I went up to her and said the only thing I could say, "I'm sorry, Eufemia."

Eufemia sighed and said softly, "I forgave you a long time ago, Gabby."

CHAPTER V

She rose when I came into the tiny waiting room and said, "Mr. Garcia, my name is Rebecca Williams. I realize that I don't have an appointment, but I'd like to speak to you if I could. It won't take very long. I can wait."

She'd have to wait. There were three people ahead of her. I beckoned to the woman in the first chair and said, "*Pase, señora.*" It was almost eight p.m. and there were still three to go. Do a good job at a fee that people can afford and the word gets around. An hour later Rebecca Williams was still waiting. I was not accustomed to having a pretty, blue-eyed blonde in my office. I could only guess at what she wanted.

I locked the front door and showed her into my office. "What can I do for you, Miss Williams?" She looked too young to be married. Twenty or twenty-one. I glanced at her ring finger. Ringless.

"Thank you for seeing me at this late hour, Mr. Garcia." There was at most a fifteen-year difference in our ages. Still, she was formal. "I'll be graduating from college in two months, and I don't know whether I want to be a lawyer. I guess the question is whether I *need* to be a lawyer. Because I'm not interested in the title, the status, or the money. I just want to help people."

She paused again, disconcerted. Her eyes fell away, and she gulped and looked back at me.

"So what does that have to do with me?" I said, brimming with confidence.

"You have a reputation for helping the poor. That's what I want to do. I'm fluent in Spanish, both written and spoken. I spent a year at the University in Guanajuato. I realize that you can't pay very much, but I don't expect much. In fact, I'd be willing to volunteer my time, part-time, for the rest of the school year and then full-time through the summer. I brought my resume."

She handed me two typewritten pages. Honors everywhere. Major in sociology, minor in Spanish. A four-point average. I looked across the desk at the clear, bright blue eyes, as bright as the resume said they would be. Surely too bright for me and my practice.

"Well, I hadn't planned on hiring anyone. . . ."

"No. No. I'm not asking to be hired . . . paid. I want to volunteer."

I looked back over her resume. Did I really want someone this bright around? "Let me think about it. Let me give it some thought. . . . I'll call you."

We rose and she extended her hand. I took it in mine and felt its softness. She was more than pretty. She was beautiful.

Once she left, a wonderful warmth spread over me. A beautiful white girl wanted to work with me. A beautiful white girl had lost her composure when she looked at me. But the ranch returned, as it always did: the refurbished house and Eufemia, pulling and scratching and clawing at that which was shrinking rather than growing. Once again I shrank.

It had been sixteen years since those two dreadful nights. For the most part I had managed to put them behind me. Eleven years to complete college and law school while working at an assortment of jobs to sustain myself left little time for anything except my studies. Now in my fifth year of a law practice, I routinely worked twelve-hour days, six days a week. On Sundays I allowed myself to sleep and lay in bed as long as I cared to. A late leisurely breakfast with the Sunday paper was followed by an afternoon movie and dinner downtown before I returned to my storefront office, which was located across the driveway from my house, for four or five hours, preparing for the week to come. During my first three years, there had been attempts to match me with a suitable partner. I had rebuffed them all. Rumors circulated that I was gay. Indeed, there were times when I wished that I were gay, rather than lusting and longing for women that I knew I could never penetrate. On those occasions when I found myself hopelessly alone with a woman and an opportunity, the fear of failure became so great that all I felt was a numbness around my groin, provoking ugly, awkward excuses before I fled.

Over the years I had conditioned myself to accept the fact that all of the mating rituals that surrounded me daily were simply not for me. I convinced myself that my disadvantage was actually an advantage, one that saved me countless hours in meeting and keeping a mate, one that in the end would allow me to be a better lawyer and help more people. Occasionally, I would slip and find a woman desirable. It was an odd feeling, like allowing myself to enter a room filled with food when I was hungry, knowing that I couldn't eat. A void would set in, filling me with its own special ache. Fear and shame followed: fear that I couldn't do it; shame that I would be found out. And my member would shrink to a stub and sometimes, I felt, to a button on the base of my pelvis. That night was one of those slips. But it ended as quickly as it began, and I suspected the reason even then: she was a white girl.

I didn't call her. By the second day I wasn't even thinking of calling her. But she called me. Seven days to the day, a week exactly. Martha, my part-time secretary, answered the phone, which enabled me to say, "As you can see, I already have a secretary. I really don't need another one." I thought that was the end of it. I didn't know Rebecca then.

Three nights later, just after seven, while I was meeting with clients, I heard the rapid clatter of Martha's typewriter in the waiting room. For a moment I thought it was one of my client's children playing on the typewriter. But the clatter was too smooth, fast, and uninterrupted. It wasn't like Martha to return in the evening, even when she had fallen far behind. She was on salary.

When I stepped out of my office, the waiting room was overflowing. All six seats were taken and three men were standing. I greeted several of them and was starting back to my office with my next appointment when I noticed her, when the blonde hair registered. I looked back and saw her busily typing away, completely at ease among a room full of dark-skinned people who spoke little if any English. I stopped and stared. If she saw me, she gave no indication. Not once did she look up at me.

The next appointment was excruciating. The sweat-stained man had been arrested on a driving with a suspended license charge. That much was clear; the rest was a blur. When was his license suspended? Why was it suspended? What notice had he received of that suspension? When was he eligible to have his license reinstated? All the standard questions. I must have asked each five times, and each time I was only able to grasp a fragment of the answer. My confusion was completely confusing the poor man. The fragments changed. *He* was asking *me* questions, trying to understand what I wanted to know. Finally, embarrassed, I asked to see his paperwork, hoping to make some sense of my mess. But not before I looked down at my notes and saw random words on different lines at different places on my legal pad, all incomprehensible. I looked at his arrest papers and court papers. They might as well have been blank because I saw only black lines. What the hell was she doing here?

I knew I had to confront her, deal with her. So I told the man that I would have to review his court file before proceeding and asked him to return at the end of the week. I had resolved to see her next: I would accomplish nothing if I didn't. But when I stepped into the waiting room, I stopped short. She was consoling an old Mexican woman, complete with black shawl, who was quietly sobbing for her son who had just been arrested. "He's a good boy. He's a good boy," the woman repeated. And Rebecca, in a Spanish that surprised me, kept agreeing: she was sure that he was, assuring her that she had come to the right place because I was a very competent, dedicated lawyer who truly helped people. I looked around the room at all the other open, trusting brown faces and sighed.

I raced through the others, spending little more than five minutes with each, making a quick determination that they needed to bring me more documents, more paperwork, or that I needed to review the court docket before we could proceed. Because I had to talk to her, I had to put an end to this.

I locked the door after the last one. It was not quite 8:30. Still early enough for someone to come looking for "*el licenciado.*" Then I turned to her and said, "What are you doing here? What do you want?"

"I want to help people."

"What?"

"Do you think you're the only one who wants to help people?"

She took me by surprise. "What?"

She was sitting at Martha's desk, her stark, straight blonde hair falling well below her shoulders, her eyes wide and unafraid.

"I said I want to help people."

Crestfallen, I looked away. I must have assumed that she had returned because of me. Now she had told me, as plainly as she could, that she had come to help people.

"Does that surprise you?"

"No," I said quietly. But not looking at her, afraid that she might see my disappointment.

She came the next day and for the rest of the week too. She came exactly at five as Martha left and stayed until nine when I left. She came at nine o'clock on Saturday morning and stayed until I locked the door at six. I felt like a prisoner in my own office. I kept my office door closed when she was there, and yet I was aware of her, painfully aware of her, aware of the nonstop clatter of her typewriter, of her quick certain steps to the filing cabinet and back, of the squeak of her chair. I instructed her to knock before entering. That gave me time to ready myself, to plant my feet firmly under my desk, and sit squarely in my chair with my arms on the armrests and rehearse the words I would use: "Come in. . . . What is it?" Words designed to make her speak, make her explain, make her be the awkward one. And awkward she was, bumbling and stumbling through her sentences, reddening when I wouldn't help her, when I would sit and look up at her under the rims of my eyes without so much as blinking as she stammered through a question or explanation. And awkward I let her be.

Still, her work was far superior to Martha's. In two, four-hour days she was able to do what Martha did in five, eight-hour days, with a tenth of the mistakes. Her Spanish was grammatically correct, and she could spell, in English and Spanish. She began organizing the unorganized, which was everything. She embarrassed me with her questions and suggestions, most of which indicated that neither Martha nor I knew anything about running a law office.

At the end of three weeks, as I let her out of the office, I blurted out, "Please don't come anymore. I can't pay you."

As agitated as I was, I could see the hurt on her face. It was a while before she answered. Then she said, "You don't like my work?"

"Your work is good. It's too good. I just don't have the money to pay you for it."

"The money doesn't matter. I want to help people. I told you that."

My clients called her "*La Rubia*." The blonde one. Seldom seen in the Mexican villages from which most had come, and seldom seen on the east side in which most of them now lived, she was a rarity. They were astounded by her Spanish and her warmth and her decency. She cared and it showed. Soon they were calling and asking for "La Rubia" even when Martha was there. They trusted her. They sought her advice. *Muy amable.* You are so kind. I must have heard them direct that phrase to her a thousand times. There was an eagerness on their faces when they talked to her. They were unaccustomed to being treated like that by a white person. They loved her.

Within two months my office was transformed. The files I now carried to court looked like files: organized, stapled, and two-hole-punched instead of the assorted, loose papers that laid unidentified in the file folders that I had routinely taken to court for five years. Now my pleadings could have been typed in any of the high-rise law offices.

I had always told myself that appearances didn't matter, that what was important was providing quality services for my clients no matter how poor they were. But it felt good to look like a lawyer.

I marveled at Rebecca's capabilities and wondered how a twenty-one-year-old could know so much about running a law office. But all I could do was wonder. Because all I knew about her was her address and phone number, both of which Martha had given me, and because I still spoke to her only when it was necessary and usually the only words I said to her that were unrelated to business were "hello" and "goodbye."

Gradually, she established our comfort levels. It was all about pleasing me. She watched and listened attentively. Every decision was mine and mine alone. She openly boasted about me and my legal talents to anyone who would listen. It was some time before the suggestions came. But once she had relaxed me, they came in increasing numbers and regularity. And I increasingly found them more and more helpful.

Two weeks into the summer Martha came into my office and gave me an ultimatum. "Get rid of that blonde bitch or I'm outta here! Take your pick! Me or your fucking blondie!"

Martha had never spoken to me like that before, and I had never seen her so angry. She was snorting: her nostrils wide and her eyes round and her arms tightly folded across her breast.

"What's the matter?"

"What do you mean what's the matter! You know damn well what's the matter! That bitch corrects everything I do! Everything I type for you I see redone the next day! Who in the hell does she think she is! Phony white bitch! She's so nice to everybody with her perfect Spanish! If they only knew what a scheming witch she is! Get rid of her or I go!"

Martha didn't give me much of a choice. Rebecca *was* routinely retyping everything Martha did. The errors she pointed out each day *were* embarrassing. I was paying Martha for nothing and paying Rebecca nothing for everything. It didn't make sense. But was I ready to be alone with Rebecca?

When I told Martha that Rebecca had become a valuable asset

to the office and that she, Martha, was free to stay or leave as she pleased, Martha erupted. "You goddamn Mexicans are all the same! Give you a little money, a little education, a little status, and all of a sudden you're too good for us Mexican women! You want your white bitches! You want to parade around with them like their shit don't stink!"

If Martha only knew.

Once we were alone, Rebecca was all business. She came at nine and left when I did, which was usually around nine on weekdays and six on Saturdays. Everything she did was designed to make me more productive. She took over my calendar and began screening all calls. Did they really need to see me or was it something she could handle? If it was the former, I had a concise summary of the client's problem on my desk when she showed him in. If it was the latter, she would handle the problem in the waiting room or, if it was a sensitive matter, would schedule those appointments for times when I would be in court so that she could use my office. She became a notary public, filling that desperate need that Mexicans always seemed to have to have everything notarized. Soon she was known as *La Notaria*. She translated documents from English to Spanish and vice versa. It wasn't long before she was taking in more money than what I was paying her. She never mentioned that.

My business boomed. The waiting room was always full. Somehow she squeezed two more chairs into it, and, when that wasn't enough, she bought six white plastic chairs that she put out on the sidewalk each morning and stacked in our waiting room at night. I had started her at Martha's salary and promptly doubled it and soon increased it again. She purchased a new, state-of-the-art typewriter, and ordered a set of law books that she managed to stuff into my office, and convinced me of our need for a copy machine. Efficient, efficient. Sometimes I found myself wishing that she wasn't so damn efficient, so businesslike.

I don't know if it was what I perceived as a reluctance on her part to leave, or whether it was the fact that it was an early Saturday evening in late October and the few free hours I allotted

myself each week were beginning, and the person I was now closest to was leaving, that led me to say, before she could say goodnight, "You never talk about yourself."

She had been gathering her purse and jacket and stopped,
looked up and blushed, blinked and looked away for a moment
before looking back and answering, "Neither do you."

Now I blushed, and she blushed some more, and for several
moments we dangled in discomfort, exacerbating it by our inertia,
neither wanting to leave.

"I guess that's true," I heard myself say. "Maybe it's because
I didn't think there was too much to tell about myself that was
very important."

"Oh, you know I'd listen."

It was something that had to be said, but once said was obvious. Yes, I did know she'd listen. Yes, I did know she cared. So I
told her about growing up on a ranch outside Delano and about
wanting to be and becoming a lawyer, but briefly, and then asked,
"And what about you?"

She blushed again and shuffled a bit, but I knew that she
wanted to tell of herself. She said that she had been born and
raised in San Jose, that she had had a happy childhood, that her
father had made a comfortable living, that she had always been
bothered by the plight of the poor, that she had gone away to college for two years, had not liked it, and had returned home to
complete her studies. When I asked her what kind of work her
father did, she said, "He's kind of a consultant for some corporations." When I asked what kind of a consultant he was, she said,
"About business." That was all.

We stood, waiting and wanting, chancing a look at each other,
and then looking away, desperately wanting the other to make the
first move, to do something. She smiled nervously. I was too
frightened to smile. Eufemia and the refurbished house were near.
Then the smell of new carpet filled my nostrils, as stale and distinct as it had been years before, and I could feel Eufemia grop-
ing and pulling for what couldn't be. The numbness and shrinking began. I turned, saying as I began moving, "I gotta go," and

hurried to my office and closed the door behind me.

I heard the outer door close, not right away, but after a minute or two, after I was seated behind my desk with my face buried in my hands, remembering what I didn't want to remember, but remembering nevertheless, and listening too, listening for the sound that I somehow hoped would never come, and then hearing it, the door and the doorjamb engaging, brief, clear, and final. She was gone. She had waited, stayed. Had she hoped, too? . . . Yes. . . . No.

I sat in the darkness for a long while, mostly pitying myself. It wasn't the carnal. I would have gladly surrendered the carnal, if a woman could have held me, if it would have been enough for her, too. When the sea of self-pity passed, I chastised myself. I had wanted what I could not have. I had been ready to give up everything, all I had worked so hard for, to be with someone. I would have deserted all my causes, all my rationales, in an instant . . . for her, for what couldn't be. When I finally left my office, I had resolved that if it ever happened again, if I let myself go again, I would have to ask her to leave.

For the remainder of the weekend I worried about how I would face Rebecca on Monday, convinced that I had made a complete fool of myself and that she had seen me for what I was: alone and needy. But like so many of my worries, these too fizzled into nothing because on Monday Rebecca was herself: formal and businesslike. If anything had happened Saturday, she probably hadn't noticed. By the end of the day I was bothered by two thoughts: nothing had happened Saturday, and I was all too ready to believe that something had. When Rebecca said goodnight to me that evening in her cold, formal manner, I was certain that for her nothing had happened. I was embarrassed and disappointed.

When I told Rebecca that the office would be closed for Thanksgiving Day, she asked, "Where are you going for dinner?"

She had taken me by surprise. I had no place to go, but I said, "I'm having Thanksgiving with friends." She said nothing, but I was certain that she had seen the lie on my face.

I slept in on Thanksgiving morning and, once awake, lay in

bed for the rest of the morning, staring at the ceiling and dozing off, enjoying the luxury of doing nothing. At noon I cooked myself breakfast, ate, and walked over to the office just after one.

She came unexpectedly at three bringing a large plate covered with aluminum foil. "I brought you some turkey," she said. I gulped and said as quickly as I could, "Thanks, but I've already had my turkey." "That's okay, a little more won't hurt you." She set the plate on my desk and left, but only my office, because I could hear her uncovering the typewriter and then her steady clatter began.

I sat at my desk for more than an hour, staring down at whatever it was that I had been reading, occasionally looking over at that silent mound of aluminum foil two feet from me. Finally, I rose and put on my jacket and went to the front door and said, "I'm locking up now." She covered the typewriter and came to the door without once looking at me, which embarrassed me all the more, and walked out into the orange dusk saying, "Goodnight," as she always did.

Once she was gone, I went back to my office and removed the foil, unveiling a large slab of white meat, which covered a generous portion of dressing. Alongside that were green beans, mashed potatoes, and cranberry sauce. I wondered about her family; I tried to picture them but had no success.

She had to have known that I had no place to go.

I carried the plate across the driveway, elated and disturbed. I placed it on the center shelf of my refrigerator where each time I opened the refrigerator door I would have to see it. There it remained, untouched, for three weeks. Sometimes I opened the door just to look at the plate. She did care about me. . . . Beyond that I couldn't go. At the beginning of the third week something under the foil began to stink. I tightened the foil around the plate's edges. But with each day the stench got worse, so bad that I began opening the refrigerator door only when it was absolutely necessary. At the end of the week I carried the plate, arms outstretched and head turned, out to the garbage can.

She was pretty. There was no denying that. Her fine mouth

and gentle nose had a dignity all their own, and her blue eyes lit up her face. More and more I caught myself staring at her fine bare legs as she left my office or had her back to me. Beyond that I couldn't go even though I knew that her hips and butt were full, her waist small, and her breasts round and soft.

Just as The Big Bear helped me through adolescence, so too did the Mayas help me through early manhood. I had heard of the Aztecs early on. After all, the Marines were always fighting from the halls of Montezuma to the shores of Tripoli. In high school we learned that the Aztecs were the Indians that Hernan Cortez sorely humiliated and conquered in claiming Mexico for Spain. But I had not heard of the Mayas until my third year in college, and then, only by way of a footnote in a history text which said that the Mayas had the most advanced civilization in pre-Columbian America, one that was comparable and even superior to some European civilizations of that time. That was all I needed. Within days I acquainted myself with all the works on the Mayas in Mesoamerica in the college library. For the next several years whatever spare time I had was spent studying the Mayas. I learned of the magnificent cities at Tikal and Copan and Palenque. At Palenque the tomb of the great ruler, Pacal, had recently been discovered, prompting comparisons to Egyptian and Asian cultures. The murals at Bonampak and the seaside splendor of Tulum captured my fancy. They were great mathematicians, architects, and astronomers. Their calendar was intricate and advanced and their hieroglyphics undeciphered. The sculptures that adorned so many of their buildings were breathtaking. I longed to be a Mayan. But it was hopeless: I had neither the long, thick, pointed nose, nor the almond eyes, nor the flattened forehead. Nor could I get past Papá's frequent recitations that on his side of the family we were Tarahumara Indians, and on my mother's side Tarascans.

Just after my discovery of the Mayas I thought I saw their descendants everywhere. Every dark-skinned Mexican with a thick, pointed nose had to be one. I'd approach them in Spanish. Occasionally, I'd get an irritated response in English: "What do you mean where am I from? That's none of your goddamn business!" Usually, they were from the non-Mayan parts of Mexico: Oaxaca, Michoacan, Sinaloa. Yes, some may have heard of the Mayas, but they had never been to the states of Chiapas and the Yucatan. For a while I was convinced that Eufemia had been a full-blooded Maya, and for that time I wished that I had stayed with her and that somehow we could have had a child. Gradually, I abandoned my vigil, or at least the questions that accompanied it. By the time I began practicing law I was almost content to simply admire the strain in an individual that had been passed down through generations and mixed marriages, an individual who most likely would never know or care about the accomplishments or intelligence of his ancestors. Every now and then I would ask someone who carried that nose and those features if they had ever been to Chiapas or the Yucatan. No.

On the day I threw out the turkey, Manuel Orozco, a neighborhood organizer and the source of many clients, invited me once again to his annual Christmas party at his home. What surprised me was that he also invited La Rubia.

When she came for me on Christmas day, she was dressed in high heels and stockings and a skimpy but expensive dress that I looked at only briefly because her exposed thighs made me uncomfortable. And when I saw that her car was much better than mine, I wondered where the money had come from.

That Christmas afternoon in California was warm and sunny, and Manuel Orozco's party was in full swing when we arrived. The doors and windows to his house were wide open, and kids were streaming and screaming about everywhere, draped in T-shirts and laughter.

There were joyful shouts when we entered, not unlike those that usually greeted me when I went to one of my client's parties. Except that this time the shouts were for Rebecca as well. "La Rubia! La Rubia!" they exclaimed. As promised, there was food and drink of every kind, and everywhere I went I was, as always, the center of fawning admiration and attention. But so was Rebecca, and as the afternoon wore on, the party-goers seemed to be making a bigger fuss over Rebecca than they were over me. That annoyed me, and the annoyance stayed with me for the remainder of the afternoon, was with me still on our way home when she asked, "Is something wrong, Gabby?"

"No," I managed to answer.

When we pulled up to my house, I opened the door, but she said, "Wait. Stay a minute. I have something for you, Gabby." I turned and under the door light saw more thigh than I had seen earlier that afternoon. I shuddered and closed the door, more to shield myself from those thighs than to stay.

In the darkness she said, "What's the matter, Gabby?"

"Nothing," I said, thinking it had to be the drinks she had at the party.

Then she turned on the overhead light and repeated, "I have something for you, Gabby."

I looked straight ahead, not wanting to know or see what she had for me. My body shook and my member shrank.

"Look, Gabby."

I didn't look, until I felt an edge pressing against my hand. Then I looked, but down, not over, and saw a small gift-wrapped box lying beside my hand.

"Open it," she said. "Open it. I want to see if you like it."

I raised it, brought it to me without turning my head, struggled with the ribbon and the paper, sending loud, crackling sounds through the car. I didn't know what to expect and never expected what I saw. It was a small green, jade-like figurine. When I raised it to the light, I saw the gigantic, grotesque teeth and the long crooked nose of the ugly, yet beautiful Mayan rain God, Chac Mool.

"Do you like it, Gabby?"

I couldn't answer. My eyes and throat welled with tears. I nodded and opened the door and fled, with my tears and my tiny rain God.

There was no working that night, though I sat at my desk for a long time looking at, and losing myself in, that little green monster's evil, mocking grin. Finally, I pushed aside the stack of files before me and said, "You win, my little man," and turned off the lights and locked the door and walked across the driveway with him.

There was little sleeping that night either. The questions were: why had she given me Chac and how did she know?

The week between Christmas and New Year's Day was traditionally the slowest, quietest week of the year, and that year was no exception. The courts, for all practical purposes, were closed. Many Mexicans returned to Mexico for a visit, and the rest of my clients and potential clients were only too willing to take a week's vacation from their legal woes. As a result, I was in the office much more than usual, and the clients who came into the office were few.

I didn't know what to expect that week, but I must have been expecting something because I was disappointed on that Monday when it was business as usual. The skimpy dress was gone, and we spoke only of clients and cases. My spirits fell: the green god had only been a Christmas gift, something an employee gave her employer. How or why she knew about the green god no longer mattered.

It took most of that first day to get over my disappointment. I did so by distancing myself from her, withdrawing more and more until by late afternoon I was hardly speaking to her, using nods to communicate whenever I could. She left without saying "Goodnight." Still, the next day I was listening for her in the next room. When she brought in papers for my signature, I noticed the delicateness of her fingers and the whiteness of her skin just inches from my brown coarse fingers. And then I waited for her to turn, waited for that split second when I could gobble up the bareness of those legs and the thickness just above the knees, suggesting that there was so much more. I told myself that I had to get a hold of myself. But I kept on listening for, anticipating her. By noon I admitted that I wasn't getting any work done. Still, I wouldn't leave, wouldn't go to the law library or walk across the driveway to my house, even though I kept reminding myself that if she so much as winked at me, I would shrink to a button.

At mid-afternoon when she went out for a sandwich, I tried to understand, articulate what it was that I was doing, what it was that I wanted, and decided that I wanted to enjoy her in my limited way, without her knowing or suspecting, without even the remotest threat of performance. I listened for her the rest of the afternoon. When she said "Goodnight" just past six, I was exhausted.

That night I convinced myself that I had to come to my senses, that there could not be a repeat of that day's insanity. The next morning I was in the office before seven, closing my door even though it was two hours before her arrival. Just before nine she knocked for my signature. As she left, I asked that she close the door behind her, mumbling that I had a motion to draft and that I didn't want to be disturbed the rest of the day.

At noon she was at the door again. This time she closed it once she entered. She stood directly across the desk from me. I suppose that if I had looked up before she began speaking, I would have had some inkling about what was to follow.

"Why are you afraid of women?"

The words stunned and stung me, forcing me to look up at her. "What?" having heard what she had said but not knowing what to answer. Until finally I mustered, "I'm not afraid of women."

"Why are you afraid of me?"

Her eyes were both accusatory and certain. I could feel my eyes darting but couldn't stop them. "I'm not afraid of you." Still, my eyes couldn't meet hers.

"Then kiss me."

"What?"

"Kiss me."

I could feel myself hot and churning, but my mind was frozen. "What?"

She stepped around the desk, around to my chair with her bare leg touching mine, ever so slightly. "Kiss me."

I looked up at her again, and her eyes and face were open and calm, matter of fact, as if there were nothing else we could or should do. "Kiss me," she repeated. Her words were at once a statement and a command, but quiet, even, firm.

I rose and she pressed herself to me and I to her. I could feel the softness of her breasts and the fullness of her thighs. Our eyes were but inches apart, speaking a language of their own. She put her arms over my shoulders and cupped the back of my head in her hands and brought my lips to hers. We kissed, a wet kiss, her moist lips moving, covering mine. I brought my hands to the narrow part of her firm back and held it and then caressed it. We were locked in that kiss for what seemed like hours. It had been years since I had touched and been touched, and the wonder of intimacy overwhelmed me. When we broke apart, she said, "I love you."

I couldn't look at her. I couldn't accept it, hear it, see it.

"I love you," she repeated, hardly more than a whisper but as resolute as any thunderclap.

She came to me again. We kissed once more, her lips teaching mine, introducing me to wonders I had never known, sending my head swirling. She pressed closer. There was no mistaking her breasts. Her stomach was just under mine, rising and falling, her thighs flush against mine. Her breathing grew heavier. She ground her hips against me. Her tongue flickered and I pulled away. Because I couldn't, and I knew it, and I was shrinking, and more than anything, I didn't want to be found out.

"What's the matter?"

"Nothing."

"Then why are you pulling away?"

"We can't."

"Why? I love you, and I'll show you that you love me."

"I can't."

"Why can't you?"

"You . . . you work for me and it's not right."

"What's not right? I love you. . . . Look at you. You want to as much as I do."

"I may want to, but I can't." And with that I moved past her, out of my office, into the hall, and into the restroom, needing to hide, but more than anything wanting to return to her. Fear prevailed, and I didn't dare touch myself because I knew what I had to be. Still, she was in my office, waiting, wanting me. And I thought of all I had accomplished through sheer grit and determination and told myself that this, too, I could accomplish, that if I tried as hard as I had with everything else, this too could be accomplished. I began manipulating myself, gently, thinking of her wanting me. Nothing. I kept at it, telling myself not to get discouraged, to concentrate, she wanted me, to try harder, she wanted me. Nothing. I tried to envision her nakedness, as beautiful as anything I had ever seen in magazines. Nothing. I recalled a specific photo, as blonde and as blue-eyed as she, and as big and curvaceous as she had to be. Nothing. I applied more pressure, stroked harder, until it hurt and I saw Eufemia and stopped.

When I came out of the restroom, she was gone. I dreaded the next day. Because she knew. She had to know. I couldn't get it up. How I hated that phrase: he can't get it up, always accompanied by smirks and derision. All that night it taunted me: *You* can't get it up. *You* can't get it up. Once I had come upon a homeless man masturbating in the sun along a riverbed. Even the lowest of the low could get it up. She had said that she loved me. That night those words were no more than a mirage.

She had a certain coolness toward me in the days that followed. I thought I understood; I had expected worse. By the end of the week, things were almost back to normal. Not once had she alluded to my impotency. No one else seemed to know, none of the many people she dealt with daily. Maybe she didn't know.

By the following week our eye contact was what it had been. Then our eyes locked, twice. Each time they scurried, ignoring, or at least pretending to ignore, those contacts. And I began looking at her again, when she was turned or not watching or even when she was standing next to me at my desk asking if what I said in a brief was really what I meant to say. She was beautiful. "I love you," she had said.

She was brilliant. "I love you." With clients, whomever they might be, she was gracious and charming. "I love you."

For days those words tormented me. Because there was little in me to love. How could a woman love me, if she really knew me, if she got close enough to see me? Besides, I was neither strapping nor handsome, and whatever success I had attained was purely the result of overcompensation. How long would it take her to find me out? And sooner or later, she'd learn that I couldn't get it up.

Then I dared look past her face, past her brains, past her grace and her charm. I dared look at her body again. I dared admire what I couldn't have, lick what I couldn't eat. And she seemed to know, sense that I was looking. Because her skirts and dresses got shorter, the thighs got fuller, the fine golden hair on those thighs suggested that it became finer and softer the further it went up. The breasts were fuller, too, rounder, freer, the nipples plain and bold.

As I look back now, it all seems so predictable, so inevitable. But then only our bodies knew. Because they were locked in that dance, that eternal tease, that give and take: her lead, my response, my lead, her response. We waltzed around that office for weeks without ever touching. Twice, as we were locking up the office, we all but kissed. Fear of being exposed kept me from moving those few final inches.

When we kissed again, it was at the copy machine with the lights on and the shades open for all the world to see. It was a long, wet, wonderful kiss, the warmth and closeness of her body, a body so different from mine, warming and soothing me, telling me that everything everywhere was wonderful. I could have gone on with that embrace forever except that I felt her increased breathing and I felt her thighs rubbing against mine, searching, maybe, for what was never to come, and I pulled away, smiling, hiding my fear.

"What's the matter? Why are you always pulling away? What's so funny?" her face contorted, puzzled. "What's the matter?" she repeated. "Can't you see that I love you?"

She did love me. And for that moment I accepted it.

"Wait a minute," she said, going to and locking the door, turning out the lights, and returning to me through the shadows of the streetlights. "Kiss me," she said. I kissed her, not pulling away as she pressed closer and closer, as she explored the inside of my mouth with her tongue, as she buried her fingers into my back and moaned softly, and then unzipped me and touched me as no one had ever touched me, caressing me, and I felt myself hardening and stretching, and I gasped both in pleasure and disbelief.

"I want you," she said.

I grappled with my pants, able only to drop them to my ankles. I grappled with her, touching her and feeling her. We fell to the floor beside the copy machine. I hurried with her panties, trying to remove them before I lost it, keeping her hand on my size, and then finally just pushing the fabric aside and entering that wonderful, wet, warm cavern, a stranger in a strange land, a pleasure so sharp that it bordered on pain, still knowing that I had to, wanted to, move in and out, up and down, to enhance what was not enhanceable.

And she moaned, "Oh, Gabby, I love you! Don't stop! Don't ever stop!"

CHAPTER VI

"**I** love you, Gabby."

She had first said it in my office. I had heard it then, and I heard it thousands of times thereafter. But I never really understood it until I no longer heard it.

She, on the other hand, understood, knew, appreciated exactly what she was saying. Not once did she doubt it, at least not until the end. It seemed also that once she said it, she set out to prove and explain it to me forever.

"I love you, Gabby."

Those words always surfaced in our foreplay. She said them when I penetrated her, almost without exception, as if it were the reason, the purpose, the essence of what we were doing. I heard them, but, in my eagerness, in my hunger, I brushed them aside. For me they had little relevance. Occasionally, I would be struck by them, interrupted by them, just long enough to note the oddity of their presence.

"I love you, Gabby."

She would speak of our lovemaking. I would speak of our fucking. She never argued: she knew that lovemaking was lovemaking. I disagreed: "We fuck, we don't make love." Love was the furthest thing from my mind when I was in her. I no more thought of love then than when I was eating a burrito or drinking a beer. To color our moans, our grapplings, our cries, our thrusts, with that quaint word, lovemaking, was too much for me. Was there something dirty about what we did, something that needed glossing over, a cover-up? What we did was no different than what dogs, horses, flies, fish, birds did every day from the beginning to the end of time.

"I love you, Gabby."

That word. What the hell did it mean? They all said it, they always said it. It was the key to their hearts, the key to their. . . . They said it so quickly, so easily. Often it seemed a word of convenience, without any meaning at all. I could certainly use it as a word of convenience, but never with her.

"I love you, Rebecca."

Those words dripped out of my mouth for the first time months after we began. They seeped out as I climaxed, a surprise and even a shock to me later that day as I remembered them. In the months that followed, they came more often, more regularly, always at climax. I told myself that I was simply accommodating her and, ultimately, making it better for myself. Still, months later, when they came before climax, I told myself that they were a way of expressing my thanks and, perhaps, my appreciation. But my words never carried the certainty, the conviction, the commitment that hers did.

"I love you, Gabby."

It was a giving and a taking. "I just want to give myself to you, Gabby. I want you to take me, Gabby, take it." I was more than happy to take. I took and I took and I took, seldom giving her words much thought, much interpretation except that it was mine to take. She said that, too. So I took, as simple as that. "Is it mine?" "Yes, it's yours." "Only mine?" "Only yours." "Nobody else's?" "Nobody else's" But as our fire calmed, when I began to see how much she had given me in so many other facets of my life, I began to wonder about my taking. "But I want you to take it. I want you to take me. Don't you understand?" It was even better when I understood. She enjoyed the giving as much as I enjoyed the taking. She enjoyed my taking as much as I enjoyed her giving.

"I love you, Gabby."

We had just climaxed when she said, "I heard someone say yesterday that some things can only be said through sex. I think that's true."

"Do you?"

"Yes."

"Why?"

"Because that's how you always tell me you love me."

As we were packing her dishes, I asked, "Have you told your parents?"

"Told them what?"

I wanted to answer: About me. Instead I said, "That you're moving."

"No."

"Aren't you going to tell them?"

"Sure I will."

"How will they know how to contact you?"

"Gabby, I'll be twenty-two next month. I've been on my own almost four years now. I'll tell them once I'm settled."

As we drove in the rented truck, I faced the fear that I had been dodging, that had been licking at me for weeks. Now it said, quite clearly and plainly, that I had no business being with a white woman. Growing up in the southern San Joaquin Valley, I had never seen a white woman with a brown or black man. In northern California I had seen some, but not enough to make my situation more comfortable. Blonde, blue-eyed Rebecca was as white as she could be. She was as light-complexioned as I was dark-complexioned. Standing together before a mirror, the contrast was stark. The first weeks of our new love had been confined to the office and my house. We had little need or thought to go elsewhere. Then Rebecca began suggesting that we go out to a movie or to dinner. I ignored those suggestions just as I ignored the fear that those suggestions kindled. Now she was actually in the process of moving in with me, and the fear would no longer be restrained. That afternoon I saw hate and racism everywhere.

It was on the face of every white man, woman, or child we

passed on the street. It was the reason for the turning of every white head in passing cars. The intersections were rampant with it. There they acted as if they hadn't looked, hadn't seen, when I knew they had. I saw hot hate in men's eyes. And I found myself shaking my head, no, no, it's not what you think; I barely know her; I'm just helping her; I'm just doing her a favor. I saw contempt in women's eyes and startled looks in kids' eyes.

"Gabby, the light's green. People are honking. Are you okay?"

"Yeah, I'm okay."

It raged in the neighbors, too, white and brown, as we unloaded, not one of them in sight, but all watching, from behind their curtains or hedges or from the corners of their windows. I could hear the white neighbors' anger as blonde, blue-eyed Rebecca stood in full view on my open porch, telling me in her loudest voice where each of her boxes should go as I slunk in and out of the truck, in and out of the driveway, and in and out of my house, hearing them behind their closed doors and windows as clearly as I heard her. "Who does that fucking little greaser think he is! First, he comes in here and makes an office out of a store in a decent residential neighborhood. Then he brings all his dirty spic clients into our neighborhood, cluttering up our street with their beat-up old cars and their trash, and now he has a white whore move in with him. I can tell you one thing, I'm out of here! Sure as hell, as soon as I can sell this fucking place, I'm out of here!" I could hear the frightened brown neighbors. "He should stick to his own. Even if he is a lawyer, the white people around here aren't going to like it. There's plenty of pretty young Mexican girls around who would love to marry a Mexican lawyer. He should stick to his own. Everybody will say that he thinks he's too good for Mexican women. Besides, I know they're not married, and any white girl who would move in with a Mexican man without being married has got to be white trash."

When we finished unloading, I was exhausted, more from all the eyes that had watched and all the unsolicited cracks they had made than from my labor.

"What's the matter, Gabby?"

We were sitting in the front room surrounded by boxes.

"Nothing," I said. Because everything was the matter. Not only was I afraid to be seen with her, I was also terribly afraid that she was ashamed of me. She said that she had been estranged from her parents for four years now, that she and her father had parted after a bitter fight and that she didn't care if she ever saw him again. That was as much as she would say. On that evening I doubted even that. It was simply a pretense. That way she would never have to introduce me to her parents, and they would never have to know that their daughter was living with a Mexican. Why else hadn't she told her parents that she was moving? "What's the matter, Gabby?"

"Nothing." Because if I said any more, it would all come out. . . . It came out anyway. "Maybe this isn't right."

"What isn't right?"

There was no stopping now. "You living with me. Me living with you."

"What? We just moved all my things over here! I gave up my apartment! And now you tell me this!"

"Didn't you see the way they looked at us?"

"Who? Who are you talking about? Who looked at us?"

"The people on the streets on the way over here. The people in the cars."

"What?. . . . How did they look at us?"

"They looked at us funny, weird."

"I didn't see anybody look at us funny. Who, tell me who?"

"The people we passed on the streets. The people at street corners when we were stopped. The people in cars that passed us."

"I didn't see anybody look at us funny."

"You weren't watching."

"There was nothing to watch."

"You're white and I'm Mexican."

"I've known that since the first day I walked into your office. No, even before that. Big deal."

"Then why haven't you introduced me to your parents?"

"My parents. You want to meet my parents. Okay. Let's go

over there right now. I'll introduce you to my parents. Come on, get up, let's go."

"I don't want to meet your parents. What do I want to meet your parents for?" I couldn't meet her parents. Imagine what they would think when they saw me.

"You just said you did."

"Don't you understand, Rebecca, people aren't going to like seeing a white girl with a Mexican."

"I'm not a girl."

"All right, white woman then. . . . Don't you understand?"

"You're the one who doesn't understand. I love you. That's all I need to understand. I love you, and if somebody has a problem with that, then that's their problem, not mine. I love you, and I don't care what anybody else thinks."

Her eyes were clear and steady. There was no doubting what she said. She loved me. How or what that meant, whatever problems I might have with that didn't matter, not to her at least. She loved me.

"And you love me."

It was a statement, but my hesitancy in answering made it a question.

"You love me, don't you?"

Her eyes were as intense as I had ever seen them. This was not the time to ponder.

"Of course I love you."

"We love each other. We have no problem with that. And anybody who does, well, that's their problem, not ours. It's that simple, Gabby."

From then on, Rebecca insisted that we go out, that we be seen in public. We went out to dinner at least once a week and to movies and to an occasional concert. We went on Sunday afternoon walks in the park and visited with friends in their homes and in our home. Whenever we walked, Rebecca would take my hand, or if my hand was in my pocket, would take hold of my arm. Her show of affection in public probably made me more uncomfortable than anyone.

For the most part, people were polite. If they did notice us, they would generally look away when I noticed them. Gradually, I came to believe that the majority of people didn't notice us, and if they did, paid little attention to us. But at first I was suspicious and vigilant. A few were openly hostile, staring persistently and flaunting their disgust. I quickly learned not to mention these to Rebecca because she would confront them loudly and defiantly. "What's your problem? What are you staring at? You got a problem?" Only a handful ever answered. "Yeah, I don't like white women hanging all over dirty greasers!" "You're a disgrace to our race!" Those she went up to. "Do you know what a racist is? Look it up! See if it fits!" I should have admired her, but more often than not, I was embarrassed.

Nothing embarrassed me more than the incident at Li Lum Restaurant. I loved Chinese food, and one Sunday Rebecca decided that we had had enough Formica- and linoleum-covered Chinese restaurants and that we deserved the best Chinese restaurant in town, Li Lum. "The food's great. None better. I used to go there with my folks. It's expensive, but we really worked hard this week, Gabby." We had worked hard that week.

I felt my first misgiving when I learned that it was located on the edge of the most exclusive part of town. It was a large building whose façade was adorned with two great gold pillars behind which two giant, gold, fiery dragons loomed against a bright red backdrop and two huge gold doors. "Wow," I said when I saw it. "Don't worry, Gabby, it's not that expensive." It wasn't the money I was worried about.

Inside the dimly lit foyer a woman in a long, tight-fitting dress stood looking down at the cash register before her. The foyer opened onto a large dining room with tables covered by white tablecloths and softened by candlelight. It was a far cry from all the family-run Chinese restaurants that I had become accustomed to, where whoever was closest to you waited on you in his everyday clothes while the rest of the family cleaned mounds of snow peas at a back table. The woman looked up at us, paused, and then looked back down at the register. We waited. The woman continued with whatever she was doing. Rebecca cleared her throat. The woman didn't look up. I felt a tinge of humiliation. Rebecca persisted. "Excuse me," she said softly, "we'd like to have a table for two." The woman didn't respond. "Let's go," I whispered. Rebecca walked over to the woman and said in a matter-of-fact tone, "Excuse me. We'd like a table for two." Just as matter-of-factly the woman looked up. There was no hint of any emotion: her slanted eyes gave nothing, her mouth was little more than a slit. They stared at each other. Then the woman nodded once, took a menu from the register, stepped around the register, and without a word walked toward the large room with Rebecca close on her heels and me, after some hesitation, closely behind both.

The large room appeared to be full. Its patrons were older affluent white couples. Some of the men wore ties and the women were dressed for an evening out. Rebecca and I wore slacks and sweaters. The woman led us around the far side of the room. The diners at every table inspected us as we passed. Their looks were cold, condescending, and annoyed. What am I doing here? I kept thinking. The journey around the large room seemed never-ending. Where was she taking us?

At the far end of the large room was a set of double doors that opened onto a smaller dining room of about fifteen tables. It was into this room that the woman led us. Three tables closest to the double doors had people seated at them. They too gave us cold looks. Instead of seating us at any of the tables near these people, the woman led us to a table at the furthest corner of the room, away from the others, next to a door over which an illuminated red EXIT sign glowed. When the woman stopped at that lone table, I wanted to bolt, run out that back door. I looked at Rebecca, who only looked at the woman. Rebecca asked, calmly, evenly, "Can't we have one of those tables over there by the others?" The woman answered, just as calmly, "Sollee, all leeserved," as she gestured toward the lone table.

I gave Rebecca a "Let's go" look. But Rebecca wasn't looking at me. Instead she took a seat at the table. The woman stopped gesturing and stood motionless, staring past us. Only after I sat down did she place the sole menu before Rebecca and leave without a word.

I leaned over the table and whispered, "Let's get out of here. I don't want any more of this. Let's go."

"Not yet, not now," in that same calm, matter-of-fact tone.

"Are you crazy?" whispering. "Can't you see what she's doing to us? She doesn't want me here. She didn't even give me a menu. Look at where she put us. They're all laughing at us! I don't want to be where I'm not wanted. Please, Rebecca, let's go."

"If you want to go, go."

Her answer hurt.

I leaned even further over the table. But I saw the others watching and I sat up. I couldn't leave alone. They would know, and Rebecca would never forgive me. It was hard to believe. I had just come for dinner and now all of this. The air was becoming thick, heavy, yet Rebecca seemed so unaffected. How could she understand? She wasn't a Mexican.

We sat. Nothing happened. No one came. No waiter. No busboy. We waited. With each second the waiting grew in importance, grew more humiliating. Each second added to the shame. The room grew hotter. I was suffocating. I wanted to take off my sweater, but I was wearing only a T-shirt underneath. But wouldn't they expect that from a Mexican, a T-shirt?

"Please, Rebecca, let's go. I can't wait any longer."

"No," she said calmly, completely unaffected by the wait, by everything. I watched her, resenting her calmness, her unaffectedness. But then, it was I they didn't want there.

"Here she comes," Rebecca said.

I turned, elated and relieved that someone, anyone was coming; I turned, forgetting about the others, to watch someone come to take our order. It was the woman in the long silk dress, and she was indeed coming, but behind her was another couple that she smilingly seated near the others, with two menus, and then bowed and left. Only then did I see that Rebecca had raised her hand for service.

"Let's go."

Rebecca shook her head.

A busboy in a white smock and black trousers emerged from a doorway in the opposite corner of the room with a water pitcher, slithering past several empty tables in the center of the room and going directly to the newcomers' table without so much as glancing in our direction. Again, Rebecca waved her arm.

"Don't do that, Rebecca. You're just making it worse. Please don't do that. He's not going to come over here."

Wasted words. She continued waving even after the busboy had finished pouring and turned his back on us before walking past the empty tables again and out of the room. Each new humiliation cut deeper.

"Let's go, Rebecca." Now she either didn't hear me or ignored me.

Then a waiter in a white coat and black tie appeared at the newcomers' table and began taking their order, nodding and smiling. This time Rebecca stood up and waved, and when everybody in the room except the waiter looked over at her, she said loudly, "Hey, Mister Waiter, you forgot about us! We want to eat, too!" Now the waiter did turn, but just long enough for him to dismiss us with a look of contempt and return to the diners at hand.

Rebecca bolted, half-running, half-walking, knocking over chairs at the empty tables in her haste. The waiter was a short, slight Asian, who, by the time Rebecca reached him, was giving her his full attention. Rebecca grabbed the waiter by the lapels and pulled him to her. "Hey, mister! I mean you, mister! I was talking to you, mister! Don't you understand English? You don't turn your back on me. Never! Never!" She was shaking him. Women screamed. Men rose to help the waiter. The busboy reappeared with his water pitcher and, with his free hand, while saying something to Rebecca in what must have been Chinese, tried to pull Rebecca from the waiter. Rebecca wheeled and pushed the busboy away from her, and he stumbled and fell, dousing water on two customers who were coming to the waiter's aid. There were more screams. Rebecca had hold of the waiter again but released him as soon as she saw the woman in the silk dress approach and grabbed her instead, bringing her face to face, and then shouted, "Who do you think you are? Tell me, who do you think you are? Have you already forgotten that your people were brought here as coolies, as slaves? Have you forgotten that your people's houses were burned down and that your men were lynched by white people for no other reason than that they were Chinese? Do you think for a moment that your fine customers would have you in *their* homes for dinner? You of all people should know what it's like to be discriminated against! You should be the last people to discriminate, not the first!"

We drove home in silence, she angry and I humiliated. We got ready for and into bed, each self-absorbed; she, I thought, in her victory and my defeat, and I in my loss and humiliation. We lay awake for a long time, silent, letting the darkness purge us. Toward morning she touched my back with her fingertips and then kissed the back of my neck lightly and said, "I love you, Gabby," breaking the darkness.

I went to sleep, still smarting from the restaurant's humiliation. But there was more, and sleep unraveled it and presented it, clear and inescapable: I had humiliated myself. Instead of whining and begging to leave, I should have done what Rebecca did; I should have demanded that we be served. It was my fight, and I had let her fight it. It was my fight, and I had been afraid to fight it.

I saw little of Rebecca the next day. Court, counsel, and clients filled my day. We had a late dinner, and I went to bed immediately after saying I hadn't slept much the night before. Rebecca followed.

"What's the matter, Gabby?"

"Nothing. I'm tired." It was easier to hide in the dark.

"Something's bothering you, Gabby. Tell me."

I didn't answer.

"Is it about last night? Are you mad at me for what I did?"

"How could I be mad at you. You did the right thing."

"Then what's the matter?"

I searched for the right words. None of them fit. Finally, I just said it. "You're always saying you love me. But what's there to love? Especially after last night."

"Why shouldn't I love you after last night?"

"You saw me. I was a coward."

"How?"

"I should have done what you did. It was me they wanted out of there, not you. I'm the one who should have stood up to them, not you."

"I love who you are and what you've made of yourself. It took plenty of courage and strength and discipline to become who you are. There's a lot to love in you."

Rebecca and I had been living together a little more than eight months when the Li Lum incident occurred. Except for occasional gawkers it was an aberration because by then we had established a circle of friends and acquaintances. We patronized certain businesses and restaurants. With these people and in these places we were a couple. Most important, we saw ourselves as a man and a woman, nothing more, nothing less, who loved each other.

There was, however, still the issue of Rebecca's parents. I had not yet met them. We had broached the subject many times and had always left it with the implicit understanding that we would visit them soon. But there was an unspoken ambivalence on both sides. For me, it was the right thing to do, and I didn't want to feel that I was running from another racial conflict. On the other hand, even I was now convinced that Rebecca was not ashamed of me, and the fact that Rebecca had broken off with her parents some four years before had nothing to do with me. On Rebecca's part, she also acknowledged that I should meet her parents. But the resentment she bore them, and in particular her father, was very strong, and I doubted that she would have even considered seeing her father if I weren't in the picture.

Three days after the Li Lum incident, Bill Brady came up to me in Department 3 before the calling of the calendar and said, "I need to talk to you."

Once I passed the bar examination, I rented an abandoned grocery store on the east side of town, and painted over the fading "Merced St. Market" lettering above the front door, had a telephone installed, had a wooden sign made that said, GABRIEL GARCIA—ATTORNEY AT LAW, hung it beside the front door, and went off to court to watch what lawyers did before getting my first client a-week-and-a-half later. I knew I wouldn't want for clients because I was the first Mexican lawyer in San Jose, and the first lawyer who spoke Spanish. Given the large Mexican population in the county, I had a ready made market.

But sitting and watching what lawyers did in court for a week and a half was not much of a foundation for representing a client in court. Had it not been for the language barrier, I would have probably appeared more confused and flustered to my clients than they were. As it was, out in the hall, after the case had been called, I could put the best spin on what the judge had said in translating his English into their Spanish, being careful to omit any remarks the judge may have made about my inexperience or ineptitude, since, after all was said and done, those had nothing to do with the case.

On Friday afternoon at the conclusion of my third week of practicing law, I appeared in court with Andrés López, a man who was being arraigned on three counts of armed robbery. The courtroom was full. The arraignment itself should not have taken more than two or three minutes. A minute or so into the proceeding, the judge stopped in mid-sentence and said, "Mr. Garcia, these are serious charges. If your client is convicted of these charges, there's a very real possibility that your client could be sentenced to state prison for a substantial period of time. Have you informed Mr. López that you have been practicing law less than a month?"

"Yes, your honor." I may not have been that specific, but I did tell him that I had just opened my office, and he could have easily drawn the inference that I had just started practicing law.

"And did you tell him that he might want to at least consult with a more experienced lawyer in a case as serious as this?"

"Yes, your honor." I had done no such thing. But I had heard the guffaws in the audience, and I was certain that some of them had come from lawyers, because I had heard and even seen some of them snicker at my responses in court over the past three weeks, and a "no" answer only promised to bring more of the same.

"Mr. Garcia, let's do this. I'm going to put Mr. López's case over until Monday. In the meantime, I want you to sit down with Mr. López and carefully explain the gravity of the charges against him and his potential prison exposure. Then I want you to candidly outline what your experience as an attorney has been, and specifically what experience you've had with these types of cases. If Mr. López then wants to continue with you as his attorney, that's fine. He has an absolute right to the attorney of his choice. On the other hand, you tell him that I would advise him to at least talk to another attorney experienced in these matters, just to get a second opinion. Tell him that on Monday I will be making inquiries of him regarding his decision. And, by the way, Madame Clerk, please make certain that we have a Spanish-speaking interpreter here to help me with my questions of Mr. López. That will be all for now, gentlemen."

Outside in the hallway a bewildered Andrés López asked, "¿De qué se trató eso?"

Before I could answer, a thin, erect, grey-haired man in his sixties approached us and said, "Mr. Garcia, my name's Bill Brady. I'm a lawyer here in San Jose. I heard the judge's remarks, and I think you and I should talk. Why don't you go on and finish with your client. I can wait. Then we'll talk."

On the day we met, Bill Brady had been practicing law in Santa Clara County for thirty-four years. I had heard about him and had read his name and seen his picture in the paper many times in connection with high-profile criminal cases. The word was that in the days before public defenders, whenever the court had before it an indigent defendant facing serious criminal charges, the court would as often as not appoint Bill Brady to represent him. Bill Brady was well-respected in the legal community.

We walked out and sat on one of the benches in front of the courthouse.

"Most everybody calls me Bill. How about you?"

He was leaning toward me and his eyes held mine, but there was nothing threatening or offensive about him.

"Gabriel's my name but nobody uses it. They either call me Gabby or Gabe, mostly Gabby."

"Where you from, Gabby?"

His eyes were soft, gentle, and keen, bringing life and grace to a markedly wrinkled face.

"I grew up on a ranch ten miles outside Delano in the San Joaquin Valley."

"Is that home?"

"No, I left there eleven years ago and never have gone back."

"Got family down there?"

"Just my Dad." I was revealing myself to a total stranger without the slightest hesitancy. I liked him.

"Where's home?"

"I guess it's San Jose now."

"Where'd you go to school?"

"San Jose State."

"Where'd you go to law school?"

"San Jose School of Law."

"Been here eleven years, too. Sounds like this is home."

"Yeah, I think so." Despite his reputation, I was completely at ease.

"Is that why you opened an office here?"

"That and the fact that I think there's a big need here."

He slapped his knee and sat upright, his eyes twinkling. "You hit the nail right on the head! I can't tell you how happy I am to see you starting a law practice here. For years I knew this had to happen, and now it's happened. You're absolutely right, there's a tremendous need here. I'm sure you know that almost 20 percent of the county's population is Mexican, many of whom speak little or no English. Yet damn near 70 percent of the defendants in criminal cases are Mexicans." He used the word without hesitation, without affecting the flow of his sentence, without making either of us uncomfortable. "There's a tremendous need. It's not only the language. These people need somebody they can identify with, be at ease with. This fellow you were just in court with. How many lawyers do you think can come straight out of law school and hang up their shingle all alone, and within a couple of weeks have a man come to him and ask him to represent him on some serious charges?"

"I don't know."

"Well, I do. Not very damn many. I'm probably looking at the only one in this county. You put yourself through college?"

He didn't need an answer. He was nodding before I said, "Yeah."

"Law school, too?"

"Yeah."

"First one to graduate from high school in your family?"

"Actually, I was the first one to go to high school on either side of my family."

"Look, if you work as hard at being a lawyer as you did at becoming one, you'll be a huge success. It doesn't take a rocket scientist to be a good lawyer. It's all about hard work and discipline, and about being honest with your clients and yourself. But you've got to be careful, especially in the beginning. You may not have understood what Judge Evans was doing in court this afternoon. Believe it or not, he wasn't just trying to protect your client, he was probably every bit as interested in protecting you. You see, if your client gets convicted and goes to prison and appeals, your competency, your qualifications for representing him would probably be brought up on appeal. The court of appeal could take you to task, and so too could the State Bar. You don't need that, especially at the beginning of your career. Do you see the problem?"

"What should I do? I already took his money."

"How much did he pay you?"

"Two hundred dollars."

"Two hundred dollars! You gotta be kidding. Two hundred dollars for three counts of armed robbery!"

"That's all he had. And, besides, he said he didn't do it. And my rent's due next week."

"How much is your rent?"

"Two hundred dollars."

"That's still not going to pay for your secretary."

"I don't have a secretary."

"Who's going to do your typing?"

"I don't have any typing."

"You will, believe me."

"I can type."

"It's not the same, Gabby, it's not the same. And once you get going, there won't be any time."

"But if I give him back his money, I won't be able to pay the rent. Plus, I already used some of it to pay for the phone. I don't have two hundred dollars to give back to him."

"That all can be easily remedied. Let's do this. Let me come into the case with you."

"But I don't have any money to pay you."

"Don't worry about that. I don't want or expect any money. If I associate with you as co-counsel, it'll do two things. It will satisfy the judge's concern about your client's representation, and it will let me help you get some experience representing folks."

"That's good, but why are you doing this? You don't even know me."

"I've already told you. This community needs you."

Not only did Bill Brady associate himself in my case, he also had the court appoint me as second counsel to him in a similar case, and in other cases as well. That allowed me to watch the best criminal defense attorney in the county try a case. But watch during the first case only. Because thereafter Bill Brady had me progressively question witnesses first on direct and then on cross-examination. He had me make an opening statement and then a closing argument. Then he sat at counsel table with me and watched as I did an entire misdemeanor trial, counseling me each step of the way. He was wonderful.

Bill Brady made his secretary available to me on a daily basis at no cost. Little by little he had her come to my office and set it up with office supplies, with legal forms and used furniture, with books and eventually a part-time secretary. Bill Brady would *always* be my friend.

Three days after the Li Lum incident, Bill Brady and I sat on the same bench outside the courthouse that we sat on the day I met him. He was thinner now, almost as if his flesh were sinking into his bones, and far more wrinkled. Age was beginning to take its toll. But his eyes were still warm, alert, and strong. He leaned over toward me, as he always did, as if what he was about to say was very personal, very private. That day he leaned even closer, and after his eyes met mine, they flitted from side to side as if looking for a place to begin.

When he looked back at me, he said, "I hear you and Rebecca went out to dinner at a Chinese restaurant over in the Sun Garden part of town last Sunday night."

I nodded.

"Well, you probably don't know, but you're the talk of the legal community."

A lawsuit, I thought. Rebecca had pushed the busboy and grabbed the waiter, and the lady in the silk dress and somebody had fallen. Some bastards would sue over anything.

"So?"

"Rebecca was with you, and there was quite a scene."

I nodded. A chair had been knocked over in the scuffle, people were screaming, some had run out of the room and maybe out of the restaurant too. But a lawsuit?

"Gabby, do you know who Rebecca Williams is?"

"Come on, Bill. We live together. We work together. I've introduced you to her. Of course, I know who she is."

"But do you know who she is?"

"I don't know what you're talking about."

"Rebecca Williams is Walt Williams's daughter."

"So who is Walt Williams?"

"Gabby, you know who Walt Williams is. Probably the best damn personal injury lawyer in northern California. We've talked about him. I've pointed him out to you. Ruthless, tough, shrewd, brilliant, will stop at nothing to win. Rich, filthy rich. Has invested wisely. Owns two banks, a string of real estate, and has his fingers in some of the biggest corporations in the area."

That Walt Williams. It was as if something had fallen on me, flattened me. Consults corporations. That's all Rebecca had said. Consultant to corporations. That Walt Williams. Bill Brady was watching me, waiting for some sort of explanation.

"I didn't know that," I said, stunned.

"I didn't know that either until Walt called me."

"So what's that got to do with anything?" I said, as nonchalantly as I could.

"Gabby, you're like a son to me. I love you. You know that. There isn't anything I wouldn't do for you. I've shown you that. I've always talked to you as if you were my son, and that's how I'm going to talk to you now. . . . Apparently, some of the people in the restaurant knew Rebecca, knew she was Walt Williams's daughter. She used to go there with Walt and her Mom not that long ago. The word got back to Walt that Rebecca was in that restaurant with a Mexican raising hell about racism and discrimination and threatening to sue everybody for being bigots. Well, Walt was humiliated and then infuriated. He did some checking and found out that the Mexican is you, and worse, that you're a lawyer, and that Rebecca works for you, according to him for peanuts, and lives with you, and that you're quite a bit older than she is. Kind of like you're taking advantage of his daughter."

"Me? Take advantage of Rebecca? You don't know Rebecca."

"Maybe not, but I do know Walt Williams. Besides, that's not the point."

"What is the point?"

"That he's furious. He could crush you, Gabby, if he wanted to. And I don't want to see that happen. That's the point."

"Come on, Bill, let's be straight with each other. He's mad because I'm a Mexican. I'm with his daughter and I'm a Mexican.

That's really why he's mad, right? That's what you're saying, right?"

"That's part of it, but not all of it, not all of it by any means. You see, Walt Williams and I go way back. He called me about this. He heard I was close to you. I think you should know that as successful as Walt Williams has been in his business life, his personal life has been a complete disaster. A couple of broken marriages, a few nasty relationships with younger women. Probably the only thing he's ever really loved in his life, unfortunately for you, is his daughter, Rebecca. There isn't anything he's loved more. But, as you might well imagine, he's a huge control freak. And I take it Rebecca is no weakling herself. Anyway, a few years back Rebecca apparently bolted, wanted to live her own life. There was a big falling out, and she refuses to have anything to do with Walt. The long and the short of it is that Walt wants to talk to you."

"When?"

"As soon as possible. This afternoon. He's cleared his calendar. He said he'd see you anytime this afternoon that's convenient for you."

"What does he want to talk about?"

"I don't know. He didn't tell me. But I assume it's about Rebecca and you."

"Rebecca's twenty-three. She works for a living. I pay her. I don't think anything about Rebecca and me is any of his business." I could feel the fight taking hold. It had been there all my life. First, the fear and then the panic and then the conviction that I wouldn't be able to accomplish what I had to accomplish, that I would fail, only to have the fight kick in.

"I think you should talk to him, Gabby."

"Why?"

"He's a very important man in this community. He could make or break most people here."

"I'm important, too."

"Don't play with me, Gabby."

"How's he going to hurt me? I represent people on the lowest socioeconomic level: Mexicans. What's he going to do, run out to the fields and tell the farmworkers not to come to me? And in Spanish no less."

"No, but he can certainly influence most anything that he chooses to influence."

"Why are you acting on his behalf, Bill? Why are you trying to convince me to talk to him? You're my friend."

"Gabby, it's because I do care about you that I'm talking to you. He's very angry right now. He thinks you're taking advantage of his daughter, playing on her, as he calls it, 'white guilt.' If he met you, talked to you, I'm sure he'd change his mind."

"Boy, that's clever, turning it around on me like I'm playing on his daughter's white guilt. What he really doesn't like is that his daughter is living with and working for a Mexican. You can tell him for me that I'm not talking to him about my personal life or any other part of my life. And if he can't respect or appreciate that, he can go take a flying fuck."

"I'm not going to tell him that. If you want to, you can."

Bill left, and I sat and tried to calm myself and gather my thoughts before I went back to the office. I was still trying to decide why Rebecca hadn't told me who her father was when one of the clerks came out and said, "Hey Gabby, you've just been assigned out to trial."

"Oh, shit!"

"You want me to tell the judge that?"

I spent the rest of the day arguing pretrial motions, reviewing my file, picking a jury, and talking to my client. It was almost 6:30 when I got back to the office. My client had driven back to the office with me, and I was still immersed in his case when I opened the door and saw Rebecca at her desk typing. Bill Brady's revelations came rushing back.

Before I could say a word, Rebecca said, "Walt Williams wants to see you."

I looked around the room and saw three small, wide-eyed brown men and my client, all of whom came to attention.

"Is he on the phone?"

"No."

"Where is he?"

"He's outside in his car. He told me that you know he's my father. And I told him that you had other appointments, and I didn't think you could see him. He said he'd wait, anyway. So I said I didn't want him waiting here and that, if he wanted to wait for you, he'd have to wait for you outside."

"How long has he been here?"

"Since five."

All of the morning's emotions returned. Walt Williams. I looked around at my shabby office. It was getting shabbier by the second. I looked at my client and my three prospective clients, poor and needy, and getting poorer and needier, too. Everything spoke volumes about my limited abilities as a lawyer.

"Tell him to come in." What else could I say.

"I'm not speaking to that man. If you want him in here, you tell him."

"But he's your. . . ."

"This is *your* office, not his."

I looked out the front window and saw a big, shiny, expensive car parked at the curb with a man seated behind the wheel. As I tried to make out the man, he turned and looked directly at me. Walt Williams. I was caught. I opened the door and motioned him in.

He was a big, square-shouldered man who, despite his white hair, appeared to be in much better physical condition than I. He was impeccably dressed in a dark suit and white shirt and the thought flashed through my mind that his tie probably cost more than my flimsy, wrinkled suit. He stood with his back to Rebecca, not once having looked at her. His blue eyes were sharp but friendly, his ruddy face pleasant. Still, the longer he looked at me, the shakier I got.

"Won't you come this way, Mr. Williams," gesturing toward my office.

But Rebecca would have none of it. "Gabby? These men have appointments, and one of them has been here since before five."

I stopped. Gabby. Did she have to call me Gabby? I was sure that in his office the secretaries didn't call him Walt. Even if she was his daughter, that was all the more reason to call me Mr. Garcia. I looked at the three waiting men and my client and said, in my best English, "Gentlemen, you'll have to excuse me, but an emergency has arisen. I'll be with you momentarily," even though I knew they spoke little or no English.

My office had never seemed so small and cluttered and dirty. When he sat in one of my two wooden chairs, I couldn't close the door without asking him to move. My desk was covered with papers, and as I tried to clear a space so that I could take notes if needed, a stack of papers fell off the desk, which really served to show how much my hand was shaking when I tried to pick them up. Then, as I turned to begin our conversation, I saw, or rather noted for the first time, how badly smudged the door was, smudges from the menial labor that his clients would never do, but smudges that he had already seen. And I worried about his expensive suit, which sat in my filthy chair.

"What can I do for you, Mr. Williams?" I said bravely.

"Everybody I care anything about calls me Walt, and I'd like it if you'd call me Walt. And I'd like to be able to call you Gabby."

I was surprised by his easy, down-home manner. But I reminded myself that he had come for a reason and that he had been in this one-on-one setting thousands of times, that he had to be a master at it, and that I had to be careful.

"What can I do for you, Mr. Williams?"

"I've come for my daughter."

"What?"

"I've come to get my daughter."

"You've got to be kidding," dropping all guard, all pretense.

"No, I'm not kidding. I'm very serious, as serious as I've ever been about anything. Probably more serious. I've come to get my daughter."

His eyes were as matter-of-fact as the tone of his voice, and neither was demeaning, hostile, or threatening. He wasn't concerned with my desk, or my suit, or the size of my office. He had come for Rebecca.

"Rebecca's twenty-three, Mr. Williams."

"Walt, please."

"She's twenty-three, and she's here because she wants to be here. She came here asking to be a volunteer. I didn't go to her, she came to me. I didn't even know her. And believe me, I pay her. She may not be making what she could be making in other offices, but I pay her the best I can. She's free to leave whenever she chooses."

"Yes, I know that. And I also know that she lives with you and thinks she loves you."

Thinks. Thinks. I was caught on *thinks.* He was the enemy.

"Mr. Williams, I don't want to discuss my personal life with you or anyone else."

"I'm sorry, Gabby. I didn't come here to intrude or interfere or offend you. I came because I love my daughter. I love her more than anything in this world."

He winced, and for a moment I thought that this hulk of an accomplished man was going to break down and cry in my little office. He had disarmed me again.

"Bear with me, Gabby, please bear with me. I won't be long."

He stopped and sighed and composed himself.

"You know, Gabby, I come from pretty humble beginnings myself. I've accomplished many things, I've acquired many things. I've been driven, driven, driven. But I never loved until Rebecca. I'm married to a good woman. But I haven't been much of a husband, much of a partner. She's an unloved woman. But I do love Rebecca. People talk about dogs giving them unconditional love. And I think for a lot of men, no, let me speak about me. For me, the only unconditional love I'll ever experience is for my daughter. That's why I'm here, Gabby.

"I gave her everything, everything money can buy. I know she thinks that everything I gave her was designed to keep her, not lose her. In some ways she might be right. I guess the hardest thing for a parent is to lose his child. I guess I was afraid of losing her, and because of that, I did try to control her, control everything around her, so much so that she finally bolted. You saw her out there. She won't even look at me; she won't speak to me. I'm sure she thinks that by coming here I'm trying to control her now. Doesn't she understand that every father loses his daughter?

"Gabby, I mean no personal affront, but it kills me to see her working as a secretary when she could be so much more. That's really why I'm here. That's why I came. I came to ask you to set her free, just like I've set her free, for her own sake. She was accepted at Harvard. She was all set to go. Days before she was to leave, she decided that the education at Harvard was just another means on my part to try to control her, to keep her. So she left our home, went out on her own, would have nothing to do with me, and ended up here instead. She can be so much more, Gabby, if you let her, if you too set her free.

"Gabby, you're a very successful man in your community. I'm sure you know you can have most any woman you want in your community. I don't need to tell you that. Besides, you're almost twice Rebecca's age. You've seen enough of life to know that what Rebecca's going through now, her love for you, her dedication to your people, is just a fad, something she'll outgrow and then she'll move on. I'm convinced that she's put herself in this situation out of white man's guilt. I saw plenty of it in San Francisco a few years back. All those white women taking up with Negroes and having their babies, becoming slaves to those Negroes. Anything to make up for the sins of their fathers. Rebecca's doing the same thing. I know her. She's always been concerned about the way your people have been treated in this community. And she feels guilty. She wants to purge that guilt. That's pretty obvious. I am from Texas, and I'm not going to tell you that I have some of your people over for dinner on occasion. But I've never been cruel to your people, I've never discriminated against them. Hell, I can't tell you how many. . . ."

There was a loud bang. The door had slammed into his chair, and then Rebecca screamed, "Get out! Get out! I love him, and I'm going to marry him!"

We were married at St. Geneve's Church two months later. I wasn't much of a Catholic, and Rebecca had been to a Baptist church a few times, but when I told her that I wanted to be married in the Church because most Mexicans believed that to be married in the Church meant to be married forever, she agreed. It was a brief ceremony with a handful of people attending. Bill Brady was my best man, and Delia Ortiz, an organizer for a women's support group, was the matron of honor.

Before we left, the church's custodian came up to me and said, "You know, Señor Garcia, there was a suspicious white man who came to the wedding. He came in after the wedding started, sat in the back all alone, and left before it ended. What made me suspicious of him was that he had been parked across the street all morning watching the church. Another thing, I thought he was crying during the wedding."

"How was he dressed?"

"Real nice."

CHAPTER VII

Once we were married, my law practice exploded. The judges began appointing me to high-profile criminal cases, which put my name and face in the media almost monthly. The base of my clientele, Mexicans who worked in the fields and in the canneries and in the service industries, doubled. And, something I would have never thought possible, we began getting white clients. I smelled Walt Williams in the background, but I said nothing to Rebecca. Walt Williams was also somewhere behind the deference I now received from the judges in the courthouse and the newfound respect the court personnel showed me and the new importance many of my colleagues gave me. Some of the lawyers were blunt. "Boy, you really married into it." "Tell me, Gabby, how does it feel to be the heir apparent to an empire?" I didn't mention my new status to Rebecca. If she ever thought that Walt Williams was meddling in or influencing our lives in any way, there was no telling what she would do.

"We need another lawyer, Gabby."

"Why do we need another lawyer?"

"Because you can't keep doing this. You're making all the appearances. You're reading all the files. You're doing most of the research. You're seeing all the clients. You're making all the decisions on all the cases, no matter how big or how small. You're sleeping four or five hours a night, and you're working seven days a week. We have no life. We're always working. We need another lawyer, and we have enough business, and we're making enough money to justify having another lawyer."

I didn't want another lawyer. The good ones would be a threat and the bad ones a waste. The good ones would see how incredibly hard I worked and know that with half the effort, they could accomplish more. I would simply be paying them and grooming them to expose me and eventually take some of my business when they left. I wanted no part of that. The bad ones would be more of a hindrance than a help. To Rebecca, I said only, "I disagree. I think we're doing just fine."

"Are you out of your mind? You're going to kill both of us!"

So we put an ad in the legal newspaper and interviewed six of the applicants, three of whom had more than five years of experience practicing law and three just out of law school. From their resumes and cover letters I had the impression that the three experienced lawyers had tired of the hard hustle of practicing law and wanted the security of a weekly paycheck. The other three were hungry and ambitious. I wanted none of them but said nothing to Rebecca, who insisted that she sit in on the interviews.

"What did you think of him?"

"Not aggressive enough. I think he's already been beaten down after only six-and-a-half years of practice. He's looking for an eight-to-five job, a steady paycheck. Someone like that around here would drive me crazy."

"But you said the last one was too aggressive."

"He was. But that doesn't mean we have to hire someone who's not aggressive at all. Don't forget, I'm the one who's going to be busting my butt to make his paycheck every week. Then you have employer contributions, benefits, health plans, vacation. No, it would kill me to think that I'm working day and night to put food on this guy's table."

"You're not going to be satisfied with anyone, Gabby. You're never going to find your 'Mr. Perfect.'"

"Oh, I don't know. We still have two applicants to go."

We concluded the interviews in a week. Rebecca was satisfied with two and would have hired either of the two. I was against hiring any of them. We reached a compromise of sorts. We would hire another full-time secretary, with Rebecca handling the entire process herself, including the ultimate selection. Rebecca would take night courses at the college and become a certified paralegal and do all of the research and legal writing and the bulk of the client interviews. She would continue to manage the office and make the final decisions on all the lower-level cases.

Rebecca whizzed through the paralegal courses in a year. There was little in the courses that she hadn't done already. Relieved of her secretarial duties, she was certainly the equivalent of another lawyer. The only thing she couldn't do was appear in court. We soon contracted out routine court appearances to a lawyer who specialized in making those appearances. I couldn't have been happier. Our business continued to boom. Our productivity and the quality of our work continued to improve. We were as fulfilled as we could be.

Or so I thought. Because, just after Rebecca had completed her first full year as a paralegal, she came into my office one evening and said, "Gabby, I want to start a family. I'll be thirty in three months, and I want to start a family."

"What?" I had been hunched over a brief on my desk. I sat up and pushed the chair away from the desk to give myself some room to breathe. I could hear my entire practice collapsing around me.

"I want to start a family."

"You can't . . ." I stopped. I had been a lawyer for thirteen years then, and there was at least one thing I had learned: in times of crisis, in times such as these, it was absolutely best not to say anything, to buy some time, not to say anything I would regret later.

"Rebecca, this is the first chance I've had to read the D.A.'s response in Mendoza. We argue the motion tomorrow morning at 8:30. It's an important motion, as you well know. I still have to read the cases. I'll be here late tonight and be gone early in the morning. Can we talk about this tomorrow, tomorrow evening?"

"Okay. We'll talk about it tomorrow evening," she said. But her look said more; it said: This is not negotiable, Gabby.

I didn't want a baby. I already had a family. Rebecca and I were as much of a family as I wanted and needed. But it was a lose-lose situation. If I said no, she would resent me and probably not forgive me until she was pregnant. And Rebecca was not to be taken lightly. Carrying her resentment around would be too much of a heavy load for anyone, especially me. A yes meant the demise of everything I had worked for, everything I had accomplished. She was the backbone of the office; she kept the office together. She was a better lawyer than any I could hire. My success was her success; I wasn't going to find that in any other employee. I thought and thought. By late the next afternoon I thought I had a solution.

Rebecca came into my office after the last client had left. "You wanted to talk," I said, beating her to the punch, wanting to appear as open and concerned as possible.

"You better believe it," she said firmly. She was sitting across from me, upright and erect, with her eyes keyed directly on mine.

"You want to have a baby?"

"That's how most couples start a family, isn't it?"

I wanted to answer with some sarcasm of my own, but the firmness of her jaw convinced me otherwise.

I leaned back in my chair, trying to soften the air. "I suppose they do." That didn't soften her one bit. "But why do we have to do it now? Why not a year from now or even two? That way we could plan and prepare ourselves for the huge void that I'm going to have around here with you gone. There's nobody more important, more essential to this office than you. And you're probably not going to want to stop with one kid. So the changes we make will have to be made with an eye to some permanency. My guess, from the things you've said, is that you're going to want to have two or even three kids."

"I didn't say I wanted to get pregnant tonight, Gabby. But I don't want to wait two years either. We should be able to find suitable replacements or alternatives within a year. . . . Frankly, Gabby, I'm bored. I know we're doing well, but I don't want to be doing this the rest of my life. It's not enough for me. I know it's your life, but it's not mine. You're the lawyer, I'm the paralegal. Most of this I can do with my eyes closed."

That came as a surprise. But it fit perfectly into my equation.

"Why not go to law school? In four years you'll be a lawyer. There's a fifteen-year age difference between us. You'll probably outlive me by twenty-five years. If something were to happen to me in the next few years, you'd have a rough time raising two or three kids as a paralegal. You'd be in a much better position to raise them as a lawyer. Sure, I'll have a family with you. But let's do it the right way. Let's start once you're a lawyer. You can take a couple of years off then and come back full force. You'll make a hell of a good lawyer."

I had caught her completely off guard. Her eyes and mind lightened and drifted. She liked the idea. As much as Rebecca claimed to despise Walt Williams, there was still that connection and what I had always thought was a desire to outdo him in some way. Her look was far away, but it was saying "I like it."

"I'm hungry. Let's go get something to eat," I broke in.

"No, stay. Get back to what you were doing. I'll get some takeout. Be back in twenty minutes."

Alone, I was satisfied. It was seven months before she could start law school. Four years to complete law school. Three months to prepare for the bar exam. Four months waiting for the results. All the while she would be working days in the office and going to classes at night. A good five years before she could become a lawyer. A lot could happen in five years. In five years I stood to gain a lawyer and lose nothing in the interim.

Rebecca devoured law school with the same facility she had her paralegal courses. She studied only on weekends, and that concerned me at first. Remembering my long hours of study, I warned her again and again that law school required much more study than she was giving it. She listened politely and went on with her weekend studies. Two weeks before semester finals I told her to take the next two weeks off from the office. "What for?" she asked. "To study," I said. "I've been studying," she said. After her first final exams I stressed the importance of not becoming discouraged, that not doing as well as one hoped was nothing to be ashamed of, that one had to persevere. "Look at me," I reassured her. "I flunked the bar the first time I took it." Rebecca finished first in her class.

I was shocked. I should have been overjoyed. Instead, I was

disappointed. I had wanted Rebecca to learn at the school of hard knocks, just as I had. Instead, she had made a mockery of my experience. Once I got over the initial shock, I felt a tinge, a hint of apprehension. But I reasoned that she had an unfair advantage over her classmates because she had been working in a law office for years and now was essentially doing the work of a lawyer; once the others became familiar with the concepts and the program, she would have to study much harder to maintain her status. She studied even less the second semester and finished even further ahead of her class. Within days Rebecca had an offer for a summer job in the second most prestigious law firm in San Jose. I told myself that Walt Williams was behind it. But that wasn't enough of an explanation even for me.

"I don't see how we can afford to have you work for Fletcher and Thompson this summer."

"Why would I want to work there? I saw that brand of law growing up. I have no desire to spend my life making and saving money for corporations and wealthy individuals."

I couldn't argue with that. But then, I was in no position to argue. No law firm had ever offered me a summer job. For the first time I began to be wary of the day she became a lawyer.

That was probably the beginning of the end. I began examining Rebecca's work in a way that I had never done before: I was looking for mistakes. When I found one, I was quick to point it out loudly to her and to our secretaries, Teresa and Belen. I'd ask myself what the hell was I doing. I was supposed to be trying to help her, not tear her down. But I couldn't help myself. It was a compulsion, a daily need to find and announce that she had made one or several mistakes. On the other hand, when she corrected me, I was quick to answer with something like, "That may be the way they teach you in law school, sweetheart, but believe me, that's not the way we do it in court." When she corrected my written materials, I now returned them to the secretaries with snide remarks like, "A good law student doesn't necessarily make a good lawyer." I stopped that practice only after two deletions of her corrections cost me decisions in court.

When Rebecca's second year began, instead of lightening her office workload as I had for her first year, I increased her workload. I told myself that I wanted to teach her a little humility, give her a reality check, and that, in any event, we were busier than ever and that she had to carry her fair share, especially since going to law school was strictly for her benefit. Today I can say that I wanted her to fail. She didn't fail. She increased her law school extracurricular activities, signing up for moot court and working on the law review. She studied only on weekends and seemed to do even less than she had the year before. She finished far and away first in her class.

Some nights Rebecca came home after I had gone to bed because she said she stayed at the law school to study in the library or with a study group. One night I was awakened by her at the front door. I looked at the clock and saw that it was after one o'clock in the morning. Where could she have been? Classes usually ended by nine, and study groups would have passed out by then and the library long since closed. I was full of suspicion but decided not to say anything. I pretended to be asleep when she came to bed a few minutes later. The next night I lay awake waiting for her return. It was after midnight when I heard her at the front door. She was involved with someone. She had been with him. It was probably a young law student. Our sex life had dwindled to near nothing. She had seemed awfully perky since the start of her second year. It all made sense. But I didn't want her to know that I knew, not yet. I didn't want to be confronted with bold-faced denials. I wanted to catch her in the act. So I pretended to be asleep again when she came to bed.

The next day I contacted a private investigator, one I didn't know and had never used. I asked about his fees for tailing someone and his guarantee of confidentiality. I was to call him back the next day. That night as I ate alone, I decided to have Rebecca followed. I felt good about the decision and went to bed hoping to get some badly needed sleep. I couldn't sleep, and the later it got, the angrier I became. By two I was seething. I had had enough. At 2:20 when she came in, I was in a rage.

"Where in the hell have you been?"

"What do you mean, where have I been?"

"Just that! Where in the hell have you been? Classes are over by nine! Where have you been?"

Rebecca looked at me and sighed. "I've been next door working. Go check my typewriter. It's not only warm, it's hot. Go check the piles on my desk. In fact, I forgot to turn off the copy machine. Check that, too, while you're at it."

Rebecca did look worn out, and I must have looked embarrassed. Because I was embarrassed. But not enough to keep me from getting out of bed the next two nights at twenty-minute intervals to tiptoe over to the dining-room windows and carefully move the edges of the curtains back, ever so slightly, so that I could see into the office. Yes, she was at the filing cabinets. Yes, she was at her desk typing. No, she wasn't on the telephone. Yes, she was using the copier. It had to be the Robles brief because she was making at least five copies of a multipage document. Oddly, as I watched her, I hungered for her in a way that I hadn't in months, years maybe. But when she came to bed, I was too afraid that she would suspect that I had been watching her to do anything but pretend that I was asleep.

The next night, Saturday, I was determined to have sex. I was determined not to go to bed until Rebecca did. When she did, I promptly followed. I kissed her on the back of her shoulder. "Hmpf," was her response. But then, we hadn't kissed in weeks. I kissed her again on the back of the shoulder. This time there wasn't even a "Hmpf." I touched her. Not a stir. I rubbed her shoulder and moved down her arm. Nothing. She couldn't be asleep, not so soon and with my touching her. My hand moved toward her breast, and she turned and said, "Gabby, I'm exhausted. But it's been weeks since we have. Maybe we should." I wanted more of a response, but that was all I needed. I caressed her, kissed her, fondled her, and entered her. She let me, but that was all. Still, the less she did, the more I wanted and needed her, the more I clutched and grabbed her and wanted to remain one with her long after the act was over. But she quickly fell asleep and turned from me. I laid awake for a long time, startled by my need. On Sundays Rebecca studied all day and went to bed early. That Sunday I found one reason or another to be with or near her throughout the morning as she studied, whether it was in the office or in the house. She moved from place to place until early afternoon when she said, "Gabby, please. I study better when I'm alone. Are you going to work in the office or in the house? Pick a spot so I can have a spot." I was angry and hurt, but soon the need and the want reminded me that she would be going to bed early that night. I let it pass.

That evening I watched and waited for the first signs that she would be going to bed. I was in the bedroom moments after she went in. But I had no sooner entered when she said, "Please, Gabby, not tonight. I'm totally exhausted." I lay next to her angry, frustrated, and needy, but afraid, too, afraid of losing her. And that fear made me want and need her all the more.

I began talking about myself in a way that I had never done before. It started in the office and for the most part was limited to the office. Every court success, no matter how small, I dressed up and dramatized for the adoring eyes and ears of the captive secretaries and sometimes Rebecca. I talked about my motions and appearances in detail.

Every risk was underscored, every threat enlarged, the odds were always insurmountable only to fall time and again before my brilliance, skill, and courage. It was during one of those demonstrations about a cross-examination that Teresa said, "Rebecca's going to have her first trial in three weeks."

"Trial? How can she have a trial when she's not a lawyer? She's just a law student, not a lawyer, Teresa."

"She's talking about my moot court," piped up Rebecca from her desk around the corner.

"Moot court's not a trial," I explained. "There's no jury, there's no cross-examination, or direct examination. All the student does is stand before someone who acts like a judge and then argues back and forth about a set of facts. It's a training. It's nothing like what trial lawyers do. It's more like what appellate lawyers do, and that's pretty boring stuff."

"Are you going to go watch her?"

"No. I've got a jury trial set for the next morning, and I'll be working on it that night."

I changed my plans when I received a personal invitation from the dean of the law school. "Dear Mr. Garcia, I would be deeply honored if you could find time in your busy schedule to . . ." After fifteen years of practicing law in San Jose it was my first invitation ever to a law school function. There was a small group of lawyers and judges, some of whom considered themselves to be part of a select group, who regularly attended law school functions. To me, the invitation was further proof of my growing stature in the legal community. I wore my best suit and Rebecca wore her best dress, and together, we entered the law school smiling, arm in arm for all to see, the successful, loving couple.

The dean met us just outside the moot courtroom. He was a beaming, balding little man who wore round wire-rimmed glasses and a walrus moustache. "I'm so glad you could make it, Mr. Garcia," clasping my hand in his like an old friend even though I had never met the man. "I see your name in the paper from time to time, and I know that you must be extremely busy. So, thank you so much for coming." Then, turning to Rebecca, "Ah, Rebecca, my dear, so good to see you," hugging her, "I'm sure you'll be your wonderful self tonight." Rebecca smiled and excused herself and went into the courtroom. The dean watched her go and then said, "I'm sure I don't have to tell you, Mr. Garcia, you've got a wonderful young woman there."

"Yes. Yes."

"But come, I'd like you to sit with me. I've got some seats reserved for us."

We entered the already crowded moot courtroom, he nodding and smiling and waving and stopping to say a few words to different people and introducing me to most, and I walking and standing alongside him, enjoying being his guest and the rarefied atmosphere of academia.

The setting was very different from the only other moot court debate I had seen, at a local high school, and very impressive. There was a three-judge panel, two of whom were sitting judges in our Superior Court, the third a law professor. The moot court-room itself was beautiful, far more elaborate than any of the courtrooms we had downtown, complete with rosewood paneling and hand carvings. The audience was well-scrubbed, smartly dressed, and well-educated, a stark contrast to the audiences I played to every day.

The dean had arranged to have two seats placed to the right of the judges's dais, far enough away so that it was clear we were not judges, yet close enough so that we had an excellent view of the student lawyers as they made their presentations. When I realized that I was not only the dean's guest but his only guest and that, aside from the judges, we were the only persons facing the student lawyers, I was very pleased. When I looked out at all the fresh refined faces in the audience and felt the air of civility emanating from them, I thought to myself that I could get used to this very quickly. I had finally arrived.

As the students were making their last-minute preparations and the judges were arranging their papers, the dean leaned over to me and said, "You know, Mr. Garcia, I've been a lawyer for almost forty years. I've tried cases in eight states. I've taught in four law schools and been a dean in two. And I have to tell you that I've never seen a law student as extraordinarily talented as Rebecca. The sky's the limit with her. She can go as far as she chooses." I felt as if a four-hundred-pound boot had stepped on me. Good thing I had leaned over to listen to him and that he couldn't see my face. He straightened himself, and I thought it was over. He was just beginning. He leaned over again and said, "That's why I wanted to make sure that you came tonight, just so that you could see for yourself what an incredible talent you have on your hands. You should start planning now. Rebecca will be a lawyer in two years, and the judges tell me you're a pretty fair lawyer yourself. Together, the two of you can have the best law firm that San Jose has ever seen. I kid you not; she's extraordi-nary. And it doesn't hurt that she's not only Walt Williams's daughter but his *only* child. She's certainly a chip off the old block. Start planning now. Set your agenda. You can't aim too high. My guess is that Walt Williams would take the two of you in as full partners the day she passes the bar."

The room was hot. My shirt collar seemed to be choking me. I tried to control my face, put on the plainest of looks, hoping that no one was looking at, worse, watching me. Because there was no way I could hide what I was feeling. I was back in those dens in the ranch houses outside of Delano almost forty years before. I was present here, as I was there, under false pretenses. There it had been J.J.; here it was Rebecca. I wanted to run and hide, but I couldn't do either. How long would it be before I belonged? Or would I always be a house nigger?

The dean couldn't leave it alone. He leaned over again and said, "You're a lucky man, Mr. Garcia. Look at her—she's not only brilliant, but she's absolutely stunning, beautiful." I wanted to turn on him and punch him squarely in those wire-rim glasses, smash them all over his lusting eyes, and prove once and for all to all of them that it was true, I didn't belong in their quaint, polite, white gathering. I couldn't run, I couldn't hide, and now I couldn't lash out. I would always be a house nigger.

The first of the law students rose and began his presentation. He was a well-spoken, well-dressed young man. I watched and heard him speak for at least twenty minutes.

Yet, when he sat down, all I remembered was that he was articulate and well-dressed. Because all I could hear, all I could think of was: What the hell am I doing here? How long am I going to continue pursuing this madness, pursuing something that I will never have, hoping to lose what I could never lose?

Then Rebecca went to the podium, and I could feel eyes shifting to me, and I could feel their questions: What the hell is she doing with him? Say it! I wanted to shout. Get it out in the open! Put it on the table! I tried not to listen to her, not to look at her. But I had to look. Because people would be watching for my reactions. So I looked, and in looking, I listened. She was beautiful, stunning, and her words were clear and concise, her delivery smooth, her eye contact wonderful, and she was completely at ease. When one of the judges interrupted her with a question, one I could not have answered, she immediately asked him to clarify the question, pointing out its ambiguity. Once he rephrased it, she answered fully and precisely and then paused and asked the judge, "May I proceed, your honor?" The most the judge could do was nod. She continued her presentation and was completely convincing. When she was finished, there was a burst of applause that continued for a full twenty seconds even though the audience had been asked to refrain from applauding until all four presentations had been made. I sat stunned. As a second-year law student, she was not only as good as I was now, but better. The sky for *her* was the limit. But what about me?

There was a reception following the presentations in the faculty lounge. A large congratulatory crowd gathered around Rebecca in the moot courtroom. I slipped past them and out of the courtroom as quickly as I could, hoping that some form of alcoholic beverages would be served. There was, and I was the first in line. When the server filled my glass with Chardonnay, I shook my head and said, "Fill it." I was on my second full glass before most had their first. I needed to numb and fortify myself. A large crowd gathered around Rebecca in the faculty lounge as well. As it turned out, most of the people in attendance were not aware of any connection between Rebecca and me. As Rebecca stood in her adoring circle, I stood next to the bar fortifying myself. The handful of people who knew we were married said, "You should be proud." They were right. I should have been.

Satchel Paige was a pitching teammate of Mike Garcia. He had been a superstar in the Negro Leagues for many years before he was allowed to play in the major leagues. Some say he was fifty before he threw his first major league pitch. Satchel Paige was a colorful personality who was quoted often in the media. My favorite quote of his was "Don't look back, they may be gaining on you." For me it had become a motto, a general rule of conduct that I had fallen back on over the years. For me it meant: don't worry about the competition, work harder. The problem now was that the person I lived with, my wife, had become the competition.

The night after the moot court, as I lay next to a deeply sleeping Rebecca, the choices seemed clear. Continue practicing law the way I had been since Rebecca entered law school, and I'd lose her the day after she passed the bar exam, or sooner. Start trying high-profile criminal cases again, and she might not leave me and I might not be so threatened by her.

Most criminal defense attorneys lost money taking cases to a jury trial, and I was no exception. Over the past two years I had tried one case before a jury. Plea bargaining was the name of the game. You tried a case before a jury only when there was absolutely no other alternative or, in the beginning, when you were trying to establish a practice. On the other hand, Rebecca had now reached the point where she could do practically everything I did in the office and, in many instances, do it better. She would only improve in the next two years, and once she passed the bar, it would be tough to walk around the office with an air of authority when it was clear that she was the better lawyer.

But a good lawyer was not necessarily a good trial lawyer. Well over 90 percent of lawyers would never try a case before a jury, and more than half would never see the inside of a courtroom as lawyers. Most lawyers were buried in depositions, research, arbitrations, negotiations, drafting legal documents, and advising clients. Over my first ten years I had tried many cases before a jury primarily out of need and ignorance. I had become an above-average trial attorney through hard work and determination. Soon after Rebecca began working with me, I had all the business I could handle, and it was clear that there was no need to continue trying cases. There was a need now. Rebecca wouldn't be able to try a case for another two years. By that time I would have established myself as the trial lawyer in the office, and an office our size didn't need two trial lawyers. The ease and smoothness of her delivery, the ability to think on her feet in arguing a hypothetical case in a rarefied atmosphere after months of preparation was not the same as a cross-examination or a closing argument when a man's life was on the line. I shuddered at the thought of the hard work and pressure of trying cases. But it was the only way I could think of to survive and preserve my dignity and self-respect around Rebecca the lawyer, and, in the end, the only way to avoid losing her.

As the only Mexican-American lawyer in the county who had tried any serious criminal cases, the Alternate Defender's Office was delighted to have me back on their panel. We agreed that I would handle no more than three serious violent felony cases at one time and that I would be allowed to screen and select the three that were assigned to me. I was careful in my selections. I always chose the defendant who had the highest-profile case and the best chance for an acquittal, which was not often.

Those cases did exactly what I hoped they would do. A day after the assignment of the first case, the phone began to ring: reporters wanting a quote for their deadline. Television news people were at the door hoping for a sound bite. It wasn't long before clients who were waiting to see me began asking the secretaries and Rebecca and me about my latest "big case." Rebecca might have been the most promising law student in history, but I was the only lawyer in the office. From the waiting room I could hear, "I saw your boss on TV last night." "Your husband must be a very good lawyer because the court keeps putting him on all those terrible cases." Wherever I went, "I saw your picture in the paper this morning." "I heard you on the radio yesterday." Yes, there was only one *real* lawyer in the office.

But I paid dearly for that identity. At forty-seven, I felt the four or five hours of sleep a night that ambition and the need to prove had fueled in those beginning years were now fueled by fear. I was more of a zombie this time. My body was worn, and my mind was clogged with too many years of cases. I sipped on black coffee from early morning until late at night, and when that failed me, I turned to those stark white No-Doz pills. I ate my only meal of the day between ten and eleven o'clock at night, fearful that eating at any other time would slow me down or put me to sleep. I interviewed witnesses at night knowing that I couldn't absorb anything off the written page at that hour and that all I had to do was be awake for most of them and that those little white pills would widen my eyes and raise my brow and tingle the nerves in my arms and fingers so that there was no danger of sleeping.

It meant trying to be in bed by midnight and keeping the alarm set at five, and then reminding myself as I sat on the edge of the bed in that deadening morning stupor that I had to get up, that she was still sleeping, that it would make me stronger, and that I would feel worse that evening if I weakened, then staggering to the shower and letting the cold and hot water shock and soothe the stinging numbness from me. I gave myself ten minutes to shower, shave, and dress. Because I needed the next three hours before court when my brain could best absorb and retain written materials, to read the volumes of reports and transcripts that the three appointed cases brought. At 8:15 I would pack those materials in my briefcase and take them to court with me so that I could read them in the courtroom while waiting for my other cases to be called, and then take them with me to parks and riverbanks and sloughs, where I wouldn't be found or disturbed during lunch hours that never saw food, outlining and graphing and comparing those reports and transcripts instead, because there wouldn't be any more time that day. Once I was out of court in the afternoon, the office and other cases beckoned. There were phone calls to return and clients and witnesses to see and cases to prepare, other than the appointed three, for court the following day.

Three nights a week I went to the jail. The clients in those three cases were always in jail. I went in after 6:30, after the counts and the feedings and the showers and guard shift changes so that I wouldn't have to wait in those mindless cell-like interview rooms for an hour or more before my client could be brought to me. I set aside three hours for each of those interviews and saw each of those clients once a week. Some of the time was spent discussing their cases; most of the time was spent attempting to gain their trust and confidence. These were hostile, angry, cynical, mistrusting men. But the more they saw that I cared about them and their cases, the easier it was to work their cases.

Most nights I ate at 10:30. Since it was my only meal of the day and since I had worked hard all day, I rewarded myself with as much as I wanted of whatever appealed to me on any given night. I began with appetizers, then the main course, and dessert, sometimes two. Of course I had something to drink to relax me. White wine while I ordered, a martini while I waited, more wine with my dinner, and port with my dessert. It wasn't long before I hungered as much for the alcohol as I did for the food. It relaxed me.

In Rebecca's final two years of law school, I tried six major cases: three homicides, a serial rapist, a kidnap/rape in concert, and a case of bestiality involving a man and his three young daughters. The trials averaged about four weeks, four weeks of hell, or rather six weeks of hell, because an all-consuming fear set in about two weeks before each trial date. It was the fear of failure, the fear of being exposed or found out. "I saw you on television last night, Mr. Garcia. You're such a good lawyer," an admiring client would say in his heavily accented English as he sat across from me. If he only knew. If he had only seen me at four o'clock that morning, bolting out of bed without the benefit of an alarm because by then I believed, and had convinced my body to believe, that we only needed four hours of sleep, that one second more could lead to disaster, because I wouldn't be prepared and everybody would see me for what I was, a slow, plodding, dull Mexican who had come this far, unexposed and still surviving on backbreaking burro hours. I didn't need a shower to wake me. Fear had wakened me and wired me. I was so awake I was jittery. All I needed was my file, to calm me. I went to the back porch, the coldest room in the house, because I didn't want to get warm, comfortable, and maybe even yawn. I turned on the tiny desk lamp and no other light so that I would have to focus, get close up to the page to see, to read, to concentrate. Then I would go over a police report that I had already read fifteen times and compare that to my handwritten condensation and both to a time line and a graph and continue drafting my ten or fifteen or twenty pages of cross-examination notes for one of the People's witnesses. I would work for exactly one hour and fifteen minutes, hunched and shivering over that old desk, my first desk, which was a wooden door set on four wooden fruit lugs, a desk that I kept for times like these to remind me where I had come from, how far I had come, and how I had gotten there. Hard work. Nothing else. "You're a really good lawyer, Mr. Garcia." If they only knew.

I allowed myself ten minutes to shower and shave and was back at my desk by 5:30 to work another hour and fifteen minutes before I went back inside to put on my suit and tie and make a pot of coffee. Ten minutes for that as well. Because I knew that my brain could work at its maximum capacity for seventy-five minutes and then needed a break, even though I thought of nothing but the case as I showered and shaved and dressed and poured myself my first cup of coffee and then returned to the porch for my final hour and fifteen minutes.

Rebecca would be up when I went into the bedroom for my suit. "Good morning." There was nothing good about those mornings, each of us said, self-absorbed, to wherever the sound of the other had been. More often than not those were the only words we said to one another until late that afternoon when I returned from court. If she said more to me, it was in servile tone, which I enjoyed, because she knew the state I had worked myself into. At some level it frightened her. The secretaries saw it, too. At times, just the sight of me took them aback. There'd be a pause, maybe even a little gasp, a hand to their breast and a step back before they caught themselves and gave me a little nervous smile or quickly looked away.

The trial would be a war. I told myself that over and over again. What I couldn't articulate then was that it was not only a war against the prosecutor and the police but against fear itself. During those two weeks preceding the trial, fear was really the enemy. Almost everything I did in some way or another was designed to combat fear. I framed my acts as acts of self-sacrifice, self-discipline, and mortification to prepare myself, strengthen myself for the war, when I was simply using them to cope with the fear.

Once the trial began, once the jury was selected, there was a

lull in the fear, for a day at most, when it became clear that I was
better prepared than the prosecutor, which only served to put the
vast investigative resources of the State to work again. More evidence was garnered and added to the existing evidence to form a
giant wall over which there would be no escaping. I worked harder. I dealt exclusively with the trial. I slept even less, and those few
hours were devoted to reliving the trial. My body began twitching,
different parts at different times. I couldn't control the twitching,
and I worried that it would be visible in court. I stayed out of the
office. I avoided anyone not connected with the case. I was short
with the secretaries and made at least one of them cry during each
of the trials. Rebecca kept her distance. When we did speak, it was
near midnight when I was bloated with food and drink.

"How'd it go today?"

"Fine."

"Anything new and exciting?"

"Not really."

"How much longer?"

"The judge told the jury two more weeks."

"Goodnight, Gabby. I'm exhausted."

"I know the feeling."

It is expected that defendants will be convicted. Hung juries
and convictions on lesser charges are considered victories. But I
was fighting for myself as well, fighting to keep from being
exposed, seen for what I was, an imposter at best, a fraud at worst.
I needed the facade. It had become me. Each prosecution witness
became a battle. Most were minor skirmishes. But the principal
witnesses, the victim, the eye witnesses, the investigating officer,
the expert witnesses, were major battles, sometimes wars within a
war. The prosecutor would question first, building his case. Then
I would cross-examine, trying to tear down that case. The prosecutor would try to repair whatever damage I had done and I would
have another chance to undermine. Always when I finished, and
sometimes during my cross-examinations, I would look to my
client for his reaction, his approval and steal glances at the jury
and the prosecutor to gauge the impression I had made. The vast

majority of the time I was able to preserve my facade, remain unexposed because of my exhaustive preparation. But there were witnesses that completely destroyed me, and then there was nowhere to hide as I longed for the day to end so that I could try to regroup, cover my exposed wounds, cover my shame. Those days of annihilation brought with them nights of numbness in which my eyes were closed and my body lay prostrate and the scene of the shame repeated itself throughout those four or five hours. In the end my client was usually convicted after a process in which he had become all but irrelevant. Because the trial very quickly became a struggle between two egos, two wills: mine to survive and the prosecutor's to conquer. And the defendant's guilt, justice, and the victim were too often forgotten in the daily battles for our identities.

In the third case I tried, the jury found the defendant, Mónica Torres, not guilty of murdering her husband. It was undisputed that Mónica Torres had shot her husband at point blank range in their home and killed him. It was undisputed that three hours before the shooting the couple had quarreled, that Mónica had been badly beaten and had fled the home, going to the home of her parents who were in Mexico at the time, only to return three hours later when the shooting occurred. The prosecution claimed that Mónica armed herself at her parents' home and returned to kill her husband. Mónica said that she was tired of being beaten, was afraid of her husband, and had returned to their home, thinking her husband had gone to work, to get some clothes and belongings in order to leave him. As she was gathering her things, her husband startled her. He was still at home and still in a rage and, after a few words, came at her again. The gun was on a shelf next to her. Afraid for her life, she took the gun and shot him.

Two days before Mónica was to testify, her cousin came to see me saying he wanted to do anything he could to help Mónica. He said he was at Mónica's parents' home when Mónica arrived, badly bruised and bleeding on the morning of the shooting. He asked her what had happened, but she wouldn't say. Given the history of Mónica and her husband, he knew what had happened.

Mónica locked herself in one of the bedrooms for several hours. When she emerged, she said she was going back to the house to get some things. She was no longer crying but she was upset. He decided to go with her because he thought something might happen and he wanted to help her if it did. He said he thought he saw a gun in her bag when they got in her car. When they got to Mónica's house, she asked him to wait in the car. When I asked him how certain he was that he had seen a gun in Mónica's possession before she entered her house, he said he was positive because once she got out of the car, she loaded a revolver at the end of the driveway just before going into the house. In fact, he said, some of the bullets had fallen to the ground while she was loading the gun and might still be there. A couple of minutes later he heard gunshots and got out of the car and ran because he was on parole and couldn't afford to be around a shooting of any kind. He said he was coming forward now because he had completed his parole just the day before.

Having no criminal records, Mónica Torres was a beautiful, diminutive, demure young woman of twenty-three who had immediately succeeded in charming the judge and three male members of the jury by simply sitting at counsel table during the first days of the trial. When I went out to the jail to discuss her cousin's allegations, she erupted. For a full fifteen minutes she railed against her cousin, calling him every curse word I had heard and some that I had not. She repeated again and again that he was a punk and a pimp and a drug addict and was not to be trusted. She never gave me an answer as to why he said he had seen her with a gun before going into her home except that her husband's family may have given him some drugs or money and put him up to it. I hadn't seen that side of Mónica Torres, but I couldn't help thinking that her husband had. I did not call the cousin as a witness.

Mónica Torres cried and cried when she testified. She cried so much and so convincingly that both the judge and the bailiff stopped the proceedings long enough to provide her with Kleenex, and one of the male jurors rose and asked for a recess during the prosecutor's cross-examination to allow her to gather herself. She spoke so softly that the judge and the jurors were on the edge of their seats straining to hear her, but not once did the judge ask her to speak up. I concluded my questioning by asking her why she had shot her husband. She stopped crying for a moment, looked up at me with eyes red and swollen from a full day of crying, and said, "Because I thought he was going to *kill* me." The *kill* rolled and rose and broke, followed by a new wail of tears. The jury found her not guilty in less than two hours.

The next morning I went to Mónica Torres's home when I knew she had an appointment with her husband's insurance carrier. Except for Mónica, I had told no one about the gun and the bullets. I had deliberately waited until the trial was over to go out to the house. I walked up the driveway to the place where the cousin had said they parked. I walked a few feet further, looked in a flower bed and found three unspent, rusted bullets. I drove to the river and threw them as far as I could into the moving water.

The media bash was wonderful. I was on the front page of the newspaper. I was on the morning and evening news. I was on two talk shows. Everywhere I went people congratulated me on a great job. The secretaries wanted a complete rehash of the trial. I was a legitimate, accomplished lawyer. Everyone said so. Rebecca didn't bother me in the least. Let her be the greatest law student since sliced bread. She would never catch me now. In fact, when I saw her buried in work at the office with her law school texts close beside her, she looked tired and worn. "You're working too hard," I said to her as I bounced in from an interview. "You have to take time to smell the roses." Three days later, smelling the roses was the furthest thing from the presiding judge's mind. He wanted a firm close trial date from me on the kidnap/rape in concert case. "A trial date sixty days away is simply not feasible, Mr. Garcia. I understand that you were in trial for the past month, but you did have time before you started the Torres case to devote to the preparation of this case and . . ." The kidnap/rape in concert case was a brutal, ugly case. There was absolutely no defense to it, and the mere mention of it outraged the community. That old feeling of fear and discomfort settled in. "Well, your honor, as this court knows, the charges in this case warrant a life sentence. This is a very serious case, and because of my other court commitments I have been unable to . . ."

In a week's time the Mónica Torres case was forgotten. It was the only case of the six that I won. Without it, I don't know how I would have gotten through the remaining three cases. In a way, it mirrored life. You need that one good day to forget the five bad days that have just passed and to encourage and help you take on the next five bad days waiting in the wing.

The last of the six cases involved a hanging death in the jail. One inmate had been hung by six other inmates. We had just completed jury selection in that case, and I was hurrying out of the courthouse to talk to a witness when I ran into Walt Williams. I had seen Walt Williams just a handful of times around the courthouse in the seven years since our marriage. We had nodded to each other, but nothing more. That day Walt Williams was entering the courthouse surrounded by a group of well-heeled lawyers or clients when we made eye contact. I was past him before I could think to nod, fear and survival propelling me as fast as my feet could carry me. "Hey, Gabby!" I heard. I tried to walk faster, act as if I hadn't heard. If I didn't talk to this witness before he testified . . . "Hey, Gabby!" The voice was louder, closer; he was running after me. Oh, shit! If I don't get to. . . .

"Hey, Gabby, hold up a minute. I know you're in trial but I need to talk to you for just a minute or two."

I stopped. "Hello, Mr. Williams."

"Christ, Gabby, like it or not you've been my son-in-law for seven years now. You can at least call me Walt."

My head was throbbing, and my body was tingling. I didn't want to call anybody anything. I just wanted to talk to that witness.

"Slow down, Gabby, this won't take a minute. I know you're in trial. I know what that's like, believe me."

Did he? Could he know what it was like for *me*? I looked at him and thought only of the witness.

"Gabby, I'm not getting any younger. I was sixty-two last week. I've made all the money a man can want. I have everything a man can need. To buy one more thing, anything, would be a sin. But you know, Gabby," putting his hand on my shoulder, lowering his voice and searching for my eyes, "I need my family."

It was not a plea. It was a statement, as real and as human as the hand that lay gently on my shoulder. At that moment the hysteria that was churning inside of me left me and I looked at him and listened.

"Margaret's not very well. Oh, hell, let's leave Margaret out of this. It's about me. I need my family. I need my daughter, as she is, as she wants to be, with you. So I need you, too, Gabby. And I need your children. I don't want to leave this world without knowing my grandkids, without knowing that in some small way I will continue, that for me death wasn't as final as it could have been."

"So what are you trying to tell me . . . Walt?"

"Talk to her, Gabby, get her to let me make contact with her. I want to see her. I want to make things right. I don't want her to hate me. I want you to be part of my family. I want to know and love your kids, my grandkids. I want the chance not to make the same mistakes with them that I made with their mother. I want to love them and let them be. That's all I ask of you, Gabby, talk to her. Let me into her life again. I won't interfere, I won't intrude. Please talk to her." Now it was a plea, a plea for what was perhaps the most important thing in Walt Williams's life. He made it quietly and with dignity.

"I'll talk to her, Walt, I'll talk to her."

As I watched Walt Williams walk away, I felt a strange calm, and I knew that none of this mattered, the fear, the scurrying, the hysteria, and yes, even the case itself, none of it mattered. Family mattered. Love mattered. But an hour and a half later, as I paced the halls waiting for the afternoon court session to begin, I cursed myself for having passed up the opportunity during the noon hour to talk to the witness I would be cross-examining in a matter of minutes.

I did talk to Rebecca. I talked to her after my client was convicted of first-degree murder with special circumstances for the hanging of his cellmate. The night of the verdict I came home drowning in alcohol and collapsed. Rebecca had taken the bar exam the week before, and the next night it seemed that for the first time in four years there were no classes, no clients or witnesses, no cases, no studies that had to be dealt with. It was awkward. We closed the office together and then looked at each other.

"Want to go out for dinner?" Rebecca asked.

"Sure."

"It's been a long time."

"It has."

We went to Li Lum's on Rebecca's dare. It had been at least seven years, and much had changed. I was in a suit, and Rebecca was in heels. The woman in the long dress was gone. In her place was a maitre 'd who greeted us with, "Ah, Mr. Garcia, I saw you on television last night." Yes, hanging my head alongside my client as we took the verdict. We were quickly seated in the main dining room, and several people recognized and greeted us. No sooner were we seated when a young man in a white smock served us water and presented us with menus. Close behind him was our waiter who smiled and bowed and took our order and smiled and bowed again. Much had changed indeed.

Then we were alone in a room full of people, sitting across from each other after five years of reasons not to linger and be together. Rebecca looked at the tablecloth and then made markings on it with her fingernail. I waited for her to look at me. She made more markings. She knew I was watching. Finally, she looked up and said, "How did your client take the verdict?"

"It wasn't unexpected."

"When's the sentencing?"

"Rebecca, let's stop it. Let's get to the point."

"What is the point?"

"The point is that I want to have a family."

"You what?"

"I said, I want to have a family."

"Huh. Just like that." She was stunned. "I wanted to have a

family years ago and you said to wait."

"Yes, until you finished law school. You're finished with law school and I'd like to have a family."

"Wait a minute, Mister, I didn't just go to law school like taking a walk around the block. I worked hard for four years, real hard, while working full-time at the office, too. And I've done well, real well, so well that I have offers pouring in from law offices all over the state."

"Oh, so you're going to leave our practice and run off to some fancy corporate law firm?"

"I didn't say that."

"What *are* you saying?"

"That I want to have a career."

"So have your career after the kids come."

"Who said anything about kids? I remember saying I wanted to start a family and that could be one kid."

"So start your career after you have one kid."

"That's easy for you to say, Gabby. You've been practicing law for eighteen years. "I'm thirty-five and you want me to start a family now and when I'm forty start being a lawyer. That's ridiculous."

"Well, I'm forty-nine, and if we don't have kids now and you start practicing law now, we probably won't have any kids. And I want kids."

"Since when?"

"Since now."

"Well, why don't you go have some?"

"I don't appreciate your sense of humor, and I don't want to die without having had kids."

"Gabby, I want a career. I want to be a lawyer, and that's what I'm going to be."

There was nothing more to say. We sat in silence, looking away. The waiter brought our appetizers. They went untouched. After a while Rebecca said, "I'm not hungry."

"I'm not either." I called for the check and we left.

The silence followed us home and remained with us for

almost two weeks. For the first time ever, I slept on the couch. The memory of Eufemia had kept me in our bed even in the worst of times. I tried to remember how long it had been since we had had sex. Nine weeks and two days. And before that? At least ten weeks. And before that? A long time. And each at my insistence. I wanted her more than ever, but I would have castrated myself first before I went to her then. Not after her choice. As obstinate as I was, so too was the question that dogged me: Did I really want kids or was I afraid of losing her? As much as I tried to evade it, the answer was simple. I was afraid of losing her.

For the next thirteen days we spoke to each other only in the presence of the secretaries and clients. The rest of the time it was an ugly little game of who was going to speak first. On the evening of the thirteenth day, Rebecca walked up to my desk and handed me a small brown paper bag. "Here, I won't be needing these anymore." Then she turned and left the office. When I opened the bag, it contained a small flat oval plastic case that I knew but couldn't immediately place. Inside the case were Rebecca's contraceptive pills.

She wasn't home when I went next door, but she came home about an hour later.

"Thank you," I said when I saw her. She turned from me and shook her head. "Thank you," I repeated. She shook her head again as if to say, "Don't thank me." I went to her and held her. She kept her head down and then sighed and whispered, "I guess I still love you."

"What?"

"I guess I still love you."

Guess! Part of me wanted to press the issue. Guess. Another part of me had better sense. I let it be. Her pills were in my pocket. I didn't want to jeopardize that.

I watched Rebecca for the next hour, my desire rising with every minute, waiting for the first sign that she was going to bed. When she went to the bedroom, I followed. When she got into bed, I got into bed. I pressed myself against her and began caressing her and kissing her. She didn't move. But the pills were enough of an indication of what she wanted. I continued caressing her and then turned her on her back. But as I lifted myself to my knees, our faces brushed, and I felt the heavy smear of tears on hers. Anger ran through me. But I wasn't about to be denied. What was mine was mine. But once I was over her, I heard the snivel of her tears and I felt myself become limp. Still I tried, but the more I tried the smaller I became until I got out of bed and, with a groaning, guttural sound, rushed from the room.

The next day I moved into the spare bedroom where I slept until Rebecca left.

We never talked about that night, and we never talked about the fact that I was sleeping in another room. We were pleasant and courteous to each other, especially in the presence of the secretaries and clients. But we avoided each other by burying ourselves in our work. To the outsider, we were the perfect working couple.

I had expected Rebecca to leave when she passed the bar exam. She passed but stayed and hope sprung eternal. She accepted three court-appointed misdemeanor cases. I knew she would do well and was only mildly surprised when she won her first case. A hung jury and a subsequent dismissal of her second case were much more of a surprise. I was astounded when she won her third case. Three successive victories by any criminal defense attorney was unheard of. I worked harder on the next homicide case I was about to try.

Within a year, Rebecca was court-appointed to represent a defrocked medical doctor who was charged with twenty-eight felonies for over-prescribing narcotic medications to patients. The case had drawn a lot of media attention when it was first charged, but, thankfully for me, the media had lost interest in it by the time Rebecca was appointed. It was a difficult, complex case. There were volumes of reports and medical records, a large number of expert witnesses, the medical issue of chronic pain, the legal issue of when prescribing was excessive in cases of chronic pain, and the fact that the doctor had long since publicly lost his license to practice medicine. I watched with glee as she worked long nights and weekends on the case, certain that she would get her comeuppance in this trial. But I was less than gleeful when the jury acquitted the doctor on twenty-two of the twenty-eight counts and couldn't reach a verdict on the remaining six. Five days later my client in the homicide case was convicted of torturing and beating to death his girlfriend's baby. Ironically, there was no mention of the doctor's case in the media, while my name and face were everywhere.

About four months later Teresa came to my door and said, "There's a Dr. Browning out here to see you."

"Who?"

She closed the door and in a hushed voice said, "His name is Dr. Browning, and he doesn't have an appointment, but I think you better see him."

"Why? Who is he?"

"He's the doctor that teaches at the university and is the head surgeon at Presbyterian Hospital. The one whose patient died from the medication he gave him. It was in the news. They played it up big."

I had read the first two articles in the newspaper and then lost interest. An affluent white client had yet to retain me. "What does he want?"

"He needs a lawyer."

I was flattered and began straightening out my desk, wondering how long I could remain in these shabby offices with this type of client coming in. Apparently, the publicity I was generating in the court-appointed cases was beginning to pay off.

He was a tall, handsome, distinguished-looking man in his early forties who was impeccably dressed. As he entered the room and looked around my small, cramped, soiled office, I remembered my meeting with Walt Williams years before in that same room and, like then, was embarrassed.

I shook his hand, gestured for him to sit down and said, as coolly as I could, "What can I do for you, sir."

"My name is George Browning. I'm a surgeon and, as you may have read in the papers, I need a lawyer. But I think your secretary made a mistake. I'm here to see your associate, Ms.

Williams. I testified for her as an expert witness in the Brandt case several months ago and was very impressed with her. I was hoping to explore the possibility of retaining her services."

Rebecca wasn't in, but I had Teresa make an appointment for Dr. Browning to see her.

I didn't go home that night. After my usual late dinner I didn't stop drinking. When the restaurant closed, I walked down the street to a bar and drank there alone with the bartender. When the bar closed, I stumbled to my car and slept. Garbage trucks woke me in the morning, and after vomiting, I was able to drive home.

Rebecca not only represented Dr. Browning, but she had the case thrown out of court at the preliminary examination without ever having to go to trial. The next morning it was Rebecca's picture that was splashed all over the front page with an ecstatic Dr. Browning.

When I got home that night, there was a note on the dining-room table. It said, "Gabby, I'm leaving. I don't love you anymore." She took only her clothes.

CHAPTER VIII

As much as I feared Rebecca leaving me, as certain as I was at times that she would leave me, as much as I did to avoid her leaving me, when she left me, I wasn't ready. But then, I couldn't have been ready. I couldn't have anticipated the loss. She was gone and nothing else mattered. It was as if everything in my life had been leveled, and I stood in the center of a vast wasteland. Everywhere I turned, there was nothing but crumbled grey rock. Whether the sun shone or not, the days were grey, and no matter where I went or what I wore, I was cold, a cold that seemed to rise from the rubble and seep through my shoes and socks because my feet were always like ice. She was everywhere except with me. She was in every room of the house, in every inch of the office, in my car, on the street. There was no escaping her but no having her either. I couldn't eat and I couldn't sleep. I drank myself into a stupor at night, but she was in my last conscious moment and then howled through what must have been sleep, howled without making a sound, howled by smiling or looking at me as she did when she loved me. Sometimes I slipped from that state of unconsciousness to consciousness without knowing because she was there, too, the only difference being that my eyes were open and I could hear the endless solitary ticking of the clock in the darkness. I knew I was awake when the jolt came, like a blow bringing pain, the real live recognition for the first time in a few hours that she was gone and she would not be coming back. I removed my clothes from our bedroom and then locked the door and flushed the key down the toilet so that I wouldn't have to see or go near our bed again.

Reading was impossible. I would sit with a report or a brief or anything and run my eyes over the words on a page, come to the end of the page without having absorbed a single word. I would start at the top of the page again, slow my pace, decide to concentrate on one paragraph at a time. Concentrate. By the second sentence, the loss registered again. She was gone. Forever. I read on. She was such a good, kind, caring person. I would never find anyone like her again. I read on. There were so many things I could have and should have done differently. Like . . . I read on. I never took the time. Everything else was more important. I had to go here, I had to go there. I had to answer this call, see that person, while she waited her turn. I read on. Maybe someday we would accidentally meet, and I would convince her that what I had done, whatever it was, was not intentional, that it was the pressure of work, and she would see how wrong she had been to leave. I read on. Then she would always be first, and I would always appreciate her, always show her how much I loved her. I read on. I don't love you anymore, Gabby. I was at the bottom of the page, and again I had retained nothing.

Clients came and I wouldn't see them. Teresa and Belen were beside themselves.

"What do you mean he's not in? I had an appointment! We go to court tomorrow!"

I could hear them out in the waiting room as I sat paralyzed at my desk, filthy and drinking, unable to stay in the house, too ashamed to go out into the streets and worse, court. "If he's not in now, when will he be in? . . . What do you mean, you don't know? This is his office, isn't it? You're his secretary and you're trying to tell me you don't know where he's at?"

Some were smarter then others. "He's not here! That's his car out there, isn't it? You mean the man's out walking around town with his briefcase! Where is he? When will he be here? I have a right to know. Do you know how much money I've paid that man? . . . Sure you know. I gave you the money. My money is paying for you standing there, and you're trying to tell me that you don't know where he is! Bullshit!"

As the days passed, Teresa and Belen came up with the only

answer that wouldn't be thrown back in their faces. "He's sick."

"Sick? What's the matter with him?"

"Nobody knows. The doctors are running tests."

"Where is he?"

"In the hospital."

"What should I tell the judge?"

"That he's sick."

One returned saying, "The judge wants to know what hospital."

"I can't tell you that. That's confidential."

"And the judge wants to know why you can't send another attorney."

"Because there's no one else here to send."

I listened to them and didn't care. What could anyone do to me that was worse than this? I took another swig of the tequila and thought: the judge had asked why we couldn't send another attorney. He hadn't said send Rebecca. They knew. It hadn't taken long. She was probably working for one of those big law firms downtown.

The court called. The fear and deference in Teresa's voice caught my attention.

"Yes, your honor."

"No, your honor."

"I don't know, your honor."

"I'm not at liberty to say, your honor."

"Can I have Mr. Garcia's doctor call you, your honor?"

"Thank you, your honor."

The next morning Dr. Richard Chang walked into my office unannounced. Dr. Chang had been my physician for more than twenty years. I was originally seen by him only because his associate was away on an emergency. During that first visit Dr. Chang had told me that he had just come to San Jose after practicing medicine on a Navajo reservation for ten years. The image of a Chinese doctor attending to and living with Navajo Indians in the Arizona desert fascinated me, and I became his patient. Over the years he had become more than a doctor to me.

"Oh, my God, what's happened to you, Gabby?"

I hadn't showered or shaved for a week, and during that time my diet had consisted of tequila, Milky Way candy bars and water, in that order.

I motioned for him to close the door. When he did, I said, "Rebecca left me," and I cried as I had never cried before or since.

Dr. Chang committed me to the Mount Madonna Sanitarium high in the coastal range overlooking the Santa Clara Valley. He told the court I was suffering from exhaustion and that a thirty-day stay at the sanitarium was imperative.

They kept me sedated and under watch for the first week. The following week they allowed me to go out onto the grounds, at first with one of the staff and then alone. The sanitarium had been someone's country villa. It was a large two-story structure that stood in the center of a clearing on forty wooded acres. Beyond the gardens and fountains and old carriage houses were thick sloping forests of redwoods and madrone and scrub oak. Except for the birds there was absolute silence. It was under those trees and among their foliage and next to their stream that I began to accept the fact that she was gone.

When I told Dr. Chang that I wanted to be released a day early, he looked at me, and in his quiet, thoughtful manner said, "Why?"

"There's something I need to take care of before everybody knows I'm back."

He knew. "Are you sure you're well enough?"

I nodded and added, "I have to."

I didn't recognize that part of downtown San Jose anymore. Better, I was beginning to forget what that part of downtown San Jose had looked like. It had been the business section of San Jose's barrio when I had first come to town. Most of the two-story brick buildings had been razed and giant skyscrapers had replaced them. The entry doors to 185 North Center Street were ten-foot panels of polished glass. The lobby walls and floor were of soft-

colored marble, and behind an ornate desk facing the front doors
some twenty feet away sat a man in a brown uniform. When I was
three steps into the lobby, he was asking, "Can I help you, sir?"
He knew I didn't belong there. I ignored him and went to the
directory instead. I had as much right to be in that building as anyone. I looked for the name but at first couldn't remember it in my
rush to evade what I knew was coming at any second and then,
remembering it, couldn't find it in that jumble of names on the
wall before he said what I ignored again, "Can I help you, sir?"
The directory became a blur but I stood before it and looked at it
anyway. "Can I help you, sir?" I could feel myself beginning to
burn, and I warned myself: Not here, not now.

"The Fletcher firm," I said with my back to him.

"The Fletcher firm is on the twenty-eighth floor, sir."

Sir. He no more meant that than the Texas Rangers had.

The elevator was twelve feet of mirror paneling with gold rail-
ings. It was soundless and motionless. Only the fleeting light on
the floor panel indicated that we were moving. I stepped out onto
carpet so thick that my feet sank. I started to my left and found that
part of the elevator hall sealed off. I turned, looking for a sign or
directory but found instead that the hall opened onto a gigantic
room that extended to a far wall of windows overlooking the valley and the coastal range beyond which I had left just hours before.
In the center of the room sat a receptionist behind a solitary desk.

"Can I help you, sir?" She looked like something straight out
of *Vogue* magazine.

"I'm looking for the Fletcher law firm," I heard myself say.

"This *is* the Fletcher law firm."

"Where?"

"The entire floor."

I stepped forward and found myself on marble again. The
walls had tapestries and paintings. There were three separate sitting areas with plush couches and stuffed chairs and oriental place
rugs. Fresh-cut flowers adorned every table. Superimposed on all
this was an image of my office, small, cramped, soiled, and worn.
She belonged here.

"Can I help you, sir?"

"I'm looking for Ms. Rebecca Williams."

"And you are?"

"Gabriel Garcia."

"Do you have an appointment, sir?"

"No, but it's urgent."

"And the urgency?"

"She'll know."

"Please have a seat, sir. I'll check with Ms. Williams's secretary to see if she's available."

I sat on one of the couches. Real leather, not the imitation stuff I was accustomed to. I looked around the giant room at its opulence. I had worn my best suit, my best shirt, and my best tie. I had shined my shoes an hour before, and I wore new socks that weren't falling. But I didn't belong. I'd never belong.

"Ms. Williams's secretary would like to know the nature of the urgency, sir."

"Tell her I don't want to discuss it in public. Ms. Williams will know."

They don't even know she's married. Not to any Garcia, anyway. Not to me. They have no idea who I am. And who *are* you? Oh, stop.

I fingered the 3x5 cards in my pocket. While I was in the sanitarium, the *Times* had done a feature article on Rebecca. It told that she was a local girl, the daughter of Walt Williams, mentioned her education and academic honors, told about her recent victories in the criminal courts and her new position with the Fletcher law firm. There was no mention of me. After reading the article I decided that I had to see her, had to have a face-to-face meeting with her and get some understanding and maybe even resolve some misunderstanding that had led to her leaving. I spent several hours putting my thoughts on paper, as I would a closing argument, and then reducing them to 3 x 5 cards, which I memorized. It was those cards that I fingered as I waited. I felt the need to review those cards one last time but was afraid the receptionist would know what I was doing.

I waited. Would she see me? Probably not. Over the past five weeks she had made no effort to contact me. There had been no message at the office, nothing at the house, and there had been no calls at the sanitarium except from Teresa. I felt bites of shame. The secretary had probably told the receptionist to get rid of me, and she was probably waiting for enough time to pass to make it appear that they had looked for Rebecca. I caught the receptionist looking at me. She looked away. I didn't belong there.

"Mr. Garcia." The words came from a tall, comely woman who was standing in a hallway to the left of the receptionist. "Mr. Garcia, Ms. Williams will see you. Please follow me." She wore horn-rimmed glasses and her blonde hair was pulled back tightly in a bun. She was as self-assured as I was nervous. She waited until I was past the receptionist's desk and then, without a word or smile, turned and began walking down a long, well-lighted hall. Her legs were long and shapely, and as I began watching the movement of her hips, I saw myself kneeling over Rebecca on that last night in our bed, and my stomach sank and my eyes dropped.

The secretary stopped beside an open door and gestured with her head, and my heart beat faster. Rebecca was standing behind a large, polished mahogany desk, and my breath caught. Behind me the door closed. "Hello, Gabby." It was a different Rebecca. Her hair had been cut and hung neatly just below her ears, emphasizing the fine lines of her jaw and chin. The glasses she sometimes wore had been replaced by handsome horn-rimmed glasses not unlike those of the secretary. She wore an elegant grey silk business suit. Her small, old scratched oak desk had been replaced by an elaborate expensive piece of furniture that seemed to take up half the room. Behind her, instead of the soiled whitewashed wooden slats, was a huge window that opened onto a panorama of the valley and the bay beyond. Standing there, Rebecca exuded an air of confidence that I had never seen.

She was waiting for my response, but I was seeing the woman I thought I would never see again, the woman I had loved as I had loved no other, as I would love no other. She was more beautiful than ever. She had been mine to touch and kiss and love, and I would have done anything to have her back, for a day, for an hour, a minute. There was too much to say. Too much for hello.

"How are you, Gabby?"

I was mesmerized.

She motioned for me to sit and I sat.

I couldn't take my eyes off her. What I was seeing was the hundreds of thousands of moments we had had together. They were better now than they had ever been. Forgotten completely were not only the words on the cards I had memorized, but the cards themselves.

"Teresa said you were in a sanitarium. I was sorry to hear that. She also said that you were fine now. I was glad to hear that."

I heard what she said but none of that mattered. What mattered was that I was with her again.

"Gabby, I've got to go to a deposition in just a few minutes. I did want to see you. Is there something you want to say? I'm going to have to leave very soon."

"Please come back, Rebecca." It came from every part of me, from the deepest part of me. It was all I had to say, all there was to say.

She sat down and looked at me, but her eyes were far away. The passing of seconds, minutes gave me hope. Then she saw me again and said, "Gabby, I care deeply about you and I always will. The years we had together, both the good and the bad, I will never forget. But I don't love you anymore, Gabby, and I was beginning to live a lie. I don't want to live a lie. I can't go back to you."

She kept her eyes on me, but they were seeing other things, things present, past, or future I did not know. There was so much I wanted to, needed to say. So much that was running through my mind. But my tongue was frozen and I said nothing.

The phone rang, breaking the silence. She answered. "Yes, I know. Tell them I'll be there in a minute." She put the receiver down and said, "Gabby, I have to go."

The office was a mess. Rebecca and I had been gone a full month. Rebecca was the biggest loss and a permanent one at that. She had been the office manager, the paralegal, and a lawyer, too. She had supervised the three secretaries, and had been the fiscal officer as well. During our absence the newest secretary quit, saying she could not work in an office as chaotic as ours. Once I returned to work, I hired two secretaries through a temp agency, but at the end of two weeks I was still overwhelmed, and things seemed to be going from bad to worse.

I had never been an administrator, and now I was acting as an administrator and trial lawyer and doing poorly at both. It soon occurred to me that I didn't need a practice as large as I had. I was alone and my needs were simple. Rebecca hadn't taken a cent from any of our bank accounts. I had plenty of money with no one to leave it to except the State of California. I could close the office, take Teresa with me, and move downtown, limiting my practice to court-appointed high-profile cases. That would give me all the money I needed. But in doing so, I would be turning my back on my clientele base: low-income Mexicans that I had always said I wanted to help and work with, although in recent years it was Rebecca who had been handling the bulk of those cases. Still, I was reluctant to let them go. It was those clients who had attracted Rebecca to me in the beginning. Moving to an office downtown and specializing in high-profile criminal cases would give Rebecca fewer reasons for returning. But how long could I keep the door open?

That question was answered for me shortly. My landlord of twenty-two years died suddenly in his sleep. One of the few things his survivors could agree on was that they wanted to sell the old store and my house. I toyed with the idea of buying the property mainly because I thought it might help me convince Rebecca to return. I had examined and reexamined her reason for leaving a thousand times. She was beginning to live a lie. We were no longer helping the people we had set out to work for. I was trying high-profile criminal cases, and she was beginning to do the same. If we bought the property, we could remodel the store and bring in another lawyer, or even two, and an office manager, and return to helping people in a much bigger way than before. I was excited and was about to call her with my idea when I saw her picture in the paper. She was arm in arm with Dr. George Browning at the opening of a new medical wing at Presbyterian Hospital. The look she had on her face, the look she had for Dr. George Browning, was markedly different than the look she had for me just a few weeks before. Like it or not, the lie may have involved something totally different than her need for helping the disadvantaged.

I called Dr. Chang, and he agreed to see me. I took the newspaper with me.

"I'm afraid that I'm losing it again, Richard, that I may start drinking again tonight. I've looked at this picture a hundred times, and I've made and have tried to make all sorts of things out of it. Please, Richard, I want your honest, frank opinion. What do you make of it?"

He took the newspaper, looked at the photo, and then began reading the long article on the new wing. He was a small, deliberate, thoughtful man. His office was decorated with Navajo rugs, tapestries, and paintings. I once asked him if he had had trouble relating to the Navajo. "Not at all," he had said dryly. "We had a lot in common. They came across the Bering Straits." When he finished reading the article, he looked at the photo again, and then at the article again. What the hell was he reading the article again for? But there was no one else I could have gone to with that article, and he was thorough. When he finished rereading the article, he looked up and said, "I think you should know that Rebecca is living with George Browning."

"What? . . . Are you telling me that you can tell that from that photo?"

"No. George Browning and I have a very close mutual friend. She told me that Rebecca moved in with George the day she left you."

I shook my head in disbelief. I can only imagine what my face must have looked like.

"She said that Rebecca is very much in love with George

Browning. She doesn't think Rebecca will ever come back to you. Believe me, Gabby, it's not my intention to hurt you or to pass on idle gossip. In the long run, I think the sooner you hear this the better. The sooner you begin dealing with the fact that Rebecca is now living with another man and may very well not return to you, the better."

I didn't drink that night. I think I was afraid that this time I might not come back, that this time it was hopeless. Not only had she left me for another man, but a man that seemed far beyond my reach. I was in shock. The thought that Rebecca might have been involved with another man had never crossed my mind. But Richard Chang was right. Once I got over the additional blow to my ego, over the new shame and bouts of self-pity, I began to heal, not completely, never completely. Slowly I began to function as I had with and before Rebecca. Except that now I had something new to prove: that I was better than Dr. George Browning.

Two days after my visit to Dr. Chang, I rented a condominium two blocks from the courthouse. I moved the following day, taking only my clothes. Everything in the house was Rebecca. She had chosen most of it and had lived with all of it. When the landlord's son asked me what I intended to do with what I had left behind, I told him to keep it or sell it; whatever he didn't want I'd give to the Salvation Army. He kept everything.

Leaving the storefront office was not as simple. The most difficult part was informing clients, past and present, that we would no longer be practicing there, and to many, that we would no longer be representing them. Disengaging myself from clients with open files required at least one face-to-face meeting with each person. Ironically, although I was the attorney of record in most cases, they were more Rebecca's clients than mine. Still, there was guilt on my part in leaving them. And I was bitter. Look what she had done to them. Look where she was at now. She couldn't have been further away from the people she had always claimed she wanted to help. Blame her as much as you want, she's never coming back. Looking at the large stack of files that had to be closed reminded me how hard she had worked. Mope over her all you want, she's not coming back. Many of the bewildered clients asked about her in the same Spanish they had always spoken to her. "Where did *la Rubia* go?" "Where's the *Secre*? She was such a good person." Yes, she was. But she wasn't coming back. Leave Dr. George Browning for you? You've got to be kidding.

It took me two months to leave the storefront office. Teresa and Belen had found other jobs so I went alone. I moved into a modest old building downtown and shared space and two secretaries with three other lawyers. There were no fancy trappings; none of the rooms advertised success. I had always despised fancy furnishings defining the lawyer.

I stuck to my plan to take only high-profile cases. Money was not a problem. Rebecca still hadn't gone near the bank accounts. I increased my contract with the Alternate Defender, doubling the number of serious violent felony cases from three to six. Then I went to work, spending all of my time on those six cases and any other high-profile case that came through the door. I worked as hard, if not harder, than ever. I was up by five-thirty and reading by six. Court, jail visits, briefs, memos, reports, research, meetings with my investigator, interviews with witnesses, potential witnesses, and family members took the rest of my day, which ended each night, six days a week, at exactly ten. Then I would walk to Sam's, the only restaurant downtown open after ten, for my dinner. It was my only meal of the day. Black coffee and cigarettes kept me alert and awake throughout the rest of the day. Dinah had my table, a glass of Chardonnay, and the morning paper waiting for me as I walked through Sam's front door. By nine o'clock each night I began thinking about that Chardonnay, and as I walked that block and a half to Sam's just after ten, I could taste and feel it. Four minutes after Dinah seated me, she brought me my second glass of Chardonnay as I read the paper. As much as I enjoyed my liquor, I had a strict rule that I wouldn't drink before ten. Dinah brought me a martini with my appetizer. Halfway through my martini, I was completely relaxed, thinking only of what I was reading in the sports page and needing no one. I had two and sometimes three glasses of red wine with my main course and port with my dessert. I managed the two-and-a-half-block walk to my condominium quite nicely. Once there I would watch what was left of the late night news with a nightcap: Scotch on the rocks. Most nights I fell asleep on the couch. On Sundays I slept until noon and began preparing for the coming week at one; on Sundays I left the office at eight, and Jennifer, Dinah's weekend fill-in, was ready for me then.

Four months to the day after Rebecca left me, I transferred all the money in our joint bank accounts into my personal account. She wasn't coming back. I hadn't heard a word from her. But three days after I transferred the funds, I was served with divorce papers. My initial reaction was that she was angered by my transferral of the funds. But on closer reading of the divorce papers, she wanted nothing, only her freedom. I gave her that, letting the divorce proceed uncontested. She wasn't coming back.

Within the first year, the reduced caseload and the long hours spent on a specialized area of the law began paying dividends. In every case I handled, no one was better prepared than I, which led to some acquittals, hung juries, and convictions on lesser charges. Prosecutors became wary. There was a new respect for me and my work that fostered some excellent offers of pretrial dispositions. Fear would always plague me, but in the back of my mind, I now knew that by the time we reached trial I would know the facts and law of my cases better than any prosecutor. My name and face were in the media constantly, and the media was beginning to call me for comments on criminal cases in which I was not involved. People on the street would stop me and say, "I know who you are. You're . . ."

But everything has its price, and part of the price I was to pay for the media attention came from an unexpected source, my associates. By the third year they were not happy with me. They complained that the receptionist was spending too much time, the majority of her time, answering my calls and attending to the host of people that were constantly coming to see me. Perhaps, they suggested, I should get my own receptionist. Two of the three lawyers had very little business, but I thought better of mentioning that. They complained that the people who came to see me and sat in the waiting room were well-known criminals and were frightening their clients and the secretaries. In fact, almost without exception, every one of my clients was in jail, and the various family members and potential witnesses often had no records. They complained that the secretaries were spending too much time working on my cases, talking about my cases, and reading reports from my cases instead of working on their cases. The sad truth was that they were envious of me and shamed by my success. By the fourth year the end of my association with those three lawyers was in sight.

The end came sooner than I expected. It came in the form of Terry Kennedy, a senior partner in the law firm of Jones, Kennedy, and Marcus. At that time Terry Kennedy was the big name in San Jose personal injury cases. I had known him only by sight until he took on the representation of one of five young defendants who were charged with the murders of three teenagers in a drive-by shooting. He was representing the driver of the car, whom the prosecution was trying to implicate on a conspiracy theory. I was court-appointed to represent one of the two alleged gunmen. The trial itself lasted just under a month, but various court appearances brought us together many times over the course of a year. As often happens in lengthy cases involving several defendants and lawyers, Terry and I paired off. Before, during, and after court sessions, we were usually together discussing what was about to or what had just happened in court. I liked Terry. When the trial ended, Terry Kennedy asked me to join his firm. I was flattered but protested that I couldn't afford their overhead. Terry said that they would match whatever my overhead was then, and I agreed.

That evening when I returned to my office, Joel Schwartz, one of my associates, was waiting for me. Our antiquated copier had broken down again, and this time was in need of major repairs. Joel was firmly convinced that since the majority of copies made on that machine over the past four years were mine, that I should pay for the entire cost of the repairs. If it weren't for me, the machine would still be in very good working order. I told Joel Schwartz to shove his copier where the sun don't shine.

The following evening Terry Kennedy and I left court together and went to his offices. They were gorgeous. The space they would be giving me was every bit as good as Rebecca's had been and had a better view. Besides, it came with the territory.

It was as if Rebecca had dropped off the face of the earth. She never called and I never saw her. Then, a few months after our divorce was final, I learned that she had married George Browning. I saw a large photo of Rebecca and George Browning in the Sunday paper. They were on church steps waving and beaming. She was in a long, flowing white gown complete with veil and bouquet, and he wore a tuxedo. The caption described the ceremony as "elegant" and said that the couple would be honeymooning on a private island in the Caribbean. I smelled Walt Williams. Rebecca was finally in her element. She was never coming back.

I had naively expected to see Rebecca in the criminal courts. So certain was I that I repeatedly practiced my greeting before the mirror. "Hello, Rebecca, it's good to see you." Every day of that first month back from the sanitarium was sure to be the day. But the first, second, and third months came and went and no Rebecca. I finally asked Bill Jacobson, a deputy public defender, whose wife worked at the Fletcher firm. "She's been assigned to work with Tom O'Grady on a multimillion-dollar lawsuit against San Jose Gas and Electric. It looks like they'll be going to trial in six months." Of course, why waste that kind of talent on paltry criminal cases. The following year Rebecca and Tom O'Grady were on the front page of the *Times* under a headline that blared: $30 MILLION VERDICT AGAINST UTILITIES. I must have sat staring into space for some time because Dinah came up to my table and asked, "Is anything wrong, Gabby?" I shook my head. No, the only thing wrong was that once upon a preposterous time the woman in that photo had said she loved me.

A few months later Teresa called me. I hadn't heard from her in more than two years. "How are you, Gabby? I see your name in the paper all the time."

What did she want? Whoever she was working for probably had a case involving one of my clients.

"I see you're still taking all those big cases. I don't know how you do it. I could never do it. It takes a special person to do what you do."

She was out of a job and wanted to come work for me. I was doing just fine sharing a secretary. I didn't need the added overhead.

"You look real good on television. You've gained a little weight but you look good. I mean, you know how to do it now. You come across like a real professional."

Maybe she only wanted a letter of reference. I could do that. Then she got to the point.

"I guess you don't see Rebecca very much these days."

"No." My body tingled.

"Well, you probably don't know that she's pregnant then."

"No."

"The baby's due in four months."

She went on but the words just bounced off my ears. There were several uh-uhs and uh-huhs on my part until she said, "Well, I'd better get back to work. Nice talking to you, Gabby."

"Uh-huh."

I never understood why Teresa did that. I always thought that I had treated her well and that we got along well.

I went to Bill Jacobson again, not caring what he or his wife or anybody else would think, or who it would get back to. I asked him directly. "Oh, yeah, she's pregnant. Baby's due in three or four months. She's already taken a leave of absence. They want her back as soon as she has the baby. But she won't commit to that or any other definite time. She's such a good lawyer that she can get away with something like that." It took me weeks to get over the fact that Rebecca was carrying another man's child. Three months later I began scouring the *Times* daily birth listings. It was some time before I read it in small print: Born to Rebecca Williams and Dr. George Browning at Presbyterian Hospital, a seven-pound, three-ounce baby boy. Dinah was within ear range when I put the paper down and said, "Can I have another martini, Dinah?"

I should have been numb by then, but I was soon to learn that when it came to Rebecca, I would never be numb. Not only did

Rebecca refuse to return to work immediately after the birth of her first child, but four months later she was pregnant again. I stopped going to Bill Jacobson. Ignorance was better, no matter how short-lived. Within two years of her return to the Fletcher firm, the legal newspaper reported that she had been made a partner. Once again I smelled Walt Williams. My suspicions were confirmed some time later when the *Times* did a feature article on THE SUC-CESSFUL PROFESSIONAL FAMILY. There were several photos of Rebecca and George Browning and their two towheaded pre-school sons in and around their mansion. In one of the photos, Walt Williams was holding one of his grandsons. Some years later when Rebecca was sworn in as a judge, the *Times* photo showed George Browning on one side of Rebecca and Walt Williams on the other. Walt Williams couldn't have been happier.

After Rebecca, I never had another woman, not even a date. This was the subject of a running dialogue Dinah and I had.

"You ought to meet someone, Gabby."

"I meet people every day."

"You know what I mean. A woman. W-O-M-A-N."

"And you know what I mean."

"It's not good to be alone."

"I read that somewhere in the Bible."

"We weren't meant to be alone."

"Who's alone? I'm surrounded by people all day, every day and half the night, except Sundays. I've got people waiting to see me when I get to the office, people waiting for me at court, peo-ple trying to interview me, phone calls by the dozens, secretaries complaining, the jail calling that clients want to see me. By ten o'clock every night I'm tired of people. Fed up."

"You're always alone here."

"Dinah, it's the only chance I have to be alone, to have a lit-tle privacy, to relax, to enjoy myself. I don't need another person and another set of problems. Here I can have a drink or two while I eat and read the paper and just plain unwind."

"But you go home to an empty apartment."

"Dinah, when I get home, I'm so exhausted that all I want to do is sleep. I'm ecstatic that there's no one else there to bother me, to have to contend with, to keep me from sleeping."

"Suit yourself, Gabby, but I still don't believe you."

Occasionally, an old bag about my age would just happen to be sitting across from my table having dinner alone at ten o'clock at night. I smelled Dinah. The poor thing would be all painted up covering every cream conceivable, wearing perfumes that smelled like rotting vegetables, and turning elevated breasts toward me that were threatening to pop out of her low-cut dress at any moment. The sight of her would take me back to Rebecca, to what I had once had, and I would bury myself in my paper, not even looking up at Dinah to order.

Once Rebecca became a judge, it afforded me an opportunity to see her, watch her, admire her at least once or twice a week without anyone knowing. I would wait for her arraignment calendars because then her courtroom would be packed, standing room only, and I could step in unnoticed and unseen and stand in the back and watch her. Her hair was turning white, unadorned and free from those jillion sprays sold everywhere. She had let it grow back to the length I had known. Her face was unpainted. She did nothing to hide the wrinkles that were settling in. She had never been afraid of growing old. In fact, her face had softened, and she was obviously a kindly woman, kindly but firm. I admired the way in which she dealt with those who came before her: patient, respectful, concerned, and considerate, but firm. She had always been intelligent, but now she was wise as well. What to do with the person before her. I could see her mind turning, those keen blue eyes searching. Seldom did I disagree with her decision. She was not only wonderful but beautiful still. But I learned early on not to go into her courtroom for the Friday-afternoon calendars. By then the week had worn and exhausted me, and to watch her on a Friday afternoon was to invite tears to an old fool's eyes.

There was no way I could have known or even suspected. Nothing like it had ever happened to me. I was selecting a jury in an attempted murder case in which a masked armed robber had shot his victim in the head but the victim hadn't died. The selection of a jury had always been a difficult phase of the trial for me. The law said that every defendant was entitled to a fair and impartial trial by a jury of his peers. Most defendants were young brown or black males from impoverished and dysfunctional homes. Most jurors were middle-class, middle-aged whites who, until that day, had never been in a room with someone who looked like or had the background of the defendant. As far as impartiality, the prospective jurors brought their biases with them, biases based on fear or race or hate or a combination of the above, and all believing that the accused wouldn't be sitting at counsel table in front of a judge in a courtroom with two or three armed deputies in it if he hadn't committed some criminal act. Unless, of course, they believed the police were out running around arresting innocent people. Over the years I had come to understand and expect these biases. What I couldn't accept was the sanctimonious labels the judicial system continued to cloak itself in.

I had just begun questioning the third juror, who had already learned from the previous questions to and the answers given by the preceding jurors what he had to say either to stay on or be excused from the jury, when it happened. I was standing about a foot from the jury box railing looking up at the third juror, trying to get some idea of who this man was in the few minutes allotted to me, when all of a sudden my breath caught, stuck. I couldn't breathe. I couldn't get any air into my lungs, and my mind swirled in panic. I took a few steps toward the judge's dias and managed, "I can't breathe," and then rushed to the nearest door, which was to the judge's chambers. Once inside I fell on the judge's couch and breathed. And all the contortions that were raging through my mind and body eased.

The judge declared a recess, and I took a walk around two blocks, more embarrassed than anything. I knew what it was: lack of sleep. I had been up working on the case since four that morning even though I had gone to bed after midnight and then had laid awake strategizing. The lack of sleep had caught up with me, and I promised myself that I would get at least five or six hours of sleep that night. I returned to the courtroom, completed the selection of the jury, and then the two-week trial, without a problem, aside from the fact that the jury rejected my client's and his family's alibi and convicted him on all counts. For the next seven months I went about my normal daily routine without any reason to think of the breathing episode again.

That August I was court-appointed to represent one of several defendants who had been involved in a jailbreak that resulted in the deaths of a deputy sheriff and two inmates. The case had attracted national attention. It was a hot, muggy day as I walked up the courthouse steps, and my pant legs were sticking to my skin. For security reasons the defendants were to be arraigned in a basement courtroom. There was a large gathering of spectators and media outside the courtroom door. I knocked on the door and a deputy within lifted the piece of fiberboard covering a small glass window on the upper part of the door, recognized me, and let me in. I was surprised by the ten armed deputies in the courtroom. But then a deputy sheriff had been killed and the attempted escape had occurred while the defendants were being transported to an outlying court. The air was warm, stagnant, and stuffy in the courtroom. It would be unbearable once those in the hall packed the courtroom. At exactly 1:30 the deputies opened the doors and there was a push for good seats. Once everyone was in, the deputies closed the doors, and the air became warmer, thicker, and scarce. We waited ten, fifteen minutes. The air was beginning to feel like another substance rubbing against my face. The court was twenty minutes late in starting and the defendants, who were usually brought out before the judge took the bench, hadn't been brought out yet. "Where are they?" I said to one of the deputies. He simply shrugged. I had been exchanging small talk with the other lawyers and had run out of small talk and interest. I looked to another deputy. "Where's the judge?" He shrugged, too.

Then the word came. The courtroom was to be cleared of

everyone except the attorneys. There were murmurs of protests as the deputies started herding everyone out.

I looked at the first deputy, and this time he said, "There's been a threat of another escape attempt." Then the spectators and the media were gone, and another ten armed deputies took their places. The courtroom air remained thick and stuffy. Then, from behind the dais, a captain emerged from the judge's chambers and said, "Can I have your attention, please? The judge has ordered that from now until the upcoming proceedings are completed, all the doors to the courtroom will be locked, and no one will be allowed to enter or leave the courtroom until the proceedings have been concluded and the prisoners are back in the holding cells." Locked and not permitted to leave. Those words reverberated in my brain and all of a sudden I couldn't breathe. I got up from my seat. I had to get out of there. I had to breathe. I ran to the hall door. Four deputies surrounded me. "I can't breathe! I've got to get out of here! I can't breathe! I've got to get out of here!"

I came to in the Presbyterian Hospital. A nurse was at the foot of my bed.

"What am I doing here?"

"That's what we're trying to find out, Mr. Garcia."

"What happened?"

"Apparently, you collapsed in court. An ambulance brought you here."

It came back to me. The fear, the panic. I thought I was going to die, and they wouldn't let me out, they wouldn't let me breathe.

"Dr. Chang's already called. He said he'd be here around 5:30."

I was afraid and ashamed. Everyone would know. At least the media was out of the courtroom. No cameras. No reporters. But the deputies loved to talk to the media, and so did my colleagues. And I had lost an opportunity to handle a case that would have been in the media for months. The scuttlebutt around the court-house would be that I was afraid of the big cases. Judges would be reluctant to appoint me. But what happened?

What was wrong with me?

Richard Chang wanted to know as well. I told him what I

remembered, and he examined me, and then my words, looking up a bit, his dark eyes reflecting the mulling over in his mind. "Has anything like this ever happened before?"

I thought of the attempted murder case. But I hadn't collapsed there. "No. . . . No." I didn't want to appear any sicker than I was. I needed to get back to work as soon as possible.

"I'm going to keep you here for a couple of days and run some tests on you. I'm sure you could use the rest."

The next morning I had a number of files brought to me, and I worked on them in between tests. Late that afternoon I was sitting in bed reviewing a file when I felt someone watching me. I looked up and saw Rebecca standing in the doorway. She smiled and said, "Hello, Gabby."

Emotions erupted in every part of me. It took me a while to say, "What are you doing here?" The words were curt and the tone harsh. They were not what I expected or wanted, but I had no control over either.

"I heard what happened in court yesterday, and I was concerned. I came to see how you were."

"You? Concerned? Huh."

"Gabby, I do care about you and always will. I will always respect what you've done with your life."

"Huh."

"I did love you. I loved you very much. But we reached a point where we were damaging each other. Things were bad between us, and they were getting worse. I have a family now that I love deeply. But I will always care about you."

Anger, hate, love, yes, even desire, jealousy, self-pity, and above all, a sense of loss raced through me. Anger must have provided the most protection, because I said, "Look, I'm fine, and I don't need all your proclamations about how much you care for me. That's not going to make me any better. Besides, I've got a lot of work to do. So if you don't mind, I'd like to continue with my work."

"Gabby, I know I hurt you. But I do care about you."

"You've had a funny way of showing it. Please go."

"All right, but if you need . . ."

"Go!"

She left and I cried until Richard Chang entered, either ignoring or not noticing my tears.

"The good news, Gabby, is that all the tests are negative, at least for any major illness. Your blood pressure and cholesterol levels are high, but we've known that for some time. Still, they're higher than they were six months ago, and I'm going to be changing your medications a little. But those you can control, Gabby, by your eating and drinking and work habits and exercise. How much alcohol are you drinking now?"

"Only at dinner."

"Daily?"

"Yes, but only at dinner. Please don't ask me to give that up. It relaxes me."

"Well, a glass of wine at dinner won't hurt you."

"So, what's wrong with me, Richard?"

"Gabby, I think what you experienced was a panic attack, nothing more, nothing less."

"Panic attack?"

"I'm sure you've heard of them."

"Sure I have. But those are mental, and what I experienced in court had nothing to do with my mind. I couldn't breathe. It was my body that couldn't breathe, not my mind." Catalina Garcia raised her contorted head once again. "There's nothing wrong with my mind."

"I know what you're thinking, but I believe it's best to refer you to a psychiatrist."

"Richard, my mother was a paranoid schizophrenic. I know what mental illness is. I'm not mentally ill."

"I didn't say you were. But the mind is incredibly strong. It can trigger physiological reactions in us that we're not aware of."

"Richard, I don't believe in sitting down with some shrink once a week for the rest of my life reflecting, on my navel and every bowel movement I've had since I last saw him."

"I understand. But the psychiatrist I will be referring you to emphasizes the pharmacological side of psychiatry. I'm certain that after a visit or two he'll be able to prescribe medication that will allow you to function as you always have without any danger of repeated attacks. . . . I want to say some other things to you, Gabby, as much as a friend as anything else. You have to stop working so hard. You've got to get out and have some fun. Enjoy life. Meet people. Make new friends."

"I deal with people every day."

"That's not what I mean, Gabby. The mind is a powerful thing, and if you're alone, it can play cruel games with you. Ever since Rebecca left, you've withdrawn further and further into yourself. As far as I can tell, you've excluded everyone. That's not healthy, it's not good. It may very well have played a significant role in your collapse this week. You've been here three days, and, aside from me, the nurse tells me that you've had just one visitor."

"Nobody knows where I am."

"Not true. The newspaper reported your collapse and the fact that you had been brought to Presbyterian Hospital. The nurse told me that there have been no calls inquiring about your condition."

All I could do was look at him. If I tried to do any more than that, I might have fallen apart.

"It's occurred to me that perhaps you should consider a change in professions, or at least stop being a trial lawyer. I'm sure there are other kinds of work that a lawyer can do. The stress you're apparently putting yourself through in dealing with these cases is not healthy."

"It's the only thing I know how to do." It was more than that. It was me. It was my identity. Being a good trial lawyer was what set me apart from others. It gave me value, worth. Without it, I would be nothing, nobody. But I couldn't say that, even to Richard Chang.

"Well, it's something you should consider. I'm not trying to hurt you or humiliate you with these comments. Some of us do care about you. The nurse said that Rebecca left in tears."

It was just as Richard Chang said. After one visit, Dr. White prescribed Xanax for me and told me that these attacks were often the results of a chemical imbalance, which could be effectively dealt with by pharmaceuticals. A follow-up visit was scheduled for sixty days. When I asked Dr. White about the possible psychological origins of these attacks, he referred me to a psychologist who dealt with that school of thought. I attended a group session conducted by that psychologist. It was held in a large bare room with fourteen chairs arranged in a circle. Beginning on the psychologist's left, each person told of his or her latest encounter with panic attacks, followed by comments and suggestions from the others until the entire circle had been heard. I heard a woman describe her fears of going outside her house, a man's fears of standing in lines, a man's fears of crossing streets, a woman's fears of driving over bridges, a jewelry salesman's fears of closing large sales that he had routinely made for twenty-five years, a woman's fears of driving alone. When it was my turn, I passed, saying I would "share" on my next visit.

The group sessions weren't for me. I had lived with fear all my life. I would always live with fear. But fear of failure had taken me to heights of success that few, if any, of those whom I had grown up with would ever know. Whether I was happier than they was a moot point. I had long thought that fear was the worst of human emotions. It severely limited and stunted people. It killed dreams and aspirations. Oddly, in my case, it had propelled me. I had to be betting that I could still channel it enough to drive me. I never returned to the group sessions.

I took the Xanax instead. I learned to regulate it and use it only in tension-filled situations, which were usually trials and important evidentiary hearings. It calmed me but I had to be careful. If I used too much, I reached a state where I worried about and feared nothing.

I was a confirmed user of the drug when I took Alan Newsome's case.

PART II

CHAPTER I

I had anticipated the vans and the trucks with their high antennas. I had visualized them right where they were, in the no-parking zone in front of the courthouse. But I had no idea there would be so many. Twenty or thirty cameramen and reporters were appended to them in small groups around the courthouse sidewalk. "There they are," I said, pointing my chin. "Remember, try to relax, appear as normal as possible, look straight ahead, and don't say a word." Fear tightened his face. If anything, I had frightened him all the more.

They hadn't seen us yet. In a few moments they would and the circus would begin. Pigs, I thought, there to protect the public's right to know. Every day of the week a homicide of one kind or another—a stabbing, a drive-by shooting, a drug rip-off or retaliation, a plain old-fashioned robbery gone awry—was being played out, tried in an empty courtroom. Where were they then? They knew the public well. A successful doctor coldly killing his invalid wife: that raised ratings, that sold newspapers.

The nursery school case flashed in my mind. Ten years before, eight women and two men were accused of sexually abusing thirty-three preschoolers. I had represented one of the women and watched as the media had its day. Headlines and front-page material for over a month. Lead story night after night. In-depth stories of the innocent toddlers and their grief-stricken families. Editorials. Histories of the school and the first telltale signs of decadence. Why adults perpetrate horrifying crimes on children. Investigative stories on the defendants and what drove them to commit these atrocities. The school was closed. The teachers became unemployed and unemployable, as were their spouses in some cases. The children of two of the defendants were beaten at school by other children. Neighbors picketed three of the teachers' homes, demanding that they move out of their neighborhoods. In fact, all but two left San Jose and some left the state. Six months later, after an extensive preliminary examination hearing, the charges against eight of the defendants, one of whom was my client, were dismissed. A year later a jury acquitted one of the two remaining defendants and could not reach a verdict on the other. The District Attorney elected not to retry that defendant. Not a word of retraction was written or heard. The media had ably protected the public's right to know.

Two cameramen started toward us, their eyes on the lenses of long cameras propped on their shoulders. "Remember, not a word. They don't give a damn about you. They're here to sell copy." The others noticed the first two and rushed to join the feast, blocking the sidewalk. "Look straight ahead and walk through them."

"Doctor, can we have a word with you, please." "KZVU Evening News, Doctor, we'd like to get your side of the story."

"Doctor . . ." They wouldn't budge. I leaned into them. "Gentlemen, please, we're due in court now." Grudgingly, their bodies shifted, as did their questions. "Doctor, is it true that your wife had never used a gun in her life, didn't know how to use one?" "Doctor, we understand that you recently purchased the gun used to kill your wife. Why did you need a gun?" "The police say that there were no signs of any intruders at your house the night of the shooting. Would you care to comment on that?" I glanced at him. His head was down a bit. Other than that, his face was impassive, pale but impassive. "Doctor, your wife had been bed-ridden for three years. Had that produced a strain on your marriage?" "Is it true that you were about to file for a divorce?" We were wedging our way through them, and the courthouse doors were in open view. Still they flanked us, hoping to provoke him. "These are very serious charges, Doctor. Here's your chance to refute them. Are you sure there's nothing you want to say?"

We hurried up the steps into the courthouse and watched the carnival recede behind us. "We'll be okay now," I said, "at least until we leave."

When I had first begun practicing law, the courthouse and the courtrooms were the exclusive province of the court. Cameras were simply not allowed in the courthouse or courtrooms. In the seventies a clamor arose that courts were soft on crime. Watchdog committees sprang up and scorecards were kept on individual judges. The media fanned the fire. Judges ran for office every six years, and it wasn't long before there were cameras and reporters everywhere, in select cases to be sure. In the nineties, the O.J. Simpson trial appeared, and the public was appalled by the media's circus atmosphere. Once again the courts took control: written application for limited access by the media was now the rule. The majority of the media was required to remain outside, with their equipment and big black cables extended across the front sidewalk.

We took our place in the metal detector line, another court-ordered phenomenon of the nineties. Every day hundreds were searched as they entered the courthouse for that lethal weapon that had to be lurking somewhere. The line wasn't moving. It was beginning to wind its way outside the courthouse. Next to the electronic archway a sheriff's deputy who spoke no Spanish was motioning to a wide-eyed man who spoke no English on the other side of the counter. "Your pockets! Your pockets! Empty your pockets!" Alan Newsome watched. His reaction to the metal detector and the everyday indignities suffered by his newfound contemporaries was one of disdain, disbelief, and affront. Then too, we were surrounded by Mexicans, blacks, and poor whites, the core of the criminal justice system, and he looked with disdain at these people as well. "Your pockets! Your pockets! Don't you understand! These! Empty them!"

Another Mexican stepped out of line, went to the befuddled man, and spoke to him in Spanish. The first man then quickly emptied his pockets, keys, coins, wallet, papers, and a few dollar bills, putting them in a plastic container. The deputy waved him through the archway, but the alarm sounded. The deputy waved him back and pointed to his belt, watch, and glasses and the plastic container. The man complied but the alarm still sounded. The deputy leaned over the counter and said, "What you got in your shoes?" The man's eyes widened even more. Someone in the line said, "*¿Qué tienes* in *los zapatos?*" The man shook his head in earnest denial. The deputy sighed and said, "Go through again." The man blinked. From the line came "*Vete.*" The alarm sounded again. Now the man looked in every direction, pleading his case with his eyes to anyone who would look. "Come on back!" the deputy said angrily. "I said come on back!" But the man only blinked. "Oh, shit!" the deputy said. "Wand!" pointing to another deputy who stood at the far end of the counter with a metal detector in his hand.

The man looked in the wand-carrier's direction but didn't move. He turned back to the deputy and blinked some more. From the line came directions in Spanish. The man looked to the line and then to the wand-carrier and back, again and again. Finally, he walked to the wand-carrier and then stood on a rubber pad, bewildered, as the wand skimmed over every part of his body. The wand found nothing, and the man was set free. Once again he turned to the deputy and blinked.

As Alan Newsome emptied his pockets, the deputy examined him with grudging deference. He had to have seen the reporters and cameras hounding us outside. As Alan Newsome felt and looked at his pockets a second time, the deputy's eyes searched for some explanation: how could this man, who probably had everything the deputy could want, have killed his wife? In a few more visits to the metal detector line, there would be little difference in the way the deputy looked at Alan Newsome and the way he looked at the others who passed his metal detector daily: with thin-lipped contempt.

But now he spoke softly, "Go on through," still puzzled. The alarm remained silent, and the deputy turned his attention to me with a bored nod, and I wondered, as I often did, if he got some perverse pleasure out of witnessing me empty my pockets for the ten-thousandth time.

"All right, try it."

I did more than try it, I passed it for the ten-thousandth time.

We walked down the long corridor to Department 10, the felony arraignment court. The doors to Department 10 were still locked even though it was after nine and the hallway was packed with people. We stopped at the edge of the crowd, and the smells and heat of people crammed together in an enclosed space filled my nostrils. I glanced at the doctor and he glanced back. He was uncomfortable, and I produced a smile of sorts, which did little to relax him. Most of the crowd were women, short, dark, heavyset women dressed in their Sunday best, which only confirmed how poor they were. They came for their men who were locked up somewhere inside the cells and tunnels of the criminal justice system. They came for a glance or a nod or a wave or a smile or a brief mouthed message. They came in spite of whatever new heinous acts their loved one was charged with this time. Over the years I had heard some ask the question, "If we were the ones who were locked up, would they come for us?" Those who answered their own question invariably answered no.

The doctor leaned closer and whispered, "Do you think I'm overdressed?"

"No, it shows the court some respect, and it won't hurt to stand out."

The doors rattled and the crowd stirred. Behind the steel doors, locks were being jostled. The crowd gathered its things, readying itself. It was the seats, their locations, that were important. The prisoners would be brought out, fourteen initially, and seated in the jury box along the right wall until their cases were called; then another fourteen would replace them. Two signs in the courtroom reminded the audience of the verbal warning that the bailiff gave before the beginning of each session: that it was a misdemeanor to communicate in any way with the prisoners, violators would be ejected from the courtroom and could be arrested. Despite the familiar warning, these women had come to communicate, and where they sat too often determined how much communication there would be, whether with eyes or lips or hands or the flashing of thighs or breasts.

Most of the seats were already taken when we entered. "Have

a seat anywhere, Doctor, and once your case is called, come up to the podium and join me." Then I took my place behind six or seven lawyers at the podium.

It was Monday morning and the courtroom was packed. The jail had been stacked with unarraigned defendants since Thursday night. I looked for and saw no cameras, and just as I was beginning to feel relieved, I saw a lone cameraman rise in the far left corner, raise his camera, and focus on the jury box.

"He's getting ready for your boy, Gabe," said Bill Johnson, who was two ahead of me, pointing with a nod at the cameraman.

"Have you got the doctor, Gabe?" asked Frank Swift, turning.

I nodded. The less said, the better.

"They got much of a case?"

"I don't know. I haven't seen any of the reports yet."

A small semicircle formed around me. We spoke quietly.

"That's him back there in the suit and tie?"

I nodded.

"What's he like?"

"Decent enough. But I really haven't had that much contact with him."

"Sounds like you're going to have your hands full. According to the papers, no one had access to her, or a motive, other than him. No signs of an intruder. His gun and, according to relatives, she didn't know how to shoot a gun. The shot was to the left temple, and she's right-handed."

"You believe everything you read in the papers?"

"No, but none of that helps you."

The bailiff rapped his gavel and announced, "All rise! The Municipal Court of the State of California is now in session, the Honorable John Franklin presiding. Please be seated and remain quiet."

A stooped, white-haired man in his early sixties stepped from one of the back doors, took three quick steps up to the bench, seated himself, and without looking at anyone or in any direction began calling the calendar. "People versus José Ramírez." We called him "Lightning" because, once on the bench, his sole purpose in life was to get through the calendar, no matter what its size, as quickly as possible.

I had known John Franklin since his first days in the District Attorney's office. An above-average trial deputy, he had been appointed to the bench after he had been an attorney for less than ten years. His uncle had been the governor's appointments secretary's college roommate. He had remained on the Municipal Court for almost thirty years, despite repeated efforts to have himself elevated to the Superior Court. The Municipal Court was a court of numbers, the entry-level court. Everything from failures to pay tickets or fines to the first stages of serious felonies were heard there. The calendars could easily reach one hundred cases in the morning session and another one hundred in the afternoon session. Reading defendants their rights and the charges against them and obtaining their pleas day after day was far removed from the contemplative photos of Learned Hand and Felix Frankfurter. In short, the calendars had worn John Franklin down. And there was no relief in sight, despite the dramatically longer sentences the legislature was increasing each year.

"You're charged in count one with a felony, possession of methamphetamine, in count two with a felony, possession for sale of methamphetamine, in count three with a misdemeanor, being under the influence of methamphetamine and with a prior conviction of possession for sale of methamphetamine. How do you plead, guilty or not guilty, and do you admit the prior conviction?"

It was only when there was no answer that "Lightning" looked up, looking first at the jury box, because most felony defendants were in custody, and, seeing no one standing in the jury box, added, "If your name is called, please stand." Only when no one stood in the jury box did he look to the podium and see the apparent Mr. Ramírez standing alone to one side of it.

"Are you José Ramírez?"

"Yes."

"Do you have a lawyer?"

"No."

"Are you planning to hire one?"

"Well . . ."

"Are you working?"

"Not now, but . . ."

"I order that you go to the Public Defender's office when you leave this courtroom to have them determine whether you qualify for their services, and to return to this courtroom one week from today at nine o'clock either with your own lawyer or a public defender. Failure to follow my instructions will land you in jail. Next case. People versus Ramiro Mendoza. Mr. Mendoza, you're charged in count one with a felony . . ." And so it went, with "Lightning" blistering through case after case, conducting his own private war on calendars, determined that no matter how large the calendar, he would finish long before noon and well before four, leaving bewildered defendants in his wake.

John Franklin called our case, "People versus Alan Newsome," in the same drab tone, with the same speed. There was a stir in the courtroom, murmurings and then a hush. I had hoped for just such a reaction and turned, just as everyone else had, to where Alan Newsome was still seated, as impeccably different in his brown tweed suit and striped tie as the others would have been in his world. "Yes, your honor," I said, motioning to the doctor who seemed stuck to his seat, not wanting to run the risk of slowing down Lightning. "The defendant is present, represented by Gabriel Garcia. Please come forward, Dr. Newsome." Alan Newsome rose and the courtroom stirred again. The camera whirred and followed him, along with all the other eyes, as he stiffly made his way to the podium.

John Franklin looked up from the complaint, and for several moments peered over his bifocals at Alan Newsome, hushing the courtroom again. He looked at Alan Newsome as if he were trying to recognize or understand him, looked a full fifteen seconds. Only then did he return to the complaint and begin a slow, deliberate, word-by-word reading.

"Dr. Newsome, uh, Mr. Newsome, you are charged in count one as follows: that on February 25, 2000, in and for the county of Santa Clara, you did willfully and unlawfully kill another

human being, to wit, Amy Newsome, with malice aforethought."
He stopped and looked over his bifocals again. The only sound in
the courtroom was that of the camera. Then he went on to a word-
by-word reading of the armed allegation, stopped and looked up
again, and said, "Do you wish to enter a plea today?"

"No, your honor," I answered. "There is the matter of discovery and . . ."

We left the courtroom to the stares of all, which pleased me.
John Franklin had always shown me as much deference, however
small that might be, as he did anyone. I, in turn, had always suspected that had something to do with his fondness for Rebecca.
But today had nothing to do with Rebecca or me. It was all about
Dr. Alan Newsome. If Dr. Newsome and the charge that he had
shot and killed his wife could stymie John Franklin, what effect
would those same factors have on a jury?

"We met fifteen years ago last month in the emergency room
of the Valley Medical Center. Amy was a psychiatric social worker, and she had brought a client in who was hearing voices. The
client was a woman named Lupe Rodríguez. Amy was very beautiful then, and I was immediately smitten."

Alan Newsome paused and looked warily at the tape recorder
on my desk. I had asked him to come to my office that afternoon.
I told him that I wanted to learn as much as I could about the relationship with his wife, that, if need be, we could have dinner
together. Now I ignored his look of distrust as he stared at the tape
recorder. I had already explained that anything that was recorded
fell within the attorney-client privilege and could be used only by
me. If he protested again, my answer would be the same. What I
hadn't said was that, aside from memorializing everything he told
me, the machine freed me to watch him as he spoke, to evaluate
him and what he said without the distraction of note-taking. It
also eliminated the numerous times I would have to ask him to

repeat himself, as well as the number of opportunities that gave him to correct and embellish his answers. When he looked from the machine and saw my impassive look, he continued.

He told me that Amy had been reluctant to date him until she learned that about a third of his patients were poor Mexicans. He caught himself just after the word Mexican, as if he had uttered an obscenity, and there was an awkward pause as he readied himself to look back at me for my reaction. I had been in this situation so many times that now it was more amusing than anything. Naturally, Alan Newsome felt compelled to assure me that I wasn't one of them. I laughed to myself and asked myself: then what the hell am I? Outwardly I didn't react, and when he saw that, he continued.

Once they began dating, the match seemed made in heaven. In a matter of weeks they began living together. They lived together for six wonderful years. During the week they worked long hours. They had breakfast at six and left the house immediately after. They met every afternoon for a late lunch/early dinner so that when they got home at seven they would have three or four hours to be with each other: talking, reading, listening to music or watching television. On the weekends they took frequent trips to the Sierras or the central coast where they could hike in the mountains or along the beaches. When he spoke of the mountains and the beaches, there was happiness in his eyes.

They had few friends, but then, they didn't seem to need friends. When he said that, his eyes moistened, and I thought: he couldn't have killed her.

Caroline was conceived unexpectedly on a weekend trip to Yosemite. Three months later they were married. Once Caroline was born, their lives changed dramatically. Amy's maternity leave went from six months to five years, until Caroline was in kindergarten. Alan's work hours increased. He still left before seven, but came home closer to eight in the evening. He worked all day Saturday and often for a few hours on Sunday. Caroline became Amy's first priority; she was the light of Amy's life, and Alan made sure that he was home before Amy put Caroline to bed. After dinner, Alan read the morning paper in his easy chair where, as often as not, he fell asleep. Despite the changes Alan never regretted having Caroline. She had brought him another side of love.

No matter what he said, there was regret in his eyes, and nothing he had said so far would have given him a reason to kill Amy.

When Caroline started school, Amy went back to work. She tried to be as dedicated and competent as she had always been with her clients while continuing to be a full-time mom. She was home by four each afternoon but brought a briefcase full of work with her, which she would pour over once Caroline was in bed. Amy went to bed long after Alan and was up long before him. She kept this up for a little more than a year and then the illness struck. Her symptoms were flu-like: weak, aching, cold shivers, burning eyes, and headaches. But this flu went on for weeks and the symptoms grew stronger. She was bedridden and began losing weight. Alan scoured the medical journals but with no success. He took her to several specialists and had test after test run at Stanford Hospital. Nothing.

Here I couldn't help myself. I picked up a pen and jotted down: get M.D.'s reports/test results.

Alan hired a day nurse and extended Caroline's caregiver's hours. Aside from being the breadwinner, husband, and father, he now also became cook, maid, nurse, and caregiver. Amy became irritable. She drove people away. She became jealous of Alice, the caregiver. She accused Alice of having an affair with Alan.

"Were you?" I asked.

"Absolutely not," he answered.

 Six months after the illness began, Alan took Amy to the Centers for Disease Control in Atlanta. They were there a week. She was examined by some of the most respected physicians in the country. More tests were administered. But they too found nothing. In Alan's mind that was the turning point. Amy lost more weight. She aged before his very eyes. Her skin sagged, her eyes sank, and her cheeks hollowed. She looked more like a woman in her sixties or seventies than a woman in her forties. She developed a foul odor, but would only allow Alan and Ella Mae, her nurse, to clean her with a washcloth. She refused to bathe. She was convinced that Alice was stealing not only her husband, but her daughter as well. She ordered that Caroline go directly up to their bedroom as soon as she came home from school. Alice was not allowed upstairs. When Alice did go upstairs, she was screamed at and belittled from behind a closed, locked door. Alice quit, and Amy chose as her successor a Mrs. Wilson, a frightened sixty-seven-year-old woman who spent her time each day sitting downstairs twisting a handkerchief while her charge, Caroline, lay upstairs in bed with her mother until Alan came home.

I was on guard for any attempt by Alan Newsome to make himself a victim, but I had heard none yet. There was sadness in his voice, but it was more like he was now reading from a chronicle in a flat, matter-of-fact tone.

Amy could not see the harm she was causing Caroline until Caroline's teacher, at Alan's request, paid a visit to Amy and Alan in their upstairs bedroom. The teacher was very concerned. Caroline had become completely withdrawn at school, staying in the classroom during recesses and lunch hours, refusing to have anything to do with her classmates and ignoring her studies. When the teacher left, Amy cried, and three days later Caroline went to live with Amy's sister, Claire, in Ohio until Amy recovered. Amy's illness was then in its second year, and once Caroline left, Lupe Rodríguez, Amy's old client who had been visiting Amy several times a week, began visiting Amy daily, from the time Alan left in the morning until shortly before he returned in the evening. Soon she was the only person, besides Alan, that Amy was seeing.

"Are you certain that no one other that this Lupe Rodríguez and yourself had access to Amy?" I asked.

"Yes."

"What about her nurse?"

"No. What Amy had done to Alice, she now did to Ella Mae. She excluded her. Except for taking a lunch tray up once a day, Ella Mae was no longer allowed upstairs. And while Amy spent the entire day behind a closed door in our bedroom with Lupe Rodríguez, Ella Mae sat downstairs waiting for me to come home."

"Could Lupe Rodríguez have killed Amy?"

"No. I don't like Lupe Rodríguez, never have. But she loved Amy very much, even if it was a twisted love. This was a suicide. I'll always believe that."

"Believe what you want, Alan, but the police report says that Amy was right-handed, yet the bullet wound was to the left temple. The report says that you told the police that Amy was afraid of guns and had never fired one in her life. The gun was fired inches from Amy's temple, yet there was no gunpowder on either of Amy's hands. Somebody else fired that gun, Alan."

Alan Newsome sat silently, looking far off into the distance, shaking his head.

"Tell me about this Lupe Rodríguez," I said.

"She's a paranoid schizophrenic. Amy met her in the jail about a year before we met. Amy liked her from the very beginning, thought she was very bright . . ."

"What was she in jail for?"

"Theft. She was hiding in big shopping complexes that have pharmacies and was stealing from the pharmacy once the store was closed. Amy said she was self-medicating. I always thought that was Lupe's way of having a good time. I met her the same night I met Amy and was never as impressed with her as Amy was. Rather than bright, I thought she was manipulative. But then, she didn't care much for me, either. I'm sure she saw me as a threat to their relationship. She had made great strides under Amy's care. There wasn't anything Amy wouldn't do for her, and I know Lupe loved her in her own twisted way. I saw Lupe a few times after Amy and I started living together. She had nothing to say to me, and the looks she gave me were hostile, to say the least.

"It turned out that Sylvia Macías, an old patient of mine, was Lupe Rodrígez's sister. When Amy left her job at Mental Health, she stopped seeing Lupe altogether. Several times after that, Sylvia told me that Lupe was having a difficult time making the adjustment, that she stopped taking her medication and became very ill, locking herself in her room by day and disappearing into the banks of the Guadalupe River by night. When Amy returned to work, she had Lupe put back on her caseload. It took months for Lupe to warm up to Amy again. Then Amy became ill and didn't see Lupe again for almost a year.

"It was Ella Mae who told me that Lupe had begun visiting Amy . . ."

"When was this?"

"It was several months, ten maybe, into Amy's illness. Ella Mae was very impressed by that first visit because apparently Lupe had walked to our house from hers, which was some ten miles away. After that first visit she began coming two and three times a week. Within three or four months she was visiting almost every weekday.

"I didn't pay much attention to her visits, at least not before Caroline left. I guess I thought it was better that Amy was seeing somebody rather than nobody at all, even though Ella Mae was always telling me how weird those visits were. Amy had this old wooden chair in our bedroom, uncomfortable as hell. Her grandmother had brought it over from Poland. Amy loved that chair, and, of course, that was the chair that Lupe took to. Every morning she'd take the chair and put it next to the bed, next to Amy, and every night, a little irritated, I'd put it back across the room, out of the way, only to find it next to the bed the following evening. Ella Mae said they would sit there, or rather Lupe would sit and Amy would lie in bed, saying nothing, Amy with her eyes closed and Lupe staring into space for two or three or four hours, the only communication being Lupe's hand resting on Amy's arm."

"You mean they never talked?"

"Ella Mae said that for the most part they were silent. Every now and then she thought she heard a few words, but never when she was close by. She always had the feeling that they always stopped whatever they were doing, if they were doing anything, or saying anything as soon as they heard her coming.

"She is a skinny little thing, looks more like a teenaged boy than a young woman. Five-foot-one or-two, not more than a hundred pounds. But she had them all intimidated. No, that's not entirely true. Ella Mae was a giant of a woman, as strong as she was tall, but even she had a healthy respect for that little thing. Alice just stayed away from her, and Mrs. Wilson was terrified of her. I suppose it had to do with her schizophrenia. She did look and act strange. Just looking at her, you know there is something wrong with her, that she is of a different species. Her hair ranges from long to stub-length to almost bald, and her eyes are always fixed in a wide, unflinching stare.

"It all changed when Caroline went to Ohio. Once Caroline was gone, she extended her visits, from just a few minutes after I left to just a few minutes before I came home. How she managed to get there when she did or where she went to when she left probably should have had some significance for me then, now that I look back. But, of course, it meant nothing to me then. Ella Mae was forever commenting, 'Seems like she's always here. As far away as she lives, it seems that by the time she gets home, it's time for her to turn around and come back.' I paid little attention because by then Ella Mae's resentment was high. They had pretty much relegated Ella Mae to the kitchen downstairs, letting her know, in no uncertain terms, that she wasn't welcome upstairs.

"When Ella Mae quit she said, 'I don't know what you're paying me for, Doctor. I don't do anything all day long except stay in the kitchen out of their way. If I go up there, Missus yells at me. You don't need me here, Doctor.' Her successor, Rachael Lemke, was lazy at best and only too happy to stay out of their way. I don't know what she did all day, but whatever it was, it wasn't with Amy. Which gave Lupe free run of the house. How free I didn't know, or didn't want to know, even after I came home one evening and found that she was still upstairs in our bedroom with Amy.

"I was totally shocked to find her there. I know now that I had assumed and accepted as a fact that her coming and leaving just minutes after I left or before I arrived was an indication that she was at least wary of me, that she knew and understood that it was my house, and that she had no business being there when I was there. After all, she never came on Saturdays or Sundays. But I was in for a rude surprise. Anyway, on that day Rachael's car was parked out in front, as it always was, and Rachael had her bag and purse ready, as she always did, waiting for that moment when she could leave. 'How'd everything go today?' I asked, as I always did. 'Fine,' she said as she always said and left.

"I went upstairs to change my clothes before I started dinner without the slightest hint that Lupe was up there. She was waiting for me, no doubt about it. She had decided it was time to confront me, I know that now. The room was almost dark, and I didn't see her until I was about to enter. She was sitting in that old wooden chair, hunched and stooped next to Amy, who was sleeping. I stopped in the doorway, shocked. She didn't speak or move or even nod. Instead, she stared at me as if I were an intruder, as if it were her house, her bedroom. She stared a flat, hostile stare that was as much open as it was truthful, making me smirk at first, making me stare back for a moment until I told myself that it was insane to try to out-stare the insane. So I looked away and entered the room, uncomfortable and angry. Not only was it *my* house, it was *my* bedroom. I wanted to chase her, but I couldn't justify a scene when all she had done was sit and stare. I started to change, take off my shirt. With that she rose, slowly, giving Amy's arm two pats, and then moved sideways, and then down toward and around me, facing me, even when she was behind me. Then she was gone.

"About three or four weeks later we heard the noises . . ."

The phone rang. It was Rebecca. My breath caught, and my head and hands tingled. After all these years she still had that effect on me. She wanted to see me, have an early dinner. I palmed the phone and said to Alan Newsome, "I'm afraid we're going to have to continue with this at another time."

CHAPTER 11

She was already sitting in the far corner of the empty, darkened restaurant when I arrived. Didn't want to be seen with me was my first thought. Had to avoid even the slightest appearance of impropriety was my second, with a snicker.

"Hi, how are you?" looking up at me over the flickering candle.

"Fine. And you?"

"Fine," she said, nodding little nods, her chin resting in the crevice of her thumb and forefingers, watching me adjust myself. "It's been a while."

"You said it was important," brusquely, dispensing with the niceties.

"Oh, Gabby," she said, reaching across the table and touching the back of my hand, "why can't you be yourself around me?"

I was about to say, "Why ask ridiculous questions?" but I saw her eyes, still bright and blue and beautiful, unmarked by the many lines that radiated from their corners, and I saw how all of her blonde hair had slipped to white, making those eyes more striking still, and I sighed and felt myself sink, winded almost. I still loved her.

"Gabby, you know I still care about you and always will."

"You have a unique way of showing it."

"Don't be hostile, Gabby, please."

If I were being hostile, it was so I wouldn't cry. I asked myself why I had come again when I had promised myself so many times that I wouldn't, why the slightest pretense brought me running. I asked myself, knowing the answer full well. "You said it was important."

"Yes," still gently fingering, as only she could, the back of my hand.

"Well."

"I see you've taken on that doctor's case, that Newsome fellow."

"Yes."

"Gabby, you're going to kill yourself. You know that. You have to know that."

"What am I supposed to do, stop eating?"

"You can't be that financially strapped."

"That's easy for you to say. You and your husband have to be making well over a half a million dollars a year."

She sighed and looked down at that immaculate white table-cloth, and I longed to reach for her and raise that wonderful chin to mine and kiss her as I once so often did.

"Gabby, I wanted to talk to you about this because I don't think anybody else can. You're not well and you're not taking care of yourself, and a case like this is not going to make you any better. George ran into Dr. Chang and Dr. Chang was concerned . . ."

"Please don't insert your husband into my life again. Don't you think there's been enough of an insertion?"

She sighed again and said, "Gabby, you're not well. This case will kill you."

"Rebecca, I think I'm old enough to make that decision. If that's all you came to tell me, you're wasting your time. You really should be home having dinner with your husband and children. After all, you female judges don't get to spend much time with your families, do you?"

I stood and looked at her again, angry but longing, and then turned and left.

"We left off at the noises, as you called them. . . . When did they begin?"

"They started after Caroline was gone, a good while after Caroline was gone. You know, Caroline never returned. . . . But the noises started in the second year of Amy's illness. Ella Mae was gone. Rachael was her nurse, doing as little as she could. Lupe Rodríguez was visiting every day, probably all day by then.

"One night I woke to a scratching sound that seemed to be directly above us. It was almost as if something were trying to scrape its way through the ceiling. Amy was sleeping. I listened and it stopped. And I decided to let it pass, to get up into the attic in the morning or call a pest control man. But as soon as I closed my eyes, it started again, louder and more persistent. I nudged Amy and whispered that there was something in the attic. She stirred but that was all.

"Whatever it was must have heard us because it stopped, waiting, I thought, for our silence, our sleep. I listened as intently as I could. It had to be a big animal. Its scratchings were big. I had read accounts of possums and raccoons slipping into people's homes, but we had no such animals in the neighborhood and somehow it sounded bigger than a possum or raccoon. I listened and listened to the silence and must have finally fallen asleep because I was jerked into consciousness again by the scratchings, but now they were over Caroline's room or the stairs. I nudged Amy again. When she grumbled, I nudged her harder. When she said, 'What?' I said, 'Nothing.' Because it had stopped.

"Two nights later I said, 'There's somebody or something in the house.' She was breathing deeply in the darkness. It was movement, a shifting of weight in some part of the house that creaked. At times it seemed to be coming from the attic again, at the farthest end, then it seemed to be coming from the spare bedroom and then from downstairs. 'I hear it,' she said.

"Then we lay in the darkness, listening. The creaking continued. I got out of bed and went from room to room quietly turning on light after light. The noises stopped. I looked behind beds and closets but found nothing. I looked in the attic. Nothing. I went into the kitchen and took the biggest knife we had back to bed with me. There was not another sound for the rest of the night.

"But the noises continued. Not every night, nor even every other night, but enough so that I knew they would be returning. There was no pattern except that they came at night and only after I had gotten into bed. After my first search, they were always in some other part of the house, never near us. For a few nights I slept in other rooms. But the noises seemed to know where I was. Because they avoided me, sent me creeping into other parts of the house, never to be found.

"For the most part they were creakings, like the base of a big tree or a mast in the wind, low mournful sounds that always indicated movement. 'I've talked to the builders,' I'd say, as I returned to our bedroom, knife in hand, tense, 'and they've all assured me that there's nothing to worry about, that it's just the house settling in.' Sometimes they sounded like careful, deliberate steps in the darkness.

"Sometimes it was a loud scratching, like that of an enormous rodent. Sometimes it was the faint vibration of distant movement. But the pest control man said, 'There's nothing up there in your attic. There's nothing in your walls. The kind of creatures you're talking about aren't borne in houses, they come from the outside. I've checked your house, top to bottom. It's airtight. There's no way anything like you're describing could get in.'

"After a couple of months I was on the verge of insanity. I had searched the house more times than I could count. I had muttered every obscenity that I could think of. When I went to bed at night, I didn't expect to sleep, rather, I expected another night of torment. I would sit on the edge of the bed and grip and regrip that huge knife and then check and recheck my flashlight before placing the two of them in ready positions on the nightstand next to me. By then I had taken to stalking, searching silently in the darkness with my knife and flashlight at every hint of a noise, and sometimes without the hint of a noise.

"Much of that changed when I bought the gun. It was a .357 Magnum, a big gun, as big as any I had ever seen. Amy feared it from the beginning. She had never been around guns.

"'Hold it,' I told her. 'Get used to it. With these goddamned noises, you never know when you might need it. I'll keep it loaded,' showing her the long, thick projectiles. 'These are hollow-point bullets, designed to explode when they make contact. Blow a hole in the bastard the size of your fist. He'll wish he never saw this house. . . . Here, it's empty now. Put your finger on the trigger. Pull it. Feel how it works.' She shook her head no, but as much as she feared the gun, she also had a kind of awe for it. It took days for her to finger the gun, pull the trigger. 'Pull it harder,' I told her. 'Harder.' She did, struggling, and the hammer finally rose and fell with a dull slap. 'Great,' I remember saying. 'From now on it will always be under my pillow, loaded.'

"After that I would rise calmly out of bed at the first sound and move silently and confidently toward that sound with gun in hand and with the conviction of a man who knew his day would come.

"When I found Lupe Rodríguez in the closet under the stairs . . ."

"You found Lupe Rodríguez in a closet in your house?"

"Yes."

"The same woman who was always with your wife?"

"Yes."

"When?"

"About four or five months after the noises began."

"Tell me about that."

"By then I think I had a suspicion that the noises might be Lupe, that I was really searching for Lupe, and no one and nothing else, when I was tracking the noises."

"Why?"

"Probably because right after I told Amy that I didn't want Lupe Rodríguez in our house when I came home from work, the noises started."

"Tell me about the closet."

"Most of the stairwell closet actually runs along the first flight of stairs for about eight feet and then doubles its three-foot width over the last three feet forming an 'L' at the far end of the closet, which falls directly under the stairs as they turn overhead. I used that closet mostly for storage of old medical records in cardboard boxes. In my pursuit of the noises I had turned on the closet light and looked into that closet a hundred times, although, as I reflected later, I had never actually stepped to the base of the L because I could see from the closet door the edges of cardboard boxes stacked from floor to ceiling, completely filling the space under the stairs.

"Early one morning, while I was waiting for Rachael, I went into the stairwell closet searching for an old chart. My search took me to the boxes under the stairs at the L and I was shocked to find that the first row of boxes, the ones against the inner wall, were gone. Instead, there was an open empty space where the boxes should have been. Against the back wall of that empty space I saw a cracker box and two empty Diet Pepsi cans. I screamed and screamed, and, with the cracker box in hand, I banged my way out of that crampness and screamed some more, wild cries of anger and anguish and ran upstairs screaming, 'Where is she! Where is she!' at a trembling Amy who had pulled the covers up to her eyes to protect herself.

"'Who? Who?' came from under the covers. 'Your friend, Lupe Rodríguez, that's who!' When she said she didn't know, I ran to the nightstand to retrieve what I had come for. Then I ran out of the room, down the stairs, through the kitchen, and into the garage. I got into my car and sped to and then circled the bus stop, finally parking far enough away so that she couldn't see me as the bus approached, couldn't see me until she was heading toward the house. I waited, sweating and breathing rapidly, my hand and my trigger finger twitching occasionally. Each second seemed a minute, each minute an hour. At times I felt my heart would catch. Finally, I heard the bus in the distance and I lowered myself in my seat, just to be sure. The bus passed, continued on, and then stopped. The end of the line. Slowly I rose, and was rising still when I saw her step down out of the bus. I told myself that I had to wait until she was at least a block from the bus so that no one would see me. But as soon as she cleared the rear of the bus, I jumped out of my car in a dead run, gun in one hand, cracker box in the other.

"She was walking head down and didn't see me or even hear me until I was just a few yards from her. When she looked up, she stopped, frozen, and I was on her before she could take another step. I stuck the gun an inch from her forehead and, holding the cracker box up, said, 'You ever set foot in my house again, and I'll blow your brains out! I'll blow your brains out!'"

He was silent again, his eyes far off on that moment past.

"Have you ever told anyone this?"

"No."

"Don't. . . . Did anyone see you?"

"No."

"How can you be certain?"

"I can't."

"Did the police question you about it?"

"No."

"Are you sure?"

"Yes."

"What did Lupe do?"

"For a long time she just stared at me, scared. But then there was nothing else she could do with that big gun an inch from her forehead, an inch from her eyes. When I lowered the gun, she turned and ran and jumped back on the waiting bus."

"That was the end of the line. Did you see anybody else on the bus?"

"Not that I remember?"

"How about the bus driver?"

"I didn't see him."

"Then what happened?"

"I ran to my car, afraid that the police might come, and left. Rachael was at the house when I got there. My wild condition must have scared her. She didn't hesitate when I told her that she had the day off, that I had to do some work on my stored charts, and that there was no need for both of us to be there. I went upstairs and found Amy crying. She was always crying. It seemed like those days she lived to cry. I remember her sobbing, 'She's my only friend, Alan. She's my only friend.'

"I couldn't have cared less then, and I told her, too, pretty emphatically, that if I ever found Lupe Rodríguez in my house again, for whatever reason, I would blow her brains out. I also told her that I knew that she knew that Lupe was always in the house, that Lupe was the noises. She only shook her head and cried that Lupe was her only friend. I searched the stairwell closet again. This time I found signs of her sitting, if not sleeping, against the walls: grease spots where her head had rested and woolen fibers along the baseboard and strands of thick, coarse black hair on the floor. She had probably spent at least parts of days and nights in that closet. When and for how long, I didn't know. But never again.

"Then I searched and researched every part of the house, every part of the garage, and found human stains on the walls of other closets, found strands of that same thick black hair in other closets, too, and in the loft and even under Caroline's bed. When I moved Caroline's bed, I found an oval absence of dust about the size of Lupe Rodríguez in the center of that otherwise dust-laden patch of carpet. And even as I gasped at the thought of that lunatic sleeping under my daughter's bed, the thought occurred to me . . . something I didn't even want to think about, let alone accept. I ran to our bedroom and carried a terrified Amy to Caroline's bed and returned and moved the bed, flashlight in hand, and saw what I didn't want to see: directly under Amy's side of the bed was the same oval absence of dust, and at the head of it, four strands of thick, coarse black hair. I screamed until all the scream in me was gone. Then I pulled out my gun from my waistband and aimed for the head of that oval absence and fired, but the gun only clicked and clicked and clicked. I dropped to the floor, sat with my gun next to the oval absence, and cried.

"After that, the noises stopped and, according to Rachael, Lupe had not been around. I made random checks of the house that week, coming home unexpectedly at different times of the day, and rushing upstairs to find only Amy in bed, alone and red-eyed. By the end of the week I gloated: Lupe was gone and with her the noises.

"Two weeks to the day after I found the box of crackers, the noises returned. It was almost midnight and I had just gone to bed, just laid my head down when the creakings began, as if someone were coming upstairs. I grabbed my gun and jumped out of bed and ran to the stairs, flipping each light switch as I did. Nothing. I ran downstairs into the stairwell closet. Nothing. I dead-bolted all the doors, wanting to keep her inside or at least know where she made her exit. Then I went to every place that I had found a trace of her. Nothing. I searched every room downstairs. Nothing. I checked the doors again. Still dead-bolted. She had to be upstairs. Slowly I went upstairs, listening. Upstairs I locked each door, sealing off each room and then began a systematic search of each room. Nothing. I ended in our room, mumbling to myself, clicking the gun, my shirt soaked with sweat, sitting beside the bed, beside a curled Amy with the covers pulled over her head, sobbing and twitching. My search of our room was a blur. I kept returning to the closets, to the bed, to the dressers, to make certain that my search had been complete. Exhausted, I went back to bed.

"I no sooner covered myself when the noises began again. I sprang up in bed. Amy whimpered. I sat motionless in the darkness, holding my breath so that I could pinpoint the sound. Again, they were creakings, movement above the hall outside our room. The attic, I hadn't searched the attic. But the only entry to the attic was a trapdoor high up in the spare bedroom's closet, and I had long since removed the required ladder. I had looked in that closet just minutes before. The trapdoor had been shut, and there had been no sign of a ladder. Then the creakings shifted, down and to the end of the hall. I placed my feet on the hardwood floor and was certain that I was feeling the shifting of weight. I ran into the hall, gun in hand. Nothing. I looked in the spare bedroom's closet. Nothing. I listened. Nothing, always nothing. It was almost as if she knew when I laid myself down on the bed. But how? I went back to our bedroom and sat on the floor with my back against the bed, gun in hand, and waited. Nothing, or at least nothing that I heard. Because I woke up the next morning in that position, sitting and cold.

"I asked Amy for the tenth time if Lupe had a key to the

house. Her answer was a straightforward no, and I had no reason to doubt her. I checked all the dead-bolts. They were still bolted. Was she still in the house? I reexamined every place that I had previously found a trace of her. Nothing. Again I was totally confused. Was it really her? That night when the noises returned, I ran down the hall with my gun and then stopped at the stairs and walked slowly back to our bedroom, took a blanket off the bed, wrapped it around myself, and sat down on the floor propped against the bed. The noises had never come when I was not in bed. I fought off tears for a while and then fell asleep.

"The next morning the dead-bolts were all in place. I scoured the front and back yards, mainly for any signs of entry through the windows: footprints in the flower beds, smudges and fingerprints on the windows. Nothing. I looked around the shrubs and bushes in the backyard, the gazebo, the barbeque area. Nothing.

"She didn't come again for about a week . . ."

"Why do you say 'she?' How certain were you it was Lupe?"

"I'm getting to that, Mr. Garcia, I'm getting to that. I didn't hear the noises for about a week. Then . . ."

"So you never actually found Lupe Rodríguez in your closet?"

"No, but who else could it have been? I can't think of anyone who's been in my house, let alone had access to my closets and loft and my daughter's bedroom and my bedroom, other than Lupe Rodríguez, who has thick black hair. She certainly didn't deny it at the bus stop."

"I might not have denied it either with a .357 Magnum inches from my forehead."

"No one else has ever had the kind of access she had to my house."

"All right, assuming Lupe Rodríguez was creeping around your house at night a few months before your wife's death, so what? What does that have to do with Amy's death?"

"Mr. Garcia, everybody, including you, has raised the fact that Amy, who was right-handed and had little experience with guns, was shot in the left temple as proof positive that I shot her. If Lupe

Rodríguez was the only other person in the house on the night Amy was shot, then maybe she did shoot Amy."

"What evidence do you have that she was in the house on that night?"

"I'm getting to that, Mr. Garcia. . . . About ten days after Amy's death, a few days before I first saw you, I was storing boxes in the garage, boxes filled with some of Amy's belongings that were making it impossible for me to live in the house. As I was stacking the boxes, I noticed scrape marks high up on the wall just below an opening to a crawl space over the garage. I had never searched the crawl space because I knew, or thought that I knew, that it was sealed off from the rest of the house. The opening was closed off by a plywood board that was latched shut. I climbed up on a ladder to examine the marks and then swung the board open. I was stunned and then outraged to find a sleeping bag, a flashlight, empty Diet Pepsi cans, cracker boxes, and lunch meat wrappings up there. I was shocked again to discover that Lupe had managed to squeeze herself upward between studs to the attic. You ask how I know that it was Lupe. Well, not only were the studs replete with tufts of black hair stuck to their sides, but one of the studs had ripped off a piece of a sweater that Lupe always wore. I was in for yet another surprise when I went into the attic. Pieces of cardboard and newspapers and two blankets were laying on the floor directly over our bedroom. By measuring I was able to determine that the blankets and cardboard had been placed directly over our bed, over Amy's side of the bed.

"Last but not least I found a plastic container of orange juice, the fresh-squeezed kind, that had a little more than three ounces of juice in it and had printed on its side, 'Enjoy by 2/26/00.' Amy was killed on February 25. Lupe had to have been in the house that day."

"Why haven't you told me about this before?"

"Because I was having the liquid tested to see if it was orange juice and when it was bottled. I just got the results this morning."

"And?"

"It is orange juice, and it was probably bottled around the

twentieth of February."

"Does anyone else know about this?"

"No."

I parked across the street from her home along the bank of the Guadalupe River within shadows of the new high-rises of downtown San Jose. The river had been the lifeline of the Indians who had first settled there. It had fed the Spaniards and Mexicans who came next and, later, the white man. I climbed up onto the bank, onto the fresh green grass. An old mattress was strewn just inside the bank. Papers and cans and rags and bottles were everywhere. The homeless lived here now, and it was hard to see how the green stagnant water served them except as a cesspool.

I looked across the street at the old lopsided grey house. It was tired and worn. Lupe Rodríguez lived there with her craziness. And I thought of Mamá and all her craziness and smirked at the platitude that everything happens for a reason. Had I been blessed with Mamá so that I could deal with Lupe? I looked up and down that short, quiet street waiting for the others.

Alan Newsome had resisted coming, insisting that Lupe hated him and would never talk to me if she saw him with me or knew that I was associated with him. On the other hand, Lupe's sister, Sylvia, was his patient and apparently very fond of him, and I was betting that Sylvia would answer the door. I wanted Alan Newsome to introduce us to Sylvia, to put us on our best footing with Sylvia, whom I considered a potentially valuable source of information and influence, if not a witness.

I would have preferred interviewing Lupe Rodríguez alone but case law mandated otherwise. By interviewing a prospective witness alone, I made myself a potential witness, and if the need for my testimony arose, I would have to withdraw as my client's lawyer. Therefore, Barbara Benson, my investigator of many years, had to be present. I would have enjoyed taking my time with Lupe without another person's questions, insertions, or interruptions, letting Lupe run through her craziness, neither startled, awed, or frightened by that craziness. Because I had lived with craziness for fifteen years. I was confident that I could sit and let the craziness run its course, and at some point, once she began revealing herself, because she, like everyone, needed to reveal herself, I could get her to tell me what happened. Not taking anything away from Barbara Benson: she was as good as they came. "I don't intimidate and I'm not intimidated," she loved to say. She could get more out of a female witness than I could ever hope to get. She put both male and female witnesses at ease quickly and in a way that I couldn't. With women, her look said: Yes, I know, I understand, we women are in this together. With men, it was: You can tell me, you can trust me, I'm taking you very seriously. But she hadn't had a crazy woman for a mother. Lupe Rodríguez was my challenge.

It was a quiet Saturday morning. Occasionally, I could hear the clanging of the light rail a few blocks away. Standing on the bank of the Guadalupe, I alternately looked at the green mossy water for any sign of movement and then across the street at the old grey lopsided house for any sign of life. At exactly 9:03, Alan Newsome pulled up in a big, boxy Mercedes, a car I had not expected from him. He saw me on the bank and came quickly. He was in a hurry.

"Let's go," he said.

"Go where?"

"Across the street to talk to Sylvia Macías. That's what you wanted me for, wasn't it?"

"I'm waiting for my investigator."

"Why wait? Can't we get started without him?"

"No, I need an investigator present whenever I interview a potential witness."

"Why?"

"Because a witness may recant or lie on the stand about what she's told me out of court."

To the extent that he stopped asking questions, he accepted my explanation. Instead, he began pacing up and down the bank.

He was a thin man who seemed to be getting thinner. He did not wear anxiety well.

"You know, you told me you were afraid that there'd be an ugly scene if Lupe saw you. My guess is that if they've seen us over here, your pacing is not helping matters. Relax. She'll be here in a minute."

"Who's she?"

"My investigator, Barbara Benson."

"You have a female investigator?"

"Best investigator I've ever had and I've had several male investigators. Thank God women fall in love and want to have children, or we men would be in a whole lot of trouble."

Alan Newsome continued pacing, his face tight, its creases extended, looking over at the grey house with each turn and then in between turns, too. He had told me that Lupe Rodríguez did not like him, hated him even. Still, I didn't expect to see what I now thought was fear. Anxiety, yes, but not fear. There were beads of sweat on his forehead. I doubted him for the first time.

Barbara drove up. Late as usual. Her broad smile acknowledged that. "Hi," she said, still smiling when she was almost directly below us.

"Nice of you to come."

"Thank you. I knew you wouldn't start without me." Her smile was soft and easy, and her hazel eyes gleamed. She was a tall, big-boned woman who exuded gentleness. We were friends, and, with the exception of Rebecca, she was probably closer to me than anyone.

I introduced her to Alan Newsome. Then we crossed the street. When we reached the gate, a short, squat Mexican woman appeared from behind the darkness of a dirty screen door, hurried across the rickety porch and down the shabby steps, arms outstretched, palms open, fingers extended. "Don't come in! Don't come in, Doctor!" she shushed. "If she sees or hears you, I'll probably have to call the police!"

"What's the matter, Sylvia?"

"Nothing's the matter, Doctor, except that she really doesn't

like you right now, and if she knows you're here, it could be
bad. . . . I'm sorry, Doctor, you know how much I like you. But
she's not in her right mind. You know that." Her eyes continued
to plead even after she stopped speaking. An old faded cotton
dress covered the rectangular block of her body. Over the dress
she wore a soiled, colorless apron, which she fidgeted with as she
looked up at Alan Newsome, her spindly bare brown legs shifting beneath her, giving her an odd nakedness.

Alan Newsome looked at me: I told you so.

"I don't see any reason for you to stay, Doctor, but please
introduce us to Ms. Macías before you leave."

He introduced me as his lawyer and Barbara as my investigator and left her with, "Please tell them everything."

Sylvia Macías watched Alan Newsome go, delaying for a few
more moments having to deal with us. When Alan Newsome's car
sped off, she looked down at her apron for several moments.
When she looked up, she said, "What do you want me to tell you,
Mr. Garcia?"

It was a weary look, one numbed and bewildered by life's
daily misdeeds, no more prepared to deal with another one of those
misadventures than she was to talk to us. Please leave me alone,
the look said. She kept the gate closed and did not make the slightest move to open it. She was content to keep us on the sidewalk.

"I want the truth. That's what you can tell me, the truth."

I saw her stiffen. It was my brusqueness. I knew that even as
I spoke, but I was annoyed and impatient, wanting to step past her
to Lupe Rodríguez. I had succeeded only in damaging my cause.
Because now she stood silent and bowed, looking at the bottom of
the gate rather than at me.

"Sylvia," came the voice behind me, gentle and honest and
soothing, "we've come only to try to help Dr. Newsome, not to
hurt you or Lupe." I resented the intrusion. "You've known Dr.
Newsome for years. You know what kind of a person he is. Do
you really think he's the kind of a man who would kill his wife?
I don't think you do. We know that he has helped you, treated you
when no other doctors would. Now we ask that you help him."

Sylvia's eyes rose and her head tilted. I had seen Barbara's magic many times. It had taken me years to grow comfortable with it. There were fewer and fewer times that I resented it. This was one of those times. I reminded myself that the case was mine, that I had the final say on everything.

"How can I help?" the squat woman said, still abusing her apron.

Barbara was quick. "We think Lupe will be called as a witness. We also think that she could be the most important witness in the case. We need to talk to her."

I wanted to reassert myself, take control, but I didn't know how then.

"She won't talk to you. She won't talk to anybody. Most of the time, she won't even talk to me."

"You mean about the case?"

"No, I mean to anybody about anything. The police have been down here three times. They've stayed for hours. One time they took her down to the police station. Kept her there for ten hours. She never told them anything."

"How do you know that?" I asked.

She answered my question without looking at me, but rather at Barbara. "They're always threatening her, telling her that they're going to lock her up if she doesn't start answering. They were still threatening her when they brought her back from the police station. But she's been like that with everybody, about everything, ever since her sickness started. She's worse now that Mrs. Newsome's gone."

Barbara wouldn't be denied. "Sylvia, it's not like we have to see her now, or even tomorrow. If we could see her next week for a few minutes or even in a couple of weeks. That would give you time to convince her to talk to us. Today it would be enough if you could just tell us about her."

I was irritated. Barbara was taking a good thing too far. But she was making progress, and I didn't know how to retake control.

"What is it you want to know?"

"Things like where she was born? Why have you raised her?

Was she always like this? If not, when did she get sick? What was she like before and after she got sick?"

Sylvia lowered her head, weighing Barbara's request. I had no idea there could be so many variables in that request. When she looked up, she looked at Barbara, not at me, and I thought she was about to begin. Instead, she stretched her lips, rubbed them against each other, moistened them, sighed, and turned and looked back at the house, a quick look, and when that apparently produced little, she looked again, now studying the porch, the door, and the windows. Then she turned to Barbara again and, in a voice that was little more than a whisper, began.

She told Barbara that she was the oldest and Lupe was the youngest in a family of nine children that followed the crops in California and Arizona. When she was twenty and Lupe three, the family went to Mexico in their pickup truck for a winter visit, leaving her behind to finish high school and care for Lupe. One night, somewhere in Mexico, their father hit a cow in the middle of the road, sending the pickup over a steep cliff, killing everyone. Sylvia never finished high school. Instead, she began cleaning houses to support herself and Lupe. Because Lupe was cute and smart, she was always able to take Lupe with her to clean houses. By the time Lupe was in the sixth grade, she could clean houses as well as a grown woman.

She paused again and looked back at that worn house once more, and turning and leaning closer to Barbara, said, "You know how ugly she looks? Well, she used to be beautiful. She still is beautiful. But she does everything she can to make herself look ugly. When I ask her why she does that, she says that she feels ugly, so why shouldn't she look ugly. I guess that makes sense."

The sickness started in the ninth grade. Lupe brought home an all-F report card. Before that she always had straight A's. The teacher said that Lupe just sat and stared at her desktop all day. In a way, that came as no surprise because at home at night, instead of doing her homework, Lupe had started sitting for hours staring at the same page of a book. The staring spread to the housecleaning. One Saturday morning while cleaning a house, Sylvia found

Lupe sitting on the floor of a darkened room staring at the wall. When Sylvia pulled open the shades to show Lupe what a beautiful day it was outside, Lupe said, "You don't understand, Sylvia. You don't need all that out there. Everything's right here," pointing to her head.

Then the voices came. Lupe loved them at first. She laughed with them, joked with them, listened to them as she had never listened to anyone. Now she didn't even need Sylvia. But the voices changed. They began giving Lupe orders. They became angry with Lupe. They became disgusted with Lupe, finally telling her that she had to kill herself because she was worthless. Lupe ran from them, but they were everywhere. Lupe clung to Sylvia, begging Sylvia not to leave her alone with the voices. One night Lupe's screams about the voices brought Sylvia running to Lupe's room to find Lupe curled into a ball in the furthest corner of the room shaking and crying. Sylvia could only calm Lupe by spreading herself over and on top of Lupe's curled body so that the voices couldn't get at her.

At this point Sylvia didn't know what to do. The parish priest advised her to take Lupe to a psychiatrist. When Sylvia learned that psychiatrists were medical doctors, she went no further. She couldn't even pay Dr. Newsome; how was she going to pay another doctor.

The voices let up. They told Lupe that she wouldn't have to kill herself if she killed homeless people. They knew that Lupe hated homeless people: they were dirty and smelly and lazy. Never mind that Sylvia was always telling her that someday she could be homeless, too. When Lupe began going on "night hunts" along the banks of the Guadalupe River, Sylvia threw up her hands. On second thought, it was better than dealing with a screaming, crying curled-up ball. But when Lupe returned from one of her "night hunts" with a bloody knife, Sylvia called the police.

They put Lupe in a padded cell at the hospital for six days. When they released her, "she looked like a zombie." Here Sylvia paused, tucked in her lips, and looked up at that memory, as much in the grey sky as it was in her mind. I thought she was going to cry. Her lips reappeared and disappeared again and again before she continued. Sylvia asked the doctor what was wrong with Lupe and the doctor told her that Lupe was on medication. When Sylvia asked what kind of medication, the doctor said that Lupe was a paranoid schizophrenic and would probably be one the rest of her life and would have to take medication for the rest of her life. Sylvia had said, "She's what?" "A paranoid schizophrenic." "You mean she's crazy?" "I guess you could say that." Sylvia would never forget those words: "I guess you could say that."

Lupe took the medication for a while and then announced one day, "I ain't taking no more of that medication crap." She had discovered street drugs. They at least were fun to take. They made her feel good, not dead. To get them, she stole from drugstores and sold herself, even though she had never liked men. But the street drugs brought the police and eventually jail. "That's where she met Mrs. Newsome, and you probably know the rest."

She looked directly at me for the first time, and I shook my head no and said, "We don't know much about the facts of the case yet, and we know very little about your sister's relationship with Mrs. Newsome."

Her eyes stayed with me. "So you're Gabriel Garcia. I've read your name in the paper. I didn't know you were such an old man."

"Neither did I."

Just then, from the house came a voice, flat, quiet, and yet strong. "Sylvia. Sylvia."

Sylvia whirled around, fear on her face. "I'm coming. I'm coming," and started toward the porch.

I looked up at the porch and, behind the darkened screen door, saw a boy-like figure, thin and with close-cropped hair. It was impossible to make out anything more. Sylvia Macías hurried up the porch steps. When she reached the door, there was an exchange: irritated mumbles from behind the door and repeated apologies and apologetic gestures from our side. Then Sylvia turned and, without looking at either of us, said, "I can't talk anymore," and was gone.

Lupe Rodríguez, I thought.

CHAPTER III

A week after my first visit, I returned to Lupe Rodríguez's home. I went alone. Two days before, I had gone to Alan Newsome's home, again alone. There I saw the grease spots on the wall in the stairwell closet. I saw the box of crackers and the strands of black hair and woolen fibers. I saw the oval absence of dust under Caroline's bed. I saw the attic studs that still pinched strands of thick black hair and a piece of torn fabric. I read the lab report that said that the liquid in the sealed plastic container was orange juice and that it had probably been bottled on February 20, 2000. As I read the report, the weight of Alan's denials descended heavily upon me.

When I went to Alan Newsome's home alone, I had already decided to interview Lupe Rodríguez alone. Barbara Benson was as good an investigator as any. But I had lived with a paranoid schizophrenic for fifteen years. That experience had made a major impact on me, and I had learned something about the phenomena of that disease. Lupe Rodríguez was the most important witness in the case, if not the actual killer. She would not be fooled, eased, or cajoled by Barbara Benson's approach. At best, Barbara would be an awkward intrusion into my quest for the truth; at worst, she might permanently seal Lupe's lips. No, Lupe was mine. She would not escape me. I would wait her out. I would get the truth from her. My obligation to have an investigator present whenever I interviewed a potential witness could wait until I had made headway. This time I got as far as the porch. But before I could knock, the front door swung open, and the same squat nervous woman in the same worn dress and the same soiled apron intercepted me. "What do you want?" Her words were hushed and tense as she stepped out onto the porch, pushing the screen door out and pulling the front door closed behind her.

"What do you want?" She was plainly annoyed, but afraid, too.

"I want to talk to Lupe."

"Are you crazy?"

"*I'm* not."

"Well, *she* is, and she's not talking to nobody."

"Have you told her that I want to talk to her?"

"No."

"Then how do you know that she won't talk to me?"

"Because ever since Mrs. Newsome died, she won't talk to nobody, not even her social worker. I don't know who she thinks is going to feed her, because I barely get enough to pay the rent, and if she doesn't start talking to that man pretty soon, they're going to cut her off, and we're both going to be out in the street."

"Sylvia, this is very important. We're talking about Dr. Newsome's life here. If we . . ."

"Shhhh!" crossing her lips with a finger. "If she hears us talking out here, she'll probably call the fire department."

Even though I too had been speaking in hushed tones, I spoke more softly. "Sylvia, think of all Dr. Newsome has done for you. You're still walking, and they say that there was a time when everybody thought you'd be bedridden. He treated you when nobody else would treat you. Money was never a problem. He believed in you when nobody else did. Now he needs you to help him. He's fighting the biggest fight of his life. And you can help him in a way that nobody else can. You can get Lupe to talk to me. Your sister is a very, very important witness."

She looked down. Our eyes had yet to meet; now hers were completely taken from me. She said nothing. Her feet shuffled, as if reacting to her eyes. Then she sighed and said, "How can I help you?"

"By getting Lupe to talk to me."

"But I told you, she won't talk to nobody."

"She talked to the police, didn't she?"

"They talked to her, but I never heard her talk to them."

"What did they say?"

"They kept asking her about the night Mrs. Newsome was killed. Was she there that night? Where was she? Had she ever been at the house when Dr. and Mrs. Newsome were together? Did she ever see a gun in the house, or in Mrs. Newsome's room? They asked and asked, but Lupe didn't answer, she didn't say a single word. And they got madder and madder because she wouldn't answer. Then they took her down to the police station. She was down there ten hours, and when they brought her back, they were really, really mad, cussing and talking loud about how the next time they were going to put her in jail if she didn't talk. I didn't know the police could talk to somebody like that."

"Did they ask her anything else?"

"Not really. . . . You know, they did ask her about a girl named Kathleen. Kathleen. . . . I forget her last name."

"Powers? Kathleen Powers?"

"Yeah, that's it. Kathleen Powers. But Lupe didn't answer that either."

She stopped. She had nothing more to say. But I couldn't leave it there. Lupe was too important.

"Is she here?"

"What do you mean is she here?"

"Is Lupe inside the house right now?"

"Sure she's in the house. She's always in the house. She never goes out except real late at night, like three o'clock in the morning, and then she sneaks out. Since Mrs. Newsome died, she never goes out. It's not that I don't want to help, but she's really strange now."

"What does she do all day?"

"She just stays in her room."

"All day?"

"All day."

"So you never see her?"

"I never see her."

"Besides staying in her room, how is she strange?"

"For one thing she's not taking her medication. It's stacking up in the bathroom. And that's bad. But that's just the beginning. She does some strange things in her room.

"Before Mrs. Newsome died, she used to talk to me. She wasn't always nice, but she talked to me at least. She never listened to me, but I didn't expect her to. And she still had things in her room. Not that she wanted me in her room even then, because mostly she kept it locked when she was here and always when she was gone. But she still had things in it. When I'd knock, she'd at least talk to me through the door or even open it if she was feeling okay. And when she'd open it, I could see that she still had things there. But she loved Mrs. Newsome. God, how she loved that woman. And Mrs. Newsome had helped her. That I can tell you. She practically brought Lupe back from the grave. She breathed life into that girl. So when Mrs. Newsome died, it was like Lupe died, too. She was always over there helping with Mrs. Newsome. At first, one or two times a week and then every day, Monday through Friday. Then she started staying overnight, sometimes not coming home for three or four days at a time. She said that her job was to take care of Mrs. Newsome. She always said that. I was happy to hear that. She needed a job. She needed something in her life.

"Since Mrs. Newsome died, she won't come out of her room. She won't unlock the door. When the police came, I thought they were going to break down the door. They almost did. You can still see the footprints on the door. The welfare has sent her I don't know how many letters telling her that if she doesn't talk to her social worker they're going to stop her money. But she still won't do it. I don't know who she thinks is going to feed her. But she doesn't worry about those things. Clothes, friends, eating, none of that matters to her. All she cares about is her room."

"But there have to be times when she talks to you."

"Not anymore. Like I told you, she won't come out of her room, and she won't talk to me through the door anymore. Since Mrs. Newsome died, I've only seen her twice in the hall and she didn't say a word to me either time, didn't even look at me, just like we've been going up and down the hall all day, every day, and there's no reason to talk or look anymore. And when you came the other day, all she said then was 'Get rid of them.' But you were already gone.

"Oh, I know she comes out of her room and she eats some things, and I know that she went to the store and cashed her check, because I can see that things have come and gone in the refrigerator. But she does everything at night, when I'm asleep. She moves in the night. With these twenty-four-hour stores, she never has to come out in the day. And in that room of hers it's never day. For a long time I thought she took to the night just to avoid me. Now I know it's to avoid everybody and everything.

"Because one night I couldn't sleep and I heard her, or thought I heard her. No, I didn't hear her because she knows how to move without making a sound. She knows every loose board, every squeak in this house. I felt her, I felt this poor old house move. And then I felt the front door close, and I ran to the front window and watched her. The moon was out and you could see the trees and the cars across the street. She didn't walk right out, not right away. What she did was stand right next to the hedge and look up and down the street as if she was looking for someone or something. But what's going to be coming up or down our little dead-end street at three o'clock in the morning? Then, all of a sudden, she ran across the street and up and over the bank down toward the river.

"I've seen her do some pretty crazy things, but I couldn't imagine what she'd be doing down in that dirty water at that hour of the night. I waited. But she didn't come back up. I thought of calling the police, but I didn't want her to get mad at me. She's hell when she's mad. I waited until just after 4:30. Then she came out of the river with two shopping bags in her arms. I ran to my room and pretended to be asleep. I could feel her in the kitchen. Next morning I went out to the garbage can and found stuffed way down in it two Safeway shopping bags. I don't shop at Safeway. Never have liked those stores and, besides, there's none around here. And then I found the receipt. It was dated that day at 3:47 a.m. at the Capitol Safeway. So the next day I took a bus out there and do you know that the Guadalupe runs right behind that Safeway. Imagine that girl walked all that way along the river at night to Safeway.

"She's my baby sister and I love her and she's got nobody else. When I'm gone, I don't know what will happen to her. Who's going to put up with her roaming the river like that at night?"

"You said she used to talk to you."

"Yes, before Mrs. Newsome died. The way I knew she wanted to talk to me was that she'd leave her door open, just a crack, just an inch or two. I guess she was too proud to come up and say, 'I need to talk to you,' after all those days of not talking. So I'd knock and she'd say, 'Come in,' and I'd go in, and she'd be sitting where she always sits, over in the corner, next to the closet, away from the windows. And we'd talk, mostly about Mrs. Newsome and how nice she was and how much Mrs. Newsome needed her now that she was sick and how she would do anything for Mrs. Newsome.

"Once Mrs. Newsome died, she started taking things out of her room, not all at once, but probably something every night. I started finding things out in the back yard. Dresser drawers, then the dresser, her two chairs, her mirror, her two pictures and one book, her bed frame and then her box spring and finally her mattress and clothes. I yelled at her through the door, 'What are you doing?' All she would say was 'I don't need it.' When I kept on yelling, she just wouldn't answer.

"Then I started hearing this rasping sound coming from her room. I must have heard it in my sleep for I don't know how many nights. You know how you'll remember a dream for the first time days or weeks after you've had it? Well, it was the same thing. Once I found out what she was doing in there, I remembered that I had been hearing that rasping sound for weeks in my sleep. I even remembered waking up to the rasping and thinking, 'What's she doing now?' and going back to sleep. One night I didn't, or couldn't, go back to sleep. So I lay there listening to the rasping, thinking it had to stop soon. But it didn't. After a couple of hours I got up, but as soon as I did, even before I started toward her room, it stopped. She must have heard me or felt me getting out of bed. When I banged on her door and said, 'What's going on in there, Lupe?', there was no answer.

"So the next night, about 9:30, about the time I usually go to bed, I acted like I was going to go to bed. I made the floor creak, I made the bed creak without getting in. Instead, I creeped real quiet, real slow, out of my room, down the hall, and sat on the floor across from her door. About forty-five minutes later the rasping started. Only from there it was much louder and clearer. Still, I couldn't figure out what she was doing. I waited, ten, fifteen minutes and then I jumped on the door and pounded on it before she could stop and yelled, 'What are you doing in there?' The rasping stopped. But that was all I heard. "She didn't rasp anymore. Or not at least while I was in the house or awake. Because I didn't hear anything, not a sound, at least for a couple of weeks. And I was listening, believe me, I was listening. I was dying to know what she was doing. I was dying to get into that room. But she kept it locked tighter than a drum. And I didn't once hear or feel her come out of it even though I knew she was, because of the refrigerator. As hard as I tried to stay awake, she had to know when I was asleep. In some ways, she's smarter than anyone I know.

"Then, just as I was starting to sleep full nights again, I started hearing these loud creaks coming from her room. They were loud, too loud to be the floor, and different, like something big tearing. But even before I could get out of bed, they'd stop. After a few nights of creaks, I slept a whole afternoon, and then that night I waited near her door in the hall, ready to wait all night if I had to, to find out what those creaks were. Nothing happened until about two o'clock. Then all of a sudden her door opened. I didn't hear it or see it. I felt a draft and looked in that direction in the dark and knew the door was open. But she didn't come out, not then. I don't know if she was standing in her doorway smelling or feeling for me. But about five minutes later I felt her in the hall. I say felt because she didn't make a sound and I couldn't see nothing. Then the floor gave, and I knew for sure she was in the hall and moving. I turned on my flashlight and caught her halfway down the hall carrying boards. 'What the hell are you doing?' I said. But before she could say or do anything, I saw that her door was still open, and I ran into her room and turned on the lights and almost fainted.

"There was *nothing* in the room. I mean *nothing*. I knew she had taken everything out, but somehow I never imagined, never understood, until then, what it might be like living and sleeping and never coming out of a room with nothing in it. I take that back. There were some things in it. In the corner was a neat stack of sandpaper sheets and on top of the sandpaper was a putty knife, a crowbar, and a can of putty. She stood right behind me, saying nothing. And then I saw what all the rasping was about. All of the walls and ceiling were white, real white, plaster white. She had sanded away the paint. She had taken out the boards that go along the floor and the walls and the boards that go around the windows and the closet and had filled the cracks there and the nail holes with putty and sanded that, too. What I didn't notice at first was that she had sanded the floor, too, taken all the varnish and dirt off the wood, sanded so much and so deep that the wood floor was almost pure white too.

"'It's my room,' she said, and I just stood there. It was her room, and, besides, I couldn't speak; I couldn't think of anything to say. Then after a long time of just looking at the walls and the floor and the ceiling and the windows and the closet, and then looking some more, I said, 'And what about the landlord? What will he say?' And she said, 'It's my room.' And, as usual, she was right.

"I let it go. It was her room. Actually, in one way, the room never looked so good, so clean. I let it go. I went back to sleeping at night, even though I could hear the rasping in my sleep. Whether I was hearing Lupe do it or hearing it in my dreams, I didn't know. Then one day I was outside, and I happened to go by the side of the house that I never go on, that side, the side over there, the side that Lupe's windows are on. Over on that side of the house there's just a fence and a bunch of bamboo that's grown wild, big and tall and thick against the fence. It's grown so much that you almost need a machete to get through. Anyway, I just happened to go that way, and I couldn't believe what I saw. Her two windows were boarded up.

"That was it, that was too much. I ran back in the house and beat on her door and yelled, 'Damn you, Lupe, you better open this door before I break it down! You've gone too far!' And she did open the door and I was shocked again. The room was completely dark. I mean dark. I went in, past her.

"'Turn on the light!' I said, because I wanted to see what she was up to. 'What light?' she said. So I went to the light switch myself. But there was no light switch. She had taken it out and covered it over and, of course, had sanded it smooth, so smooth that I really couldn't tell where the light switch had been. Now I was really mad, and I said, 'Don't play games with me, Lupe, turn on the light!' and she said, 'What light?' And I looked up, and I could see from the open door that she had taken the light out, too, and had puttied it over and sanded it over so smooth that I couldn't tell where the light had been either. Even the boards that she had used to cover the windows were flush with the wall and sanded smooth and clean, too. It was like you were in one big empty, smooth, clean box. Except that she still had her stack of sandpaper in the corner. But that was all.

"'It's my room,' she said before I could say anything. 'Are you craaazzeeee!' I screamed, trying to control myself, trying not to use the word I always promise myself I'll never use again but used it, anyway. 'Yes,' she said. Then there was nothing more to say. Except that she said, 'It's my room. It's me. And if you ever try to change it, I'll leave.'

"So I let it be. I didn't want her living in the river under the bridges or under the trees like those other crazies or homeless or whatever you call them. But I still hear the rasping. Now she does it anytime she wants. What I think she's doing is sanding, cleaning everything she touches or walks or sits on. Because the two times I've been in there, as soon as I leave I can hear her sanding, sanding away my footprints. . . . But the thing I worry about most is that she sits and sleeps on the floor in the same place in the

same corner of the room, and now when I hear her sanding, I just
hope that she doesn't sand down through that part of the floor.
Because what am I going to do then?"

"Will she talk to me?"

"I don't know, Mr. Garcia, but I'll try."

I waited on the slanted porch, staring at boards that had either
been painted grey or worn grey. Would she talk to me? A cold
March wind continued winter. I wound my way back many years
to Catalina Garcia. I remembered how she had sealed herself off
from the world in that tiny uninsulated house in the blistering heat
and in the freezing cold; how she ran and hid in their room whenever anyone came to our door; how she found the darkest corner
to sit in as soon as Papá began opening the shades and windows.
Would she talk to me? I tried to recall how Papá and I had best
dealt with her. Directly and firmly. There could be no deviation.
She would manipulate. She would use her condition to her advantage. She would be crazy, certifiably crazy. She would cry. She
would be silent. She would be pleasant. She would be well. No
matter: directly and firmly. Not always successful, but by far the
best approach.

I waited. Somewhere in the bowels of that frail structure they
were discussing me. She had closed and locked the door behind
her as she left to speak to her sister. Not a good sign. A biting north
wind swept down from the lead-colored sky. The porch made a
mockery of shelters: it was nothing but a conduit for the cold. I
thought of Catalina Garcia and the way she would sidle up to the
lowest corner of the front window to watch Papá talk to someone
outside. I shifted my eyes to each of the front windows on either
side of me. I couldn't tell and I didn't dare look directly at either
window. If I caught her peeping at me, it might jeopardize any
chance I had of talking to her. I chided myself. Be real. She's not
going to talk to you. Even she has to know, or at least sense, the
danger she would be placing herself in by talking to you. Still I
waited, shifting my weight from one foot to the other and back
again, apparently believing that the motion would warm me.

She had to know that I knew or at least suspected her. Even

with her craziness she had to know. They were taking too long. It was quite simple: do you want to talk to him or not? Not a good sign. I strained to hear but could hear nothing. I was about to knock when I felt movement, the movement Sylvia had described. Then Sylvia was at the front door, rolling her eyes and twisting her hands.

"She'll talk to you, Mr. Garcia. But only to you. Alone. Never with Dr. Newsome. She hates the Doctor. My, does she hate him. Please come in, Mr. Garcia."

I entered a large, lopsided, high-ceilinged room that had a worn sofa, a small stained coffee table, a television set on the floor's faded floral linoleum and nothing else. To the right was a darkened hallway. All of the doors that led off the hallway were closed except for the last one. Slits of light knifed their way from under the closed doors but only darkness came from the open door. I followed Sylvia Macias, thinking of Catalina Garcia and the countless times I had sought her out in the darkness of our tiny house.

As we neared the open door, Sylvia Macías chirped in a pleasant, nervous voice, "Lupe, Mr. Garcia's here," as if I came every day. There was no answer.

When we stopped at the open door, I saw nothing but darkness. I felt darkness. But I smelled the perfect cleanliness of freshly sanded wood.

"Lupe, this is Mr. Garcia." I had no idea if there was anyone in the room at all. "He's a lawyer. He wants to talk to you." And with that, Sylvia Macías brushed past me and left.

I stood there with absolute darkness before me. I had no conception of the room itself. If Lupe Rodríguez was in the room, I knew not where. There was no hint of sound or movement. After a full two minutes, I said, "Lupe, I need to talk to you."

"Come in and close the door, Mr. Garcia." The flat quiet voice was before me and off to my right.

I closed the door and waited for my eyes to adjust to the darkness. But there was no adjusting, there was just smooth darkness.

She didn't speak or move or breathe. I waited until I realized that I would have to speak or there would be no speaking.

"Lupe, I have to talk to you."

"I know."

The flatness of that voice, the sparseness of those words left no doubt. She knew.

"Lupe, I have to talk to you," I repeated.

"About what?"

Mamá. I should have remembered. I should have known. There would be no niceties, no middle ground even. I moistened my lips and set and reset my teeth. The voice had come from below me. She had to be sitting on the floor as Sylvia had said. I looked down, trying to focus on what I could not see. I moistened my lips and reset my teeth again. If I didn't speak, we wouldn't speak.

"Lupe, I know how much you loved Mrs. Newsome, and I also know that, for whatever reason, you don't like Dr. Newsome very much. I want you . . ."

"What is it you want, Mr. Garcia?"

It was as direct and final as final could be. I heard myself sigh in the darkness.

"Lupe. Dr. Newsome is . . ."

"What is it you want, Mr. Garcia?"

The flatness and sparseness said it all: say what needs to be said, nothing more.

"Lupe, you know as well as I that Dr. Newsome didn't kill his wife. I want you to help me defend an innocent man."

Those words alone had been enough to lift my load. Now it was she who paused.

"Will you help me, Lupe?" If I could have only seen her eyes then.

"You think he's innocent?"

"Yes."

Again she paused. I wanted to say, and you know he's innocent. But I thought better of it.

"Has he told you about Kathleen?"

"Kathleen?"

"Kathleen. That young girl who used to work for him."

"Kathleen Powers?"

"Yes."

My heart stopped, and a numbing fear, panic shot through me.

"He hasn't told you, has he?"

"No." But at that moment I very much wished that he had.

"When he does, maybe we can talk again."

She had dismissed me, but the panic held me. After a while she said, "Just turn around and take five steps. The doorknob is about three feet off the ground. It's the only thing that sticks out in my room." She was more than Mamá.

I called and left a message on his machine. He came in at 3:30.

"What's the matter?" He was apprehensive. He knew I had gone to Lupe that morning.

"Nothing."

"Did you see her?"

"Yes."

"And?"

"Our meeting went fine. A little on the strange side, which is to be expected, but otherwise fine."

"Then why the call? What's so important?"

I had anticipated this scene. Now was the time.

"Who is Kathleen Powers?"

Despite his apprehension, I caught him by surprise. The answer stuck in his throat. His eyes fluttered. He flushed. "She's a college girl who worked temporarily in my office as a receptionist."

"You told me that the first day we met. Is there anything more?"

"More! What do you mean more? Absolutely not!"

"All right then, when did she work for you? What exactly did she do in your office? What was your relationship with her?"

"My relationship with her?"

"Calm down. What I'm asking is how much contact did you have with her on a daily basis and under what circumstances?" I didn't like it either. He had lied to me. How much, I didn't know. How much it would hurt the case, I didn't know either.

"What did Lupe Rodríguez say?"

"Very little. I need *you* to tell me about Kathleen Powers."

He paused. He was sorting out his facts. I didn't like it.

"Kathleen Powers was a college student who filled in as an office receptionist while our regular receptionist was out on maternity leave. She was with us four or five months, something like that. I saw her probably every day that I was there, saw her at the front desk. We exchanged everyday pleasantries. That's about it."

He sat across from me, avoiding my eyes, his thin, pale face still flushed but now puffed as well. I had not seen this side of him.

"Why would Lupe Rodríguez mention Kathleen Powers? Why would she tell me to ask you about Kathleen Powers?"

"How should I know? The woman's crazy. You can put as much stock into what she says as you want. I certainly wouldn't."

I thought it best to leave it there.

I talked to Barbara Benson that evening about finding and interviewing Kathleen Powers.

"Yes, I noticed that, too, in the police report. That they were looking for her and hadn't been able to find her. Any idea why they want to talk to her?"

"No. Probably just routine investigation. They've talked to everybody else in the doctor's office except her." I didn't dare mention that I had seen Lupe Rodríguez without her.

"Why should we look for her? Why not let them find her?"

"Just trying to be thorough. Who knows, they may *not* want to find her. They may know that she might say something that could hurt their case. . . . But remember, don't go to the doctor's office, don't ask anyone there. The doctor's shook up enough with all those search warrants. And I'd like you to make this a priority. She's the only person mentioned in the police report who hasn't been talked to yet."

What Barbara Benson found was interesting indeed. Kathleen Powers had turned eighteen the day before she began working in Dr. Newsome's office. She had been a recent high school graduate and had been in her first semester at City College. In some ways she had been an extraordinary girl who had emancipated herself from her alcoholic parents three years before, supporting herself ever since. She had lived alone in a small apartment near the college and managed to purchase an old car. She had been as stable and responsible as any adult. Then she disappeared, three days before Amy Newsome's death. She left a note for her apartment manager saying only that she was leaving the area and would let her know where to send her deposit once she was settled. The apartment manager had not heard from her since. She withdrew from City College without any explanation. The job at Dr. Newsome's office had ended that week, and she had failed to report to her new job the following week.

"What do you make of it, Gabby?"

"I don't know. It may all be just a coincidence, but I can understand why the cops are looking for her." I didn't like it. There was something there, something that now made me reluctant to find her for the police.

"You want me to keep looking for her?"

"No, better not now. Let them look for her. They have more resources than we do. Sooner or later they'll find her. Unless something's happened to her."

The morning after I received Barbara's report, I returned to Lupe Rodríguez. Sylvia greeted me with that same nervousness and again locked the door behind her as she left to see if Lupe would speak to me. I waited. March was now promising a wonderful spring. The sky was blue and the sun shone brightly. Birds were chirping and hopping from limb to limb. After a while I wondered what it was that Lupe was doing, besides sitting in the dark, that was taking so long to get a response. Yes or no? Do you or don't you want to talk to him? When Sylvia unlocked the front door, she was less nervous. That was a good sign.

"She will talk to you, Mr. Garcia. Please come in."

This time I paid particular attention to the voice. "Come in and close the door." Again, she was sitting on the floor before and to the right of me. She spoke immediately.

"Did you ask Dr. Newsome about Kathleen?"

"Yes."

"What did he say."

"That she worked in his office as a substitute receptionist and that the only contact he had with her was when he spoke to her in the office."

"Liar."

That too was flat, even, emotionless, but convincing nevertheless.

"Did he tell you that he used to meet with her at night and on the weekends in his office?"

"No. Did he?"

"Yes."

"How do you know that?"

"I was there."

"You were there? In the office?"

"I was there."

"In the office?"

She stopped. She wasn't going to give me more.

"Did he tell you that he used to follow her around at night and peek in her windows?"

"No." But there was a horrible ring of truth to it. "How do you know this?"

"I was there."

"Where? How?"

"I was there. . . . Did he tell you that he used to drug Amy so that he could leave the house at night and follow his little love thing?"

I shook my head, but not in disbelief.

"Did he?"

"No."

"You better talk to him some more. You better tell him that he shouldn't lie, that I was there. . . . Did he tell you that Amy knew he had a young girlfriend?"

"No."

"She knew. I told her. You better talk to him some more. Tell him if he doesn't start telling the truth, I'll start talking to the police. They tried to make me talk, but I wouldn't. But I will if he keeps on lying."

No, she was not Mamá. But she wasn't lying either.

At the front door I motioned Sylvia out onto the porch.

"How far is it from here to Dr. Newsome's office?"

"Oh, it's far. I have to take the bus, and it takes me about forty-five minutes."

"You don't have a car?"

"No."

"Does Lupe have a car?"

"Where is she going to get a car from? She doesn't even know how to drive."

"What did she say?" His eyes were fastened tightly on me, and his lips had disappeared.

"She said you were lying about Kathleen Powers."

"Lying! She's the one who's lying. That lunatic doesn't know what the truth is."

"She said if you don't stop lying, she's going to talk to the police."

"Let her. Let her. She's got nothing to tell them. Nothing that has to do with the murder of my wife."

"She said you were meeting with Kathleen Powers at your office at night and on the weekends."

"What? This is insane. How could she possibly know what went on in my office?"

"She says she was there."

He stopped, sat back in his chair and absorbed it, sighed, turned to the far wall and absorbed it some more. For a long while he said nothing. Then slowly, slightly, he began to convulse. The convulsions grew stronger and then became sobs and tears. Through the sobs he garbled, "I didn't kill her. I didn't kill her. You have to believe me. I didn't kill her."

I had seen men cry before. Not often. On most of those occasions there had been a breakdown, a complete abandonment of taking it like a man, being a man. Such was the case that afternoon in my office. I let Alan Newsome cry for several minutes. Then I went to him and patted him as gently as I knew how and said, "I think we've had enough for today, Alan."

He returned the following afternoon. He was calm, embarrassed, and withdrawn. He said that he had been smitten by Kathleen Powers but that nothing had happened, that she was not attracted to him and that there was more than a twenty-five-year difference in their ages.

The meetings at his office were tutoring sessions for her chemistry course and nothing more. He did not follow Kathleen around at night and did not know where she lived. He did say that he had accidentally met Kathleen at The Rendezvous one evening and had followed her around the dance floor for a few dances, but attributed that to having had too much to drink. He had never drugged Amy. Not only would that have been a violation of his professional ethics, but also a violation of the law. Amy was not aware of his fantasy, and that's all it had been, a fantasy. He concluded by saying that he had not murdered his wife.

I believed some of what he told me, but not all. I left it pretty much as he presented it, knowing that we would have to revisit this area again and again before the trial. In the meantime, it *would* be best if we could find Kathleen Powers before the police did.

CHAPTER IV

"There's been a change in plans, Barbara."

"Which is?"

"We've got to find Kathleen Powers. The sooner the better. And by all means before the cops do."

"Why the change? You just told me on Monday to let them find her, that they had all the resources."

"It turns out that the good doctor was smitten by little Kathleen."

"What?"

I had to be careful here. "He came in yesterday and said there was something he had to tell me. He said he had tutored Kathleen Powers in his office at night and on weekends for a chemistry course. He said that he was smitten—that's the word he used— smitten by her and that he developed this fantasy about her. But that it all came to nothing because she wasn't interested. Nothing except that one night he made an ass of himself at this place called The Rendezvous. It's a bar that has live music. Apparently, on that night he had been drinking and she showed up, and he followed her around the dance floor. That's it. That's all I know." That's all I could tell her.

"Are you serious?"

"I felt the same way you do when I heard about it yesterday. Now it's not just the fact that she disappeared three days before Amy Newsome's death, now it's all this 'smitten' business, too."

"You mean he just walked in here yesterday afternoon and made that announcement?"

Barbara Benson had been an investigator a long time. No one

232

knew better than she that one lie led to another. If she found out
that I had cut her out of the loop with Lupe, she would be furious
and at the very least would walk out on this case and maybe on
others as well. I made sure that my look was blank and casual
when I said, "He didn't just walk in out of the blue. I had given
him all the police reports and asked him to review them so we
could discuss them. We were doing that on Tuesday when Kathleen Powers's name came up. I mentioned that the police were
looking for her and would probably find her before the trial, but
that we had nothing to hide, nothing to worry about. The next day
he's in here telling me about this 'smitten' business."

"What do you make of it?"

"I don't know. It's a problem. It could range from nothing to
a homicide. A kidnapping. No, she would have surfaced by now,
or her parents would've reported her missing. That's a thought.
Find her parents. See if they've heard from her. The good doctor
has made little Kathleen potentially a very important witness. I
don't think the cops have any idea about a personal connection
between the doctor and Kathleen. If they did, my guess is that
they would have located her by now. Which makes it all the more
important that we find her before they do. If they get to her first,
there's no telling what they'll get her to say."

"I agree. But it's clear we're not getting the full picture from
the doctor. It's one thing to lie. In this business we expect that
from our clients. But to lie *and* conceal, that's a little much. I hate
working with a client who conceals. I hate working with anybody
who conceals."

She was looking right at me. She knew. It had to have been
Sylvia. She must have gone back to their house on her own. They
had no telephone. She hadn't had any contact with Alan. I held my
eyes on hers steadfastly. To blink or blush or look away would be
total capitulation. There had to be a reason, an explanation, an
excuse, something that mitigated my deceit, something to soften
the blow.

Her eyes shifted, and she said, "I've already put in a lot of time
trying to track her down. I've been to her old apartment. I've talked

to the manager there. I've . . ." She went into detail chronicling her efforts to locate Kathleen Powers. She didn't know. She had abandoned the subject of concealment. She wanted appreciation not confrontation. As she went on with her recitation, I searched for ways to tell her. Because if I didn't, she would eventually find out. "Barbara, there's something I have to tell you. . . ." "Barbara, I haven't been completely truthful with you. . . ." There was no easy approach, no easy entry.

She completed her listing, paused and said, "This has already cost the doctor one heck of a lot of money. And it's going to cost him a lot more."

"He doesn't have a choice."

"Well, where do you want me to begin?"

"Is she home?" Silly question. Where else would she be at that time of the day except in her darkness.

"Yes. Yes. Come in, Mr. Garcia. She's been expecting you."

"Will she see me?"

"Of course she'll see you. She even came out of her room this morning and told me that you were coming today and to let you in."

"She knew I was coming?"

"Yes, she did."

Mamá knew before Papá and I ever knew that someone was coming. She'd run from the kitchen or close the door to her room before they drove up or knocked.

"How did she know?"

"I thought you told her the last time you were here."

I shook my head absently.

"Lupe's very intelligent, Mr. Garcia. She knows a lot of things that I don't even know how she knows them. But come in, Mr. Garcia. I know she's waiting. She knows you're here. I'm sure she felt your footsteps on the front porch."

I had no sooner closed the door when she asked, "What did

he say?"

The voice came from the same place that it always came from. I tried to visualize her: small, thin, dark, sitting on the floor with her legs crossed in the right back corner of the darkness.

"What did who say?" I found myself toying with her.

"The doctor."

"About what?"

"About what we talked about last time."

"We talked about a lot of things last time."

"About the girl and the drugs and that Mrs. Newsome knew."

"He said it was all true."

"He did?"

"Yes."

"Good. Because it is all true. . . . Now you know why she wanted to die. Now I can talk to you.

"I live in darkness because she met me in darkness and took me out of darkness. She taught me to see. Now that she's gone, I've returned to darkness until the time comes, until I'm ready, like she was. Then I'll join her.

"She was the only person I ever loved. She knew me. She talked about things that mattered. She made sense and I listened. I did what she said. It gave me structure. She led me out of that darkness. It's easy to love someone who loves you. No one's ever loved me. Not like that.

"Then he showed up. I hated him from the beginning. As soon as he showed up, things changed. She changed. She started talking about him, about how nice he was. 'Mr. Wonderful' this, 'Mr. Wonderful' that. I bet she doesn't think he's so wonderful now. She talked so much about him that I finally puked all over her carpet. She stopped talking about him then. But it was too late. Because the next thing I know they were married. She didn't tell me, Sylvia did. 'Mr. Wonderful' was bragging to all his patients about his new bride, showing them pictures and things. But she never said anything to me. We played this game with her acting like it never happened and me acting like I didn't know. Things got worse. Now it was like she never had any time. Like I was a bother to her. Like she would lose patience with me. 'I've already explained that to you, Lupe.' 'We've been through this fifteen times, Lupe.' When the fifty-five minutes was up, it was up, like right now. Boom! Before, she would always stay and talk and joke and laugh and have fun, but once she got married, once she was with 'Mr. Wonderful,' when fifty-five minutes hit, she was out the door. I hated the bastard. He made my life miserable again.

"And then she got pregnant. Boy, what a shock. I guess I used to think about them like Mary and Joseph, just real good friends who maybe every now and then kissed. But when that belly kept getting bigger and bigger, I knew it wasn't just kissing. I even tried to think of them like Jesus, Mary, and Joseph. But that whole trip about an immaculate baby barely fit Mary and Joseph. It sure as hell didn't fit 'Mr. Wonderful' and her.

"When the baby was born I hated it, too. Because she quit working. She stopped seeing me. The welfare department sent out some silly old white guy to be my worker. I wouldn't talk to the man. He wouldn't have understood anything I said, anyway. Then one day I decided that if she wouldn't see me I would go see her. I took a bus way across town to where she lived. But when I got there, I saw his car in the driveway, and there was no way I was going in that house while he was there. So I hid in the back yard between some bushes waiting until she came out. But she never came out and it got dark and I was still there, and I decided to stay there until he went to work the next day and then ring the doorbell. Then all the lights went out except for one upstairs, and it stayed on for a really long time, and I knew that that had to be their bedroom, and I didn't want to think about what they might be doing. And I didn't know if they did what they did with the lights on or the lights out. It had to be with the lights out because that's the only way she could do it with someone as ugly as him. I didn't want to stay for that. I couldn't stay for that, stay and see the lights go out and then know, but try not to think about, try not to imagine what they were doing. So I left. There were no buses running then and it took me three hours to walk home.

"I didn't see her for five years, but there wasn't a day that went by that I didn't think of her, even when the voices came. In fact, when the voices came, sometimes I could hear her voice mixed in with theirs, too.

"She came back and worked for a little while. But it wasn't the same. He would never let it be the same. Then she got sick. Sylvia told me. And it kept getting worse. She couldn't get out of bed and nobody could figure out what was wrong with her. I knew what was wrong with her right from the beginning. It was him, he was making her sick. Sylvia kept telling me that she was getting worse and worse. I knew that she needed me. So I went over there again. This time I went in, past the baby-sitter and nurse. She was so happy to see me that I stayed all day. Then I started going every day.

"She was better when I was there. She wanted me there all the time. She gave me a key to the house. I told her not to worry, that I'd be there for her all the time. Instead of coming home, I started hiding in different places just before he came from work. I hid in closets and under beds and outside in the barbeque pit and up in the attic in a part that nobody could get to except me.

"She got scared because he started to be gone all the time. He would come home from work, cook, and then leave, saying he was going back to the office or the hospital. He was gone on Saturdays, too, even though his office wasn't open. She thought it had to be another woman, and I didn't put it past the creep. Then she started crying and begging him not to leave her so much. So he drugged her. I saw the funny powdery stuff in the glasses the next mornings, and I couldn't wake her up for nothing. After a couple of times of seeing her all drugged out, I decided to find out what he was doing. I started following him."

"How could you follow him? You don't have a car."

"I didn't need a car. I used his car. He has one of those big expensive cars with a big trunk, and she had a key to his car on her key ring. I took the key off the key ring and used a rag to jam the lock and hold the lid down. Everywhere he went, I went. But I only went at night because I was with Amy during the day. The first place we went was to his office. I thought he was going there to work until she, this Kathleen girl, drove up. She was carrying a bunch of books with her. When I peeked in his window, he had books, too, but his were already open. At first they looked at their books and talked real serious like, and then they started smiling at each other and laughing and talking and not looking at the books anymore, until he got up and walked around his desk to point at something in her book. But he stayed there next to her and they laughed and talked some more, and he touched her as much as he could, little touches on her arm and hand and shoulder and face. This went on every other night for a couple of weeks. Then she came in one night with her books and just started crying, and he went over to her and held her and rocked her and stroked her like he was her daddy. Shame on him! The dirty old dog! He was old enough to be her grandpa. He had his dirty old paws all over her that night playing daddy.

"She didn't come back anymore, not at night anyway. But he expected her to, because for the next two or three nights he had his books open, and when she didn't come, he'd look at his watch and then look at it again and again. Then he'd get up and come to the window and look right past me at the parking lot. But he was out of luck. That dirty old man, that 'Mr. Wonderful,' had been stood up. Then he'd get on the phone and you could tell by the way he was dialing that he was calling her. But she wasn't answering, and he kept banging the phone down harder and harder.

"He got weird then and that's when I told her. If you love someone, you have to tell them, you have to tell them the truth, you have to tell them how things really are. You have to. After three nights of her not showing up, we went on this really long ride. He had me scared. I thought he knew I was in the trunk and was taking me out to the tullies to do me in. Because he had a gun. It was a big old ugly thing. It was the one that killed Amy. Anyway, we drove and we drove. When we finally stopped, he didn't get out of the car for a long time, and that scared me even more. I thought he was waiting for me to crack or trying to decide where to shoot me. But when he did get out of the car, he walked and then ran away from the car. I thought he had planted a bomb or something, so I jumped out and found myself in the middle of a million apartments, with him running across the street and me and the car in some kind of a carport. I moved as far away from the car as I could without him seeing me. The car didn't blow up. Instead, he started walking up and down the sidewalk across the street. He'd walk two blocks one way, stop and turn around, and walk two blocks the other way and then do it again. He did this for at least half an hour. And I'm thinking: *I'm* the one who's supposed to be crazy. Then, after that half-hour, during one of his two-block stretches, he stopped and looked all around. The place was pretty well lit over there, and when he didn't see anyone, he got right up next to a window at one of the apartments and peeked in, stepped back, looked around again, and then peeked longer. He did this for about ten minutes until he heard a car coming. Then he pulled back, walked away from that apartment for about a half a block, and then crossed the street and headed back toward our car.

"I didn't know whose apartment it was until a couple of nights later when she came out, when this Kathleen girl came out. This time he only walked up a block and then down a block and peeked. He peeked for about five or ten minutes. All of a sudden he jumped back from the window and walked away all hunched up like it was really cold. And she came bouncing out, all perky and dressed up in real tight clothes—she didn't look like no schoolgirl then—and got in her car and took off. When she zoomed past him, he put his head down even more so she wouldn't recognize him, and then he stopped and stared after the car for a long time.

"That's when I told Amy. She already knew, or at least thought she knew. She knew and she didn't know. She didn't want to hear it. She didn't want the truth. She thought there was another woman and was living with that. So when I said, 'Amy, that's not half of it,' she started crying and begging me to stop, not to tell her. But when you love someone, you have to tell them, tell them how things really are. She had to know what 'Mr. Wonderful' was really like. She had to understand that the only person who really loved her, who hadn't abandoned her, who came and sat with her all day, every day, was me.

"So I told her about the schoolgirl and her books first, and she cried and cried. Then I told her about the long drive and how he walked up and down past this apartment and that the apartment was the girl's. And when I told her that he stopped at her window and looked all around and peeked in, it was like she knew the peeking was coming. Because the minute I said the word *peeked* she started screaming and shaking and yelling and I couldn't tell her anymore because she couldn't hear anymore. Just crying and shaking and screaming. And I couldn't tell her about the drugging either, not then.

"We went back again two or three nights later, only this time he didn't get out of the car. He just sat. I thought we were at the apartments, but I didn't know for sure. He sat and he sat, and I started thinking again that maybe he knew I was in the trunk. But then I heard a car door and a car start and then leave and we left. I didn't know it then but he was following her. He followed her a long way to this bar where they have music. He got out of the car and walked away. I got out and saw him standing at the end of the parking lot, looking across the street from where she was standing, talking to a bunch of guys where you go in.

"Then he got really crazy. For a week we went to the apartments every night. But now when he got out of the car to go peek, he was wearing a trench coat and hat. Then one night when she came out all bouncy and perky and wearing her tight clothes, he didn't get all shook up. He just walked away real casual-like in his trench coat and hat, and when she left, he came back to the car real casual-like, and we went to the bar with the music. But this time he walked across the street and went into the bar. The kicker was that old gramps was dressed up like all the youngsters at the club, or trying to be dressed up like them. No more trench coat and hat. He had on jeans and tennis shoes and a baggy sweatshirt. I laughed and I laughed when I saw him standing in line with all those youngsters trying to be something he could never be. But it wasn't funny after he went in because he stayed for a couple of hours, and it got cold in that parking lot and people started staring at me, thinking that I was looking for car stereos to steal so I had to get in the trunk where I couldn't move and froze.

"It got so that he knew exactly where she was every night. Because on Thursday, Friday, and Saturday nights we didn't go to the apartments anymore. We went straight to the bar or the club or whatever you want to call it."

"Was it called The Rendezvous?"

"I don't know how you say it. I just know that it started with an R and had a lot of letters after it. . . . It got so that I didn't go with him on those nights because I knew where he was going and I couldn't go in, and I didn't like freezing in the trunk for three or four hours.

"But I told Amy. I told her what he was doing. She had to know. She had to know the truth. She couldn't keep living a lie. And since I loved her, I had to be the one to tell her. So I told her. How much she heard I don't know. Because she fought it. She'd shake her head and start sobbing and say 'No, no, no,' and let out these moans. Then one Saturday while he was downstairs, I took the juice that he always drugged and poured it down the sink so that at 11:30 that night she was still awake. Then I told her she was going to call his office, because he always said that he was going to his office or the hospital. I brought the phone to her, and she started crying and shaking her head. She wouldn't dial, so I dialed, and when it started ringing, I brought the phone to her ear, and she started yelling and screaming as it rang and rang. It took her a while to calm down, but when she did, I told her that we were going to call the hospital and ask for him. She started crying again, begging me not to. She finally said she knew he wasn't there, that it was a lie, that he was a lie, that her whole life was a lie, and that she just wanted to die. She begged me not to embarrass her with the nurses. And when I put the phone down, she hugged me and kissed me.

"From then on she kept saying that she wanted to die, that she had nothing to live for but that she was afraid. I tried to tell her that now that she knew, things would get better and she would get well, and we could go off and live together someplace.

"But 'Mr. Wonderful' didn't stop there. He wasn't satisfied. He kept at it. This is what ended it. This is what made her die. I wasn't going to go with him that night. I went with him only because I hadn't gone with him for a couple of nights and because he was getting weirder around the apartments and this was his night to go to the apartments. This time he ran across the street. He didn't bother to walk or look around. He went right up to her window and peeked. But he jumped back, like he'd been stung by a bee or something, and leaned against her wall, and looked up at the sky even though there were no stars that night. He peeked again and jumped back again, like he couldn't look. Then he did it again. Then he just leaned against her wall not looking in any direction, not caring if anyone saw him. Then he went around to the side of her apartment to this fence that made a tiny box around a big window. That fence was taller than him, but he jumped right over it. There was light coming from the top of that big window, and I thought he was really crazy. I couldn't see what he was doing behind the fence, but then I heard screams, a woman screaming. He jumped back over the fence and started running. Lights were going on all over the place, and people were looking out their windows to see what was going on. He ran further into the apartments, and I couldn't see him anymore. This big, husky dude came running out of her apartment pulling up his shorts, and I mean underwear shorts, and it was colder than hell and him all naked except for his shorts, running back and forth trying to find 'Mr. Wonderful.' She was in her doorway, fussing with her robe, crying.

"The police came. They searched all over with flashlights. They even came to the carport where I was, and I thought they would for sure see that the trunk wasn't closed tight and find me and think I was the guy because I was hiding. But they went right past me. He didn't come back until it was getting light and I was freezing.

"I went with him the next two nights, but all he did was drive and drive. He didn't stop once. I couldn't figure out what he was doing, but later on when the cops questioned me, they told me that that Kathleen girl used to work for the doctor. They asked me if I knew her. I didn't say one word to those pigs all the times they questioned me. They said she left town just a few days before Amy was killed. So I think he was driving around on those nights trying to find her.

"I didn't tell Amy about the fence until the day before she died. I guess I was holding back because of how much it hurt her the other times I told her about him. But people have to know the truth, especially if you love them. You have to tell them how it is. You can't let them live in fairy tales. So I told her. But this time she just lay there. She didn't cry or move or blink or say anything. Finally, I asked her, 'Did you hear me?' And she said, 'Yes.'"

She stopped, and I became aware of the darkness and the room again. I waited but she was silent. When she did speak, she said only, "Now you know why he killed her."

I waited some more in the darkness. When she spoke again, she said, "You can go now."

"But how did it happen? How did she die?"

"You know all you need to know. You know why he killed her. That's all you need to know."

"But how?"

"Ask him. He's your client. You can go now."

"I'm leaving. But can you tell me one thing? How did you know I was coming today?"

"It was just a matter of time, and time was running out. You couldn't wait any longer. And you'll be back. After you talk to him. Maybe I'll talk to you and maybe I won't."

"Depending on what?"

"You can go now."

As I felt for the door handle, she said, "Mr. Garcia, I want you to know that I will never testify. When the trial comes, I won't be here. And even if you or the police find me and drag me into court, you'll never get a word out of me."

I drove to the apartments. They were a sea of grey two-story wooden structures located on several acres of land that had previously been an apricot orchard. The orchard had been split up into the equivalent of city blocks. On each block there were several elongated units of apartments. Each unit backed up onto another

244 RONALD L. RUIZ

unit, which faced its own street. Each unit was identical; each apartment seemed identical. Carports abounded. They were situated across the street from the apartment units both on the perimeter and interior streets. There were directory signs on the corners of each block with rows of letters and numbers squeezed into the centers and arrows pointing in four different directions on the edges. I drove around the perimeter of the apartments several times looking for E1-1765 and then drove through the interior streets. That's when I began going around in circles and couldn't find my way back to the perimeter. I was lost. "Goddamn low-income housing," I mumbled to myself. "If *I* can't find my way around here, how in the hell can the poor bastards that live here find their way?"

I saw a boy of about nine or ten trying to shimmy up a carport pole. I pulled alongside him and rolled down my window. "Hey, kid." He ignored me, as if my three-thousand-pound car hadn't just driven up within inches of him. "Hey. Kid." He turned, gave me a blank stare, and went back to his pole. I sat frustrated and annoyed, but then I noticed my striped tie resting on the edge of my suit's lapel, and it occurred to me that perhaps the only men the boy had ever seen in a suit and tie were cops. "*Órale, joven, ayúdame, por favor.*" Now the boy turned to me and his face lit up. "*Estoy perdido.*" "You lost, Mister?" in perfect English, "I don't think so. You're too smart to be lost." "Where's E1-1765?" He went into great detail, pointing and turning with his fingers and his arms. When he finished, he saw the blank look on *my* face. "Okay. Follow me. I'll show you." I followed him and he showed me, waving and smiling as he left.

Lupe wasn't lying. She had said it was a downstairs apartment with a high, small fence around a big window. Carports were across the street. The truth weighed heavily on me. She didn't drive. She couldn't have found her way in this maze at night unless he had brought her here, unless she had been in the trunk.

I returned to the apartments that night to see what I could see from the carport and see how exposed I would be there. The streetlights on the apartment side of the street supported everything

Lupe said. There wasn't much light in the carport, and she could have easily stood in the shadows, unseen from across the street. Light shone from the top of the sliding-glass door in the patio.

The following morning I stopped by Alan Newsome's office on my way to court, ostensibly to drop off a supplemental police report. I parked next to his silver Mercedes and tapped the trunk on my way to his office. It was plenty big. No, Lupe Rodríguez wasn't lying.

"I don't know what you charged your doctor client for the first case, but let's hope that he's got something left for the second case."

"What are you talking about?"

"Your doctor friend is one weird fellow."

Barbara Benson didn't like Alan Newsome. She seemed to like him even less now.

"What do you mean?"

"I mean when they find Kathleen Powers, you may have two cases on your hands rather than one. She might be dead, too."

Suddenly, I felt very tired. "So what have you found out?"

"Have you ever been down to The Rendezvous?"

"No."

"And I don't think that any man of your age and stature would be patronizing a place like that, except, of course, for Dr. Newsome. I went to The Rendezvous last night. I introduced myself to the owner as a private investigator who had been hired by the family of a missing girl to see if I could locate her. I told him that The Rendezvous had been one of the last places she had been seen and that apparently she was the recipient of some unwanted attention there. A drunken older man was seen following her around the dance floor and creating a scene, and I was trying to find out who that older man was. The owner had me talk to one of his waitresses, a Jennifer Blake, who was familiar with the incident.

"Jennifer remembered the incident very well, mainly because from the very first time the older man came into The Rendezvous, he sat at one of her tables and sat at that same table every time after that. He stood out from the beginning because he was obviously twice the age of everyone else and because he wore ridiculous outfits, trying to make himself look younger, when in fact they only made him look older. He just showed up one Thursday night—they have live music Thursday, Friday, and Saturday nights—and came in almost every one of those nights for about four weeks. She said it was obvious that he was fixated on a young girl who had been going there for some time. She had come alone at first, but it wasn't long before she had a boyfriend. The older man would take his seat on the elevated level, order a drink, order another, and by the third, he was just plain staring, drooling over the girl on the dance floor. He never danced, never spoke to anyone, except to order a drink, never shared his table with anyone. He was creepy enough that she told the owner about him. But he never bothered anyone, and he spent a lot of money and was a big tipper, so they left him alone. He'd get quietly drunk and drool over the girl from a distance and would quietly leave when she left.

"On the last night, the girl's regular boyfriend didn't come, and she was kind of like up for grabs. Different guys made runs at her as the older man quietly watched from his table, drinking his drinks. After the intermission, Jennifer said that the older man started talking to himself, but loudly, and then he began moaning. She was going to stop serving him, but realized that he had three or four untouched drinks on his table and that he wasn't ordering, didn't need to order any more; he got louder and people started moving away from him. It was pretty obvious who the subject of his words and moans was because he couldn't take his drunken eyes off the girl. She was dancing, having a great time, being sought after by one guy after another. Then he started pointing at her from where he was sitting. The girl couldn't see or hear him because of the music and the distance. Then he started crying, and Jennifer was going to call security when he stood up and started staggering down toward the girl, bumping into tables, crying, and turning angrily on anyone who protested. When he reached the dance floor, he stumbled to where she was dancing and pushed her partner away and then opened his arms wide as if he was going to hug her, slobbering something through his tears. She screamed, and the guy she had been dancing with came to her rescue, only to have a glass broken over his forehead by the older man. Someone hit the older man and there was a free-for-all. The police came, but by that time, the girl and the older man were both gone."

She stopped and was no doubt watching me, probably gloating.

"Anything else?" I said, not looking at her, not wanting to give her any more satisfaction. She didn't have to like my clients as long as she did the work she was capable of.

"No, I think that's plenty."

"Did she or anyone else there connect the older man with the doctor?"

"No."

"Didn't recognize him from his pictures in the paper or on the tube?"

"Didn't mention anything, and I think she would have been scandalized had she made the connection between the older man and the doctor. She would have said something."

"The doctor's case didn't come up in any way? No connection between you and the doctor?"

"Come on, Gabby, I know better than that. The closest I got was asking her if she had ever seen either of these two individuals before. She said no and I left it at that."

Let her gloat. She was one hell of an investigator.

No sooner had Barbara Benson left when Jim Grossman stuck his head in my office door and said, "You owe me one," flipping what appeared to be a police report onto my desk. Jim Grossman was a sergeant in the San Jose Police Department, someone I had successfully defended on a rape of a prisoner charge years before. He felt forever indebted to me.

"What's this?"

"It's the report you wanted. Don't ever say I don't do anything for you. And for God's sake, don't ever tell anyone where you got this from. I'm twice removed from the person who got it, and I want to keep it that way. See you later. I've got the patrol car outside."

I read the report. The police had been called out on a prowling incident. Kathleen Powers reported that she and her boyfriend were engaged in some intimate acts on her couch in her apartment when she suddenly saw a man standing outside her sliding-glass door in her fenced-off patio area. The man had been watching them and had a "sick" look on his face and might even have been crying. When she saw the man, she screamed, and the man climbed over the six-foot patio fence and fled. She denied knowing or ever having seen the man before, but the reporting officer was of the opinion that she knew who the man was but was either too frightened or embarrassed to say.

Of course she knew him. Why was she protecting him? God help us if she ever testified.

I had wanted to hear from Barbara before meeting with Alan. As soon as I put the report down, I called him.

"Alan? Gabby. I'd like to see you here in my office first thing tomorrow morning." I was at my best in the morning.

"Tomorrow morning's real bad for me, Gabby. I'm all booked up. Don't have a spare minute. How about late tomorrow afternoon? How about 5:30?"

"I talked to her again, Alan. You'd better do some rescheduling and be here in the morning."

"You talked to her again?"

"Yes."

"When?"

"Yesterday."

"Okay. What time do you want me there?"

In most criminal cases, time, the passage of time, generally favors the accused. Memories fade, the outrage of the community and the prosecutor dims, witnesses become unavailable, evidence can be lost, and it gives the defense an opportunity to catch up with the state's investigation. From the beginning I felt that Alan Newsome's case might be one of those rare cases in which the passage of time favored the prosecution. It was a simple case:

either Alan or Lupe Rodríguez pulled the trigger. It was unlikely that Amy Newsome had managed to kill herself, and I didn't believe that a jury would ever buy that. Lupe's involvement was huge, and it was imperative that the jury watch and listen to her testify. But she was totally unreliable. Here today, gone tomorrow. Talking today, silent tomorrow. And there was Kathleen Powers. From the start I felt that the less anyone knew about her the better. The sooner we got on with the trial, the less chance the prosecution had to find her. Those had been my reasons for initially demanding a speedy trial. Those reasons were clearer, more pressing now. If Kathleen Powers ever took the witness stand, Alan Newsome's chances of being convicted increased. We had four weeks until the trial. Alan Newsome and I had much to talk about.

"Glad you could make it."

He eyed me with apprehension and distrust. He knew I had spoken to Lupe again, and he was waiting for the other shoe to drop.

"We start picking a jury in four weeks."

"Why so soon? I've always heard of cases starting a year, even two years after a person's been arrested."

They all panicked as the witching hour approached. Now he had added reason to distrust me.

"I've explained to you in detail all the reasons for asking for a speedy trial at least twice. Nothing's changed. If anything, there's all the more reason to go to trial as quickly as possible."

"Why?"

"Lupe Rodríguez was not only following you, she was with you."

"Nonsense! The woman's insane. How does she claim to have done that?"

"She had a key to your car, and she rode around in your trunk."

The answer took him aback. He looked away and tried to visualize it. She would fit. The image discombobulated him. His response was a weak, "You believe that?"

"Yes, I do."

"Then you're as loony as she is."

"No, I've been out to Kathleen Powers's old apartment. Lupe Rodríguez doesn't drive. She has no access to a vehicle. There's no way she could find her way through that maze of apartments, especially at night. There's no way she could describe what she saw there as accurately as she did without having been there."

"Nonsense." But without conviction.

"She not only has you stalking the woman and peeping through her window, but she also has you jumping over a patio fence to spy on Kathleen Powers and her boyfriend."

"Do you believe that? Do you really believe that?" He was doing his best to appear indignant, outraged even, but he appeared more embarrassed than anything.

"Yes, I do. Take a look at this police report. . . . Notice the top line, the date. Three days before Amy's death and the day before she dropped out of sight. Read it. . . . Both Lupe and Kathleen Powers said it happened. The only difference is that Kathleen Powers can't, or won't, identify the suspect, although the police officer thinks she knows who the suspect is."

He shook his head again and again as he read. It was a while after he had finished reading that he looked up at me. When he did, his face was flushed and he managed, "Do you believe this?"

"Alan, you don't pay me to believe you or anyone else. You pay me to represent you in a court of law to the best of my ability, to give you the best defense possible. Having said that, yes, I believe that the incident in the report took place."

"But it doesn't identify me." He blinked and blinked at me as if to underscore his incredulity.

"Lupe saw the same thing happen, and she says it was you."

"What's this got to do with who shot Amy?"

"Plenty. It goes to motive. You were obsessed with a younger woman, and you killed your wife so that you could be with that younger woman."

"That's absurd. Ridiculous. Who's going to believe that?"

It was a sad disclaimer, and I shuddered at the thought of a jury witnessing it.

"No more ridiculous than the stalking itself, or the peeping, or the sick look on the face in the patio, or the staggering or crying at The Rendezvous."

"The Rendezvous?"

"Yes, Barbara Benson's been to The Rendezvous. A cocktail waitress there remembers an older man ridiculously dressed in trendy clothes who for weeks came and sat and drank quietly, fixated on a young woman on the dance floor. She remembers the last night the two were there. She remembers the older man ordering drink after drink, becoming very drunk as he watched the girl on the dance floor. She remembers him moaning and crying and pointing to the girl on the dance floor. She remembers him leaving his table and staggering to the girl, crying, pushing aside the young man the girl was dancing with. She remembers the older man trying to embrace the girl and the girl screaming and the older man breaking a glass on the young man's face.

"Alan, you told me you made a fool of yourself at The Rendezvous over Kathleen Powers. You just didn't give me the details. If a jury ever hears that waitress testify about you and Kathleen Powers at The Rendezvous three or four nights before Amy was shot, and you deny it, you're cooked, you're dead meat. Don't you think they'll know it was you on her patio, crying, peeping through her window? You stalking her? And you're going to defend yourself by saying that Lupe Rodríguez is insane? That it never happened?"

He sat silent for a long while, his face still flushed, his eyes looking vacantly at the floor beyond my desk, a forefinger pressed lightly against his lips as his head moved slightly, aimlessly up and down. I watched him, letting the facts soak in; the longer they soaked the better. Finally, as if with a last gasp, he said, "But she didn't identify me."

"The waitress?"

He nodded.

"Barbara Benson was careful. She only asked the waitress if she had seen either of you before the incident. She didn't want to suggest anything. The waitress said no. But if she's ever shown a photo of you, my guess is that she'll I.D. you."

Poor bastard, I thought as I watched him absorb that, too. We all carry our own hells around with us. At that moment I was glad not to have his. I let the soaking continue. He needed it. It was only after he looked up at me again, now with a blank, helpless look, not even a stare, like, "What do I do now?" that I said, "The cops and the D.A. probably haven't made the connection between you and Kathleen Powers yet. Or if they have, they can't find her. The longer we wait to go to trial, the more likely it is that they will accomplish one or both. The sooner we get to trial, the better."

He continued to look at me with that pathetic, blank, defeated look, no longer hostile, nor angry, nor confrontational—nothing except lost and sad.

After a while I said, "You know, Alan, I long ago made a rule for myself that I would not engage in telling my clients whether I believed them or not. My belief should have nothing to do with my job. Should is the operative word. I believe you. I believe you when you say that you did not kill Amy. Having said that, let me say something else. At the trial you must testify. There's no way around that in this case. But if you get on that stand and the issue of Kathleen Powers comes up and you lie about your relationship with her, you lie about stalking her, you lie about the patio and The Rendezvous, you will convict yourself. You will destroy yourself."

He looked at me for a few moments more and then said, "But I didn't stalk her. I wasn't in that patio, and I didn't do what that waitress said I did."

I let it pass. I would have been a fool to expect anything else.

We said only polite goodbyes when he left. Alone, I thought of Lupe.

I had to see her again. I had an urge to see her then, to drive over to her house then and there. But I thought better of it. This time I had to find out how it happened.

The next morning when I knocked on her door, I still didn't know.

"Come in, Mr. Garcia, she's been expecting you. In fact she told me this morning that you'd be coming today."

That irritated me, but I smiled nonetheless. "Where is she?"

"Where she always is."

"In her room?"

"Where else?"

As we started down the hall, I realized that all the approaches I had rehearsed, all the avenues of entry I had explored, had deserted me. I didn't know what I would say to her or even how I would begin. But I had to have the truth.

Once I closed the door, I didn't wait for the darkness to settle. "How did you know I was coming today?"

"The police came yesterday. They threatened to kick down the door if I didn't come out. I went out and they gave me a subpoena. Four weeks from today. They want me to testify, to tell the truth. That's all I ever tell, the truth. Since they came yesterday, I figured you wouldn't be far behind."

"Did they say what they wanted you to testify about?"

"No. They just said to tell the truth. And I said that's all I ever do. But they won't hear it from me. Because I won't be there. And if I am, I won't say a word."

"Why?"

"Because I hate them and I hate him. They deserve each other. I won't help either one. . . . But why did you come?"

"To get the truth."

"Why should I tell you the truth?"

"Because he's told the truth. And you say that's all you ever do is tell the truth."

"He's told the truth?"

"Yes."

"He's told you that everything I've told you is true?"

"Yes."

"He knows that he killed Amy?"

"Yes."

"That but for him, she would still be alive?"

"Yes."

"And you know that, too?"

"Yes."

"Then why do you need to know any more?"

"Lupe, like you, my mother was a paranoid schizophrenic. Like you, she . . ."

"I don't care what your mother was. Why do you need to know any more? Why does anyone need to know any more?"

"Because I need to know how he should be punished."

"How much he should be punished or how he should be punished?"

"How much."

She said nothing. In the darkness the silence mounted. But the silence favored me. Four minutes, five minutes, six minutes. Still not a word. But the silence favored me. Then she said, "I'll tell you how it happened.

"It was the night after I told her about him jumping over that Kathleen girl's fence. He was gone that night, probably still hunting for his baby-girl. I went up to her bedroom and found her sitting up in bed crying.

"'What's the matter?'

"'I want to die.'

"It wasn't the first time I heard her say that but this time she seemed to mean it.

"'Why?'

"'I have nothing to live for.'

"'You have me. I love you. We love each other. Someday we can be happy.'

"She was looking straight ahead. She hadn't looked at me. And if we hadn't talked, there would have been no way for me to know that she knew I was there.

"'We have each other,' I said again, hurt that she couldn't or wouldn't see that. I hugged her. I reached for her hand but felt the cold steel instead. I jumped back.

"'What are you doing with that thing?'

"'I want to die.'

"'Why?'

"'I'm tired and I'm not afraid now. Death couldn't be worse than this.'

"'But we have each other.'

"For a moment I thought she understood. Instead, she said, 'Do you love me?'

"'Of course I love you. I love you more than anything else in the world. There isn't anything I wouldn't do for you. You know that, Amy.'

"'Then help me die.'

"'Are you crazy?'

"'No, I couldn't be saner. Now I have no fear. . . . Help me, Lupe, I can't pull the trigger.'

"'What?'

"'I've tried but I don't have the strength in my finger. I've tried so much my finger hurts! Do you love me?' turning and looking at me. 'Do you love me?'

"I nodded.

"Her eyes were clear. The tears had stopped. They were the clearest eyes I had ever seen. They said that she saw and she knew and she wanted to die.

"'If you love me, you'll help me.'

"Together we raised the gun. Together we put it to her head. Together, with my hand over hers, with my finger over her finger, we pulled the trigger."

CHAPTER V

Jonathan Wesley Harris always introduced himself as Jack Harris. He was as much Jack Harris as Woodrow Wilson was Woody Wilson. A tall, gaunt, serious man with dark eyes that always seemed to be searching for your soul, he had come to the West Coast at eighteen to study philosophy at Stanford. The only son of a prominent, wealthy, East Coast family, he chose to live in East Palo Alto with blacks and Mexicans in a grungy, spent apartment complex instead of on campus or in chic Palo Alto.

I was in my first year of practicing law when I met Jack Harris. I had been asked to attend a meeting in East Palo Alto to give legal advice to a group of Mexican and black tenants whose rent was being summarily doubled by their landlord. I knew nothing about landlord-tenant law, but in those days of building a law practice, I was attending anything and everything, while inferentially holding myself out to be a legal expert on any legal matter. To my surprise, the young white undergraduate student who was chairing the meeting seemed to know a great deal about landlord-tenant law. He was a quiet, somber, unassuming young man who ran an orderly, efficient meeting without the bravado and bluster that I had become accustomed to. He understood and spoke some Spanish, and it was clear that he cared for the people. Several times that night, as the *licenciado*, I was asked for my expert legal opinion on matters that I knew nothing about. In those days I couldn't admit my ignorance, and I gave my "legal" opinion on everything. That night I painted myself into a corner more than once. Each time Jack Harris quietly came to my rescue. "I think what the *licenciado* is saying . . ." The group ultimately prevailed, and Jack Harris had made a lasting impression on me.

Over the following years as Jack Harris completed his under-graduate studies and went on to law school, I saw him only on a few occasions, but each time I saw him, the respect and warmth I felt for him was rekindled. I was not surprised when he joined the San Jose Public Defender's office immediately after passing the bar. But I was surprised and threatened, too, when he moved into a modest apartment in San Jose's eastside barrio because, as he put it, he wanted "to live where his clients lived." My fear was short-lived. He quickly made it clear to me that he was not inter-ested in private practice, not interested in chasing the dollar, and that he felt he could make a significant social impact in the Pub-lic Defender's office. Some time later he was to say to me, "Gabby, you and I want the same things." I wondered then if my want was as pure as his.

The last thing Jack Harris ever wanted was to draw attention to himself. Yet his lifestyle did exactly that. He drove a bare-bones Nissan that he had bought as an undergraduate. Like its owner, the car had absolutely no frills. In fact, I could almost hear the exas-perated salesman asking, "Are you sure you want a motor in it?" His wardrobe was strictly mail order with perhaps J. C. Penneys in a pinch. Every day he took his lunch to the office in a brown paper bag and ate it at his desk as he worked through the noon hour. But no one ever called him niggardly because he was always the first and biggest contributor to worthy causes. My guess had always been that he was a trust-fund baby who donated all of his salary, except for his frugal living expenses, to charitable causes. There were changes when he married Melinda Baxter, another dedicated public defender. She refused to live in the barrio or in an apartment. So they moved into a modest older home in a mid-dle-class neighborhood. Jack Harris also bought a new car, or rather, a newer car, one with only 40,000 miles on it.

Some twelve years before Alan Newsome's case went to trial, Jack Harris and I represented two brothers involved in a brutal rape case. Freddy and Bobby Rivas and two unidentified individ-uals were charged with having taken a drunken teenage girl up into the hills, where, for more than six hours, they repeatedly raped her and inserted a number of foreign objects into every cavity of her body. The girl had positively identified Freddy Rivas, whom I represented, as the principal instigator, who not only participated in most of the acts but also bullied the two unidentified perpetrators into joining him. Freddy Rivas had no prior criminal record. The girl also said that Bobby Rivas, whom Jack Harris represented, had not participated in any of the acts and had tried to dissuade the others from going forward and continuing their acts. Bobby Rivas had spent eight years in prison on sexual assault charges.

Freddy Rivas told me from the beginning that the victim was mistaken, that she had the brothers' roles reversed. According to Freddy, it was Bobby who had offered the drunken girl a ride home from a party, Bobby who had driven and had stopped to pick up two of his friends along the way, Bobby who had led and orchestrated the rapes and other barbarous acts. If convicted, Freddy was facing a minimum twenty-year prison sentence; if convicted, Bobby would receive a life sentence. Other than sparing his brother a twenty-year prison sentence, Bobby had nothing to gain by admitting his guilt and, in fact, steadfastly claimed his innocence for months.

A week before the trial Jack Harris and I met ostensibly to discuss common problems, plans of attack, and, if possible, strategies. I was convinced that Freddy was innocent and that Bobby was guilty and that Jack Harris knew that as well. I got right to the point.

"Jack, you're going to be sending an innocent man to prison for at least twenty years."

"I'm not sending anybody anywhere."

"You know and I know that my man is innocent."

"What I know or what I believe has nothing to do with my obligation to provide my client with the best legal defense possible. My client says he's innocent. The victim corroborates his claim, and it's my job to present that defense and not worry about the outcome."

But the eyes that always seemed to be searching for my soul weren't looking at me.

"Don't hand me that legal crap, Jack. We're dealing with people here, lives and real consequences. Not words, not legal principles. Look at me, Jack Harris! Look at me, goddamn it!" He looked at me but his eyes were unsteady. "Aren't we supposed to be working for truth and justice? Whether there's any truth or justice in this sorry world, aren't you and I supposed to be at least looking for them?"

Jack Harris looked away and thought. After a while he said, "Gabby, you and I want the same thing."

Later that day Jack Harris and I arranged for a private meeting between our clients and their family and Freddy's wife and us. During that meeting Bobby Rivas wilted and agreed to plead guilty.

There were raised eyebrows when Jack Harris accepted a judgeship, not because he wasn't eminently qualified, but rather because no one thought he would ever leave the Public Defender's office. "I think I can make a bigger impact as a judge," he explained. But Jack Harris's first years as a judge were not easy for him. Though we never discussed it, I saw him as conflicted in that role. Here was a man who believed that there were reasons other than birth or race for the bulk of our society's crimes being committed by minorities and the poor. He had spent a good portion of his adult life passionately defending "those poor bastards," as we sometimes called our clients. Now he had an obligation to the entire community to help keep it safe. Now he had to consider the brutal, senseless suffering "those poor bastards" inflicted daily on innocent victims. Now he had to send "those poor bastards" to prison for sentences that probably shocked his conscience.

Jack Harris had been a judge a little more than five years when the case of *The People of the State of California versus Alan Newsome* was assigned to him for trial.

"Look at them," I whispered, with my back to them and my

face just inches from his. "Look at them," I repeated. It was the last thing he wanted to do. "And tell me if you're uncomfortable with any one of them." He glanced over at them, the whites of his eyes stretched with fear, and then looked down. God, that would never do. I stood.

"Your honor, may we have a few moments, please?"

Jack Harris nodded solemnly.

The prosecutor and her investigator were at the table to our left, and just beyond them were twelve prospective jurors seated in the jury box along the wall. I sat down and leaned over and whispered, "Alan, we're down to our last challenge. If we excuse another juror, we're stuck with whoever takes that seat. So I want you to look at every one of those jurors, one at a time, as calmly and normally as you would any patient, and then tell me if you're satisfied with each and every one of them to sit in judgment of you."

"I'll leave that up to you, Gabby," with his head down.

"No. No. No. First, look at me, not at the floor. You've done nothing wrong. You've got nothing to hide, nothing to be ashamed of. But your posture's conveying the opposite. Sit up and look at me. . . . That's better. This is *your* trial, not mine. I want you to be comfortable with the people who will be judging you. Now relax and look at them."

He was much better this time. When he finished, he said, "I really don't have a standard to measure them by. They seem fine to me, but I'll defer to you."

I stood and said, "Your honor, the defense is satisfied."

Lisa Thomas stood, "Your honor, the People are satisfied." That came as no surprise. She had been satisfied for at least half an hour and had at least six challenges left. Lisa Thomas was a good lawyer, a very good lawyer. She had been in the District Attorney's office just seven years. This was her biggest case. If she wasn't the best deputy district attorney in the office then, she soon would be. She was a bright, quick, articulate young woman in her mid-thirties. The fact that she was also beautiful didn't hurt her. But her biggest asset was her ability to relate to people. She had been completely at ease with Jack Harris and the prospective jurors from the very beginning, and within minutes they were at ease with her. She had an air of credibility about her that said: You have every reason to trust me. When she said, "The People are satisfied," her words said more than that she was accepting the jury. They also said that she was not here to play games, that she didn't need nine challenges like the defense did, because she would be presenting the truth.

The jury, seven women and five men, all white, all middle-class, was sworn in. I was relieved. For me the anticipation of the trial was often more trying than the trial itself. The jury selection had gone well. I was in trial now.

It had been a unique experience those first two days to be representing a defendant who was not only innocent but who was truly being tried by a jury of his peers. So different indeed to stand before them and ask, "Ms. Robinson, the law says that the defendant is to be presumed innocent until he is proved guilty beyond a reasonable doubt. As you sit there now, is my client, Dr. Alan Newsome, innocent in your mind?" and to insist by my tone of voice and body language that he was innocent, rather than watch the prospective juror's confused eyes struggle with the presumed innocence of the young man seated next to me who looked like the photo of every criminal she'd ever seen and who was obviously in jail now and probably had been for several months and who sat alone without friends or family. And she was supposed to think he was innocent when he couldn't possibly be innocent. Then I would repeat, "The law says that here and now you *must* presume the defendant innocent. Can you do that, Ms. Briggs?" and then watch her glance over to the judge to make sure that I wasn't lying, and when the judge remained mute, she'd answer, haltingly, "Well, if the law says he is, I guess he is." If she were worth keeping, I'd soothe her a bit with, "At least up to this point because you haven't heard any of the evidence yet." "No, I haven't heard any of the evidence yet." And watch her relief: she could still convict him.

None of that had greeted me in this trial. Instead, the struggle was on the other side. Blonde, blue-eyed, well-dressed doctors who are out of custody don't go around killing their wives.

Instead, the confused looks came back to the precocious, polished, prepared prosecutor, whose skirt was as appropriately long as her jacket was loose-fitting.

Time and again as Lisa Thomas questioned them, I saw not only looks of puzzlement but an empathy for the well-groomed man sitting next to me. True, I used five more challenges than the prosecutor, but I wanted to be sure. Perhaps I was gilding the lily, but I knew that weeks from then, as the chosen twelve sat in the jury room deliberating the fate of my client, none would remember or even care to remember how many of my ten challenges I had exercised.

Once the jury was gone, I turned to Alan Newsome and asked, "How are you feeling?"

Alan Newsome looked at me, his eyes afloat in fear. He turned from me and looked around the empty courtroom as if he were hoping to find an answer there.

"How do you feel?" I repeated. As needy as he was, I was needy, too.

He turned back to me and shrugged and said, "Okay, I guess."

His look was pathetic. He had tried hard to keep a straight face for the jury, and now his face would hide nothing. I should have left him alone. I should have gathered my things and said, "Let's go." He had had enough of the courtroom for one day. But I was needy, too, and pushed on. This time I was more to the point. "How'd you think the jury selection went?"

He looked at me again. The question meant nothing to him. "Okay, I guess."

"Okay? Are you kidding me? You've got to begin paying better attention than that. *We* scored some big points during the jury selection." Alan Newsome hadn't scored anything, but that didn't matter. I began reciting some of the successes I had with the jurors. After a minute or two it was clear that he wasn't interested, listening maybe, but not interested. Let down, disappointed, I reached for my briefcase and said, "We better get going." And then, to cloak whatever disappointment was showing, added, "Remember, 6:30 in my office. We should go over her witness list."

Alan Newsome had taken off his tie; he seemed more relaxed. As soon as I handed him the witness list, he said, "Gabby, before we begin, let me thank you for the excellent job you did in selecting the jury. You were great." Now I was embarrassed, because I felt that he had recognized my need, my begging for approval, and thought that it was in his best interest to give me strokes whether I merited them or not. Rather than answer, I decided to get on with the list.

"Sergeant John Kroc. He was the first officer on the scene.

"Dr. Patrick Hirayama, coroner. Cause of death.

"Henry Burkett, ballistic expert. Gun fired at close range. Not much to dispute there.

"Claire Oliver, Amy's sister. From what you've said and from my telephone conversations with her, she should be very helpful.

"Alice Sandowski, Caroline's first sitter. Very favorable.

"Ella Mae Thompson, Amy's first nurse. Excellent.

"Marie Wilson, Caroline's second sitter. Shouldn't hurt.

"Rachael Lemke, Amy's second nurse. Shouldn't hurt.

"Lupe Rodríguez. We'll talk about her in a second.

"Sergeant William Renna. He took your statement on the night of the homicide.

"Custodian of the records, St. Luke's Hospital. That ties in with Renna's statement about your saying that you saw patients there that night.

"That's it. God knows how many she may have on rebuttal, but this is what she's going with on her direct examination. I think it's a good list for us. The names not listed are probably more important than those that are listed, with the exception of Lupe Rodríguez.

"But let's talk about Lupe. Lupe hates you, but she also hates the cops, maybe a little more than she hates you. They've been pretty rough on her, and they've subpoenaed her. But I think I've at least neutralized her. I've told her that you've admitted your guilt to me." He stirred in his seat. "Don't get excited. That's all she wanted. That's all it took to placate her and get her to open up to me. She's vowed that she won't testify, even if they find her and bring her into court. I believe her. She's got too much to lose.

"Note that your nurse isn't listed. I think the statement she gave Barbara that even though she may have cancelled your late appointments on the day of the homicide, you may well have been in the office until 5:30, has dissuaded the D.A. from trying to make anything out of what time you told Sergeant Renna you left. Obviously she's going to try to make something out of the fact that you told Sergeant Renna that you saw patients that night at St. Luke's. Let her. Joaquín Guerra, the janitor in your office, clearly remembers you being in the office when he arrived around eight and that you were still there when he left at ten. So you stopped and had a drink for not even an hour and were too embarrassed to tell Sergeant Renna that because you had an invalid wife at home. I would have preferred that you told the truth, but we can live with your first statement.

"But the big coup is the fact that nowhere on this list does the name Kathleen Powers appear. Obviously, they don't think she's important." Alan Newsome's face colored, and his eyes widened at the mention of the girl's name. "Look, Alan, I don't believe for a moment that you shot Amy. But I do believe you were stalking Kathleen Powers. You're not on trial for that, and, of course, what I believe is not relevant. Now I know we've been through this a thousand times, but if Kathleen Powers, and God forbid it, were ever to testify in this trial that you stalked her and you were to deny it, I think we'd be in deep, deep trouble. . . . But, all in all, I couldn't be more pleased. I think we've got a decent shot at this."

"What do you mean, a 'decent shot?'"

He was feeling better. There was righteous indignation not only in his words but in his tone.

When Alan Newsome left, I returned to the witness list. I stopped at Lupe Rodríguez. It would be better if she were gone, if they couldn't find her. There was no telling what she might say if they dragged her into court. It would be better if she were gone. Was she?

I thought of going to Lupe's home. Sylvia would tell me. If Lupe were still there, I would let her know that the trial had begun and that she should expect to testify by the end of the week. I could hint at how grueling that could be, scare her a little, remind her that it was the cops who wanted her to testify, get her angry, get her to leave. It would be much better that way. Until it struck me that dissuading a witness was a felony and if she did leave and if it ever came out that I had been with her just hours before she left, I could find myself on trial. Not a good idea.

I went to the window behind me and looked out. It was dark, and the city and valley were an ocean of lights. I looked up and down, far and wide, wondering who the most insignificant person in that mass of humanity might be and whether that worry-free individual had a better life than me. But I was wasting time. Only two hours until dinner and there was much to do.

I spread out reports, transcripts, outlines, memos, diagrams, and photos on my working table. I began with the police reports. I stared down at the first page of a report for several minutes before I realized that there was nothing to read; after twenty or thirty readings, I had virtually memorized it. There was nothing to absorb in that first set of police reports; it had all been absorbed long ago. The second set of police reports was even fresher in my mind. And so it went. I had spent so much time on what amounted to a simple straightforward set of facts that I had only to look at the first few words of any paragraph to recall the content of the paragraph. After twenty minutes I sat back in my chair, at a loss with what to do with the hour and a half remaining before dinner. Not only were the facts of the case simple but I had every reason to believe that the two most important witnesses in the case, Lupe Rodríguez and Kathleen Powers, would not testify. Neither had given statements to the police or testified before the grand jury, so there was nothing to review. I could have worked on other cases but, once a trial began, I refused to be distracted by any other case. So I sat staring out at the lights of the city. I had done everything I could, everything I knew how to do. But I had an innocent man on my hands. There had to be something more I could do. Another five minutes passed, and I finally thought, to hell with it, got up, took a Xanax and went to dinner.

I had been taking Xanax for more than three years then: one as soon as I got out of bed in the morning and one when I went to bed at night. Once in trial, I upped the dosage.

Before leaving each morning, I would carefully wrap two pills in separate bits of tissue paper and then neatly place them in the deepest recesses of my two front pants pockets, somehow believing that this was necessary given the courthouse metal detectors. Two minutes before the beginning of the morning session I would make my way to a washroom, and there, when no one was looking, gulp down a pill with a handful of water. I would repeat the process just before the beginning of the afternoon session unless a water cooler was closer or less exposed. At night I doubled the dosage. I often wondered about any placebo effect but gladly accepted the calming, regardless of the cause. I slept better at night with two pills, and on a few occasions I took three before going to bed. The night before Alan Newsome's trial I limited my alcohol intake at dinner to two glasses of Chardonnay, a glass of red wine, and a touch of port. I took three Xanax at bedtime and set three alarm clocks and left a message for my secretary, Debbie, to call to make sure I was up by eight.

After two days of pretrial motions, the testimony began.

Sergeant John Kroc was a twenty-three-year veteran of the San Jose Police Department who, on the night of the homicide, was in the field in charge of the patrol unit for Section E of the city. He was two blocks from the scene when the 911 call came on the air. He was at the home of the victim and the defendant in less than a minute and was admitted by the defendant. He found the body upstairs in the master bedroom. It was sprawled half on and half off the bed, with the head hanging just inches from the floor, and the feet resting upward in the middle of the bed. He identified a previously drawn diagram of the bedroom, drew in the body, and then marked with an X where he had found the gun, a .357-caliber Magnum, about a foot from and just slightly to the left of the victim's head. Blood was splattered across the bed and had oozed from a wound to the victim's left temple onto the carpet in a large pool. There was no sign of a struggle and no sign of forced entry. He saw no gunpowder marks on either of the victim's hands. All of the exterior doors and windows to the house were closed and locked, and, except for the defendant, there was no one else in the house. John Kroc was a tough, bright, tired cop who, in twenty-three years on the police force, had seen more than his share of life. I had known him since he was a rookie policeman and had cross-examined him many times. He had known from the beginning to tell it like it was. He embellished nothing and covered nothing. He had no stake in the truth other than to tell it. We not only respected each other but we liked each other. Now, as John Kroc waited for me to cross-examine him, his tired eyes on his otherwise grim face lit up. You had to have known John for twenty-three years to know that he was smiling, challenging me, and saying, just between us, "Come on, sucker, let's see what you can do." No matter what my plan of attack might have been, John Kroc would have seen me coming a mile away and make me pay dearly for any missteps.

I would have answered Jack Harris's direction to "cross-examine" with, "I have no questions of this witness, your Honor," had not the prosecutor conveniently omitted eliciting from John Kroc my client's physical condition at the time he answered the door. I knew that John Kroc wouldn't sugarcoat anything, so I asked him. He said that Alan Newsome was distraught, weeping, hysterical, and in a state of shock. As John Kroc left the witness stand, he looked at me and his eyes shined. This time they said, "Not bad, Counselor."

Dr. Patrick Hirayama had been a pathologist for Santa Clara County for twenty-six years. Most of his working hours were spent examining and cutting up dead bodies to establish the cause of death. He was a small, quiet, scholarly-looking, self-contained man who answered every question, both on and off the witness stand, as precisely and sparsely as possible and whom I had always wanted to ask what life meant to him. Dr. Hirayama testified that the cause of death for Amy Newsome was a gunshot wound to the left temple. The powder burns around the wound were such that he believed the weapon was fired at a distance of six to twenty-four inches from the temple. He established the time of death as between eight and eleven that night. He found no traces of gunpowder on either of Amy Newsome's hands.

Henry Burkett was a ballistics expert who testified that the bullet removed from Amy Newsome's skull had been fired by the .357 Magnum in evidence. He had examined the gun to determine the facility of the trigger pull. He found that a substantial amount of finger pressure would be needed to fire this weapon, which had a trigger pull at the opposite end of the spectrum of what is commonly called a "hairpin" trigger. He also testified that when this gun was fired, it emitted a certain amount of gunpowder residue that one would expect to find on the hand of the person firing it. On cross-examination, Mr. Burkett agreed that the .357 Magnum was indeed a large gun and that, given the space around the trigger, it was possible, "though not very likely," that two small fingers, one over the other, could pull the trigger.

I had spoken to Claire Oliver on the telephone several times. Claire was Amy Newsome's sister and had been caring for Caroline for almost a year. She was outraged by the "persecution" of Alan. She had been to California several times during Amy's illness, the first time about two months after Amy became ill and the last time about six months before her death. The illness had affected Amy not only physically but mentally as well. She had become irascible, suspicious, and demeaning, increasing in degree each time Claire saw her. It was very difficult being around Amy. Yet Alan was incredibly patient, loving, and understanding. Most men would have flown the coop years before Amy's death. He was husband, father, nurse, doctor, and housewife at home, as well as being the breadwinner. Claire didn't know how Alan managed, and she became so concerned about the effect Amy's illness was having on Caroline that she offered to take her niece to Ohio during an early visit. Alan declined, explaining that Amy and Caroline needed each other and that he needed Caroline. About a year later both Amy and Alan felt it was best for Caroline to live with Claire's family in Ohio until Amy's condition improved.

The police had called Claire three days after Amy's death and just before Alan was arrested. She had told them what she told me, but they had been more interested in whether Amy was right-handed or left-handed and whether she had ever owned or used a gun. Claire told them Amy was right-handed, hated guns, and would have had them banned from the face of the earth if she could have, and that Amy never owned or fired or knew how to fire a gun.

Lisa Thomas had telephoned Claire about four weeks before the start of the trial, and when Claire had expressed outrage at the continued "persecution" of Alan, told her he had been the only person who had access to Amy that night and that he had lied to the police about where he had been during the time that Amy was shot. Lisa Thomas then read to Claire that portion of her earlier statement to the police regarding Amy being right-handed and Amy's inexperience with guns, and asked Claire if she remembered making those statements to the police. Claire said she did and a few days later was served with an out-of-state subpoena.

The evening before Claire Oliver was to testify, Alan Newsome met her at the airport and brought her to my office. When I told them I wanted to speak to Claire alone, Alan excused himself, and as he turned to leave, Claire hugged him with a long, strong embrace, saying, "I'm so sorry, Alan, I'm so sorry." It was hardly the embrace one would have for the murderer of one's sister.

She carried that sentiment onto the witness stand the next day. Lisa Thomas got the right-handedness she wanted and Amy's disdain for and inexperience with guns, but she paid a heavy price for it. At every juncture possible, Claire Oliver let the jury know what a wonderful, loving husband Alan Newsome had been to her sister. Her words had the desired effect, especially on the seven female jurors, some of whom shook their heads, lowered their eyes, lowered their heads, and shifted in their seats. I couldn't have scripted a better ending to Claire Oliver's tour as a witness if I had tried. At the end of my cross-examination, as she was summarizing her sister's sad condition and Alan's unflagging devotion, she burst into tears and was crying still as she stepped from the witness stand. When she reached our table on her way out of the courtroom, she stopped beside Alan, put her hand on his arm, and, through her tears, said, "You shouldn't have to go through this, Alan. May God help you." For the next thirty seconds you could have heard a pin drop in the courtroom.

Jack Harris declared a recess, as much as anything, I thought, to break the heavy air that Claire's testimony had left. Outside in the hallway Alan Newsome was smiling in the courthouse for the first time. His eyes gleamed, and his face had lost some of its paleness.

He stood tall and upright, and I noticed that he was not only meeting and holding the jurors' eyes, but that he was also seeking them out. "Great job," he repeated to me. "Don't thank me, thank Claire. She did it all. You should drop her a thank-you note." I meant the note part.

Alice Sandowski was more of the same. She had been hired about three weeks after Amy's illness began. She watched Amy's condition deteriorate and watched her become increasingly difficult. She had nothing but respect and admiration for the way Alan Newsome handled the situation. I wondered why Lisa Thomas had called Alice Sandowski as a witness. It must have been the access: to establish that aside from Alan, Alice, Ella Mae Thompson, and gradually Lupe Rodríguez, no other adult was ever with Amy Newsome. When I asked Alice to describe Lupe Rodríguez, she said that Lupe Rodríguez was a thin, slight, short young woman in her early twenties who looked and carried herself more like an adolescent boy than a young woman. When I asked her to describe Lupe's fingers, Lisa Thomas objected on grounds of relevancy. "Oh, no," said Jack Harris quietly, "I think it's very relevant. Objection overruled. Please proceed, Mr. Garcia." Was Jack Harris beginning to take sides? Could the old public defender stand idly by and watch an innocent man be convicted? As it turned out, Alice Sandowski hadn't paid much attention to Lupe's fingers.

But Ella Mae Thompson had. "She was a skinny little thing, so skinny and tiny that sometimes I used to think she could creep around without being seen or heard. . . . Her hands? Small, real small, and her fingers were skinny little bones, no meat on them at all."

Ella Mae Thompson was a tall, broad-shouldered, white-haired, bespectacled woman whose loud firm voice carried in it a Texas drawl. Everything about her exuded truth and strength. The way she stood before the clerk as she took the oath, tall and straight, almost as if she were at military attention, her extended right hand a natural inexorable extension of that implacable body. "I do," rang out in a voice as committed to telling the truth as truth itself. The way she sat in the witness chair, upright, her back at a perfect 90-degree angle to the seat, her large, firm jaw meeting her neck in the same manner. Still, her clear, alert green eyes had a warmth to them that told of her capacity to love.

"That man did everything a man could do for that poor woman."

"By 'that man,' do you mean the doctor, Alan Newsome?"

"I'm not talking about anybody else in this courtroom."

"Is that a yes?"

"Yes, sir."

"And by that poor woman, do you mean Amy Newsome?"

"Yes, sir. And I say poor because that poor woman was tormented not only by pain in her body but pain in her mind, first locking herself up in her bedroom with her little girl and not letting any of us come in, and when her daughter was finally sent off to Ohio, locking herself up with that crazy one, that Lupe Rodríguez."

"How long did you work as Amy Newsome's home nurse?"

"Two years and eight months."

"And during that time did Lupe Rodríguez visit Amy Newsome?"

"Oh, my, yes. For the first few months she didn't come at all. Then one day she just showed up. Rang the doorbell. Strangest little thing you ever wanted to see. Didn't belong in that house or in that neighborhood. I wouldn't let her in, and she kept saying that Mrs. Newsome wanted to see her, and I kept asking for what, and she kept saying that, she was a patient of Mrs. Newsome's. And I told her that Mrs. Newsome didn't have any more patients, that she had been sick in bed for months and wasn't getting any better. And she said she knew that, and that's why she had to see her, because Mrs. Newsome would feel better if she saw her. To me, that was the shabbiest excuse I had ever heard of to try to get in the front door. Then she started whining about how she had left her house ten miles away at six in the morning and had to take four buses to get there. And I'm thinking: three-and-a-half hours to go ten miles by bus, shoot, I could *walk* ten miles faster than that. Then she was getting more and more upset and her squeaky voice was getting squeakier and louder so that I was afraid she'd wake Mrs. Newsome. But Mrs. Newsome was awake, and she must have heard that squeaky thing because she called down 'Ella Mae! Ella Mae!' And when I went upstairs, she wanted to know who was there and when I said, 'Lupe, a Lupe . . . ,' forgetting her last name, Mrs. Newsome said, 'Well, let her in, let her in! She's a dear friend of mine.'

"Well, that's how it started. After that, she just started coming a little more and a little more until she was showing up every day. But she would always come right after Caroline went to school and leave just before Caroline came home."

"Did she have a key?"

"You know, I really don't know. But she had to have something because she'd just come and go as she pleased. I mean she'd just appear. Because you never saw her coming. All of a sudden she was just there, and of course I didn't have anything to say about it because Mrs. Newsome had given me strict orders, after Lupe's first visit, that any time that little thing showed up, I was to let her in. But like I say, she never needed any letting in."

"Once Lupe Rodríguez started visiting Mrs. Newsome, how often did she visit?"

"Oh, my, every day. And it got worse once Caroline went to Ohio because then she showed up just after the doctor left for work and left just before he got home. Lots of times I didn't see or hear her leave but she was gone, long gone when the doctor got home."

"So these visits lasted up to eight or nine hours a day?"

"Yes, sir."

"Every day?"

"Yes, sir. Five days a week. I can't say what went on Saturday or Sunday, because I didn't work those days. But the doctor was home then, so I don't imagine she was waltzing in and out of there any old time she pleased like she did with me."

"What did they do during these visits?"

"Nothing that I could tell."

"Where did these visits take place?"

"Upstairs in the master bedroom. That's the only place they could take place, seeing how most of the time Mrs. Newsome couldn't get out of bed."

"Well, did they talk? Did one read to the other? Did they listen to the radio or watch TV? Tell us what they did."

"They didn't do any of those things that I saw."

"They didn't talk?"

"Well, you know, that Lupe girl isn't big on talk. I really think the only conversation I ever had with her was when she first tried to get past me at the front door. She's a strange one. She'll just look at you, stare at you, and not say a word, even if you talk to her, which I quit doing early on because I don't like talking to disrespectful people. Because that's what it was, look right at you and not answer a word. Disrespectful."

"You mean you never heard Lupe Rodríguez speak to Mrs. Newsome?"

"You know, I can't say that I did. In the beginning I used to think I could hear them talking, but the minute they heard me coming up the stairs, they stopped. That was before Caroline went to Ohio. They kept the door open then. But once Caroline left, that door stayed shut, and I had to knock before I went in."

"But there were times in the beginning when you went into the bedroom without knocking?"

"Yes, sir."

"What did you see then? Where was Lupe Rodríguez? Where was Mrs. Newsome?"

"Mrs. Newsome was always in bed. And that Lupe girl was where she always was, right next to Mrs. Newsome."

"In bed with Mrs. Newsome?"

"No, no, no. Mrs. Newsome had an old wooden chair that her grandma had brought over with her on the boat from the old country. It was the hardest, most uncomfortable thing you'd ever want to sit on. Mrs. Newsome loved that chair, and naturally, it became Lupe's favorite chair. She'd take it from the far wall every day and put it right next to the bed and sit."

"For how long?"

"Must have been for the whole visit because I never saw her anywhere else in the room."

"What would they do whenever you entered the room?"

"Nothing. Lupe would just keep staring off at the wall like she always did. Wouldn't even blink an eyelash when I came in. Just kept staring. Mrs. Newsome would be asleep or just staring, too."

"Why did you leave Dr. Newsome's employ?"

"Well, because once Caroline left, things went from bad to worse. They closed the door on me. Kept it closed all day, every day. If I went up there, I had to knock before I went in. After a while I had to say what I wanted before I could go in. Then they made it that I had to wait until Mrs. Newsome said it was okay for me to go in. It got so that all of our talking was done through the closed door, and I only went in once a day to carry Mrs. Newsome's lunch in and leave it. And that old Lupe would just keep staring at the wall. Sometimes I felt like she really didn't even see me. But what was the final blow was that as soon as Caroline left, Lupe started putting her hand on Mrs. Newsome's bare arm and just keeping it there, kind of like Mrs. Newsome was her pet dog or pet rock or pet something. I didn't like it, didn't like what it could mean. It just wasn't right. And me sitting downstairs all day long doing nothing because there was nothing to do, not even carrying Mrs. Newsome to the bathroom five or six times a day like I used to. I guess Lupe was doing that, too, though I couldn't see how, being such a scrawny little thing. So I finally told the doctor that he didn't need me anymore, that I was only seeing Mrs. Newsome for a minute a day and I didn't like taking his money for nothing. But I never did tell him that I didn't like what I thought might be going on. He had enough problems to worry about."

At the recess Alan Newsome was thankful and upbeat.

Marie Wilson was as frightened as Alan said she would be. She worked at the Newsome's for seven months. She had taken care of people's children in their homes for many years, and had always made it a practice not to meddle in other people's affairs so that all she knew about the Newsomes was that she had to be at their home at 2:45 each day when the little girl got out of school and that she left at 5:45 when the doctor got home. She only spoke to Mrs. Newsome a few times because her job was to care for the little girl and Mrs. Newsome had a nurse. She really didn't get to know the little girl that well because the little girl spent most of her time upstairs with her mother. She said hello and goodbye to the doctor at the same time each day, and on Fridays he gave her a check.

When she wasn't with the little girl, she was downstairs knitting. A few times she did see a young person come down the stairs just after she arrived. They never spoke, and she couldn't tell whether that person was a boy or a girl. She just assumed that person was a friend of the family's and didn't give it much thought, because, like she said, she has always made it a practice not to meddle in other people's affairs.

Rachael Lemke was the next scheduled witness, and after her, Lupe. Just before Rachael Lemke took the stand, Lisa Thomas asked to approach the bench. When we did, she whispered to Jack Harris that she had an urgent matter that had to be taken up in chambers as soon as possible. Jack Harris looked up at the courtroom clock and declared an early noon recess.

It never failed. Every time the prosecution's case began falling apart, there was some sort of crisis. Lisa Thomas had been taking a pounding. Alan Newsome now looked like the knight on the white horse, and the jury had to believe that there was something sinister going on between Amy Newsome and Lupe Rodríguez. But there was still a long way to go; there was still Lupe Rodríguez to go.

I was gracious and gentlemanly as I held the door open and nodded for Lisa Thomas to enter the judge's chambers. There was nothing gracious about Lisa Thomas. Once inside the chambers, she paced and scowled at me as we waited for Jack Harris. Hard loser. She wasn't used to losing. But prosecutors shouldn't be in the business of prosecuting innocent people. Jack Harris came in, and I watched her wait as he readied himself at his desk. She was a tall, dark-haired woman with fine distinct features, whose dark eyes could sparkle with warmth one moment and fire the next. She would carry her beauty into age. The moment Jack Harris looked up, she began.

"Your honor, several weeks ago I subpoenaed Lupe Rodríguez. As you can see, she has become a very important witness in this case. Clearly, the defense hopes to make her responsible for the murder of Amy Newsome. She was subpoenaed for 9:30 this morning. She hasn't shown. We've tried calling her but she has no phone. I've sent the police out to her house, but I don't think they've had much success locating her. I'm asking that you issue a bench warrant for her arrest. If we haven't located her by the time our next witness completes her testimony, I'm going to ask that this case be continued to Monday."

Gone. My heart beat faster. If Lupe Rodríguez was gone, it was all over. We were home free. We would win by default. I tried to look as indifferent as possible.

Jack Harris fingered his chin. "You're sure there hasn't been some misunderstanding on Ms. Rodríguez's part? From what I've heard so far, Ms. Rodríguez certainly has some mental and emotional problems. I'd hate to have a mentally ill person arrested just because she was confused as to the date or time."

"I can assure you that there's no confusion on her part. The police have tried to question her several times without much luck. They've reminded her repeatedly about her court date, and she has vowed repeatedly that she will never testify in this case."

Jack Harris continued fingering his chin. "You have no idea where she might be?"

"No, your honor, but maybe Mr. Garcia does."

"What?" My heart beat even faster and my breathing raced. "I resent that inference. If you have an accusation to make, make it. Don't play games with me or the court," prodding my anger as much to defend myself as anything. "I have no idea where Ms. Rodríguez is."

I glared at Lisa Thomas and she glared back. "He's been to Ms. Rodríguez's house on several occasions."

"So have the police." But I was deeply thankful that I hadn't been there since the trial began. They had been watching either the house or me. Sylvia wouldn't have told them. Nor Lupe. Fear picked at me. How much did they know? Did they know that she had talked to me? Worse, what had she said to me that I had never disclosed? I worried and waited for the other shoe to drop even as Lisa Thomas and I continued to exchange glares.

Jack Harris, who appeared to be ignoring our exchange, asked, "She told the police she would never testify?"

"Yes, your honor."

"She was in effect refusing to testify?"

If Lisa Thomas knew anything about my conversations with Lupe, it would come out at any moment.

"Yes, your honor."

"I'll issue the bench warrant."

"Thank you, your honor."

She didn't know.

I struggled to keep my mind on Rachael Lemke's testimony. Lupe. Was she really gone? Or in that crazy mind of hers had she forgotten or confused the date? Where had she gone? Where could she go? She had no money, friends, or relatives. Would they find her? If they did, would she testify? Would Jack Harris give them a continuance if they couldn't find her? How long a continuance? How long could she stay gone? The longer the better. No Lupe, no case. We win hands down. Without her it wouldn't take much for the jury to conclude that she was on the run because she murdered Amy. If they couldn't find her, would Lisa Thomas go forward without her, or would she dismiss the case? Much better if she dismissed. You never knew what a jury would do.

Rachael Lemke corroborated much of Ella Mae Thompson's testimony. Because of her own invalid mother at home, she arrived at the Newsome's promptly at 8:00 and left promptly at 5:30. After the first months the doctor was often gone when she arrived and had not yet returned when she left at 5:30. Lupe must have been in the bedroom at 8:00 and 5:30 because she was there at noon when Rachael took in Mrs. Newsome's lunch and she never saw Lupe come or go. Rachael Lemke used a key to enter the Newsomes's home and locked the door behind her when she left.

At the conclusion of Rachael Lemke's testimony, Jack Harris said he would hold the People's motion for a continuance in abeyance until the morning, when Lisa Thomas would have an opportunity to show what efforts she had made and what success she had in locating Lupe Rodríguez.

I wanted to go to Lupe Rodríguez's house during the noon recess in the worst way. Only the certainty that the place would be crawling with cops kept me away. But I had to go that evening. I had to learn for myself if Lupe was really gone. I had to talk to Sylvia. I couldn't rely on what Lisa told Jack Harris, or better, what the cops told Lisa who told Jack Harris. The house would probably still be crawling with cops, but as the defendant's lawyer, I had every right to make my own independent evaluation of this witness's failure to appear. Better take Barbara Benson with me and give it the appearance of an investigation. If the cops had seen me there before, they would surely see me there tonight. But I couldn't take Barbara Benson. Sylvia would mention my previous visits, and then there would be hell to pay with Barbara, with a good chance that she would walk away from the case now, when I needed her most. The longer I waited, the fewer the cops.

But I couldn't go much past eight because Sylvia might not open the door, especially if she was alone. If I was lucky, the cops might be convinced by then that Lupe was really gone and focus their search elsewhere.

At exactly two minutes past eight I pulled up alongside the river bank across from Lupe's house. The house was dark, and there wasn't a cop or a cop car in sight, which meant nothing because they were probably hiding in the bushes along the river bank watching the house. As I walked up to the house, I wondered if Sylvia was gone, too. I knocked and waited. I heard and felt nothing. The house remained perfectly still and my heart sank. I knocked harder. Nothing. Harder, banging. Then I felt movement. Sylvia was there. The movement grew stronger. She was coming to the door.

"Who is it?"

"It's me, Sylvia, Gabriel Garcia. I need to talk to you."

"But I don't need to talk to you."

"Sylvia, open the door. I need to talk to you about Lupe. Where is she?"

"You know where she is." She wasn't opening the door. "You're the one who told them."

"Told them what?"

"That she killed Mrs. Newsome."

"Sylvia, open the door. I need to talk to you face to face."

"Go away. Haven't you caused enough misery already? Coming here like a big friend and then telling the judge that Lupe's the one that pulled the trigger."

"Who told you that?"

"The cops did. They came here this afternoon. A whole army of them. It was ugly. They searched the river and found Lupe and dragged her out of the river, dragged her up here screaming and kicking and crying. They brought her in the house and threw her on the floor and put handcuffs on her hands and feet. Then they busted down her door, looking for I don't know what. I kept yelling at them to tell me what they were doing. All they said was they were arresting Lupe, and she was going to testify at your trial because you were telling the judge and the jury that she had pulled the trigger and killed Mrs. Newsome. Please go. I don't want to talk to you. I've talked to too many assholes today."

There wasn't much to say. I had been saying precisely that in court. I turned and left.

I had as much to drink with dinner as I ever had because I needed to sleep. There was no telling what was going to happen in court tomorrow morning. If I ever needed sleep, it would be tonight. I had three nightcaps at home and two Xanax pills. An hour later I took two more Xanax pills.

Debbie was standing beside my bed shaking me. "Gabby, it's 9:35. I've been calling and calling but you weren't answering. Is there something wrong with your phone? The court's been calling. The bailiff says the judge is pretty upset. They want to know where you are. I told them your car has been acting up, and you're probably stuck somewhere. I know where your spare key is, so I came over. Are you okay, Gabby?"

My head felt like it had been flattened by a truck. It took me a while to understand what Debbie was doing there and what she was trying to tell me. Then it returned: Lupe and Alan and the jury.

"Should I tell them you've had car trouble and that you'll be there in twenty minutes?"

I nodded.

Jack Harris was angry, and for the first time Lisa Thomas seemed smug. "The jury's been waiting an hour and fifteen minutes, Mr. Garcia. Where have you been? Why haven't you called?"

I was sluggish. My reactions were slowed. I had to pull myself together. "I went down to Madrone, your honor. I left at 6:30 this morning and thought I'd be back in plenty of time. But I had car trouble." What else could I tell him? That I had too much to drink and too many pills the night before?"

"Why were you in Madrone? You're trying an important case here."

"Why I went there is related to this case, your honor. It's something I'd rather not go into now." I felt Lisa Thomas's eyes widen. Let her send a battalion of cops down to Madrone. That stupid . . .

"You could have called."

I paused to collect myself. "My car broke down in the middle of nowhere."

"What was wrong with your cell phone?"

"You know I don't believe in cell phones, Judge."

Jack Harris fought back a smile. "Well, may I suggest that you start believing in cell phones, Mr. Garcia? These types of delays will not be tolerated any further."

"Yes, your honor, "I said deferentially, "it won't happen again." That was all that needed to be said. It was better to move on. I couldn't keep it up much longer.

In the closed courtroom the bailiff leaned over the counsel table and whispered, "Boy, have we got a pistol in there," gesturing with his head and eyes to the holding cell.

"That Lupe Rodríguez is a real firecracker. While we were waiting for you, she was kicking and pounding on the door and screaming all kinds of nasty things about you and your client. The judge finally had us clear the courtroom and take her out of the holding cell and back to the jail."

Fear spread across me in the form of a thousand pinpricks. I needed a pill. What had the jury heard, and why hadn't Jack Harris said anything in chambers?

As if to answer my question Jack Harris came out onto the bench. "Let the record reflect that we are in open court with the defendant and counsel outside the presence of the jury. It is now 10:35, and we are just beginning the morning session due to defense counsel's tardiness, which he has explained to the court's satisfaction in chambers. As is my practice, the jury was seated in the jury box at nine o'clock. The next scheduled witness was Ms. Lupe Rodríguez, of whom there has been considerable mention made thus far in this case. While the court was awaiting Mr. Garcia's arrival, and after I had sent the jury back to the jury assembly room, Ms. Rodríguez, who is in custody for failing to appear pursuant to a subpoena, was placed in the holding cell, which is normally used for in-custody defendants and which opens into the courtroom. No sooner had Ms. Rodríguez been placed in the holding cell when she began screaming epithets about the defendant and defense counsel. I was not in the courtroom at the time, but my bailiff told me that she was cursing the defendant and defense counsel.

"I want the record to reflect that since speaking with counsel this morning in chambers, I have had a conversation with Dr. William Ebbe, the chief medical physician in the jail. Dr. Ebbe informed me that, upon being removed from the holding cell this morning, Ms. Rodríguez was given a mild sedative and a dosage of the medication she takes for schizophrenia. Dr. Ebbe has just spoken with Ms. Rodríguez, and she appears to be fine now. He feels that in another hour she'll be even better. He assured me that, despite Ms. Rodríguez's previous disruption and her mental illness, given the medication she received this morning, she will be able to competently testify this afternoon. Of course, this will not preclude either counsel from questioning Ms. Rodríguez on her competency to be a witness. This court will be in recess until 1:30 this afternoon at which time Ms. Rodríguez will be the first witness."

I drove to the Guadalupe River wild with fear, hoping that wide body of eternally flowing water would calm me. I didn't know what to think. Worse, I didn't know how to plan or prepare. Would she testify? If she did, what would she say? How could she possibly say that Alan had pulled that trigger? If she was as angry as they said, there was no telling what she might say. Worst-case scenario: she blamed Alan and I become a witness, a witness to what she told me in her room in order to refute her crazy accusations. Jack Harris would die. He'd have to stop the trial, relieve me as defense counsel, and appoint another lawyer for Alan so that I could testify. Maybe even declare a mistrial and start all over again with another attorney. I should have taken Barbara Benson with me. I knew better. I knew the law.

The river wasn't calming me. Everywhere I turned, there was no escaping the current of destruction. I took my third and fourth Xanax of the morning. In less than fifteen minutes everything began to slow. In thirty minutes I was calm. All of my problems were still there, but I could only react to them calmly, slowly. If I had to testify, well, I had to testify. If Jack Harris had to appoint a new lawyer, well, Jack Harris had to appoint a new lawyer. Now when I gazed at the river, it added to my peace. I drove back to the courthouse, slowly. Lupe Rodríguez was just like any other witness: ask her a question and she had to give you an answer. I walked up the three flights of stairs, instead of using the elevator, slowly, deliberately. In a few minutes Lupe Rodríguez would be testifying.

She was still the most important witness in the trial, but now it was almost as if I would be observing her testimony from a distance, from afar. Whatever she said, she said. And when it came time to cross-examine her, well, I would cross-examine her.

At 1:30 Lupe Rodríguez came out of the holding cell into the courtroom with her head down. She was wearing a red jail jumpsuit that seemed two sizes too big for her. The bailiff pointed to the witness stand and she took her seat there. Her black hair was close-cropped and her brown skin was well scrubbed. She was very thin and looked more like a twelve- or thirteen-year-old boy than a woman in her early twenties.

Jack Harris said, "Ms. Rodríguez, do you understand that you've been subpoenaed here to testify in the case of the People versus Alan Newsome?"

Lupe Rodríguez nodded, keeping her eyes focused on the front edge of the witness stand.

"All right. Mr. Bailiff, bring in the jury."

The jurors entered in single file, each staring at the thin, frail figure in the red jumpsuit. They continued to stare even after they had been seated and until Jack Harris said, "Ms. Lupe Rodríguez. I am going to ask you a few questions directed toward your qualifications to be a witness in this case."

"There's nothing to ask," Lupe began quietly, looking up at the judge for the first time. Then she turned abruptly and, with her finger pointed at Alan Newsome, said in a voice that rose to a scream, "He killed her! That man killed Amy! Because she found out that he was fucking a fifteen-year-old! Kathleen Powers! She'll tell you! He killed his wife! He . . ." Only then was the bailiff able to cup her mouth and drag her back into the holding cell, kicking and writhing. When he tried to close the door, she screamed again, "He killed her. Bring Kathleen Powers here! She'll . . ."

Then there was absolute silence. The jurors' eyes seemed as

round as the clock above them.

Jack Harris was stunned. When he recovered, he said, "This court will be in recess until Monday morning at nine o'clock," and left the bench.

The jurors were dumbfounded. As they filed out of the jury box, each of them looked over at Alan and me in disbelief, seemingly seeking an explanation. A simple denial, a shaking of the head might have been enough, but any communication by us with the jurors was strictly prohibited. Alan nudged me under the table with his knee. "Look at them," he whispered.

"I am."

"They don't believe it. They don't want to believe it. They want to hear that it's not true."

I saw that, too, but at a distance, as if I were watching from another room or watching them on a large television screen acting out some sort of melodrama that had little to do with me.

"Can we say something to them? Anything?"

"No."

The bailiff stood at his desk staring down at his shoes. Only Lisa Thomas seemed herself, more than herself, buoyant, beaming. What had been a drawn, drained face just minutes before was now a fresh, full, beautiful face. Several times as she gathered her things, she looked over at us, brimming with confidence and almost arrogance. A huge blow had been struck in her favor. She knew it. We knew it.

"What's the matter with you, Gabby?" Alan asked as soon as we were alone in the courtroom. "Are you feeling all right?"

"Yes, of course, why?"

"You seem detached, almost withdrawn. Are you sure you're all right?"

He was detecting what shouldn't have been detected. I knew that. Somehow it didn't matter. "I'm fine. Would you rather that I had jumped up and down in outrage?"

"No, but . . ."

"In situations like these, it's almost better to appear detached, as if you couldn't have expected anything else." Those words made no sense at all. Let him toil with them.

"Well, you're the lawyer. I've never been in this situation before. But the jury was shocked. They didn't know what to think, what to believe. They kept looking over here as if they wanted you to do something, say something."

"You heard the judge's admonition at the beginning of the trial: there is to be no contact of any kind with the jury."

"Yes, but Lupe Rodríguez really hurt us. I'm scared, Gabby, scared as hell. We should talk. I'm free the rest of the day. I can be at your office any time, any time at all, just name it."

I was seeing, hearing, and understanding everything, but taking much longer to formulate my response, as if some sort of filter had been inserted between my brain and my tongue. It was the Xanax, and I was concerned that Alan Newsome, the physician, would detect much more than he already had if I spoke to him any more than need be for the remainder of the day.

"There's a number of things that Barbara Benson and I will have to review this afternoon. We'll probably have to do some additional investigation in light of Lupe's blast. I could easily be tied up with Barbara well into the evening. Yes, we have plenty to talk about. But tomorrow morning's as good a time as any. How about 10:30 in my office?"

I didn't wait for an answer. I rose and my legs felt heavy. I took a few steps. They were slow, deliberate steps, not my normal gait. I went back to the table and reopened my briefcase. "Go ahead, Alan, I'll meet you in the hall. I want to make sure I have something." At the very least he wouldn't walk behind me and notice. Alan went out into the hall. It wasn't that I was wobbly or unsteady on my feet; my legs simply wouldn't move as easily and quickly as they normally did. In the hallway Alan was waiting as close to the door as possible. Fear seeped out of every line in his face. He did his best to smile, but the effort only stretched and contorted his already contorted face. He needed me. He needed me to reassure him that all was not lost, that what he had seen was not as bad as he thought, that we would still prevail. I had seen that look on defendants' faces thousands of times.

He needed to be with me. I couldn't afford that. If he ever suspected that I had been using a drug during the trial, there might be hell to pay.

"Alan, you're going to have to excuse me. Nature's calling. I may be a while."

"Go ahead, Gabby, I'll wait."

"Alan, this will take a while. It's been a long week, and, frankly, I haven't had a bowel movement the entire time. Now I feel the urge and I'd better take care of it. I don't want to rush it. I want to relax and let Mother Nature take her course."

"That's all right, Gabby, I can wait."

At that moment there was nothing, no one more important to Alan Newsome in the entire universe than I.

"Please, Alan, once I'm finished I'll have to meet with Barbara Benson. We've got quite a bit of work to do."

He had a pitiful look on his face.

"Please, Alan, tomorrow at 10:30."

For a moment I thought he was going to cry. Finally, he nodded, pursed his lips, and said, "Okay."

The fear that was consuming Alan Newsome was not mine . . . yet. It was waiting for me, lurking, watching for that moment when I stopped taking those little white pills. As I sat on the bowl waiting for Alan Newsome to leave the building, new fears, however distant, swirled around me. For the first time the possibility that Alan Newsome could be convicted of murder was no longer a mere possibility. Lupe Rodríguez had just taken it out of that realm. If I needed pills to deal with mere possibility, how much more would I need them to deal with real danger? How many more pills would I need? How much more could I take and still function? This was a murder case, and Alan Newsome was a successful white doctor. If the State Bar ever found out how much Xanax I had already taken during this trial, I could be suspended or even disbarred. I had to cut back on the pills, cut back to the two per day that Dr. White had prescribed so that in any disciplinary proceeding brought by the State Bar he could support me. As I flushed the empty bowl, I vowed to cut back on the Xanax. Starting tomorrow.

As I washed my hands, I stopped and took one last pill. Tomorrow morning would be soon enough to begin dealing directly with the explosion of fear that Lupe Rodríguez had ignited.

At dinner that night, Dinah noted my drinking. "Must have been a tough week, Gabby." I looked up at her bleary-eyed and shook my wineglass to underscore my latest request. I have no recollection of how I got home. I woke up on the couch, fully dressed, to the telephone ringing. Debbie was calling. Dr. Newsome had been waiting twenty minutes for his 10:30 appointment. "Tell him I'm with Barbara. Tell him we're working on what Lupe said. Tell him . . . anything you want. But I can't see him 'til noon."

My head felt like it had been turned inside out and then dragged over a conveyor belt. Every movement shot pain through my skull. And behind it all was Lupe Rodríguez, laughing. I looked for my pills but something said: if you do, tomorrow will be worse, you *know* tomorrow will be worse. I tried to forget the pills. I wanted to die.

The Alan Newsome that was waiting for me in the reception room was not the Alan Newsome I had left in the courthouse hall less than twenty-four hours before. I nodded at him in a cursory manner when I entered. "Be with you in a minute, Alan," came automatically. But my glance had been enough to tell me that his face was no longer creased with fear and that his eyes were watching me, intent on watching me. Instead of going to my office, I went out a side door to the restroom. I looked at myself in the mirror. I looked like hell.

My eyes were bloodshot and my skin had a yellow hue, and every crease and line in my face seemed to have sunk and sagged another inch overnight. I couldn't have instilled confidence in a dog. I washed my face again and combed my hair again, but I still looked like hell. I was raw inside and fear was no longer at a distance. It was scraping against every inch of my rawness. I needed a pill in the worst way, but I had deliberately left them at home. Monday was just a few hours away.

"Are you all right?" Alan Newsome said as soon as he seated himself in my office.

"Of course I'm all right. Why wouldn't I be all right?" testily. "Why do you ask?"

"Yesterday you seemed completely withdrawn, so much so that just before they brought Lupe out I thought you were going to fall asleep. But today you're as tense as I've ever seen you." His eyes were keen and his manner aggressive.

"Alan, I've been in this business a long time," lecturing him, "thirty years to be exact. As a defense counsel, I'm subject to attack constantly. For the sake of my client and myself, I learned long ago to mask my emotions, my reactions in court. Believe me, I was as intense yesterday as I am today."

"Do you feel well enough to go on with the case?"

"What? Are you serious?" Anger, fear, and hurt spun in me. "You've got to be kidding. You've seen the job I've done for you, the work I've put into this case. For days you couldn't thank me enough, in and out of the courtroom. Are you crazy? And besides, what judge would ever let me out of this case now, in the middle of trial?"

He became defensive, stammered through apologies and mumbled something about only being concerned with my health. Son of a bitch. He was no different than the rest; while we were ahead I was great, but at the first sign of trouble he wasn't sure if this Mexican could do the job. He should have gone to a white lawyer. And then it struck me: of course, he had been to another lawyer, a white lawyer, and he had been told that the only way he could get a new lawyer now was if I was too ill to continue.

To add insult to injury, he took out a folded sheet of paper and said, "I have a couple of questions for you, Gabby." And then read, "Will you be making a motion for a mistrial? If not, will you make a motion to compel Lupe Rodríguez to testify and be subject to cross-examination?"

The bastard had been to another lawyer. I wondered who and at the same time tried to shake off the humiliation of a client seeking another attorney's opinion midway through trial. The specter of an appeal after a conviction on grounds of the incompetency of trial counsel raised its ugly head for the first time. I had to be calm and in control, even as my aching body and head craved a pill. I had to be careful and precise with my answer. The son of a bitch was probably wired for sound.

"To begin with, I don't believe in making frivolous motions. Lupe Rodríguez has not yet testified. She's still in custody, and it's my guess we'll see her again first thing Monday morning. What she'll do on Monday is anyone's guess. If she testifies, I'll certainly have an opportunity to cross-examine her, and that should eliminate any grounds for a mistrial. If she refuses to testify, then the issue becomes whether or not the jury was so impacted by what she said that they couldn't erase it from their minds in deciding the facts of the case. If she refuses to testify, I will make a motion for a mistrial on that basis.

"As to your second question, Lupe Rodríguez is under subpoena. No one can force her to speak, and if she chooses to remain silent, all the judge can do is keep her in custody until the conclusion of the trial. So my answer to your second question is no, I won't make a motion to compel Lupe Rodríguez to testify because she's already under subpoena and such a motion would be frivolous. If you want to take time now to write down the answers to your questions so that you can take them back to whomever formulated them, please do so."

Alan Newsome reddened, "Gabby, I didn't. . . ."

"Please, I've been practicing law for thirty-five years now, and while you're certainly entitled to a second opinion, which I'm sure is not a rare occurrence in your profession, Doctor, I'd like to say that I've never been so insulted as to have some idiot lawyer formulate questions for me of that caliber in the middle of a case that I'm trying."

"Gabby, it wasn't meant to. . . ."

"I think we should talk about something of far more importance: Kathleen Powers. Remember her, Alan? Of course you do. I'll bet the police, as we speak, are scouring the state trying to find her. If they can't find her, then we need only worry about Lupe Rodríguez and her lunatic claims. I don't think any jury would convict you on that outburst. But Kathleen Powers is a horse of a different color. If we've talked about this once, we've talked about it thirty times. Alan, if Kathleen Powers says you stalked her, what will your testimony be?"

"That it's not true. That it's a lie."

"Then I don't believe there's anything more for us to discuss this morning."

Alan Newsome left discombobulated. He deserved nothing less.

But I too was discombobulated. I had no idea what would happen Monday morning, yet all I could think of was Monday morning. And the pills.

I took no pills on Saturday. By mid-afternoon I was jittery. I went home to sit out the inevitable. Over the years I had seen some of my clients go through withdrawals in jail. It was not a pretty picture. The uncontrollable trembling and shaking, the cold sweat, the eyes squinting with pain, the curling of the body into the fetal position either in an attempt to squeeze out the pain or to present a smaller surface for it to ravage. The most unforgettable scenario had been with Manny Palomino. The guard had allowed Manny to bring his blanket with him to the interview room. Manny shuffled in, wrapped in his grey blanket, and as soon as the guard left, crumpled to the concrete floor in a corner of that tiny room, shaking violently, curling himself, moaning in pain, the blanket soaked with sweat, his head pounding against the floor and wall as he shook. I went to him and put his head on my lap and said, if not naively, then stupidly, "Manny, Manny, it'll pass. You gotta be strong."

My discomfort that Saturday did not begin to approach his pain. It amounted to a restlessness (I couldn't sit still, I couldn't lie still), some sweating, a ringing headache, and dry, hot-ice breath that burned my nostrils and mouth. But many times that day I repeated to myself, "Gabby, Gabby, it'll pass, it'll pass. You gotta be strong."

Sunday was more of the same, but by nightfall I was beginning to feel it passing, and I began looking forward to the two Xanax I would take just before leaving for court in the morning and the one I would carry in my pocket for the afternoon.

On Monday morning, Lupe Rodríguez emerged from the holding cell wearing that same red jumpsuit with the same downcast eyes and sat in the same chair as she had on Friday. But now she wore leg irons and a chain manacled her hands. The jury was not present, and three burly guards were posted next to her.

"Good morning, Ms. Rodríguez, how are you today?" Jack Harris said pleasantly.

There was no answer. Lupe Rodríguez sat motionless, staring at the floor. If she blinked, I didn't see it.

"Ms. Rodríguez, I'm going to be asking you a few questions to see whether or not you're able to be a witness. Do you understand that?"

No answer. Motionless. It was hard to tell if she was breathing under that too-big jumpsuit.

"Ms. Rodríguez, is it your intention not to answer any question I ask you?"

No answer.

"Ms. Rodríguez, do you understand that I can hold you in contempt of court and put you in jail for the duration of this trial if you continue refusing to answer my questions?"

No answer.

"All right, before I find Ms. Rodríguez in contempt of court, I'll hear from counsel. Ms. Thomas?"

"Submitted, your honor."

"Mr. Garcia?"

"Well, your honor, given the lies that have poured out of Ms. Rodríguez's mouth on. . . ."

"Lies! You're the liar! You know he's guilty! You told me he told you he was guilty! Now you're. . . ." The deputies cupped Lupe Rodríguez's mouth and dragged her and her muffled words and clanging chains into the holding cell and slammed the door behind her.

Jack Harris was visibly shaken. He glared at me with his dark, now angry eyes. But he said only, "This court will be in recess," and left the bench.

When he returned, he found Lupe Rodríguez in contempt of court. I made a motion for a mistrial. In a long, impassioned plea I said that in reality the jury would be unable to set aside the damaging words that Lupe Rodríguez had said, no matter what admonition the court gave. "Simply put, your honor, you can't unring the bell. What they heard, they heard. Keeping in mind who Lupe Rodríguez is, what role she played in this tragedy, and what she screamed out in open court, that bell cannot be unrung."

Jack Harris blandly said, "Your motion will be taken under submission. Let's move on. Before I summon the jury, is everyone ready to proceed?"

"The People are ready, your honor. However, our next witness does not appear on the witness list because we did not make contact with her until yesterday evening."

The bottom was starting to fall out.

"That witness is?"

"Kathleen Powers."

I desperately made a motion for a continuance, which Jack Harris summarily denied. The bottom was gone.

Once the jury was seated, Jack Harris said to them, "Ladies and gentlemen of the jury, on Friday afternoon a prospective witness, Ms. Lupe Rodríguez, was summoned to the witness stand. She was not qualified as a witness, and she did not testify. I repeat, she did not testify. She did, however, say things that may be difficult for you to forget. However, I admonish you that nothing she said is evidence in this case, and it cannot be used by you in your deliberations. In other words, when you sit down to decide what happened in this case, nothing that and I mean nothing that Ms. Rodríguez said or did can be used by you in any way in deciding what happened in this case. Ms. Rodríguez was not a witness in this case. Ms. Rodríguez will not be a witness in this case. Call your next witness."

"The People call Kathleen Powers." How I longed for the pill in my pocket.

There was a catching of breaths, and some of the jurors shifted in their seats and some raised their heads and several turned to watch the entry of Kathleen Powers. She entered looking like Little Bo Peep in a white fluffy dress that suggested she was too young to have developed breasts or hips. There was surprise in their faces, and two of them looked over at us with indignation. "Is that how she normally dressed?" I whispered. Alan shook his head, his face flushed. "Did she look like that at The Rendezvous?" "Hardly," he whispered, fear gripping his face. When the clerk asked Kathleen Powers with raised hand if she solemnly swore to tell the truth, the whole truth, and nothing but the truth so help her God, Kathleen Powers answered in what seemed the softest, most innocent voice I had ever heard, "I do."

She was a pretty girl, whose reddish-brown hair was brushed back emphasizing a smooth, round forehead and green eyes. She could just as well have been a high school girl instead of the gritty young woman who had been completely on her own for some three years.

"Would you state your name for the record, please."

"Kathleen Powers."

"Where do you live, Ms. Powers?

"In San Luis Obispo."

"How long have you lived there?"

"Almost a year now."

"Prior to that where did you live?"

"Here in San Jose."

"Why did you move?"

"Because that man was stalking me and I was afraid for my life."

"By 'that man,' whom do you mean?"

"Dr. Alan Newsome, the man sitting right over there, the man I worked for part-time when I was going to City College here."

That was how it began. Almost without exception every juror managed a look at Alan Newsome during those first moments of Kathleen Powers's testimony, looks that ranged from disbelief to disgust. The looks continued at different intervals with lesser frequency but with stronger hues of disapproval through Alan Newsome's offer to tutor and his first touches and embraces and ultimate kisses, through Kathleen's concerns that these were no longer signs of encouragement, through her decision to stop the tutoring lessons and the subsequent anonymous phone calls she began receiving at her unlisted number, through his slow drives and furtive walks past her apartment at night, through his drunken scene at The Rendezvous.

I didn't know how I would cross-examine without taking the third pill.

"Was there a specific incident that caused you to move from San Jose?"

"Yes, there was."

"What was that?"

"Well, I was already terrified of him and had stopped working for him, which didn't discourage him at all. I didn't know what to do. I was afraid to call the police because who would ever believe that a fine doctor who was respected by everybody would be stalking me? Then, a few nights after The Rendezvous brawl, my boyfriend and I were in my apartment, which was really only one big room with a tiny patio outside. The patio had a six-foot-high fence, and most of my wall facing the patio was a large sliding-glass door. I didn't have drapes or curtains over that glass door because you couldn't see through the fence and I couldn't afford any, anyway. Well, my boyfriend, whom I love very much—we're getting married in the fall—well, he and I were getting intimate on this night."

"What do you mean by 'intimate'?"

"Well, we were going to make love."

"Were you dressed or undressed?"

"Undressed." She blushed. "Well, I was lying on the couch, and I happened to look over and see Dr. Newsome standing behind the glass door watching us. I screamed and my boyfriend stopped and got off me. I jumped up and tried to cover myself with my arms and hands, and I was looking for anything to cover myself with when I saw that he was crying, that he hadn't moved an inch and was crying. And I screamed and screamed. But it was only after my boyfriend ran to the door that Dr. Newsome jumped over the fence and ran."

It was all over. Down to the tips of my toes I knew that it was all over. I cross-examined as if in a daze, asking questions by rote, questions I had accumulated over the years to buy time with, to put up a facade with, but not once did I go near the patio. There were several other witnesses the People called, but it was over. There was Sergeant Renna, who took Alan's statement that night in which he said that after he left his office he went to St. Luke's Hospital to check on patients. There was the custodian of records who testified that on the night of the homicide Dr. Newsome had no patients at St. Luke's Hospital. There was the police officer who photographed the crime scene. The police officer who established the chain of evidence. The coroner's investigator who photographed the body and saw the burn marks around the wound to the left temple, but saw no traces of gunpowder on either of the victim's hands. Before any of these witnesses set foot in the courtroom, I knew, though I would have never admitted it, least of all to myself, that it was all over.

That moment, the moment Kathleen Powers testified that she saw Alan Newsome standing behind the glass crying, motionless and crying, would be forever etched in my mind. Because at that moment I knew not only that it was all over for Alan Newsome, but I sensed that it could be all over for me as well. I had reached the pinnacle of my profession. True, I had handled more difficult cases. But those cases had been court-appointed, and at first glance the vast majority of those defendants were stone-cold guilty. In this case, an innocent, educated, successful, respected white man had sought me out, chosen me over three of the best county's criminal defense attorneys, all white. From that tiny shack in the blistering fields of the southern San Joaquin Valley with a father who spoke little English and a mother who seldom spoke, I had made my way past obstacle after obstacle, racial, educational, financial, professional, and personal, to reach this point. I was sixty, in poor health, and forever fighting fear. There wasn't much time left, and I didn't want to lose this case, a case that had garnered more local publicity than any I had ever had. For months, it had caught the eye of the northern California media, and once the trial started, the national media had picked it up. To lose now would be to lose so much. Ironically, I was fighting a battle that should never have been fought. Alan Newsome was innocent.

When Kathleen Powers's long testimony was concluded, Jack Harris declared the evening recess, and I waited for the courtroom to clear. When only Alan and I remained, I said to him, "I'll see you in my office in an hour." He was a broken man, but I had to pull myself together before I could begin working on him. He left with an "okay" and his tail between his legs.

Then I sat and thought of José and Catalina Garcia. I thought of Mike Garcia, The Big Bear. I thought of Eufemia and the parties and our wedding night. I thought of the day I left the ranch, of the long, hard years that I worked and educated myself. I thought of the Mayas. I thought of Rebecca and the love she had given me, the love that I had lost. I thought of my silly, desperate, endless need to succeed, to prove myself, and its bitter reward: fear and panic attacks. And I was ashamed. Ashamed of what I had become: a frightened, lonely man dependent on pills. I sat with my shame for almost an hour. When I arose, I was no longer afraid. I had always been afraid but never weak. Now I would be neither. Come what may, there would be no more pills.

In my office I said to him, "Alan, if you get on that stand and lie about stalking Kathleen Powers, you're going to be convicted of murder." Those were the first words I said to him, and the only words I needed to say to him. I said them loudly and clearly, with certainty and without hesitation. To be gentle with him then, to have said anything else, would have been a disservice to him and me. He looked at me with doe-like eyes, and I repeated myself, "Alan, if you get on that stand and lie about stalking Kathleen Powers, you're going to be convicted of murder."

"What do you want me to say?"

"The truth."

"What is the truth?"

"The truth is that you were worn down by a tragic set of circumstances that would have worn down any man. For more than

three years, your wife was wasting away. You did all you could
for her, gave her all you could. Circumstances brought you in
contact with an attractive young woman. You became infatuated
with her, obsessed with her, and in your obsession you did things
that you have never done before and will never do again. Things
that you regret."

"Isn't the truth really that I didn't kill Amy?"

He was right, of course, but I was right, too. "Yes, what you
ask is the ultimate truth, the ultimate issue. But the People's theory of the case is that you killed Amy because you wanted to be
free to pursue Kathleen Powers. Your conduct with Kathleen goes
to motive, and the judge has ruled that it is relevant and admissi-
ble evidence on that basis. It has become part of the truth. If you
lie about that part of the truth, in my opinion, you will be convicted of murder."

"But I didn't kill Amy."

"I know that and you know that. But that's almost irrelevant
now."

"I can't get up there and say I did what she said I did. If I do,
I'll lose my license to practice medicine."

"You'll lose a lot more than your license if you're convicted
of murder. Besides, even if they were to convict you of stalking
sometime after this trial, we're probably only talking about a misdemeanor, probation, no jail, and a fine. And even if the Board
took your license, with a misdemeanor conviction you'd probably
be able to get it back in a couple of years."

"I'd lose all my patients if I said I did those things. What
woman would ever come to me for treatment? What mother or
father would ever bring their daughter or son to me? What man
would respect me? Do you know that since Kathleen Powers took
the stand, five patients I was supposed to see on Saturday and
Sunday have already cancelled their appointments? Do you know
what it's like to walk down the street day after day and be recognized by everyone, convicted already by some, and, if I said I did
those terrible things, convicted by all? Where do I go if I admit
stalking her? And how do I make a living in a strange town with-

out a license? How do I support myself and my daughter? I'm not trained to do anything except practice medicine."

"The alternative is thirty-five years to life in state prison. There you'll never have to worry about where you'll live or how you'll be able to earn a living." I stopped myself from adding: even your pine box will be provided for you, because that's the only way you'll be coming out of there on this charge.

Alan Newsome and I had many more conversations before he testified. In all of them, no matter how brief the contact, I repeated, "You must admit the stalking." I prepared him as best I could for his testimony, given the fact that I didn't know right up to the moment he took the stand whether he would admit or deny the stalking. I learned about a third of the way through his direct examination what his intentions were when I asked him, "Once you left your office that night, where did you go?" and he answered, "To Joe's Place, a bar downtown." A few minutes later he recounted how he met Kathleen Powers in his office, how he tutored her in chemistry, hugged her two or three times to encourage her, and had stopped tutoring her and lost all contact with her once she left his employ. To my questions regarding the stalking allegations, he said, "That is absolutely not true." He went on to describe coming home just after eleven, watching most of the late evening news, and going upstairs where he found Amy's body. We had saved Lupe Rodríguez's omnipresence in the house for last. The thick strands of coarse black hair everywhere, the stains on the closet wall, the orange juice in the attic, the dust-free space under Caroline's bed. But by then, the jury wasn't listening.

On cross-examination, Lisa Thomas came at Alan Newsome like a barracuda. She made no effort to hide her contempt for his lies. She spent almost an hour questioning him about Joe's Place. Its size, the location of the bar, the number of stools at the bar, the number of tables, the existence or nonexistence of a band-stand and any dancing area, who was working there that night, who normally worked there and how many people worked there, the decor, the lighting, and anything and everything else anyone could possibly want to know about that miserable place. When she was finished, it was pretty clear that if Alan Newsome had ever been there at all, it must have been while he was asleep. One thing was certain, Lisa Thomas had been there, probably during the noon recess after Alan Newsome had casually dropped the name "Joe's Place" on direct examination.

Then for several hours Lisa Thomas tediously took Alan Newsome step by minute step through every detail of Kathleen Powers's testimony, as well as every reasonable inference from those details, forcing him to assert again and again and again that what Kathleen Powers had said was not only untrue but a lie, until Little Bo Peep appeared to be the biggest liar on the face of the earth. But it was only when she reached The Rendezvous that I understood where she was going. Once that dawned on me, I called Barbara Benson at the recess and asked her to drop everything and go to The Rendezvous to see if the police had been there recently. An hour later Barbara came into the courtroom and slipped me a note. "People at Rendezvous won't talk to me. They're mad. Think I misled them. D.A. & cops were there 2 days ago. Jennifer Blake, the waitress, will testify in rebuttal." I shuddered. Lisa Thomas was determined not only to hang Alan Newsome but to dismember him as well.

That night I put off eating until I could complete what had to be done. I waited until 10:30 before I went because all the lights would be out then, and all the inmates would be locked down then, and no one except Jim Freitas, the sole guard on duty in that wing, would see me. I had known Jim Freitas for more than twenty years. Ours was a friendly relationship that had grown around my evening visits to the jail. He would bring Lupe Rodríguez out for a visit without any questions asked.

When Jim Freitas saw me, he said, "Jesus Christ, Gabby, what the hell are you doing up here at this hour? Don't you ever rest?"

"I wonder about that myself, Jim. I need to see Lupe Rodríguez."

He looked at me quizzically for a moment and then said, "Okay. But be careful, Gabby, she's a legitimate nut."

"I know."

I waited in an interview room, and about ten minutes later I heard the clanging of leg irons recording each slow step on the concrete surface beneath them. I wondered if, once she saw me, she would refuse the visit. When the clanging stopped, I turned to the door. Her face was expressionless. I could have been the wall or a cupboard. It occurred to me that I had never really had a chance to look at Lupe, much less at this distance. Her skin was smooth, and her dark eyes were round and clear. Her nose was thin and fine and her mouth delicate. She could have been a pretty young woman if she had let herself.

"Lupe, I'd like to talk to you." Jim Freitas positioned himself about a foot behind her.

Lupe's expression remained the same. She could have been looking at me without seeing me.

"Come in, Lupe, have a seat. It won't take long." To my surprise she did both. Jim Freitas closed the door behind her. I took a seat across the small table from her, and for several moments we looked at each other, or better, I looked at her and she must have seen me. She was even prettier than I had just thought. Her light-brown skin was without a blemish, and her chin and jaws were superbly defined. As I looked, I also searched for the best way to begin, how best not to offend her, how to get from her what I needed so badly. But everything I thought of seemed so hopelessly inappropriate.

Finally, I simply said, "He's going to be convicted of murder if you don't tell the jury how it happened, Lupe."

"Good," without so much as a blink.

"Do you want to see an innocent man go to prison for the rest of his life? Do you hate him that much?"

"Yes."

It was as chilling and convincing an answer as I had ever heard. She needed only a word. She needed no histrionics and the tone was little more than a whisper. I could have pleaded with her in ten different languages, stayed with her until hell froze over, but I knew she would never relent. Still, I went on.

"He's innocent, Lupe, he's innocent. You, better than anyone, know that."

"No, I better than anyone know that he's guilty. He made her want to die. He made her want to pull the trigger. He made her want me to help her pull that trigger. If he hadn't been out chasing his teenager, that trigger would never have been pulled. Amy would still be here. He took her from me. We were going to be together when she got well. He took her from me and now he has to pay."

"Then just tell the jury that."

"And help him? I would never help him. You help him. That's what he's paying you for, isn't it?" With that, she began laughing, a hysterical laugh that grew louder and louder until Jim Freitas opened the door and said, "Gabby, I've got to get her back to her cell. She's on heavy medication. This shouldn't be happening."

I left the jail well past eleven. I ate little and drank little, but I slept. It was a sleep filled with struggles and challenges and mostly losses. But in the end, I had won again.

Because it was the third night I had slept without the pills, and that buoyed and readied me for the onslaught I knew was to come the next morning.

Jennifer Blake turned out to be all that Barbara Benson said she would be and more. She had been a cocktail waitress and bartender for as long as she could remember and had heard enough tales of woe to write ten books. Like television producers, she knew the suggestion of sex could sell anything. Somewhere in her forties, her body was turning from curves to bulges, but she obviously still thought if she showed a little more flesh, she could get the desired effect. The response she received from the jurors when she entered the courtroom that morning was not the desired effect. They were somewhat aghast at the figure that stood in the doorway. She had probably gotten to bed between three and four that morning and she looked it. Her makeup and creams hid nothing from the courtroom lights. Theirs was the stark white of fluorescent bulbs rather than the dim hue of the electric candles on The Rendezvous tables. Her bleached-blonde hair had been dyed and treated so much that it now hung limp in short, pointed spears just above her shoulders. Her pale, puffy bare arms seemed to belong to someone other than the owner of her painted tan face. Her skirt was too short, and there was a large dark splotch at her upper thigh hemline, which she probably hadn't noticed as she staggered out of bed after three or four hours of sleep. But when she took the stand, she was direct and deadly.

Jennifer Blake testified that she had been working at The Rendezvous for four years. The Rendezvous was a nightclub located in a converted warehouse. Three nights a week it had live rock bands. It catered to a young set in their early to mid-twenties. It was because of the clientele that she noticed and took a special interest in an obviously middle-aged man who began frequenting The Rendezvous several weeks before the homicide. Initially, she wondered what he was doing there, but it soon became clear that he was there because of a young woman who came to the club three or four times a week. Shown a photo of Kathleen Powers without the Little Bo Peep dress, Jennifer Blake quickly identified her: "Yes, that's the girl."

Like all good trial lawyers, Lisa Thomas loved the spotlight. She was on fire when she wheeled from where she was standing and pointed dramatically at Alan Newsome: "Is this the middle-aged man you've been talking about?"

"Yes."

"Was he dressed as he is now when he went to The Rendezvous? Did he look like he looks now?"

"Are you kidding? The doorman probably wouldn't have let him in. Would have thought he was an F.B.I. agent or something with that suit and tie on."

"How was he dressed then?"

"He always wore faded, baggy jeans and one of two old beat-up loose-fitting sweatshirts and canvas high-top tennis shoes that are popular with the kids and a baseball cap turned backwards. I always thought he wore the cap to hide his bald head. Now I can see that he wore it only to hide his thinning hair."

She went on to describe Alan Newsome's infatuation for "that girl." "He would always sit at the same table up in the back. We have elevated levels around the dance floor and bandstand that go up quite a ways. There are tables and chairs at each level, and the higher you go up, the darker it gets. The stage and the dance floor are well lit so that anybody sitting back where he used to sit can see everything going on down on the dance floor without being seen. That girl loved to dance and he watched every move. It didn't take long to see why he was there. He just drooled over her, slobbered over her the more he drank. He couldn't take his eyes off her. I always waited until the band wasn't playing to ask him if he wanted another drink or to serve him because then I could get his attention when she wasn't on the floor, and then I could get paid. He was a little scary at first but I'd seen old fools like him before. They're harmless. They just want to watch unseen. And until the very last night he was there, he was no different. He just sat and drank and watched and sat and drank and watched some more. When she left, he left. I will say this for him: he was a big tipper. And the more he drank, the bigger the tips."

Then Lisa Thomas reined Jennifer Blake in and took her step by deliberate, calculated step through Alan Newsome's last night at The Rendezvous. He had been drinking heavily that night, and after some two hours he started to moan and groan to himself at his table. People began complaining about him, and a couple went to the bouncer. Jennifer had decided to stop serving him when all of a sudden he stood up, grumbling to himself still, and started making his way down to the dance floor, knocking over a table and some glasses as he went. She knew where he was going, no question. He stumbled several times and almost fell once. When he reached the dance floor, he lunged for the girl. The girl screamed and her partner hit him. Alan broke a glass on the young man's face, and somebody else hit Alan. People screamed, bottles and glasses flew, tables tipped, and the police were called. When they arrived, Alan Newsome was gone.

There was a deep hush when Jennifer Blake concluded her testimony. I looked over at the jury. None of them would look in our direction. Those who were facing us had their eyes downcast. Alan Newsome sat staring into space, shattered.

As Jennifer Blake walked out of the courtroom, Lisa Thomas stood and said, "The People rest."

"Any further witnesses on behalf of the defense?" Jack Harris asked.

"May we approach the bench, your honor?" I said.

"Please do."

As we approached the dais, Lisa Thomas seemed jubilant. In her mind she had just won a difficult case.

"Your honor," I whispered up to Jack Harris. "I may have an additional witness, depending upon how you rule on a motion that I would like to make outside the presence of the jury. Frankly, I think it might be better to do this in chambers, your honor. I don't want to be accused later by the prosecution of making inflammatory statements that could be blown out of proportion by the media."

Jack Harris looked over at Lisa Thomas, who shrugged, and then out at the packed courtroom. "Very well, we'll do it in chambers. Have the defendant come in with you."

Once in chambers, I said, "Your Honor, at this time I'm making a motion to withdraw as Alan Newsome's attorney because I feel it is incumbent upon me to testify about incriminating statements that Lupe Rodríguez has made to me."

"What?" Jack Harris said, raising his head.

Lisa Thomas was on her feet. "This is ridiculous, your honor. We've completed all the evidence, and now he wants to withdraw as the defendant's attorney and become a witness."

"Please, Ms. Thomas, let him make his motion."

"I'd like at least an offer of proof and . . ."

"Please, Ms. Thomas. Your basis for the motion, Mr. Garcia?"

"On two occasions Lupe Rodríguez has admitted to me that she fired the shot that killed Amy Newsome. On at least three occasions she has indicated that she was present at the time Amy Newsome was shot and that Alan Newsome was not there."

"I'd like some particulars, your honor. When, where, who was present, and why the prosecution . . ."

"Ms. Thomas, please. You will be given every opportunity to respond. Of course, Ms. Thomas is correct. When and where did you have these conversations with Ms. Rodríguez and who was present, Mr. Garcia?"

I described in detail my visits with Lupe Rodríguez at her home and my visit with her at the jail. Jack Harris looked at me with those soul-searching eyes. He was grey now, but his face was still long and gaunt, his mouth thin. "Although you have not said so specifically, Mr. Garcia, I am assuming that on each occasion when you spoke with Ms. Rodríguez, you were alone with her?"

"That's correct, your honor."

"Was there any reason you didn't have an investigator with you?"

"I was aware of Ms. Rodríguez's mental illness. My mother suffered from a similar illness. I knew that Lupe Rodríguez would be difficult if not impossible to talk to. Given my experience with my mother's illness I felt I was better suited than anyone to deal with her. I also felt that two strangers would pose more of a threat to Lupe than one and that she would be less likely to talk to two persons rather than one."

He studied me, skeptically I thought, and I wanted to yell, Goddamn it, Jack, you know me! I wouldn't lie to you, not about something like this! Then he said, "You're aware of the law in this area?"

"Yes, I am, your honor." Wanting to add: You think I'm stupid, realizing at the same moment that, in hindsight, meeting alone with Lupe did look pretty stupid.

"But let's get to the crux of the matter. These statements you say Ms. Rodríguez made to you, and that you want to testify to, are pure and simple hearsay. How do you get around a hearsay objection, which I would sustain, keeping in mind that Ms. Rodríguez has not been a witness in this case?"

"Your honor, I respectfully submit that Ms. Rodríguez has in effect testified with her outburst before the jury. Her statements were extremely prejudicial. She was in the house daily and was with Amy Newsome constantly. The jury knows that. They've heard that from other witnesses. She said that my client killed Amy Newsome. Given her association with Ms. Newsome, the jurors could easily infer that she was in the best position to know that."

"I heard what she said, and I've ruled that Lupe Rodríguez has not been a witness in this case, and I've admonished the jury accordingly. Let's move on."

We glared at each other for several moments. His look said: I'm the judge here and I've made my ruling. Mine said: Where's your justice, Jack Harris? You know I wouldn't lie to you. You know what I say is true. How can you hide behind rules that have nothing to do with truth and justice?

"May I be heard, your honor?" Lisa Thomas interrupted. Jack Harris nodded without taking his eyes off my glare. "Mr. Garcia's motion to withdraw is not only ridiculous, it's scandalous. Mr. Garcia is a very experienced trial attorney yet he chose on several occasions to interview one of the most important, no, *the* most important potential witness in this case alone, without the help or presence of an investigator. The case law is quite clear that any attorney who does that is in danger of making himself a witness, and since an attorney cannot be both an advocate and a witness, the attorney is compromising his client's case, which may be grounds for a reversal on appeal if his client is convicted. It occurs to me that what Mr. Garcia is really trying to do here is to give his client an issue on appeal, the issue of his attorney's incompetency. If that isn't bad enough, Mr. Garcia now says that he should be allowed to testify as to hearsay statements because Lupe Rodríguez is a witness in this case and he wants to use her alleged statements to impeach her. Hogwash. Lupe Rodríguez has never been sworn as a witness in this case. Mr. Garcia knows that. Any first-year law student would know that. And you have so ruled. Mr. Garcia's motion is frivolous and should be denied." Frivolous. First-year law student. The arrogance and ignorance of youth. I had been practicing law before Lisa Thomas was born. I had handled more criminal cases than she could count.

"Is there anything else you wish to say before I rule on your motion, Mr. Garcia?"

"Yes. I've known you, Jack Harris, for almost thirty years. We each have a good sense of who the other is. I have never lied to you, and you have never lied to me. I don't lie to judges when I try cases. Never have, never will . . ."

"Your honor, this is highly inappropriate. Mr. . . ."

"Let me finish, Ms. Seven-Year-Old Lawyer."

"Let him finish, Ms. Thomas. I'll decide what's appropriate and inappropriate."

"Lupe Rodríguez has confessed to me. In no uncertain terms, she told me that she pulled the trigger. If that isn't relevant and germane to this case, then I don't know what is. But you won't let me present that to this jury. You won't let the jury hear that. It's hearsay, you say. On the other hand, that same person screamed out to the jury that Alan Newsome killed his wife. Like it or not, the jury's heard that. But you say you've ordered that out of their minds. Nonsense. You'll never unring that bell. . . ."

"Your honor, Mr. Garcia is completely out of order. His personal remarks to this court are outrageous and completely inappropriate. It is he who should be held in contempt."

"Ms. Thomas, I am very much aware of the inappropriateness of Mr. Garcia's comments. However, I will let him conclude his remarks before I rule."

"Now you have the opportunity to right the first wrong and let the jury hear the truth. You have the power, the discretion to allow me to withdraw and testify. Jack, this case is about truth and justice, not about rules of evidence. Let me testify."

We studied each other. From such different beginnings, we had wanted the same thing. Somehow we had managed to take the same path. Now we were on different paths. But it was hard to believe that we wanted different things now. Jack Harris could hold his gaze as long as I could hold mine. But this wasn't a contest. I was trying to read him, trying to decipher his thinking, hoping to find in that serious face what more I could say or do to change his mind. And he? Reviewing his ruling, wondering how he could change it without appearing to be a bleeding-heart liberal or an old crony? I didn't know.

After a long pause he said only, "Counsel, your motion is

denied. Your earlier motion for a mistrial, which I took under sub-mission, is also denied. We will begin closing arguments this afternoon at 1:30."

Alan Newsome's face was a mass of fear.

Lisa Thomas was brilliant. Her message was simple: Alan Newsome was the only person known to be with Amy Newsome on the night of the homicide, and he lied repeatedly and consistently about where he had been that night and about his motive for killing Amy Newsome, to wit: his relationship with Kathleen Powers. She made her point again and again, dressing it up with different facts of the testimony but always ending up with: the only person known to be with Amy that night lied. Amy Newsome hadn't shot herself. She was right-handed, unfamiliar with guns, and had no gunpow-der residue on her hands. The shot was fired just inches from her left temple. There was no sign of forced entry, and every attempt to put Lupe Rodríguez in the house that night was sheer speculation. A man as obsessed as Alan Newsome was with Kathleen Powers would do anything to have her, even kill his invalid wife.

When I rose and moved toward the jury railing to begin my closing argument, only juror number six, a grey-haired woman in the back row, turned to look at me. The others were either look-ing straight past me or had their heads or eyes downcast. They had heard enough. They had made up their minds. They didn't need to hear any more. Never mind that they had been instructed by the judge, and would be instructed again, that the law required them to keep an open mind until they had heard all the evidence, the arguments of counsel, and entered into deliberation with their fel-low jurors. This happened more often than not. Just another lofty legal platitude that had little to do with the human condition and was summarily discarded by all, to the surprise of none. Often I would cajole them, get them to like me, trust me, or at least not be threatened by me, so that the unpleasant task of listening to words on behalf of an absolute scoundrel could be a little more pleasant, not only for them, but for me as well. Not today. Today they were going to look at me and listen to me on my own terms because the man they had already convicted was innocent. I was representing an innocent man.

So I stood there, without saying a word, as the passing seconds enhanced the silence, and one by one, they looked at me, just
long enough to see me looking at them, and then their eyes skit-
tered away, like the eyes of children caught in a mischievous act.
When all twelve had turned and looked away, I waited a little
longer, until Jack Harris cleared his throat at the dais. Then I said,
"Look at me," softly. "Look at me," louder, much louder, and
when they were all looking, I said, "I've come to speak to you
about an innocent man, this man, Alan Newsome, and the least
you can do is look at me while I speak."

It was unlike any closing argument I had ever made. But then
I had never represented anyone whom I knew to be more innocent
than Alan Newsome and never on charges as serious as these.
"Some of you, maybe all of you, may have already decided. Well,
believe it or not, the only thing you could possibly already have
decided is that Alan Newsome is guilty of stalking Kathleen Powers. Because there's not been one shred of evidence produced here
in court that Alan Newsome killed Amy Newsome! Not a shred!"
I summarized the evidence and then asked, "Where is it? Where
is the evidence that Alan Newsome murdered his wife?

"If you want to convict Alan Newsome of something, convict
him of stalking because that's all the evidence shows he did. But
it's one thing to stalk a young woman and quite another to kill
your wife. What the evidence does show is that Alan Newsome
was a good, devoted, loving husband and father. For over three
years while his wife was afflicted with a terrible illness, he was
nurse, homemaker, breadwinner, husband, and father who cared
deeply for his wife and daughter."

I reviewed the testimony of each witness who had been in the
home and had seen the devotion and care and patience that Alan
Newsome had shown for his ailing wife and daughter. As bizarre
as Alan Newsome's obsession for Kathleen Powers had been, I
asked the jurors, without condoning it, to try to understand how
such an attraction could be borne and fester in a man carrying the
load that Alan Newsome was. Did he lie to the police about where

he was that night? Yes. Did he lie about his obsession for Kathleen Powers? Yes. "Is it so difficult to understand how a man could be so ashamed of such an obsession, have it be so out of character for him that he would deny it from the beginning and deny it to this day?"

Twice I tried to use Lupe Rodríguez to my advantage. "You will recall that the prosecutor announced Lupe Rodríguez as a witness. During her opening statement, she stated that Lupe Rodríguez would testify to 'events,' as she put it, that occurred in the Newsome household. Lupe Rodríguez did not testify. Lupe Rodríguez . . ."

"Objection."

"Sustained." Without a word as to the basis for the objection.

Then Jack Harris admonished the jury that neither side had to call every witness. "Proceed, Mr. Garcia."

"You will recall that the prosecution did, in fact, call Ms. Rodríguez as a witness. Do you think for one moment that if Lupe Rodríguez, who was always with Amy Newsome, had anything damaging to say about Alan Newsome that the prosecution would have hesitated for one second in going forward with Lupe Rodríguez's testimony?"

"Objection."

"Sustained." This time Jack Harris was angry. "Ladies and gentlemen of the jury, either side could have called Ms. Rodríguez as a witness. Neither side did. You are not to draw any inference whatsoever from that. Move on to another area, Mr. Garcia."

Years ago there had been a defense attorney who routinely cried during his closing arguments. Defense attorneys, prosecutors, judges even, privately held him up to ridicule, as did I. But as I concluded with, "Alan Newsome is innocent. I ask you to return a verdict of acquittal," I was crying.

As I sat down, Alan Newsome leaned over to me and whispered, "Great job, Gabby. Thank you."

Historically, 92 percent of the criminal cases tried to a jury in Santa Clara County ended in convictions for the prosecution. As the jury left the courtroom to begin their deliberations, I didn't expect an acquittal, but I did have hope for a deadlocked jury, based primarily on the reactions I had received from four of the jurors. Not only did I gain their attention, but I had been able to move them visibly. They were torn and uncomfortable with the case, and juror number six cried with me.

Alan Newsome was more positive. "I think you did a hell of a good job. They won't convict me. Not after your closing argument."

"Thanks. I've got to get back to the office. Let Debbie know where you'll be. My guess is that they're going to be out for a long time, maybe days. So prepare yourself for the wait. But remember, the longer they're out, the better."

Three hours and twenty minutes later, Debbie buzzed. "They want you over in court."

"A read-back?"

"I'm sorry, Gabby, but I didn't ask and she didn't say."

As I walked over to the courthouse, I thought it had to be about the exhibits. It was too soon for them to be arguing about what a witness had said. I had no sooner sat down when Alan Newsome said, "They have a verdict."

"What?" My heart pounded and fear bit at every inch of me. But it was too quick for a guilty verdict. In a case of this magnitude, with a defendant as sparkling as Alan Newsome, they would take their time, a lot of time, before finding him guilty. Not guilty? I tried shoving the concept out of my mind. But that's all it could have been, given the amount of time they had taken.

Judge Harris came out. "Madam Foreperson, has the jury reached a verdict?"

"We have, your honor."

"Please hand it to the clerk." Who handed it to Judge Harris, who read it without any indication of what the verdict might have been. "Madam Clerk, please read the verdict."

My heart was racing. This would be the biggest victory of my life.

"We, the jury, in the above-entitled case, find the defendant, Alan Newsome, guilty of murder in the first degree . . ."

That's all I heard. That's all I remembered. I regained consciousness four days later. I had suffered a stroke in the courtroom and was unable to speak. The doctors said I might never regain my speech. The world seemed huge and barren and grey. The funny gurgling sound I made when I tried to speak was real. My life as a trial lawyer was over. Now I had this part of my life to deal with. The doctors had suggested that I learn how to use a computer to communicate. In a few days I was able to communicate at a decent speed.

One evening the news had a photo of Alan Newsome in jail garb. He was due to be sentenced the following week, and every indication was that he would receive the mandatory thirty-five-years-to-life prison sentence.

The next morning the hospital chaplain stopped by. He wore a large crucifix around his neck. Holding the crucifix in one hand, he began, "Mr. Garcia, I know these are very difficult times for you, but God in His Infinite Wisdom and Goodness . . ." I stopped him there with an outstretched hand. Then I typed, "Please, Father, I've had enough of your God. Thank you."

That afternoon Rebecca stood in the doorway, feigning a smile as she fought back tears. "Oh, Gabby," she finally said and then rushed to my bed and put her face on my lap and cried. I stroked her white hair and then bent over and kissed it and then stroked it for several minutes as she cried in my lap. When she looked up, I typed, "Rebecca, you are the love of my life. But please, for my sake, it will be much better for me if you don't come anymore. I love you." She stared at the screen for a while and then rose and kissed me and left.

The following week a young man stepped into my room and asked, "Are you Gabriel Garcia?" I nodded. "These are for you." He dropped two folded pages of paper next to my hand and left. One was a complaint on behalf of Caroline Newsome, suing me for malpractice. The other was a notice of intent to appeal the judgment and conviction of Alan Newsome, filed by Alan Newsome alleging incompetency of counsel on my part.

One wanted my money, the other my license.

I read the documents over several times, put them down, and then thought of my life, thought of what it had been and what it would be. I thought of the people and things that had shaped me, and I typed those on the grey screen. "José and Catalina Garcia. The Pavlovitch ranch. J.J. Mike Garcia, The Big Bear. Eufemia. The Greyhound bus depot. San Jose City College. The Mayas. San Jose Night Law School. The Merced St. Market. Rebecca Williams. Bill Brady. Alan Newsome. Rebecca Williams. Mike Garcia, The Big Bear." Two names had kept repeating themselves, so I typed them twice. Rebecca Williams had taught me love. What more can I say? Mike Garcia taught me worth and hope—that a Mexican could be worth something and go beyond his perceived appointed lot.

I thought of the pain and suffering and human misery I had seen each day of my life as a criminal defense attorney, of the defendants and victims and the imperfect justice system. I thought of the thousands of forgotten faces I had seen in the fields covered with dust and streaked with grape juices, doing miserable back-breaking work to support their humble existences, and I wondered if their lives might have been more peaceful than mine.

I looked around my private hospital room at all its modern technology, comforts, and conveniences and thought, I've had a good life.

Fear had been my constant companion. It had dogged me every step of the way once I left the ranch. My life might well have been easier had I stayed on the ranch. But I hadn't wanted that life. I had wanted more. Clearly, each new step on my chosen path had brought me more fear. Oddly, I wasn't afraid now.

I thought of what my life would be now. Alone, old, unable to speak or practice law. On the other hand, my savings and retirement plans would provide me with enough funds for my simple needs. And I was learning to express myself in the written form. Someday perhaps I could write a book or two. Best of all, I wasn't afraid.

Under the list of names and things I had on the screen, directly under The Big Bear, I added this nine-word paragraph: "I've had a good life and I'm not afraid."

ACKNOWLEDGMENTS

My thanks to Marcial González, Nicolás Kanellos, and Morton Marcus for their time, criticisms and encouragement.